SUGAR SPRINGS

Also By Kim Law
Caught on Camera

SUGAR SPRINGS

KIM LAW

Text copyright © 2012 Kim Law
Printed in the United States of America.

Published by Montlake Romance
P.O. Box 400818
Las Vegas, NV 89140

ISBN-13: 9781612186979
ISBN-10: 1612186971

*This book is dedicated to Debra Hayes for always being willing
to jump in and help when I need it most.
The idea for this one wouldn't have sparked without you.
Thanks for being the best kind of friend.*

CHAPTER

"He's back."

Chilly November air whipped over Lee Ann London as her mother hurried through the kitchen door and slammed it shut behind her, the action rattling the copper-bottomed pots hanging above Lee Ann's head. Continuing her methodic motions with the rolling pin, she tucked her smile away and focused on the dough. "Hey, Mom. Who's back?"

"I should have said *coming* back," she bristled.

"Okay, who's—"

The thud of a heavy coat hitting the floor cut Lee Ann off midquestion and pulled her attention from the kitchen island.

Reba London's eyebrows puckered as she stood still in the middle of the room, concern etching her blue eyes and turning them a shade darker, erasing the natural twinkle normally found there. Agitation had her wringing her hands together. Over-the-top drama was one thing with her mother, but her stiff posture indicated this was actually serious.

Lee Ann pushed the rolling pin to the side and wiped her fingers on her apron. She propped her hands on her hips and studied the helpless expression on her mother's face. Rarely did anything cause Reba such distress these days. Nothing had in ages. Not since those first few years of the two of them figuring out how to make ends meet as they'd struggled to care for the twins.

At the thought of the girls Lee Ann had been raising since birth, she glanced at the clock. Five o'clock. They would be home soon. Candy from basketball practice and Kendra from cheerleading. And then another thought struck. She hadn't seen her mother this agitated since the day her half sister had proclaimed the kids' father was...

Lee Ann froze, an icy path slicing over the back of her neck. *No.*

She blinked and shook her head once, determined to shove aside the face that had popped to mind. Just because her mom's look reminded her of that day so long ago didn't mean she was talking about *him* being the one who was coming back to town. He hadn't stepped foot in Sugar Springs, Tennessee, in over thirteen years. It would make no sense for him to be there now.

But what if he was?

Her chest tightened. The thought was insane. Of course he wouldn't have decided to come back after all this time. There was nothing more for him there today than there had been all those years ago. Certainly not the possibility of having anything to do with the girls he'd turned his back on.

Reba took a hesitant step toward Lee Ann but stopped. She twisted the large flower-petal ring around her finger, hitched her mouth in an unattractive twist, and slowly nodded her head.

After several long seconds of silence as Lee Ann gave her mother a hard stare, the anxiety on the woman's face shifted and began to falter, allowing in a bit of her "everything will work out" look. She lifted one shoulder in a half shrug. She didn't seem exactly sold on the idea but more as if she was trying to convince both herself and Lee Ann that it had to be the case.

"Mom?" Lee Ann couldn't control the tremor in her voice.

Reba squared her shoulders, going for brave, but her eyes were as worried as Lee Ann had ever seen them. Sharp prickles worked their way over Lee Ann's scalp. She closed her eyes. She did not want to hear his name.

"Who, Mom?" she asked. "Who is coming back to town?"

A tiny pause, then words spoken so quietly they were almost indecipherable. "Cody Dalton."

Pain jabbed the back of Lee Ann's eyelids. *The bastard.* He had no business coming back there and disrupting their lives. She opened her eyes and moved with controlled motions until she sank into a kitchen chair, where she proceeded to stare straight ahead, focusing on the bare branches intertwined outside the kitchen window instead of the images of Cody currently daring to flit through her mind.

Okay, fine, she could deal with this. Nothing was insurmountable. The fact was she'd dealt with far worse before— those times being his fault, too, of course. She inhaled a breath into her lungs, deep enough to expand her chest as she continued to get herself under control, then she let it out slowly with the backward countdown from ten.

There was an easy solution. She simply had to keep him the heck out of their lives.

He hadn't wanted to be there before, so there was no reason she should open the door and let him come strolling in today. As she worked through the ins and outs of living in a town with less than six hundred people, she knew there was no way they could keep completely out of each other's path, but she would do everything possible to limit the run-ins. Her mom perched on the seat beside her and reached out a hand to pat Lee Ann on the back as if she were a child.

"Why is he back?" Lee Ann asked. "And why now?"

Had he experienced some lightbulb moment that made him suddenly develop the urge to be the father he'd never wanted to be before? She gritted her teeth at the thought. His children were only a few weeks shy of becoming teenagers. It wasn't as if missing the first thirteen years of their lives was going to endear him to them.

The fingers resting on her back slid away. "He's the new vet, hon, filling in for Dr. Wright for six weeks so she can be home for a spell after the baby comes."

"Veterinarian?" Shock weighted her body down as the cheerful colors of the room blended together to form a depressing blue, green, and yellow haze. Like a three-day-old bruise. "He's a vet?"

Unimaginable.

Yet strangely comforting. Warmth poked through a tiny spot deep in her belly. He'd actually done it. Then coldness slammed back into place as Lee Ann registered the other words her mother had spoken.

Six weeks?

In Sugar Springs?

Lee Ann rubbed her temples. How was she going to handle this? There was no way he wouldn't at least ask about the girls. Heck, half the population would tell him all about them, none the wiser that they were talking to the kids' actual father. Thankfully, only her mother and best friend knew that he'd even been with Stephanie that way.

The big question, though, was would he want anything to do with them? Or would he merely be curious?

And honestly, she didn't know which answer she wanted to be correct.

Reba used her thumb to wipe flour off Lee Ann's cheek, veiled hope leaking out of her now. "It'll be okay, sweetheart. Maybe he's finally grown up. The girls will get the dad they've always needed."

"No!" Lee Ann stood, dumping her chair over. She backed away until her head cracked against the cuckoo clock hanging on the wall. She righted the heirloom, then rubbed the sore spot on the back of her head as she eyed her mother. The woman may have still harbored resentment over the mess Cody had left their family in years ago, but she also managed to always hold on to that ridiculous thread of optimism that had once gotten her nothing but two kids—one not even hers—to raise on her own, and not one dollar of child support anywhere to be found. If anyone should know better, it was her.

No, they weren't going to do this. They would not hunt him down and beg him to finally be a father. As far as Lee Ann was concerned, Cody Dalton had already walked out on his responsibilities once, and he wouldn't get a second opportunity.

"Don't you dare tell him a word about them, Mother." She made it clear this was not a subject open for discussion. She'd made all decisions for Candy and Kendra since their births, just as she'd taken the lead so many times with her mother and sister as she'd been growing up. She'd had to, otherwise her mother—whose head seemed to stay in the happy clouds more often than not—would forget to make sure they had clean clothes for school or, worse, forget to pay the electric bill. It hadn't been lack of money, simply lack of concern to remember the silly details. "It will all work out" had always been her motto.

No, Lee Ann wouldn't stand for her mother closing her eyes to reality now and getting in the way of her kids' stability.

"He walked out on them, Mom. He doesn't deserve to know them. Plus, he'll be gone soon." She shook her head at the argument she could see forming. "We'll simply keep our distance while he's in town, and the kids will remain as happy and well adjusted as they've always been. I will not let him walk in here and hurt them."

She ignored the voice in the back of her head that asked if she wasn't also afraid he would walk in and hurt her. That wasn't a valid question. Doing it again wasn't possible.

"No matter what he did, sweetheart, he is their father," her mother said quietly as she bent over and righted the fallen chair. "He deserves to know them if he wants to." Reba had always believed the best in people and it galled Lee Ann every time her gullibility rose to the surface. Did she never learn from her mistakes? Then her mother's words made Lee Ann realize that even after her father had walked away when she was four, Reba would have let him back in their lives if he'd shown so much as an ounce of interest. Thank goodness for small blessings. After he'd walked out the door, he'd never glanced back.

She didn't need people who'd already turned their backs on her once. That meant she didn't need Cody.

And she refused to let him hurt her children.

After a pause, Lee Ann had herself back under control and decided to point out the likely truth, hoping that would get the point across to her mother. She softened her voice. "What if he doesn't actually want to get to know them, Mom? What then? He could be here purely for the job. And more importantly, what makes you think, given the kind of person he was when he left, that he is anyone we'd ever want around them?"

The knowledge of the kind of person Cody truly was still hurt. She'd once been his biggest supporter, certain that his crappy upbringing afforded him a bit of the chip on his shoulder he'd carried so proudly. She'd also believed she'd been the only one—aside from possibly his foster parents—who'd been able to see his real potential.

The fact that he'd ended up sleeping with her half sister instead of her, then raised complete hell on his way out of town, had actually surprised her more than it had anyone else. When Stephanie had informed Lee Ann and her mother months later that he'd declared he wanted nothing to do with his kids, Lee Ann had finally accepted that she'd been the idiot all along. He *was* the bad seed the majority of the townspeople had declared him to be.

And now he was coming back. No way had he redeemed himself, no matter what he'd done with his life since.

Her mother studied her with a mixture of understanding and regret, then gave an encouraging—though just barely—smile. "If that's what you want."

"It is." Lee Ann gave a decisive nod, glad to know she had her mother's support but also slightly irked with the tone eking out along with her mother's words. It was almost as if she were implying that Lee Ann always had to have her way. And that simply wasn't the case. It was purely the fact that if she didn't watch out for the girls, no one else would.

Stomping feet on the outside steps snagged Lee Ann's attention. The girls were home. She narrowed her eyes at her mother. "This conversation is on hold."

With a loud clatter, Kendra and Candy London tumbled through the door, backpacks, gym bags, and preteen awkwardness windmilling in with them. "Grandma!"

The girls dropped everything to give brief hugs to their grandmother, as if they didn't see her every day. Not only did Reba live next door, but whenever Lee Ann had photography appointments outside the home studio she'd added on a few years before, the girls stayed with their grandmother. And with Grandma they got away with everything. This accounted for their always being thrilled to see her.

Two sets of identical brown eyes faced Lee Ann, and a tiny shiver lit down her body as she recalled how very much those eyes matched Cody's. "You got a job tonight?"

Laughing, Lee Ann once again attempted to push Cody from her mind, and returned to the cinnamon rolls she'd been making before she'd gotten sidetracked. "Sorry, squirts," she said, calling them by the nickname she'd used since they'd been toddlers. "You're stuck with me tonight."

Good-natured groans came from both before they turned back to their grandmother. As Lee Ann spread melted butter on the dough, she fought back the clawing fear over what might happen if Cody insisted he wanted to get to know his daughters. Unless he proved himself completely inept, she knew that she couldn't keep them from him. More aptly, she couldn't keep *him* from *them*. She'd never be able to live with herself knowing that their father had been within spitting distance and she hadn't so much as introduced them.

Of course, that was assuming he wanted anything to do with them. He also had to prove that over the last thirteen years he'd learned to think of those other than himself. Because whether he was here in town or not, she would not do anything to put the girls' hearts at risk. She knew too much about what that kind of pain could do to a person.

She picked up the cinnamon and sugar mixture and sprinkled it over the butter. She couldn't help but play over the times in the past when the girls had asked about their father. The first had been when they were four. A child at their day care always got picked up by his father, and they'd finally asked about it. Telling them they simply had no father had been good enough at that point.

The subject had come up additional times over the years, mostly out of curiosity. Each occasion she'd given them a bit more of the truth. He'd chosen to move somewhere else. He was working in a different part of the country. He couldn't do what he wanted and stay in Sugar Springs at the same time.

She had never mentioned that she'd twice looked him up. The first time she'd gotten nowhere. The girls had just turned one and she still couldn't believe he was the type of person who'd turn his back on his offspring. No matter what he'd done to hurt her, she would have put that aside if he'd changed his mind and wanted to be involved in the kids' lives. She'd searched for him on the Internet but found nothing.

The last time they'd been three. She'd found a phone number registered to his name in Indiana and had almost called him that night. After a couple glasses of cheap wine long after the kids had gone to bed, she'd come close to convincing herself that Stephanie had lied. Not about him being the father. No, she'd walked in on that particular episode and had seen it with her own two eyes.

But about him not wanting anything to do with the girls.

It certainly wouldn't have been the first time her half sister had made up a story.

In the end, Lee Ann had put the phone down and had one more glass of wine instead. She'd simply wanted to talk to *him* more than anything else. Life as a single mother wasn't easy, and she was often lonely. Those times brought back memories of her high school senior year and the boy she'd once planned to spend the rest of her life with.

Instead, she was spending it with his kids.

Kendra cackled out with laughter at something Reba had said, and Lee Ann couldn't help but say a silent prayer of thanks for her daughters' health. Stephanie had come home at five months pregnant, sick around the clock and barely able to keep anything down. Lee Ann had left college on the weekends to help take care of her, yet nothing they'd tried had ever allowed Steph to gain more than a minimum of pounds.

Finally, six weeks early, the girls had been born. They'd been taken by Cesarean, and during the procedure the doctor had discovered that Stephanie's insides were eaten up with cancer. The months-long sickness hadn't been solely due to the pregnancy, and no one had known until it had been too late.

Somehow, though the kids had been born with low birth weights and had been growing alongside fatal cancer, their health—both then and since—remained relatively unscathed.

"Mom!" Fingers snapped in front of Lee Ann as Candy got her attention. "Geez, Mom. Where'd you zone off to? We asked a question."

She smiled at the long, tall young ladies standing before her, now trying their best to appear too bored to be in the same room with her. They didn't have to fake the annoyance, though. They had that one down to a tee. Swirling her fingers into a pyramid of soft flour piled on the countertop, Lee Ann lifted her hand and flicked, sprinkling both girls with powder. "What do you want?"

Fake outrage followed by instant giggles ensued as the girls dragged their own fingers along the flour-covered laminate and returned the onslaught. They may be developing teenage girl attitudes she rarely cared for, but they were still her fun little girls.

After being bombarded, Lee Ann conceded defeat and ducked her head, arms outstretched over the dough. "Stop!" She laughed as powder landed on her head. "I've got to finish these and get them in the freezer so there are enough for the fund-raiser."

With one hand propped on a hip attached to too-long legs, Kendra raised a dark eyebrow and made a face of superiority. She looked very much like her biological mother in that pose. "Then don't start what you can't finish."

Lee Ann didn't think of her sister often these days, but today seemed to be the day for a walk down memory lane. It had been almost thirteen years since Stephanie's death. In fact, five weeks from today would make it exactly so. Five days after she'd given birth to the girls. Lee Ann flicked her fingers toward Kendra one last time. "What were ya'll asking me?"

Candy laid out their plans. "Sadie Evans...You remember, her father owns the *good* restaurant in town. Well, the diner is good, too," she tacked on in a hurry, and Lee Ann guessed that had more to do with the fact her mother worked there during the weekday breakfast shift than any devoted love for the place. "She wants us to come over and have dinner at her house and then work on our school project."

"It's a school night," Lee Ann interjected.

"I told her that." Candy rolled her eyes in the exasperating way both she and her sister had picked up over the last six months. "Said you'd say no, too. Especially since we were out last night at the basketball game. But she has these really *fab* ideas, and they're going to take forever to get done." Thin shoulders lifted in a shrug. "We need to get started or we won't be finished before the Christmas break."

There were four weeks before the Christmas break, so Lee Ann wasn't buying that at all.

"Kendra and I already did our homework," Candy continued. "If we leave now, we'll be home by nine o'clock."

When Candy finally took a breath, Lee Ann opened her mouth to get in a question, but Kendra took over.

"Sadie's mom will pick us up and bring us back."

Candy shot her sister a frustrated glare before continuing, with a slightly less accommodating tone. She liked to be in charge. "Sadie's mom said she needs to get us before she starts dinner, though. And since there's only one more school day this week, can't you say okay just this once? *Please.*"

Silence fell over the room as both girls stood perfectly straight—wide-eyed and unblinking—waiting for her answer. Lee Ann peered around them to see if her mother was taking this in. They were now going for sweet, but with all the preteen running through them, they had no idea they came up short. Reba hid a grin behind her hand.

Lee Ann began rolling the dough up into a spiral as she pretended to contemplate the situation. What they didn't know was that she could use the time to herself tonight. The thought of Cody coming back to town had thrown her for a loop, and she needed to figure out how best to handle it. Good idea or not, tonight was the perfect time to have the kids out of the house. Life wouldn't end if she loosened her rules just this once.

"What about helping me with these cinnamon rolls?" she asked Candy. "I still have to make several more batches tonight. The sale is to help your team get to basketball camp next summer, after all."

She held her breath, waiting to hear the counter to her argument. She actually enjoyed their ingenuity at times. She wasn't disappointed. Kendra stepped up to answer before Candy could. "We thought about that already, too."

Out of the corner of her eye, Lee Ann noted her mother look discreetly down at her lap.

"We called Grandma after we talked to Sadie's mom."

Candy jumped in to finish. "It was our idea, so don't get mad at Grandma, but we called her to see if she could maybe help you tonight. Since she said yes, we'll put out her Christmas lights for her this weekend *without complaining.*"

"You—"

"We can do it after the fund-raiser," Kendra interrupted.

Lee Ann once again cast a glance at her mother, only to witness a guilty gleam shining from her eyes. "You were in on this?"

Wearing an innocent expression, Reba mimicked the girls' tone. "It's a really big project, and they *do* need extra time to finish."

Shaking her head, Lee Ann marveled at her total lack of control with any of them. She motioned to the back door. "Put your stuff away and call Mrs. Evans. She can pick you up as soon as you've emptied the dishwasher."

With a whoop of glee, they grabbed their bags and scrambled from the room.

Lee Ann faced the kitchen table. "Mother..."

Reba pushed her sleeves past her elbows and rose from the chair. "You know I can't say no to those girls. Besides, it is for a school project." She slid the rolled-up dough over in front of her. "Hand me the string and cookie sheet and I'll cut this batch. You can start on the next."

At the sound of movement in the rooms overhead, Lee Ann returned to their earlier conversation in a whisper. "How did you find out he was coming back?"

Reba concentrated on her task. "I saw Dr. Wright waddling up the steps to that apartment over her clinic. The building's at the end of the street, so I can see it from my house, you know. Anyway, it seemed the perfect time for a walk."

"Hmmm...I'm sure it did." And she could not see the vet's office from her house, but old Ms. Grayson, who lived across from the office, would have started calling people the minute anything the slightest out of the ordinary happened.

Ignoring the sarcasm, Reba continued. "Anyway, I went for a stroll and walked that direction—just to make sure Keri was okay, mind you. To see if she needed any help. She is due any day, you know."

"Of course."

"And there she was. Hauling cleaning supplies up and down that rickety set of stairs."

He really was coming. Pressure grew behind her rib cage. "And you're sure he's only here for six weeks?"

"By the time I got there, Beatrice"—*Ms. Grayson*—"had already grilled Keri. She filled me in. He'll be here through the end of the year. Keri wanted to take more time off, but he already had another job lined up starting the first Monday of January. She was lucky to get him last minute after the guy she had coming from Nashville canceled on her last week." Her mother nodded, proud of her sleuthing skills. "Yep, six weeks. And he should be here any minute now."

That meant she would actually have to deal with figuring out whether to let him meet the girls or not. Assuming he wasn't the boy he'd once been.

Her mother seemed to guess where her mind had headed. "No matter what he did in the past, you need to introduce them."

Lee Ann shoved the mixing bowl into the sink of water simply to have something to do that would give her a moment of not facing her mother. "I need to figure out who he is these days before I even think about anything else."

"He's their father," she said quietly. "He deserves to know them."

"Then he should have stuck around."

The quiet, methodical sound of pinwheels being sliced and placed on the baking pan lulled Lee Ann into glancing over her shoulder.

Her mother pinned her with a look. "What did he have to stick around for? Stephanie didn't know she was pregnant when he left, and he knew he'd destroyed any chance with you. If Steph hadn't gotten pregnant, would you have wanted him to stay?"

"That's not the point. We're talking about the girls now. Not me and Cody almost fourteen years ago. Plus, he could have come back when the girls were born!" Lee Ann faced her mom, hands clasping the sink behind her. She only loosened her grip when the edge of the countertop bit into her fingers. "Aren't you even still mad at him a little? He destroyed our lives, Mom."

Her mother nodded, weariness creeping in over her relatively unlined skin, and Lee Ann could tell that she wasn't purely jumping at the idea of letting the man back into their lives. "The fact he's back says something," her mother said. "And no, he doesn't deserve to be forgiven freely, but those girls do deserve a father."

"They are happy. They have a great life. Why would I risk messing that up?"

"What if he wants to be a part of it? How could you keep that from them?"

Lee Ann's heart thudded as she wondered if more than concern for the girls was holding her back. The mere mention of Cody's name had made her yearn to run down the street to watch for his arrival herself. But she knew what would happen if she opened the door of their lives and let him in.

Hopes would rise, excitement would grow, and dreams of having a father would eventually be lost forever. She curled her hands into fists to keep them from shaking. No. She wouldn't allow that. Not in her daughters' lives. Not in hers.

Hearing the thunder of feet pounding down the polished wood stairs, Lee Ann leaned in to face her mother square on. Her voice could barely be heard. "And what do I do when he decides the novelty of being a father has worn off and leaves?"

Her mother began to shake her head, but Lee Ann cut the movement off. "He won't stick, Mom. It's not in his nature. He's done nothing but run since he was old enough to move."

❀ ❀ ❀

A handful of tiny snowflakes splatted on the front windshield of Cody Dalton's SUV as he sat parked on the side of the two-lane road just outside the "Welcome to Sugar Springs" sign. What in the world did he think he was doing? He hadn't seen this place since he'd taken his foster dad's truck, tied a chain from it to the statue in the middle of the town square, then pulled the founding father over. He'd dragged a large chunk of the stone some twenty yards before the whole thing had ripped the twenty-year-old Chevy's bumper to the ground. At that point, he'd gotten the hell out of dodge.

And he'd never imagined coming back.

One lone person had crossed his mind over the years, however, though he'd never dreamed he'd actually screw up the courage to come back and face her again. Not after what he'd done.

Chances were good she would welcome neither him nor his apology with anything resembling open arms. And if he were being honest, he knew that Lee Ann wasn't the only one who would not be in line to welcome him back. He imagined the whole darned town would be more than happy to run him back out on the same path he rode in on. Probably no more than a minute after he drove through the square for the first time. He'd done all of them wrong.

He'd felt bad about it for years, but he had made amends. At least, as best he could. Whether anyone realized it or not.

And now he was back. Voluntarily. He had lost his ever-loving mind.

He reached over and patted Boss, his harlequin Great Dane, on the head and came away with a fistful of drool for his efforts. Chuckling, he wiped his hand on his faded jeans and bumped the side of his head against Boss's as the dog leaned over for a bit more love. Rescuing Boss from his previous home three years earlier had been one of the best moves he'd ever made. Unlike what this temporary assignment was going to be.

The idea of driving beyond the point where he currently sat made a spot in the middle of his shoulder blades itch, but he couldn't back out now. He'd stay for the six weeks he'd agreed upon, do his best to make amends while he was there, then be on his way to his next assignment. Where he and Boss would spend three sunny months in the Florida Keys. There, they would enjoy the beach and sand and the gorgeous lack of cold.

A few more flakes fell, these a bit fatter, and he flipped his wipers once to clear the glass. The precipitation wasn't enough to amount to accumulation yet—it was too early in the season. It was simply enough to be annoying. With a sigh and shake of his head, he started the engine and pulled slowly back out onto the highway, pointing his car toward the little tourist town that sat at the base of the Smoky Mountains. Might as well quit dragging his feet and get to it.

He would hopefully have plenty of work to keep him busy, but in his spare time he had to figure out a way to beg forgiveness for the shameful behavior he'd exhibited toward Lee Ann his last day there. He didn't deserve a second chance, and he wasn't asking for one, but he was man enough to admit that she deserved an apology. Even this many years later. Hell, the whole town deserved one for the stunt with the statue.

A long overdue one.

When he'd seen the request for a temp vet come across the listings, fitting in perfectly with his schedule and the direction he'd been headed, it had smacked of a higher power telling him it was time to grow a pair and act like the man he hoped to one day become. With a few clicks of his mouse, he'd verified that Lee Ann was still in town, then placed the call that would free him from the lingering guilt over the way he'd once treated one of the best people who'd ever happened across his path.

He'd tuck tail and grovel, not only apologizing to Lee Ann, but doing his best to give back to the community that, if he were to be honest, had been the best one he'd lived in throughout his childhood. Then he'd move on with his life and leave them all alone for good.

He only hoped they didn't run him out of town before he'd had a chance to prove that he was not the kid he'd been when he'd left.

CHAPTER

2

"You should be named Sugar. You're just as sweet as the water this town was named after." Sam Jenkins, seventy if he was a day, smiled at Lee Ann over his topped-off cup of coffee the next morning, his eyes twinkling in the wrinkled face of a man who'd done a whole lot of living. He was one of the people Lee Ann looked forward to seeing the most every morning.

She set the coffeepot on the diner's blockwood tabletop, then slid onto the chair opposite him. Leaning in, she lifted an eyebrow and gave him her best haughtier-than-thou look. The one she'd picked up from her daughters. "I'm not quite sure how to take that, Sam. It sounds like a compliment, yet you and I both know the studies showed there's nothing sweet in the water coming from our springs. I think you just told me I'm as plain as water."

One of the best parts of her part-time job was interacting with the customers, including chatting with the many tourists, whose number ebbed and flowed with the seasons. Lee Ann knew every resident in town. A large percentage of them started their mornings off there in the diner. Seeing so many friends on a regular basis made having to carry a second job easier to handle. Her dreams of being a full-time photographer could wait. Right now, she had her daughters' college funds to save for.

It was nine o'clock and the rush was over. Only retirees remained, lingering over coffee and chatting with longtime friends. Many of their conversations were about the temporary vet who'd made it into town late the night before. He'd apparently been spotted lugging two duffels and a bag they'd described as "looking like a vet kind of thing" up the apartment stairs, along with what they all referred to as a horse-sized black-and-white dog. How Cody and a dog the size of him were going to fit in the small one-bedroom above Keri's office was beyond Lee Ann's imagination, but luckily it was no concern of hers.

Same as the fact she'd caught sight of him and that monstrous dog out running in the predawn light as she'd walked to work that morning. None of it was any concern of hers. And she could simply forget that she'd had the urge to get closer purely for the reason of seeing what he looked like after all these years.

From a distance, he'd been just a man with a dog. A nicely built, very large man with a dog.

And that had pissed her off.

She'd wanted him to be fat and balding, though at thirty-two that was improbable. Especially when he'd started with the raw material he had. Still, a girl could dream.

No, the only concern of hers was to keep in mind that he was in town temporarily to handle a job that needed to be handled. Someone that—given the town's small size—she would eventually be required to have a conversation with, no matter whether she brought the girls in on the fact he was their father or not.

Ugh.

"Now, Lee Ann," Sam said, winking at her, unaware of the mental anguish she was currently slogging through as she perched in the chair across from him. "You know I paid you a compliment. This place wouldn't be the same without you." He slurped the hot liquid. "Half the people in town come in here just to start the morning off with you. When are you going to quit playing hard to get and settle down with one of them?"

She smiled. They had this conversation at least once a week. If only there was someone around worth settling down with. "None of them move fast enough to catch me, Sam. You know I'm a busy woman."

He chuckled. "Maybe if you let one catch you, you could slow down."

"Nah." Hearing the tinkle of the bell, she stood, preparing to greet the latest arrival. "I'd get bored if I did that. Then where would I be?"

Before she turned, a hush fell over the remaining patrons as every single one of them stared toward the door. Lee Ann's stomach crawled to her knees. Only one person in town could create that reaction on this particular morning. With tons of dread—and more curiosity than was healthy—she took a deep breath and steadied her nerves. She then turned to face Cody.

And crap. It might have been better not to see him up close.

Just as she remembered, his dark hair was still too long, curling a bit at the ends, and at the moment it was poking out from beneath a dark green skullcap pulled snugly over the locks. He hadn't shaved that morning. This fact highlighted the strong facial structure he'd had as an eighteen-year-old, now in its maturity making quite the impression, covered with day-old whiskers. The tension flexing that very jaw implied he was as uncertain about his being there as was every single person sitting around staring at him.

As his vision adjusted to the dimmer inside lighting, he blinked his dark eyes, and she got busy scanning over the rest of him. She shouldn't—she knew that. She was an idiot for even wanting a glance. After all, he'd not only broken off a chunk of her heart when he'd slept with Stephanie, he'd disappeared before giving her the opportunity to reclaim it.

Luckily, the years had healed that particular hurt. That meant she could take him in now with the appreciation of a photographer's eye, and her heart would be none the wiser.

Her gaze slid downward.

Her heart may be out of the picture, but her pulse was right there with her. Cody Dalton was gorgeous. And he still screamed dark and dangerous. He stood six four, one whole foot taller than her, and filled the doorway from shoulder to shoulder. Dressed in faded jeans and worn, brown boots, he could almost pass for a local hunter. Only what was above the waist gave a totally different impression. An untucked, dark blue shirt could be seen under the black leather jacket hanging open to his hips, and licking out from the edge of the collar, at the spot where his chest just met the right side of his neck, was what appeared to be the beginning of a tattoo.

Oh, yeah, this was definitely the Cody who had stormed out of her house years ago, angry at everyone he'd ever met and carrying the world's largest chip on his shoulder. She'd often wondered how he'd managed to get out of bed every morning with that thing weighing him down.

He seemed to focus and stepped farther into the room, then glanced at the "Please Wait to Be Seated" sign, frowned and headed to an empty booth away from everyone else.

Two seconds after his rear hit the vinyl, his back stiffened and his head rotated slowly in her direction. He recognized her.

Her heartbeat felt as if it had split in two. Half of it galloped at rapid speed, and the other half remained slow and steady, just daring her to try to let his presence matter.

Taking her time, she ignored the inner struggle to smooth the rumpled apron over her too-faded jeans, and headed his way. When she reached the table, a mix of the fresh outdoors and a woodsy cologne tickled her nose. She straightened her spine but remained silent. There wasn't a single thing coming to mind that she could think to utter.

Get the hell out of town? Go back to the rock you crawled out from under? Please, for the love of God, put me out of my misery and smile at me just once like you used to?

"It's good to see you again, Lee Ann." His deep voice jolted her from her own mind, and she berated herself for her last thought. He may have been her friend once, but he wasn't now.

He flipped over the porcelain cup and she filled it before dropping the menu to the table in front of him.

With a tight smile and making absolutely certain not to make eye contact, she nodded. "Cody. Welcome to the Sugar Springs Diner." Unintentionally, she let her southern accent drawl out more than usual, mortifying her when she remembered how he'd once liked it when she'd played it up. She concentrated to make sure she spoke normally. "The daily special is attached to the inside of the menu. I'll give you a minute to decide."

Without another word, she hurried to the back. She ripped off her apron as soon as the kitchen door closed behind her. The owners—friends of hers—always understood when she had to shift her schedule for photography appointments, and though she didn't make a habit out of lying, today seemed a great time to stretch the truth.

Tucking her apron into her cubby, she grabbed her purse, then headed to find Holly Marshall, the youngest of five kids and one of the owners. Holly stood behind the grill, cooking her own breakfast.

"I just remembered I have an early appointment this morning. Can you finish up for me? It's pretty slow. Only one new customer right now."

"Sure thing, sweetie." Holly didn't take her eyes off the grill as she reached for the pancake batter. "I'll just take him the special. He hasn't cracked open the menu—been too busy watching you."

Lee Ann fought the urge to peek over the prep line but lost. One little peek and yes, menu on the table, coffee untouched, and brown eyes trained on her.

Her toes curled.

As she watched, she realized she recognized the drop of loneliness she'd always seen hidden in the depths of his eyes. Weight pressed down on her. She would not let herself feel guilty for wanting him to have nothing to do with Candy and Kendra. Keeping the status quo would be in the girls' best interest. They didn't need someone like him messing things up.

When his gaze shifted, landing briefly on her mouth, she gripped the bar running along the front of the grill. A girl could go all kinds of stupid with all that trained on her. Luckily, she'd learned her lesson years ago. Narrowing her gaze, she made it as clear as possible that she had better things to do. No matter what he was back in town for, she would not be sucked in by his good looks and charm. Not this time.

Prying her fingers from the metal, Lee Ann backed away until she was out of sight of the dining room. Only then was she able to pull a full breath of air into her lungs. She had to get out of there.

She glanced at Holly, remembering her friend had made a comment she hadn't responded to, but her mind couldn't come up with whatever the words had been. Instead, she shook her head as if in apology and turned to go. "I'm out of here."

🌼 🌼 🌼

Cody couldn't get over the changes in Lee Ann. She'd always been good looking in an innocent, girl-next-door sort of way. Her pointy chin and cute little mouth reminded him of the dolls his third, or maybe fourth, foster-mother had collected. But with her long black hair now short and spiky, and the cute-girl innocence replaced by feminine curves and maturity, she was a gorgeous mix. Half tough, half fragile. He found himself with the strangest urge to discover which half was more dominant.

Something about the look she'd given him from the grill line suggested it was the tough side. And given her delay in returning, he also suspected she was avoiding him.

He couldn't blame her. Shame rolled through him at the things he'd done. Didn't matter what the excuse, he'd loved her as much as possible at the time. He shouldn't have let hatred of himself get in the way to the point that he'd hurt her. He should have just left.

Getting out of her life was supposed to have ensured she reached all her dreams. Instead, he'd been shocked to find she'd never even left town.

He'd made that discovery five years ago when he'd gotten his Doctor of Veterinary Medicine from Purdue. The pride he'd felt upon receiving his degree, and the fact he had no one in his life to share it with, had made him think of Lee Ann. She'd once pulled it out of him that being a veterinarian was his dream. She'd also been the one to convince him that he could do it. Before her, it had merely been a fantasy. So he'd looked her up that day, having zero doubt he'd find her making a huge splash with her photography, but had instead found her still living here.

It had almost been enough to send him back to Tennessee right then and there to shake her and ask why she hadn't followed her own heart. He'd made it as a vet because of her, because she'd once believed in him. The thought that something had stopped her from attaining her dream too had disturbed him on several levels.

Heading out of town after graduation had been number one on her agenda. They'd planned to go together. She would go to college in Knoxville on a scholarship, and he would work and save until he could attend as well.

Instead she'd done what?

Stayed here and opened a portrait studio? He flipped over the menu in front of him, but didn't bother opening it, still dwelling on Lee Ann. Portraits were not what she'd loved. She was good at it, sure. He'd spent a couple hours perusing the website he'd found for her studio before he'd committed to this job, and yes, she was very good. But that hadn't been her goal. She'd once loved landscapes. And animals. And exposing the two together in black and whites. And she'd been brilliant at it.

He couldn't get over the thought that she'd settled.

As he waited for her to return, he took in the décor of the comfortable restaurant. When he'd lived there his senior year, the diner had been half its current size and run by one of the oldest couples in town. As he and Lee Ann had become friends, it was often where they ended up after school, either for milkshakes with her best friend, Joanie, or he would just hang out there while she worked. She'd been his only bright spot in eighteen years of desolation.

He lifted the coffee to his mouth and took a sip.

Ms. Grayson had caught him that morning after his and Boss's run and had filled him in that the diner was the place for breakfast. He'd also discovered that ownership had passed down, skipping a generation, but he had excused himself before finding out that Lee Ann still worked there. He preferred to leave the gossip to the residents, but that was one nugget of info he wished he'd stuck around for. Seeing her when he'd come in had screwed with his mind.

He wasn't ready to see her yet.

He would eventually seek her out. He had to in order to deliver the apology he'd come to give, but he needed to get his feet under him first. He glanced toward the back again, wondering if he should go ahead and broach the idea of them getting together to talk, or if he should just wait. Bring it up another time. Of course, no time was a good time to grovel.

When he still caught no sign of her, he returned to his perusal of the restaurant. From where he sat, the grandchildren had done a good job with it, creating a warm, family atmosphere complete with roaring fireplace in the center and wooden rockers lined up across the front porch. The once-mismatched furniture had been replaced by wooden tables with cushioned slatted chairs and similarly styled booths. The place remained cozy but no longer quite as small-town unique as it had once been.

He scanned the area again, took in the odd selection of old men dotting the room, the equally eccentric women, most of whom were no longer blatantly staring at him, and had to admit that the base clientele had not altered.

Changing views, he turned from the customers and peered out the large windows gracing the front of the building. He said a silent thanks that at least the new owners hadn't changed the view.

Even though he'd never felt fully connected to the town, he'd come as close to feeling like he belonged there as he had to anywhere he'd lived. He used to sit in this very spot and look out over the town square and imagine being born to a place like this. A place that actually was his home, instead of somewhere to borrow for only a short time.

He studied the scenery, curious about the changes that had happened over the last decade. The same florist stood across the street, the "Closed" sign turned face out waiting for the day to begin, the bank—shutters drawn—stood next to it, then an empty storefront, and a new salon on the opposite corner. He squinted to bring the salon sign into focus then chuckled softly as he read the name. "Curl Up 'N Dye."

Then there was the statue standing proudly in the middle of it all.

He couldn't tell from this distance if it was the one he'd damaged, only repaired, or if they'd commissioned a new one. Either way, emotion clogged his throat as he hoped his actions hadn't completely ruined the piece of history that had always been a source of pride for the town.

Cody caught sight of a tray from the corner of his eye, and forcing what he hoped to be a welcoming expression, turned back. Only to be surprised to find someone other than Lee Ann smiling down at him.

In a swirl of strong perfume, bold makeup and shoes that seemed to have nothing whatsoever to do with the outfit, a curvy woman slid two plates of eggs, pancakes, and bacon onto the table. Next came syrup and glasses of orange juice. Then the woman herself landed on the bench across from him.

She held out her hand, equipped with cherry-red nails, and she struck him as a person who might draw blood with those daggers if someone didn't do as she commanded. Bracelets jangled on her wrist as he shook her hand.

"Holly Marshall, part owner of this fine establishment. The youngest owner to be exact." She winked, her glittery eye shadow flashing at him. "I was apparently a mistake."

Keeping his eyesight above her chin, he nodded in greeting. "Cody Dalton."

"You don't have to tell me who you are, sugar." She picked up a fork and dug into her food. "Five minutes after you hit town yesterday afternoon I knew your name. Five minutes after that I knew your history."

Sensing words unnecessary, Cody drizzled warm maple syrup over his plate. As he shoveled a sweetened pancake into his mouth, waiting to hear what the five-minute history lesson had done for her opinion of him, he was swamped by memories. He closed his eyes as his mind rewound to fourteen years earlier. Pearl had always insisted he eat breakfast, the most important meal of the day. More often than not, she would serve pancakes. He couldn't remember the last time he'd eaten them. He opened his eyes. Probably the morning of the day he'd left town.

Given the gossip no doubt running rampant in town, she and Roy Monroe, his foster parents, would know about his arrival by this point. Not that it mattered. He'd made sure their truck got back to them when he'd left it at the Memphis train station. Months later he'd sent a check to pay for the damage he'd done to the bumper. He owed them nothing now.

He scooped up another bite, but couldn't keep from drifting back in time again.

It wasn't as if the whole year he'd spent there had been bad. In fact, most of it had been fairly uneventful. The Monroes had given him chores, like all the other families he'd lived with over the years, but at least there he'd gotten to work with animals. He hadn't minded getting up mornings to feed the horses and see to the cleaning of their stalls. For some reason he'd always connected better with animals than with humans. Hanging out with them had been almost pleasurable.

He'd come to Sugar Springs right after his seventeenth birthday, after bouncing through other Tennessee counties, so he'd tried to take advantage of the new location and see the change as a fresh chance in his life.

It had lasted until the first day of school.

His reputation followed him, and no one let him forget it. The first thing to go down at school, even though he hadn't actually been anywhere near the incident, had been blamed on him. Once again, he'd become the troublemaker.

After polishing off a pancake and half her eggs, Holly propped her elbows on the table, bringing Cody back to the present and giving him a view of some impressive cleavage. She tapped one fingernail against her lips in concentration and he worked hard to keep his focus lifted high. "I'd say it's about a fifty-fifty chance of you succeeding here," she began. "Of course, with you intending to stay only through the end of the year, I'd further guess it doesn't matter so much if you're a success or not. Those who refuse to forgive your past exploits simply better hope their animals don't get sick in the next few weeks."

The thought of his presence keeping animals from needed care bothered him. Proving his worth wouldn't be easy, but it had never occurred to him that a pet might suffer simply because he existed. With the nearest vet in the next town over, many of the older residents would struggle if they had to go that far for their pets' health.

"I certainly hope no one refuses service because of me. I'm aware it'll take time for some to realize I'm a grown man now, not a self-centered kid, but I wouldn't have accepted the position if I'd thought it might cause animals not to get needed care."

Her green gaze probed his for a full thirty seconds before she nodded. "I believe you mean that."

He blinked. "Just like that? You believe me?" He'd gotten good at reading people, and he read sincerity from her. He didn't know anything about her, but if he had to put down a bet, he'd go with her being a genuinely good person.

A grin lit her face. "Just like that. I make snap judgments about people." She snapped her fingers in the space between them. "And I hold a ninety-nine percent accuracy record."

A chuckle made its way up from deep in his gut. For the first time since he'd made the decision to come, he felt he might make at least one friend while in town. "Ninety-nine percent, huh? What makes you so certain I won't bring your record down?"

She leaned back in her seat, and he picked up his glass. "Simple," she said. "You haven't stared at my cleavage one time. Well, other than that first glance, but I'll forgive you for that one. Actually, I would have been offended if you hadn't taken a peek."

Orange juice burned his nose as he choked. She sat patiently as he got himself under control. Finally, with eyes watering, he asked, "Were you around fourteen years ago, Holly? I don't remember you."

She shrugged. "I was eleven. No chest, mouth full of metal, early acne, thought boys were stupid. No reason for you to remember me."

"Well, it's nice meeting you now. And seeing as you're one of only two people who've been friendly to me so far..." And Ms. Grayson, he suspected, had been nice simply in hopes of obtaining some juicy tidbit to share. "I hope to see you around again." He cleaned his plate and held out his hand. Friendliness was one thing, but until he knew more about the town's dynamics, he'd do good to remember that obvious busybodies weren't the only people looking to share gossip. "If you'll be so kind as to hand over my ticket, I'll be on my way."

"So soon?" She appeared honestly upset. "I wanted to get to know you more. Ask a few questions and figure out if some of the things I heard about you last night are true."

He lifted a brow but didn't ask. Probably many of them were. "Maybe another time. I got in too late to meet with Dr. Wright last night, so I need to hustle on over to the clinic. Have to get acquainted with where I'm about to spend the next few weeks."

"Oh, then yeah, you'd better get to it. The woman is a walking time bomb. That baby could come any minute."

She finished her juice, still ignoring his outstretched hand, and pushed her plate away. "It's been a true pleasure, Cody. I hope you come on back in most mornings. This place could use something new to talk about."

"No doubt that would do it," he muttered. He reached for his wallet. "The bill?"

She shook her head. "How about you repay me by accompanying me to the junior high basketball fund-raiser in the morning? It's at the school."

His breath whistled through his teeth at the quick change of subject. Granted, she was good looking and funny, if a little young for his taste, but he wasn't in town to date. "I'm...uh... not sure I can make it."

"Are you kidding me?" Her red lips parted with a wide smile, and he noted that she really was a good-looking woman. There had to be many men in town who'd love to take her to the fund-raiser. "It's just down the street from your apartment, and I happen to be privy to the fact that Keri plans on working tomorrow morning. After today, you won't have to report back to the office until Monday—assuming her water doesn't break, of course."

"Of course," he agreed.

Holly tilted her head and studied him with an eye that made him nervous. "Then why else turn me down? It's not like Sugar Springs is a bustling hotbed with a plethora of options for a Saturday morning."

That was true. He opened his mouth to try another tactic but came up with nothing. Finally, he simply shrugged. "I'm sorry, Holly. I didn't come to town to date anyone."

"Hmmm...not even Lee Ann, then?"

"What? No." He shook his head and rose from his seat, feeling suddenly pinned in. "Absolutely not Lee Ann."

"But you dated her once."

God, he hated small-town gossip. "Yeah, I dated her once. Years ago. We were teenagers, we kissed, we drank milkshakes after school, end of story."

"Except from what I hear, you also broke her heart when you went ape shit off the deep end and tore the town down, then left without so much as a good-bye."

Hell. Clearly the stories were flying fast and furious. Then something occurred to him. She'd only pointed out that he'd broken Lee Ann's heart by leaving town. What about what he'd done with Stephanie? How had that not come up? It would soon enough. Unless...

He stared down at her, trying to figure out if it were honestly possible that what he'd done in the London living room that afternoon had been kept secret from the hordes of people who made gossiping a daily ritual. It was almost too unreal to believe. And then something else crossed his mind. Stephanie.

Shit, he hadn't even thought about her. Was she around? Hopefully she'd gone back to Nashville for good after that day. If she'd remained in town for any length of time, he couldn't imagine her not blurting to the world how she'd managed to screw over both the bad boy and her little sister, all in one fell swoop.

But from the obvious lack of knowledge on Holly's part, it appeared that Lee Ann had somehow managed to keep that secret hidden. Otherwise, Holly would have mentioned it. After all, his behavior with Stephanie was the juiciest part of the gossip.

If Stephanie *did* happen to be in town, he now worried that the silence from that day would change. Would his being back end up causing Lee Ann even more grief than he'd already doled out? *Damn.* He hoped not. But he couldn't imagine him being there and the past not coming back up between the two sisters. If that happened, a single conversation held anywhere but a thick, padded room would eventually be heard by the full population of Sugar Springs.

Maybe he should have thought this plan through better.

Holly was watching him silently, a gleam in her eye. "What is it, Doc? Was there more to the story than I'm privy to?"

Christ. He had to quit letting his thoughts roam across his face. Sitting back down, he went for calm and collected and focused hard not to say anything that could later be used against him. "Of course there wasn't. Simply remembering the past. I hadn't thought about it in a long time." *Liar.* "And now I really do have to go." He held out his hand again. "The bill?"

She pushed his hand away. "Don't worry. The fact you have a secret is safe with me. And please, think nothing of my suggestion about the fund-raiser. I'm not after you. I merely wanted some company." She gave him a mischievous wink. "As well as to work on one teensy secret of my own. It's something that could benefit you as well as me, actually, if you cared to hear it."

He lifted his brows in a questioning look before he caught himself, unable to believe that he was even mildly interested in hearing what she had to say. He felt like he was already being sucked into the cyclone that made up small-town living, and he didn't care for it one bit.

She tucked her hair behind her ear and leaned forward. "I'm after Tucker Brown," she whispered. "For some temporary fun—at least until I get out of town for good. He's a teacher at the junior high and he's playing hard to get. I thought a little jealousy by showing up with another man might push him in my direction."

"Ah…a woman with a plan." He couldn't fault her for that, but that didn't change the fact he didn't want to go. Doing so would place him exactly where he'd sworn to himself he wouldn't be when he'd agreed to the job. Right smack in the middle of a big community lovefest.

His plan was to express his apologies to the general population by the simple act of doing a good job. By being the guy they could depend on while Dr. Wright was indisposed. And he'd planned to do all that from the outskirts. Being involved was not in the mix. "I must admit I admire seeing a person go after what she wants, but I don't see how that could benefit me."

"I've got a plan for you, too, of course."

"For me?" He couldn't imagine a scenario that would interest him.

"It involves Lee Ann." She paused and he knew she'd said the only thing that could have gotten his attention. She snickered. "Yeah, I can see just fine from the grill line. Say what you want, but I saw the way you were watching her."

He grunted. "I wasn't watching."

She smiled, a slow movement of her mouth spreading wide across rosy cheeks, and she suddenly looked even younger. "You were watching. And she was watching, too. Maybe only curiosity, maybe more, I'm not sure. But given your past, I'm willing to bet there's something left there on both sides, even if it's merely a proper good-bye."

Cody considered the woman across from him, uncomfortable with the fact that she seemed to be keying in on him a bit too close to home. He hadn't come back to Sugar Springs to start anything with Lee Ann, but he did owe her that apology.

Given the way she'd run from him that morning, he suspected it was going to be hard to trap her anywhere long enough for a conversation. Could he do it at the fund-raiser?

"You think she'll be there?" he asked.

"I know for a fact she will be. She's in charge this year."

His jaw sagged, and he felt his shoulders slump with the action. In charge of a junior high fund-raiser? He shook his head. Wow, the woman had changed. She may have fit into the community fine when she was younger—and yes, she'd liked to take charge and bustle everyone around to her liking—but she'd also had goals that didn't involve this place. And she'd had definite plans on how to get herself there.

She'd wanted to get out of town, get away from the dependency her mother had on her, and make a name for herself with her photography. Yet years later she remained in the same one-stoplight town, with a portrait studio, leading fund-raisers for a bunch of kids?

Little about that made sense.

His heart sank with his next thought. *Oh, God.* She was married with a handful of kids. Was that it? Why she'd never left?

Holly shook her head with a knowing smile. "Nope, she's not married. Never has been."

He could see she was holding more information that she wasn't willing to share.

"Then why would she be in charge?" he asked.

She rose from the table and smirked down at him. "There's one easy way for you to find out, Doc."

Go to the damned fund-raiser myself.

He held back a groan. The last thing he wanted to do was go, but the conversation had brought up some big questions that he found himself more curious about than he should have been. "Does the entire town still come out for these things?"

"Oh, yeah."

He scanned the remaining customers. One man still openly scowled at him while the rest had resorted to stealing peeks, all probably trying to figure out if he planned to sneak out during the middle of the night and set the town square on fire. They weren't going to accept him back into their community easily, and he doubted that showing up in the middle of an annual town event and upsetting one of their favorites would win him any awards, either.

He returned his attention to Holly. "I'd better not. Looks like people don't seem overly thrilled with me being here as it is. Might be safer to stay in the background for a while."

She angled her head as if not in total disagreement, then gave a quick nod. "You think about it, stud. Breakfast's on me this morning, but you have to promise not to make yourself scarce around here."

"You got it." After eating the food placed before him, he could guarantee it. He rose to leave. "Thanks for the meal."

As he shoved his wallet back into the pocket of his jeans and made his way to the door, Holly's voice followed along behind him. "You know where to find me when you change your mind in the morning, Doc. Come on by. We'll go after the breakfast shift."

The old man to his right shot him a glare so blazing it should have singed the hair off his head. Yeah, right. Like he'd be taking any of the ladies of Sugar Springs on anything remotely resembling a date. He did not have a death wish, no matter how many stupid acts he'd pulled in his younger days.

CHAPTER

Cody took in the rounded belly of the woman making her way up the sidewalk and had to agree with Holly's earlier assessment. Keri Wright was about to pop. That baby had to be making its entrance soon.

He stood from the rocker on the clinic's front porch and moved to reach out a hand to help the lady vet up the brick steps. She looked like she might topple over backward if she didn't have something steady to hold on to.

"Thank you," she said, the words wispy with a shallow breath, and accepted his hand graciously. Her other hand pressed low on her bulging belly as she made her way up the three stairs. "Cody, right?" At his nod, she continued, "Sorry I didn't make it back over last night. I get home these days and can't seem to get myself back up to do anything."

"No problem," he said. He opened the door to the office and held it for her to enter before him. "I got in later than intended anyway and found the key exactly where you said I would. Boss and I made it fine."

"Boss?" Keri shot a wave and a smile at the curly-haired receptionist as she led the way through the narrow halls to her office.

"My dog."

"Oh, that's right." She laughed a little as she fanned her face with her hand. "Pregnancy brain. I can't keep anything straight these days. I also can't believe you're going to be okay in that little space with a Great Dane."

It wasn't ideal, but they'd had worse. "He'll spend the better part of the days down here with me, and we go for runs a couple times a day. It's only six weeks. We'll make it work."

With an audible grunt, she lowered herself to her chair and motioned across the desk. "Please, have a seat. I need to rest a minute before I show you the place."

"Looks like you need to go have that baby." The words were out before he could catch them and keep them in, and he instantly felt heat form in the back of his neck. "I'm sorry—"

Her laughter cut him off. "No need to be sorry. You're right. Only this little guy is being stubborn."

"When's he due?"

A tired smile touched her lips. "Yesterday."

"Oh."

"Yeah." She sighed in agreement. "*Oh*. I needed to keep working at least until you got here, anyway, so I can't decide if he's being helpful or stubborn. Given the doctor says I'm likely still at least a week away, I think it's pure stubbornness."

Cody couldn't help but agree. He'd been around plenty of animals in the later stages of pregnancy, but no humans. He was aware each gestation period could be somewhat unique and that babies came in their own time. He felt bad that he hadn't been able to make it to town before yesterday so she could take some time off, but the surgery he'd needed to handle in Los Angeles couldn't be scheduled before Tuesday. As it was, he'd made it cross-country in only two days. Luckily, Boss liked to travel as much as he did.

A black long-haired cat wandered into the room and wound through Cody's legs. He reached down to scratch the top of its head and it purred in contentment.

"That's Howard," Keri said. "He showed up right after I opened the doors to this place three years ago. No one claimed him, so I kept him."

"Well that answers one question. I didn't remember the clinic here when I was last in town."

"And that was what? Ten years ago?"

"Closer to fourteen." He'd learned she wasn't a Sugar Springs native when they'd talked on the phone, so anything she knew about him would have come purely from the residents. "Seems there was a guy who came to town once a week back then, but not a full clinic. I don't remember his name, though."

"That's right. Dr. Goldberg. Crotchety old man, from what I hear. He retired a year before I opened this place. Okay," Keri said, pushing herself up out of her seat. "Enough lollygagging. Let's get to it. I'm going with the theory that if I stay busy, this little guy will decide to make his entrance just to disrupt something else I have going on. We've got a couple surgeries scheduled for today, as well as getting you acquainted with the staff and equipment."

As they made their way through the treatment rooms and small laboratory, Cody learned that the clinic could handle most common diagnostic tests and treatments. Routine surgeries were performed almost daily, and only for the more difficult cases did they have to refer patients to a larger clinic, simply because Keri hadn't yet managed to afford the needed equipment.

"I'm impressed," he said. "For a town this size you've got a really good setup."

"Thanks. We're beginning to get more patients from surrounding areas, so I try to budget in as much as I can to grow. It's difficult when it's all yours and you have to make the big decisions, but I've never been more thrilled." She patted her protruding stomach. "Little Eli and I love that this is where we landed. I couldn't be happier."

As long as you didn't mind everyone knowing your business, it wasn't a bad place.

"Come on, I want to formally introduce you to the techs, assistant, and my receptionist slash office manager. I also have a groomer who comes in twice a week and a part-time receptionist who works here after school. She's a senior this year, sharp kid. The groomer doesn't live in town, but the rest of the staff does."

Cody spent the remainder of the day getting acquainted with everything in the office and performed the two surgeries on the books. He apparently passed the test, because by four thirty Keri had her feet propped on a low stool and a satisfied smile across her face. "You'll handle things just fine while I'm out, I think. Thanks for coming on such short notice. You've no idea how much I appreciate it."

"It was no problem. Worked out perfectly in fact. Especially seeing as it's on my way to my next contract."

"I just hope you don't go stir crazy while here. The pace is far removed from that of LA."

He chuckled. "Tell me about it. But I knew that coming in. Also, I'm rarely in LA anyway. It's my base, but I travel the majority of the year. I actually spend many of my weeks in towns similar to this one, so I've gotten used to entertaining myself."

"That's good. As long as you know what you're up against." She raised herself to an upright position and began gathering the papers from her desk. "There's not much going on this weekend. A bake sale up at the junior high, then a basketball game over at the high school tomorrow night, I believe. Unless you're interested in helping put out Christmas decorations with the town council. They'll finish up this weekend, so the lights will be ready to be turned on the day after Thanksgiving."

"Sounds like lots of options," he murmured. When she'd mentioned the bake sale, his mind had immediately returned to Lee Ann. He'd thought about her on and off throughout the day, unsure what the best plan of attack was. He kept telling himself that if he put off approaching her too long, that would make it even harder when he finally got around to talking to her. He preferred to deal with things head-on and get them out of the way. It was a practice he'd started some years back, and so far it had been working for him. "Actually, someone mentioned the fund-raiser to me earlier. Holly over at the diner offered to go with me."

He wasn't about to call it a date, but also wasn't going to let it be known she merely wanted to make some man jealous. That was her business and he wasn't sharing it.

"Yeah? You should go. The women of this town seriously know how to bake." She shoved a couple of notes in her purse, then she popped her head up, beaming at him. "If you go, you have to get some of Lee Ann London's cinnamon rolls. I swear, they're legendary. They seriously melt in your mouth. I'd be forever in your debt if you'd bring me one, too."

He went mute at the request. He hated to not bring the pregnant woman what she wanted, but really, he couldn't go.

"You might have seen her at the diner if you were in this morning. Short, always on the go, dark hair—"

"I know her," he said, stopping her mid-description, hoping to stop the talk about him bringing anything back from the fund-raiser.

"Really? Oh, good, I hadn't heard. Then you'll find her easy enough. Get me two, if you don't mind. I'll get you some money." She shoved a hand into her purse, but he reached over and stopped her before she could draw out any bills.

"How about you go and I work here tomorrow? You probably need to rest more than I do, anyway." He wasn't going to tell her that she looked like she needed to be horizontal, but it was the truth. He didn't know how she'd remained upright the whole day without falling over.

She eyed him from underneath long lashes that were way past drooping. "I can hold up my end of the deal, Dr. Dalton. I told you when we talked earlier this week that I would work this Saturday. That'll give you time to do your grocery run, get the lay of the place, rest up from your cross-country drive. Whatever you need to do, you take the weekend and do it. Monday is soon enough for you to start full time."

"But I don't mind."

"But I do." Her tone suggested this was not an argument he was going to win. "I take care of my responsibilities, and this one is mine. I'll work tomorrow. You bring me baked goods."

Son of a gun. Looked like he was going to the fund-raiser.

He couldn't believe he'd been there less than twenty-four hours and had already been shanghaied into attending a large community event. He slumped in the chair in resignation. Nothing about small-town living was easy, not even avoiding people. "Fine. I'll bring you baked goods. Anything else you want while I'm there?"

With a small smile, Keri heaved herself from her chair and slid a twenty across the desk. "A lemon tart bundt cake from Larissa Bailey, please. I'll call her tonight and ask her to save me one. You'll know her from her white-blonde hair and purple-rimmed glasses. She's a bit younger than you."

He scooped up the twenty and held it out for her. "Take your money back. I can get it."

"I'm sure you can, but I can also pay my own bills." She made her way to the door, both feet pointing slightly outward to accommodate her stomach, and he wondered what her story was. She had some serious pride issues going on.

Not willing to argue with her and make it worse, he shoved the twenty into his front pocket and stood to follow her out to the now-empty waiting area.

When she got to the front door, she turned back, her round face brightening. "I almost forgot. When you get the cinnamon rolls, will you say hello to Lee Ann's girls for me, please? I probably won't see them again before the baby comes. Tell them I look forward to seeing them after Eli is born."

She left, the glass door swinging closed behind her, and Cody's entire body turned cold. Lee Ann had a kid? Kids? Girls.

Well, hell. Didn't the questions just keep rolling in?

🌼 🌼 🌼

Lee Ann turned her back to the crowd and dug out another batch of cinnamon rolls. Her rolls were famous in Sugar Springs and this year's batch was apparently living up to the hype. The few remaining pastries, along with the other tables' dwindling offerings, ensured the committee would surpass its goal and close the gap on the money needed for the trip.

As she settled the box on the table, taking the opportunity to enjoy the unusual lack of customers, she scanned the crowd scattered throughout the gymnasium. Her mom had disappeared to purchase items to take home, and Candy was outside finishing up her turn holding up the sign to beckon customers in. Kendra was also out there, helping her out. Not that the entire town wasn't already aware of the event, but the planning committee had decided years ago that it would go a long way toward developing the kids' responsibility if they were required to work, as opposed to relying solely on their parents to do it.

Spotting her mother in the crowd as she purchased what appeared to be a red velvet cake, Lee Ann knew the girls would enjoy the treat after decorating Reba's yard. Lee Ann returned to her task and began strategically placing the individually wrapped treats along the table.

Worn brown boots came into her line of sight, causing every muscle in her shoulders to tense. Surely he hadn't shown up here.

Lifting her head hesitantly, she scanned over the same hard body she'd checked out only the morning before, continuing to go up until she finally came face-to-face with Cody. Yep, he'd shown up here. And just like the day before, taking in those penetrating eyes and square jaw made her heart skip a beat.

It surprised her, honestly. No matter how much she'd once hated him—or how much she still loathed him—her body apparently didn't remember. Instead, it remembered how she'd also wanted him. The bad boy and the good girl. It had been a fantasy from the first moment she'd laid eyes on him.

She had to get this ridiculous reaction under control. And she had to get him the heck out of there. She did not need the "big family reunion" to happen in front of half the town.

"You can't escape me so easily this time." His deep voice vibrated over her, reminding her how she and her friend Joanie had once made up excuses simply to get near enough to hear his low timbre.

She took a deep breath to calm her nerves before glancing toward the gym doors the girls would soon be coming through. "I'm sure I don't know what you mean."

He stared into her eyes for several seconds, then hitched up the corners of his mouth. It didn't feel like a friendly smile.

"You never were a good liar, Lee Ann." He picked up a cinnamon roll and began peeling the plastic away. "I've heard rumors about you this week."

The end of the roll disappeared between his teeth as he bit off a large chunk. When she caught on to the fact that she was standing there like a teenager gawking while the man chewed her pastry, she flushed and dropped her gaze. Sweet Jesus. Why had he come back now? She did not need this distraction in her life.

And why in the world was he affecting her this way?

Wait...What had he said? She peeked back up at him. "What are you talking about? What rumors?"

"Wow." He moaned and licked his lips, ignoring her questions. "This really is as good as Keri said. No wonder she sent me up here for them."

He scooped up four more in one hand, then finished off the first in two more bites. Again, she stood there and watched him chew.

When the last crumb disappeared, he pulled out his wallet. "Never would have believed you could learn to cook like that."

"Yeah, well, I've learned a lot of things over the years." Like how easily the supposed love of your life could turn his back on you. And his kids.

He went quiet as he pulled out some bills, then he handed the money over with a grim face. "I assume you're implying that at least some of the things you've learned came from me and my behavior."

She raised her eyebrows at the casually spoken words, anger suddenly spurting through her veins, instantly clearing any fascination she had with the way he chewed. Absolutely it had to do with his behavior! She hadn't intended to learn anything about raising kids until her early thirties, and yet here she was with soon-to-be teenagers. She'd never had the desire to waitress beyond her high school years, yet...doing it still today. Again, his fault. And she certainly had never intended to find hidden talents in the fine art of portraits. Yet, look at her now.

Yeah, she'd say that she'd learned a heck of a lot of things because of him and his actions. Dang it. Who did he think he was waltzing in here in the middle of everyone, chatting as if they were nothing but old buds?

She glanced at her watch. The girls would be back any minute and she did not want this jerk talking to them. Not today, maybe not ever. Holding up the bills he'd handed over, she gave him a tight smile. "Thanks for helping out the team."

She turned her back, making it clear it was time for him to leave. A low laugh hit her ears and a shiver streaked to her toes.

"Good to know not everything about you has changed, Lee."

She jerked around. "What are you talking about?"

With a tilt of his head, he said, "You're still here in Sugar Springs when you shouldn't be, you're running a junior high fund-raiser when you should be out opening at art galleries instead, and you're waitressing down at the diner. None of that is who you were supposed to be. But that temper..." The grin started slow and ended up covering the whole bottom half of his face. "That temper is just as I remember it. It was the only thing about you that wasn't sweet and polite. Though very few people ever got to see it." He winked. "I was one of the lucky ones."

That temper was about to throw her across the table and have her clawing his eyes out. The man better not have plans to have anything to do with her kids. He was not deserving of being their father.

"It's time for you to go, Cody. The basketball team thanks you, but we'd appreciate it if you'd find somewhere else to spread around the rest of your money."

He nodded. "I'll go. In a minute. First we need to talk."

Her heartbeat faltered. He was going to press to meet the girls now? Right here? Fear pressed in on her as she squeaked out, "I don't think so."

"Doesn't matter what you think. It's what's going to happen. So, now or later? We could have dinner outside of town, where we could have a private conversation."

"I don't want to have dinner with you."

Color stained his ears. "Yeah, well, fine. Can't say as I blame you. But that doesn't stop the fact that we're going to get together in some fashion."

She swallowed. She wouldn't be able to avoid the conversation forever, no matter how much she'd like to. "You cannot just show up here and tell me what I am and am not going to do. I haven't needed you for the last thirteen years. I don't need you now. Why don't you go on back to the clinic and hide out there for the next six weeks? We'll all just pretend you don't exist. That way, you can go on about your business when the job is over. And never look back."

Oh, please say yes.

But she knew he wouldn't. She could tell from the anger that tightened his features. He'd come back for a purpose, and she suspected the least he was going to do was disrupt her perfectly ordered life.

"Nice speech. It's not going to work. I took this job for one reason." He paused, and some of the fire leaked from his words. "It was because of you, Lee Ann. I know this is years late, but I owe you an apology. An explanation for my behavior that day." His throat rose and fell with a swallow. "I intend to make sure you've heard it."

Relief washed over her before being immediately replaced with astonishment. That was all he wanted? Seriously? He wasn't even going to bring up the girls? Well, she could end this right now. "Cody, really, don't worry about the past. It's over. We were kids. I don't need an apology from you."

He opened his mouth.

"Honestly, I'm over it." The girls entered through the far gym doors and glanced her way. Their gaze landed on Cody and their feet turned in her direction. "I forgave you years ago."

Not quite, but it was close enough to the truth. She'd accepted what he'd done and moved on years ago. That should be good enough.

Her breathing picked up as the distance between them and the girls shrunk. He narrowed his gaze on her. "Then why not give me fifteen minutes to clear my own conscience?" He shook his head. "No, sorry. This one I insist on doing. Tell me when and where we can meet, and I'll leave you alone."

"Please, just go." Her voice came out no stronger than a whisper. "There's no need for this."

Cody turned and scanned the crowd. "What's got you so upset all of a sudden? Is someone talking about us?"

Uh...*yeah*. Of course.

But she didn't reply. That wasn't the immediate problem anyway. Instead, she let out a harsh breath when her mother took stock of the situation and reached out to stop the girls as they passed. Lee Ann focused on breathing normally, but she wasn't fast enough. Cody followed her gaze and zeroed in on her family standing together about thirty feet from them.

"That must be your kids."

She blinked. *Her* kids? No words could have surprised her more.

She shook her head, amazed by his audacity. "Could you leave, now?" Her words came out low, fury making it more than difficult to contain her temper.

"I'll leave after they get over here. Keri asked me to pass along a message to them."

She counted to five as she pulled in a breath. "Give it to me and I'll pass it along."

"Nah. I'd like to meet them."

His words had come out clipped, and she pulled her gaze from the girls—who were once again heading in their direction—to study him. His features had closed down, as well as his voice. About time he dealt with the fact that he helped create those children. She just hoped he kept the information to himself until the two of them could have that talk.

"Fine," she gritted out. "Meet them and then go. You and I can talk later. Come by the diner at the end of the breakfast shift one day this week and we'll have a chat. I don't believe the vet's office opens until ten, so we should have enough time."

Kendra skidded to a stop a second after Lee Ann finished speaking, red velvet cake in her hands, wide brown eyes glowing. "You're the new vet, right?"

Candy was only two steps behind, carrying Reba's basket of goodies. She set the basket on the floor and shrugged out of her coat, a suspicious look flitting across her face. She didn't trust as easily as Kendra.

"Yes, Ma'am," he said, carefully taking in both of them. "I am."

"I knew it!" Kendra breathed. She took a step closer and bounced a bit on her toes. She was the cheerleader of the family. "Everybody at school was talking about you yesterday. They said you have a *huge* dog. What kind is it?"

Candy stepped to her sister's side but didn't join the conversation.

"A Great Dane." Cody peered carefully at both of them, then over at Lee Ann. It wasn't awe for the children who'd been spawned from him that she was seeing, but she couldn't quite put her finger on what it was, either.

What did strike her was the complete emotional distance she picked up on between him and the girls. It was almost as if he wasn't aware he was talking to his own kids. Yet that was impossible. Stephanie had not only told him she was pregnant, but when she'd told him she was dying, he would have known that either Lee Ann or her mother would raise the girls if he didn't come back and do it. And if he'd been thinking at all, he would have known it would be her.

Either way, he knew he had kids, yet he still didn't act in the slightest like he was accepting of that fact.

She keyed back into the conversation while Kendra continued to ask questions a mile a minute about his dog. When she finally slowed, Cody shot one more look in Lee Ann's direction, then picked up the cinnamon rolls he'd set down and took a step back.

"It was a pleasure meeting you two. I was asked to pass along a message from Dr. Wright."

"Yeah?" both girls asked, Candy finally perking up.

Keri was a good friend whom the three of them had "taken in," as she had no family close by but the baby she was carrying. In return, Keri encouraged Kendra's love of animals by letting her spend many Saturday mornings at the clinic helping out where she could. Candy didn't care about the animals so much but had been promised the chance to babysit when the time came. She couldn't wait.

"Yeah," he said. "She's working today, but asked me to tell you ladies hello from her, and that she is looking forward to seeing you both after the baby is born."

Identical grins bloomed on their faces as the oddest look passed through Cody's eyes.

With a hurried good-bye, he turned and headed across the gymnasium floor to the now-empty table of Larissa Bailey. She was the local librarian, and her whole body seemed to smile when he leaned down and spoke to her. Even from this distance, Lee Ann could see the blush touching her cheeks. Hard not to be flattered when someone like Cody turned his attention on you. Even furious with him, she could admit that. The man simply radiated testosterone. At that moment, every woman in the room was turned to watch him.

Larissa surprised her by pulling one of her lemon bundt cakes out from under the table to pass over to him. She'd saved one for him? Wow, he worked fast. She wouldn't have guessed he'd even met her in the two days he'd been in town. Larissa spent most of her time either at the library or her own house. She didn't get out and around too much.

Cody said something else as he took the cake, and that made Larissa laugh out loud, her cheeks growing darker. The man hadn't changed. He could charm the pants off anyone.

"You dated him, right?" Kendra's words, followed by a dramatic sigh, infiltrated Lee Ann's mind, and a tight pinch pulled at her heart. Dated? Right. The one big date they'd been saving up for had never happened.

"Where did you come up with that?"

But she knew. The whole town shared everything they knew with whoever would listen, and too many people knew she'd once done some serious mooning over him back in the day. Not to mention that she and he had once spent months hanging together every afternoon. At first as friends, but then the friendship had grown.

Of course they were being talked about now.

She peered into Kendra's eyes and had no doubt what she was thinking. She was too much like her grandmother, the dreamer. What surprised her was the matching look in her sister's eyes. They'd both recently gotten it in their minds that she needed a man, and they'd been on the hunt since. It seemed they'd come to the unanimous decision that rekindling an old flame was the solution.

She laid a hand on both their arms. "I'm sure since you heard rumors about him and me, you also heard about what he did to the original statue up on the square?"

They nodded, so she continued, "Then surely you can see that he's not someone I'd want in my life. He's trouble. Plus he'll be leaving at the end of the year."

"But—" It was Candy who started.

"Do *not* get any ideas," Lee Ann insisted.

Both girls grew pensive as they emptied the contents of the basket into one of the canvas bags Lee Ann had used to tote the cinnamon rolls to the sale. Finally Candy spoke, her voice questioning. "I thought you believed in giving people a second chance."

Lee Ann dropped into her chair. The whole day had been nonstop go from the beginning, then add on the stress of Cody and she felt as if she'd run a marathon. And the simple fact was that some people didn't deserve a second chance. But how did she explain that to her children?

A steady stream of customers arrived before she could form a reply, so she remained seated, content to let Candy and Kendra do the work.

Lee Ann snuck a glance at Cody and found he was now on the opposite side of the floor, leaning down to speak in Holly Marshall's ear. They were turned away from her, so she couldn't miss his hand pressed possessively against the lower section of Holly's back. Lee Ann's stomach clenched. He still had the ability to attract every woman in sight. The fact shouldn't bother her at all, as her only concern pertaining to him was to figure out if he was the right kind of person to be in her children's lives, but she found herself filled with another emotion she was honest enough to admit. Jealousy. And she hated herself for it.

Holly was fun and outgoing, the exact opposite of Lee Ann, and always upbeat, refusing to let anyone or anything bring her down. She was also the center of attention wherever she went.

Lee Ann was a boring, in-bed-by-nine mother-of-two.

It only made sense that Cody would be impressed. Still, his speed shocked her. First, he'd gotten to know Larissa well enough for her to save him one of her award-winning cakes, and now he was being even more friendly with Holly. How did the man move so fast?

Holly leaned back and peeked behind Cody to surreptitiously check out Tucker Brown, the sixth-grade math teacher. The smile fell from her face when Tucker laughed with the good-looking fourth-grade teacher who'd moved to town four months earlier. That was when Lee Ann remembered Holly had been after Tucker's attention for some time now. She was playing Cody. The thought brought a smile to Lee Ann's heart. Not that Cody deserved to be played. Well, maybe just a little. But it meant Holly and Cody weren't really involved.

Pulling her attention back to the table in front of her, she realized that as the girls collected money and made change, most of the buyers eyed her.

She'd just spent several minutes chatting with an old flame, and now she'd been caught staring at him across the room. No doubt they were all already wondering if a reconciliation was in the works. At least they didn't know that the kids were his. The rumor mill would be on full blast if that were the case.

When the last of the customers cleared, Kendra pivoted to Lee Ann. "We promised Grandma we'd come back and help her pick out what else we need." As if they needed anything else. She turned to go but looked back over her shoulder. "But Candy's right. Everyone deserves a second chance. You've always taught us that."

As they hurried away, Lee Ann rubbed both temples with one hand spread wide over her forehead but couldn't contain a slight smile. No matter the circumstances that made her a mother, she loved her girls and couldn't imagine life without them. Even when they said things that drove her crazy.

She rose from the chair and straightened the items on the table, then once again found herself seeking out Cody. He and Holly stood near the door, but his eyes were locked on her. He glanced again at Candy and Kendra, then with one last pointed look in her direction, left the building, Holly following close behind.

Great. His parting shot had been more like a glare, and it caused anxiety to settle in for a stay. Probably a very long one. She didn't understand exactly what had happened there today but didn't doubt him for a second when he said he intended to seek her out. Likely sooner rather than later.

She already dreaded her Monday-morning shift.

CHAPTER

4

"I skipped out early on breakfast again this morning. To avoid Cody." Lee Ann dipped her bare feet into the swirling warm water of the footbath, dropped her head against the back of the vibrating massage chair and let out a low moan. "The Marshalls are going to fire me if I keep doing that."

Joanie Bigbee, Lee Ann's best friend since elementary school, plopped into the vacant seat beside her, knocking several bottles of polish off the attached tray as she did so. They were in Joanie's salon on late Monday afternoon, completely alone. Joanie reserved Mondays for errands, administrative tasks, and much-needed girl talks. "You know that isn't true. They love you. But you are going to eventually have to quit avoiding him." She jabbed a button and the rollers started. "Ahhh...that's better. Now, fill me in. I heard he showed up at the bake sale Saturday. What did he want?"

Lee Ann forced open one eye and peeked at her. "He says he wants to talk."

"About darned time. Did he go there specifically to find you?"

"I don't know. Maybe." She shrugged. "I don't think so. Keri had talked him into bringing her back some cinnamon rolls, and then I saw him leaving with Holly as if they'd come together."

Joanie let out a little snort. "She's probably hoping he'll rescue her from what she considers a town she's outgrown."

"She deserves better than him," Lee Ann grumbled, aware she sounded petulant. The thought of him and Holly did not sit well with her. Closing her eyes, she imagined herself hiking through the mountains with nothing but her camera, wildlife, and solitude. And zero stress. She loved people, but sometimes she needed to decompress. "The worst part was he met the girls and acted like any stranger they might run into. Passed along a message from Keri, and then he was gone. There was no recognition, no shock, no...nothing. Simply nothing."

Silence from the other chair finally pulled her attention back from her fantasy of escaping. Joanie sat very still, a line pulling at her brows. "You think he didn't realize they were his?"

"How could he not know, Jo? Who else would be raising them? Plus, how many sets of twins could he possibly think we'd have in our family? Heck, twins don't even run in our family."

"So then, he's still a coldhearted jerk, same as he was when he left."

Lee Ann looked away from her friend and focused on the waning light outside the building. It would be dark soon, but she could still make out everyone outside on the streets. Locals and tourists, all going about their day, their lives seemingly perfect. Whereas her life was on the cusp of ripping open and bleeding in a way it hadn't in over thirteen years.

She nodded, sadness creeping into the movement as she realized she'd hoped to find that he had changed. "Seems like it."

Joanie was silent for a moment, seeming to decipher Lee Ann and what she really thought about the matter. Finally, Joanie reached over and squeezed her hand. "That sucks."

"Yeah."

They sat in silence for a few more minutes until the sight of a very large black-and-white dog got their attention. Behind him at the end of a leash was Cody. Tall, strong, and perfect in profile. He wore another skullcap today, this one black and pulled down low over his ears. His hair curled out the back beneath the fleece. His leather jacket was zipped against the wind, and today's jeans and boots matched the rest of his attire, all black. Like Lee Ann's mood.

As he made his way down the sidewalk on the other side of the street, both women watched, lost in their own thoughts.

Finally Joanie uttered, "He may be an ass, but you can't ever say your kids didn't come from some really fine genes."

Wasn't that the God's honest truth?

The massage rollers came to a stop, and Lee Ann fiddled with the controller to start the vibrations again. It was definitely a two-cycle day.

They watched as man and dog moved on down the sidewalk, different people stopping him along the way to chat or pet the four-legged beauty on the head, until the pair disappeared from view.

"I heard he ended up helping finish up the Christmas decorations yesterday afternoon," Joanie said. "They had a couple of cancellations and Holly ran down to his apartment to talk him into helping."

"And he came just like that?"

"Apparently so." Joanie's shoulders lifted slightly. She was clearly having the same thoughts as Lee Ann. "I don't get it, either. He doesn't strike me as someone who would easily join in, yet there he was. Staying until the last string of lights was hung, from what I heard."

A sigh escaped as Joanie pushed herself out of the chair and straddled the rolling stool in front of Lee Ann. "Give me your feet. The least I can do is give you an awesome set of toes. It won't make up for the crap going on in your life, but maybe it'll make the day a bit brighter."

Lee Ann lifted her feet onto the footstool and frowned down at the inch-thick, bright red strip of hair edging Joanie's dark, trendy cut. She couldn't imagine Joanie ever being as unsure as she felt. The woman made a decision and went after it with the force of nature. And she never failed. "What am I going to do, Jo?"

Joanie shrugged, keeping her voice low as she began cleaning off the old polish. "You can't avoid him forever. He says he wants to talk. I'd say start with that. Speaking to the man doesn't mean anything about your life has to change, it's purely one conversation."

She moved to the other foot.

"And I'd be justified keeping him from the girls if I determine he is the jerk I suspect him to be?" Lee Ann asked.

Joanie nodded. "You'd be justified."

Yet something about that didn't sit well, either. Why couldn't life ever be easy?

"It is a shame, though," Joanie continued. "The girls could use a father."

Long-ago worry flared to life, setting a flurry loose in her stomach. "Why do you think that? Have they said something? I thought I was doing okay."

Joanie sat back and peered up at her friend, her face the definition of support. "You're a perfect mother and you know it. But if anyone understands the frustrations of going through life without a father, it's both of us. Neither of us ever had anyone around, and I'm sure you can admit that sometimes a girl just needs someone other than her mother to talk to."

"I know." She tucked one hand beneath her thigh to keep from doing something childish like chewing on her nails, then she used the other to pick at a loose thread in the seam of her jeans. "But they have you. Don't they come talk to you all the time? And I don't butt in there. I give them the space I know they need."

"I know you do, sweetie." Joanie reached up and tapped Lee Ann's hand, stilling her movements. "You are the best mother I've ever seen. Honestly. I'm simply saying that sometimes..." She gave Lee Ann an "I'm sorry" look. "Sometimes having a male around would be good. They'd see the world from both sides of the coin."

Lee Ann hated when Joanie made sense. Lee Ann was the practical one. The one everybody sought out in a crisis. Joanie was...well, the flake. She was the one who jumped between businesses more often than most people did cars, and who had the audacity to name her latest venture Curl Up 'N Dye. But she had always been a pillar for Lee Ann when she needed one.

They lapsed into more silence, each lost in her own thoughts, until a sound at the door got their attention several minutes later. Both women looked up to find Cody's dog sitting on his haunches, staring in through the glass. His owner stood directly behind him.

Crap.

Though the "Closed" sign hung over the bar across the middle of the door, it was easy enough to see the place wasn't empty.

"What do you think he wants?" Lee Ann asked.

Joanie swung back around to her, one corner of her mouth lifting in distaste. "My guess? To have that conversation."

The door wasn't locked, so neither of them rose to let him in. Instead, they waited to see what he would do next. It didn't take him long to decide. With a couple quick moves, he produced a portable bowl and a bottle of water from the inside of his jacket. He then set the dog up with a drink and wrapped his leash around the top of the wrought-iron fencing surrounding the sidewalk grate—as if that would stop the animal if he decided he wanted to go.

Cody entered the salon, and Joanie started to move away, but Lee Ann pointed to her toes. "Finish."

As Joanie sunk back to the stool, Cody stopped behind her. "Hello, Joanie. Good to see you."

Joanie mumbled a hello and ducked her head as if wishing she were anywhere but there, while Lee Ann shot the man a scowl. "Have trouble reading the 'Closed' sign on the door? We're trying to have a few moments of peace here. Uninterrupted."

A muscle jerked in his jaw. "Then maybe you shouldn't have avoided me again," he replied.

She crossed her arms over her chest. "Something came up."

"Right." He sat in the chair beside her and stretched out his long legs. "Yet you seem to have plenty of time now."

He'd stepped around her to choose the seat that wasn't visible to the front door as if hoping to keep the fact he was there a secret. The dog currently guarding the doorway, however, was a dead giveaway.

"I'm in the middle of something," she stated.

"I'll wait."

God, he was irritating. She gritted her teeth together. He reminded her of Candy when she got something stuck in her mind.

"Fine." She looked everywhere but at him. "Then talk."

While Joanie worked as quickly as humanly possible to get the bright orange applied to Lee Ann's toes, Cody watched the movements in fascination. "It's good to see another part of the old you still around," he mumbled.

Joanie paused with the polish brush hovering in the air. She peeked up when neither of them said anything. "Were you talking to me?"

A smile cracked the corners of Cody's mouth. "No, but it's good to see you haven't changed, either, Joanie. I like your hair." He motioned to Lee Ann. "I was referring to the color you're applying to Mommy of the Year, here. She always had a bit of flair to her, but these days she seems to keep it more under wraps."

He shifted his attention back to Lee Ann and lifted a hand, catching a short piece of her hair between his thumb and forefinger. "Of course, this hair screams flair, too. It's the rest that's different."

Lee Ann swatted his hand away and shot him a look that should have burned the skin off the tips of his fingers. "I'm no different than the last time you saw me, just a little older."

That was actually true. She had always been the good girl, the one taking care of everybody else. The one everyone relied on. Only, she'd wanted to be different. At least for a while. She'd yearned for college and a bit of living before she settled into her final role as wife and mother. He and Joanie had been the only ones who truly understood this about her.

Eyebrows arched over his dark eyes as he continued to study her. "And the twins?" His tone was harder than she expected. "Did you have them hidden away somewhere fourteen years ago, too?"

He always had gotten right to the point. It used to be one of the things she liked about him. "I thought you wanted to apologize."

"I wanted to do that alone." He nodded at Joanie. "You seem to have a problem being alone with me. I figured we'd get the other issue out of the way."

Indignation flared, heating her from the chest up. "Candy and Kendra are *not* issues."

"Whoa." He held his hands out in front of him. "Sorry. Didn't mean to hit on a sore spot. And I didn't mean to imply they are *issues* per se. I was merely wondering about them. They've got to be, what? Twelve at least? You must have gotten pregnant soon after I left."

Both she and Joanie turned their heads to gape at the man. Literally, jaws hanging open, eyes bulging. He really did not know they were his kids. How could that be possible?

"What?" he asked.

Instead of answering, she and Joanie faced each other. Oh, geez, this meant she was going to have to tell him. Didn't change the fact he was still the jerk who hadn't wanted his kids, but she had to at least let him know who they were. Didn't she?

The slight tinkling of a bell indicated that someone else had opened the front door.

"Did ya'll know there's a giant dog on the sidewalk out here?" Melinda O'Neil, heir to half the property within the city limits, asked before gingerly stepping over the animal and entering the salon.

Under her breath Lee Ann murmured, "Does no one understand what a 'Closed' sign means these days?"

"I think he belongs to Cody Dalton," Melinda continued. "But I don't see him out there anywhere."

Joanie snared both Lee Ann and Cody in a look before motioning to the door in the corner. "Feel free to use my office for your conversation. It's a few years overdue." She rose. "I'll see what Melinda needs."

Before they could make their escape, Melinda sauntered toward the back, where Lee Ann remained seated. "I knew I'd find you here today, Lee Ann. You always head this way when you're stressed. And with Cody back, looking hotter than ever, I knew you'd be stressed. I wanted..."

When she finally caught sight of Cody sitting there, her entire posture changed. Shoulders pulled back, stomach sucked in, and breasts lifted. What was it about the entire population of single women in this town? A fresh face showed up and they immediately went into man-hunting mode.

Cody stood and held out a hand. "Cody Dalton." He dipped his head as he introduced himself, brushing his lips across the back of her hand as if he were some honorable cowboy.

Melinda giggled. "I know who you are, Mr. Dalton. The infamous bad boy of Sugar Springs." Melinda batted her fake eyelashes at him, and he graced her with one of his purely evil grins. "I may have been three years younger than you the last time you were here, but I wasn't too young to pay attention. I had one of the biggest crushes of anybody."

Lee Ann wanted to jam her finger down her throat and throw up on the both of them. She sidled out of her chair and duckwalked to the office as Cody and Melinda continued oohing and aahing over each other. "I'll be back here whenever you can pull yourself away."

Before Lee Ann fully stepped into the other room, Melinda waved a hand in her direction but didn't shift her gaze from Cody. "I just needed to tell you, Lee Ann, the central unit finally went out at the Fish and Game Club, and Daddy isn't replacing it until spring."

"Not replacing it?" That was where the twins' big "I'm a teenager now" birthday bash was going to be held. "It'll be too cold in there without it."

Melinda shook her head and finally focused on Lee Ann. "He refuses to pay jacked-up seasonal prices for a new unit when there's a perfectly good stove and a whole stack of wood to keep the place warm. You've still got almost four weeks before the girls' birthday, so I thought I should warn you in case you prefer to find another location for their party."

Right. Like another one existed. But she also didn't want to deal with stoking a fire all night long, either. After she asked Melinda to go ahead and hold the reservation while she checked around, her brain finally registered the rage tightening Cody's body. And then she realized what had been said. And what that implied.

With three large steps, Cody loomed directly in front of her, leaving a dazed Melinda to gawk at his backside. Under his breath, he asked, "Their birthday is in December?"

Lee Ann couldn't breathe. She nodded.

"I left at the end of April."

Nod.

Once-warm brown eyes now burned with anger. "So you were already a month pregnant with *someone else's* baby before I left town?"

If anyone had asked her a week ago if she was about to change her ways and begin lying on a regular basis, she would have sworn they were insane. She valued honesty. It was a priority she worked hard at every day to instill in her kids as well.

Yet now, not only had she lied to get out of the diner early not once but twice, she found herself opening her mouth to tell another one. A huge one! And it wasn't as if this was even a lie she was likely to be able to keep up for very long. But her sense of survival saw this as an opening and screamed to her that if she could get him to believe this one tiny thing, then she might have just found a way to keep from having to let him into their lives.

She took a deep breath and stared straight into his eyes. "Yes." She spoke quietly so no one else could hear. "I was pregnant before you left town."

❀ ❀ ❀

Without hesitation, Cody closed his hand around Lee Ann's slim arm and hauled her into the room, slamming the door behind them. He was hard pressed to explain his ire over something that happened more than a decade ago, but he couldn't control the anger flooding him. Realizing he still held Lee Ann, he released her. She moved silently across the room until the desk stood between them.

"Care to explain?"

She stuck her nose in the air. "I have nothing to explain."

"Nothing?" he roared and stepped up to the desk, bracing his hands on the hard surface. "I've spent over thirteen years—"

"Lower your voice, please." She spoke as calmly as if she were taking his order at the diner.

He didn't wish to share their conversation with either Melinda or Joanie, so he backed off and forced himself to do as she asked. He inhaled through his nose and started again. "I've spent over thirteen years feeling like a dog because I slept with Stephanie, and when I come to apologize, I find out you had already done the same thing to me."

She opened her mouth, then closed it. She seemed to fight with herself about what to say, then rubbed the spot on her arm where he'd grabbed her. Finally, she spoke very softly. "I can't take the blame for you feeling bad all that time. If you'd talked to me before you left, maybe..."

Maybe what? Maybe she would have said, "It's okay, Cody. I changed my mind anyway and decided I didn't want to wait until prom to give you my virginity. I gave it to some other loser." Maybe she'd even sent Stephanie to sleep with him so she wouldn't have to be the one to break it off. A sound as loud as a train roared through his head. He gritted his teeth as he spoke. "Maybe what?" he asked.

She gulped and stood stiff for a couple seconds, her wide eyes focused on him. Finally, her shoulders slumped with defeat. "I don't know."

He barked a laugh. "You don't know? That's all you've got to say?" He turned and braced his hands on the doorframe, needing to get away. She wasn't anything like he'd always thought.

Young and innocent. That's what he'd once believed. Sweet. Perfect. Too good for him.

When he'd been sent to Sugar Springs, she'd refused to accept him for the wild boy everyone else had known him to be. And he'd been surprised to find that for her he'd wanted to be different. Better.

After their friendship had grown over the winter months, they'd decided to pursue a real relationship and had anticipated making the ultimate commitment on prom night. But there was more to it than that. She'd grown to be his friend. His best friend. The one who'd believed in him no matter how many of the stories from his past he'd shared with her.

Then Stephanie had come home. Beautiful, worldly, and a woman on a mission to seduce. He'd learned ugly truths earlier in the day and had been hurting, apparently enough to let down his defenses. He shook his head, still shocked at what he'd done. He had no excuses. Bad news and feeling sorry for himself were no reasons to destroy the girl he'd dared dream with. The girl he'd dared love.

Even though he'd eventually turned his back on her, he'd truly thought he and Lee Ann had something special, something real. To discover she'd been no better than him was more than he could handle. Facing her, he had a hard time seeing the girl he'd once put up on a pedestal. Right now, even drawn in on herself and appearing smaller than normal, all he saw was another sister who'd mowed down anyone and everything in her plight to think only of herself.

Yet he couldn't just walk away without giving the apology he'd come to deliver. Whether she deserved to hear it or not, he needed to say it. Once done, no reason would exist to have anything to do with her again. No matter how much he might want to.

He glared over her shoulder just to keep from looking at her, and his gaze landed on the calendar hanging on the wall.

The pages hadn't been ripped off in three months. Tension eased from his shoulders. Joanie was still the same.

He swiped his hand across his face, then stared up at the ceiling. "I can't do it." Shifting his gaze, he eyed Lee Ann and thought he caught her eyes glistening before she focused on the floor. "I need to apologize, Lee Ann. I need to clear my own conscience, but you wouldn't believe how much finding this out hurts, even after all this time."

Her eyelids fluttered up, and he'd been right. Tears. She chewed on her top lip before speaking so softly he could barely hear her. "You seriously think I can't understand how much it hurts?" Her bottom lip trembled. "You slept with my sister."

"But you—"

"No." She sliced her hand through the air. "What I did or didn't do doesn't matter right now. No matter what else happened, we were in *love*, Cody. At least I was. At the time I thought we were leaving together as soon as we graduated. And I fully expected"—her voice broke but she managed to hang on, her entire body taut—"I thought we would be together forever. And you *slept* with my *sister*."

Fury webbed through him. How dare she pretend she'd loved...

A tiny tear bubbled up in the corner of her eye, stopping him cold. She tilted her chin up a fraction as if trying to keep it from falling. He didn't understand. Not how she'd slept with someone else, nor even why he had, but he recognized the anguish in her eyes. It was his pain echoed back at him. No matter what else, his actions that day had truly crushed her.

Lowering his gaze, he took a deep breath. He was a dog. Whatever Lee Ann's reasons for doing what she did, he'd still been the lowest form of scum that day. He lifted his head and cleared all expression from his face. "You're right. Of course you understand. And I owe you an explanation."

She shrugged, touched a finger to the corner of her eye, and moved from behind the desk. "You don't have to explain," she said. "I know Stephanie seduced you. She told me that a couple days before she died."

He slumped as the fight whooshed out of his body. "Stephanie's dead?"

She gaped at him as she and Joanie had done earlier in the other room, and he felt as if he was missing something important.

"You didn't know she was sick?" she asked.

"How would I? I left." Then he frowned at her as a thought struck. Did she think he and her half sister had continued some sort of relationship after that day? "I never talked to her again, Lee Ann. I swear. Hell, I didn't talk to her before or after. It was just that one afternoon. I couldn't possibly have known she was sick." He paused, not really interested in Stephanie, yet it felt strangely as if Lee Ann needed to talk about this. "When did she die?"

Blue eyes watched him guardedly as if waiting for him to expose a huge secret he'd been hiding. "Almost eight months after you left. She developed cancer."

Damn. "And they couldn't do anything?"

She licked her lips and shook her head. "They found it too late."

He took an automatic step forward, raising his hand to reach out to her, but she shifted backward until the back door stopped her.

"I'm so sorry." He dropped his arm to his side. Her mother hadn't been the best at nurturing or handling details, so he had no doubt Lee Ann had been forced to handle everything herself. "I know you two weren't close, but I'm sorry you had to go through that alone."

"It was a long time ago." Her voice came out strained. The threat of tears had disappeared, though.

She continued to stare at him, the oddest look crossing her face as if seeing him differently from how she had when he'd first walked into the building. He had no idea what caused the change but appreciated how the sharp edges seemed to soften.

Her anger took a turn south, too. "She admitted she'd come to town to seduce you. To hurt me."

Stephanie had been five years older than Lee Ann, living in Nashville, and working to break into the country-music scene. The two sisters had been about as opposite as two people could get. Stephanie was tall, blonde, and more classically beautiful, while Lee Ann had girl-next-door good looks and charm. Stephanie also hadn't been nearly as smart or popular as Lee Ann, from what he'd heard. She'd spent most of her high school years dating the football team instead of studying for exams. He'd always guessed he'd been played to get back at Lee Ann somehow, but he had never known for sure.

He should finish his apology and get out of there before he succumbed to the lost look now filling Lee Ann's eyes. He'd never been able to turn away from that easily.

He didn't want to tell her everything he'd found out from his foster parents that day—it didn't matter to this conversation—but he had to explain his actions somehow. "I'd gotten upsetting news earlier in the day and I came looking for you." He shrugged. "You were out on a photo assignment for the school paper, and I decided to wait. I needed to talk to you. Instead, I let her take advantage of my anger, drank the lemonade she offered—spiked, of course—and completely shut down my mind."

He shook his head. "I apologize, Lee Ann. I never meant to hurt you in any way, and certainly not like that."

She held up a hand and her head tilted a fraction. "You had a bad day?" Her tone screamed incredulity. "This is your excuse? You had a bad day so you forgot how to say no to my sister?"

"Well..." Yeah, that sounded rough, but how else was he supposed to explain it? Plus, it was true. He'd just found out things that had impacted way more than that one day. "The details aren't worth getting into, but..."

He could see that didn't soothe her any more than his first attempt at an explanation did. Out of ideas of what else he could possibly tell her, he explained it with a shrug. "It was not one of my finer moments."

A choked-off sound was her only reply.

When she said nothing else, he finally got his words going again, needing to finish and get out of there. "The fact is I wasn't the right person for you anyway. You could do better."

He glanced briefly at her flat stomach and imagined her swollen with another man's child. Children. The thought made him sick, especially when he knew that in the end she hadn't done better. She was still exactly where she'd been all those years ago, only now with children. Whoever the scumbag was that had gotten her pregnant, he clearly hadn't been there for her, either.

With his explanation out, he pressed his lips together and waited. He'd run dry on anything else to say.

"Fine." She didn't make eye contact. "I understand. Really. I do."

Only he got the feeling she didn't.

"It wasn't the first time Steph had gone after a guy I liked, anyway."

He hadn't realized that. He propped his hip against the desk and tried to look relaxed, hoping that would ease the stiffness from her shoulders as well.

"I knew I was worthless." He lifted his hands, palms up. "But that was bad, even for me. I'm still not sure how I could have hurt the one person who truly cared for me."

Or that he'd cared for.

"I'm sorry, Lee." And he really was. He had been since the moment it had happened. "No one deserves to be treated the way I did you. I don't expect forgiveness, but I do hope you can accept my apology."

She stood, stiff to the point it looked painful. Finally, he saw just a bit of the fight slip out of her, and he began to breathe again.

"You never were as bad as you imagined." Her voice edged back from glacier cold and began to soothe his raw heart. It wasn't an acceptance of his apology, but it might be the best he was going to get.

With a twist to his mouth, he tipped his head back and let out a long sigh. It was possible he was imagining it, but an air filled the room that reminded him of so many of their conversations in the past. Just the two of them talking about nothing or everything. Just being.

"You always believed the best in me," he said.

He heaved himself onto the desk until he straddled the corner, his feet dangling above the floor. Lee Ann no longer hugged the door, but she still stood several feet from him. Even though he hurt from what he'd learned about her, he found he wanted her closer. And that made no sense.

He'd arrived in town with the intention only to apologize, but every time during these past few days that he'd caught a glimpse of her or heard her light voice, his heart had twisted and he'd wanted more. Grasping the corner of the desk between his legs, he rested his weight on his arms and took in the hair spiking out in every direction and the bright orange toes. She'd deserved so much better. Still did.

"I think I got scared I would let you down," he said quietly. "That you would eventually see the real me."

Without seeming aware of it, she narrowed the distance between them until she stood only a foot away. He held his breath for fear she would realize she stood within touching distance. "I did see the real you. The day I found you trying to put a splint on that poor dog's leg."

He shifted his weight on one arm so that he leaned slightly toward her, and breathed in her fresh scent. She smelled like a flower garden. Lowering his lids, he pictured the afternoon she'd mentioned. He'd always loved animals and had come upon a dog that had tangled up with some other animal. The angry dog hadn't worried him, but he'd feared being seen brought to tears because he couldn't lessen the animal's pain. Lee Ann had come upon him and never mentioned the fragile state he seemed to be in.

"I knew the moment I saw you risking a serious mauling from a very ticked-off and hurt dog that you were a good guy."

She'd always thought the best of him. Too bad she'd been wrong. Maybe deep down she'd known, and that's why she'd cheated.

He reached out and touched a finger to the back of her hand. He needed to know. Pressure built in his chest. "Who did you sleep with, Lee? And why didn't he do the right thing and marry you?"

His words returned her from the past, and she not only jerked her hand out of his reach but stepped back and crossed her arms over her chest. She focused on something on the other side of the room. "It's not worth discussing."

He studied her stiff posture. "Is he still around? In their lives?"

If he was, Cody feared he would break the guy's nose for having once touched his girl.

"No." She followed the short word with a quick shake of her head. "He left before they were born. They don't even know who he is."

Heat crept up his neck as anger threatened to resurface. This time not for the deceit but for the man who'd deserted her. It shouldn't hurt this much.

She brought her gaze back to his, and he watched her chest rise with a deep breath. "I apologize, too. I..." She looked away. "I'm sorry, I can't explain it. But I do apologize for any hurt I've caused."

Not good enough, but he recognized it was all he would get. He probably didn't deserve more anyway. Sliding off the desk, he stepped in front of her. She had her secrets, he had his. He could live with that.

Before she could get away, he wrapped his arms around her and held her stiff body close. She barely came to his chest.

"I'm sorry," he whispered. "For everything." He pressed a kiss to the top of her head. "And for what it's worth, I did love you. As much as I possibly could."

CHAPTER

5

Lee Ann smoothed the tablecloth over her dining room table, positioned the fall-colored centerpiece in the middle, then stepped back and surveyed her work. It was perfect for Thanksgiving. She pulled her granny's silverware from storage and began wiping it down. She'd had a customer unexpectedly cancel a photography appointment this afternoon. Since there were only two more days until she'd have a full house sitting around her table, she decided to make use of the time and begin preparations.

It was better than thinking about the fact she'd blatantly lied to Cody the day before, and that she knew she had to make it right.

He hadn't come into the diner that morning, and though she wanted to believe that was because he'd simply decided to eat at home, she was also aware he'd been in each morning until today. He hadn't come in because he was furious with her.

And it was only going to get worse.

She straightened in her seat and stretched out her spine until the joints popped. Tension had found a new home since

Cody had come back to town, and she'd done nothing but add to it.

Why she'd stood there yesterday and told the man she'd been pregnant when he'd left town was beyond her. Had she wanted to lash back and hurt him the way he'd hurt her? Or was she truly such a small person that she wanted to keep him from her girls' lives?

Everything would be easier if he didn't get involved, but how was that the right thing? And didn't she pride herself on always doing the right thing?

She sighed. He may not have been her perfect idea of a father, but he clearly wasn't completely worthless. If he was, he would have given up long ago instead of putting in the hard work necessary to make it through veterinary school. He also wouldn't have sought her out simply to apologize for a hurt he'd caused more than a decade before. And she believed him when he'd said he hadn't talked to Stephanie since the day they'd had sex. Maybe she shouldn't have, but the moment the words had come out of his mouth, she knew them to be true.

Why she hadn't actually considered that an option before, she didn't know. But as she'd watched the shock cross Cody's face when he'd learned of Steph's death, she'd known a colossal mistake had been made. And she'd made it. She'd believed her sister.

Stephanie had lied and been vindictive toward her throughout her entire life, mostly because their father had left and his departure had been Lee Ann's fault. According to Stephanie, everything had been perfect until he'd met Reba and then Lee Ann had come along. Of course Stephanie also hadn't seemed to take into account the fact that her own mother had left her when she was only three. In the end, Stephanie had been left living with a stepmother and half sister, no biological parents, and a whole lot of anger.

Why Lee Ann had thought Stephanie could change in the last days of her life and show a bit of compassion toward others she had no idea. Especially after she'd practically spit out the words that it was Cody who'd gotten her pregnant instead of continuing to tell lies about it being a country star who'd fathered the babies. She'd snarled at Lee Ann that if it hadn't been for her having the boyfriend she'd had, Stephanie wouldn't have ended up pregnant in the first place. Then they would have found the cancer in time instead of during the delivery.

Only thing Lee Ann could figure for why she'd believed Stephanie when she'd said Cody wanted nothing to do with the girls was that she'd wanted it to be true. She'd wanted to believe that Cody really didn't want the kids. It made her life easier not to have to seek him out and reopen old wounds.

Because God, he'd hurt her.

She'd walked into the house that sunny afternoon, only one week before prom, knowing her world to be perfect. She was in love with the greatest guy she'd ever met, she had a full scholarship and plans to get away to college, and she would soon consummate her relationship with the man she planned to spend forever with.

Then, in one second, all that had changed. She'd stepped through the front door of her mother's home, the same house she was living in now, and had seen Cody backing away from Stephanie, who lay on the couch—a couch that was *not* still in the house today. He'd been tucking himself back into his pants, and Stephanie had been chortling with laughter, her skirt up to her waist, and her panties on the floor.

Lee Ann had caught a glimpse of pink lace shoved below exposed breasts before she'd escaped up the stairs to her own room.

She still didn't understand how he could have done that to her. What had he said? He'd gotten some bad news. Well, that was simply unacceptable. People got bad news every day. You didn't get bad news, then trip and find yourself penis-first inside your girlfriend's sister.

Irritation boiled in her. She knew she should forget about the past and move on, but he'd been the one to bring it up. She'd been perfectly content with it pushed to the recesses of her mind. But no, that wasn't good enough for him. He wanted to "clear his conscience."

So she'd kept her mouth shut about the lie she'd told.

It hadn't been right, she knew, and she would correct it. Eventually. But yesterday, as he'd been explaining how he'd come to turn his back on her in the worst possible way, she'd been unable to find it in herself to do the right thing.

Her front screen door slammed with a thwack, and she leaned over to look out of the room and down the hall. She had to get that spring fixed.

"Hi Mom," she called when she caught sight of the woman almost identical to her in size and weight. "Why are you coming in through the front?"

Her mother shrugged out of her peacock-blue coat and tossed it on the chair against the wall. Since she lived next door, she normally bopped from back door to back door between the houses.

"I picked up the chrysanthemums and pumpkins for the porch instead of waiting until tomorrow. Ran up to the nursery as soon as I got off work. My car is parked out front. Come help me unload, and we'll get them set up."

Her mother worked at city hall, which suited her perfectly. Easy access to gossip. Lee Ann was certain she was situating herself to be the town's next Ms. Grayson, holder of all knowledge of everything and everyone.

She put the spoons down she'd been working on and made her way through the house. Their family was no bigger than the four of them, but they all loved inviting over friends who had nowhere else to go during the holiday. It set the tone of thinking of others that she hoped to instill in her children and also gave everyone a nice, enjoyable day of relaxation. This year there would be seven guests. Tonight she'd do the big grocery run, and then tomorrow afternoon and all day Thursday she'd cook. It was a lot of work, but she loved every minute of it.

As she followed her mother out the door, she took in the outfit of the day. A peasant skirt in fall colors, lace-up ankle boots, and a long-sleeved, ruffled shirt. With no sign of gray in her hair, and a bounce still in her step, the woman could almost pass for being in her twenties instead of her fifties.

"Beatrice said Cody found you up at the salon yesterday afternoon," her mother stated.

Lee Ann rolled her eyes behind her. She loved this town, but sometimes it really wore on her nerves. You couldn't get a cavity without everyone knowing which tooth it was in.

"Did she also report in on what the conversation covered?"

No one knew that but she and Joanie—she'd filled her friend in after Cody had left.

Her mother harrumphed. "She didn't know."

"And what? She sent you to find out?" She went to the trunk. "Oh, Mom, these are gorgeous!"

She liked to decorate the front steps with a mix of mums, as well as pumpkins and other gourds in different shapes and sizes. At the end of the evening, all guests departed with a planted pot of their own, along with their choice of the fruit.

"Of course she didn't send me." Her mother scoffed. She then shot Lee Ann a gaudy wink. "I offered to come on my own."

Her mother turned serious. "Was it about the kids? What did he say? You know I won't tell anything about that, but I will have to come up with some reason he was seeking you out. The current theory is that he never got over you and wants to start things back up."

Lee Ann choked on the thought. "Of course that's not what's going on. Who is saying that?"

Reba shrugged. "Everyone."

And likely her mother and Ms. Grayson had started the story. Lee Ann grabbed a couple plants and scowled at her mother as she passed her on the way to the house.

Her mother was two steps behind with her own armload. "Well, it all makes sense. From their point of view, why else would he be seeking you out? And this isn't the first time he's done it, either. Everyone already saw him at the bake sale Saturday, and then he was at the diner yesterday. Word is, though, that he skipped this morning. That set everyone to thinking you must be playing hard to get."

"Well they can go on thinking it, too," she muttered. The thought of the two of them getting back together made her skin itch. It was the last thing she'd want.

"I have to admit, I encouraged that theory. I don't see you letting your guard down given how he's been absent for thirteen years. He could come up with a perfectly good reason that made sense, but you're not prone to forgiving such things."

At least her mother wasn't completely wearing rose-colored glasses for once. They finished unloading the car before Lee

Ann answered the previous question about the reason he'd sought her out.

When they had the last of the decorations positioned just where she wanted them, she took a seat on the concrete steps in the middle of them all and patted the space beside her.

"Actually, no," she finally answered. "He didn't come up to the salon to talk about the girls. He came to apologize to me for sleeping with Steph."

"Oh." The single word from her mother was spoken softly. She hadn't expected to hear that. "And did he have a good reason?"

Lee Ann leaned back, her elbows on the step behind her. "He'd apparently gotten bad news earlier in the day."

The woman who was capable of seeing the good in everyone merely turned her head in slow motion and gawked. Lee Ann couldn't help but laugh out loud, the sound making her feel better than she had in days.

"That's right. Bad news. Then Steph did her Steph thing with him, probably accidently lost the buttons on her top, brought out some 'special' lemonade, and the rest, as they say, is history." She closed her eyes and lifted her face to the breezy, slightly warmer-than-normal day. She'd come outside without a coat, and with all the anger traipsing through her, she found she didn't need one. "I've no doubt she did all the hard work to seduce him, but geez, he had a bad day, so he let it happen?"

"Well," her mom started, her tone hesitant. "Don't forget he was a teenage boy. It's hard to say no to opportunities like that."

"He'd said he loved me."

Reba paused. "He was also driven by hormones."

Clearly. But in Lee Ann's mind, that wasn't good enough. Young and stupid or not, you don't tell a girl one day that you love her, then have sex with her sister the next. Her mother didn't argue the fact further, thank goodness.

After several more moments of silence, Lee Ann could tell her mother was ready to ask the hard question. She had yet to be able to explain away Cody's selfish avoidance of the fact he'd fathered two girls and had never wanted anything to do with them. In her mind, something wasn't adding up. Wasn't she just going to love it when she learned the truth?

"So..." The hesitancy was clear in her mother's voice. "He didn't bring up the girls at all during your talk? Just like Saturday?"

Eyes open now, Lee Ann stared up through the bare branches of the overhanging tree and focused on the clear blue Tennessee sky. It sure was a beautiful day. She only wished she could have that same clear, easy feeling in her heart. Instead, she wanted to continue with the lie she'd started the day before. She knew, however, that the moment she told her mother what she'd learned, her time of pretending she could go on keeping Cody in the dark was over.

She pulled in a deep breath and let it out very slowly, still not looking at her mother. "He didn't know Steph was dead, Mom."

A small gasp hit her ears. "How could he not know? She told him that was why she wouldn't be raising the girls."

Her calm, ordered life had been so nice until now. She was going to miss it.

She closed her eyes once more. "He didn't know because he never talked to her again after running out of here that day."

"What?" Her mother shot to her feet. "But then how did he...How did she..."

Lee Ann didn't have to say anything. Instead she watched the lines of her mother's face change as realization sank in. They went from tense and stressed, making her look every bit her age, to relaxed. Relieved. Life was once again as it should be in her mind. Cody wasn't the bad guy, and she could go back to pretending life could work out perfectly.

"She never even told him she was pregnant, did she? He didn't know? All these years, we thought..." She shook her head, amazement flashing through her eyes. "And he didn't even know."

Words were unnecessary. Lee Ann merely nodded.

"Oh, my," her mom said. She turned and slowly lowered herself back down to the steps beside Lee Ann. "You have to tell him."

Surely she didn't. "I know."

"And you have to do it soon," she pressed. "People don't make it a habit anymore of talking about the fact the girls are Stephanie's, but it'll eventually come out. His being back has brought up so many things from that time. You know someone is bound to bring up Stephanie returning and having the kids. And when they do—"

"Yeah," Lee Ann interrupted. "When they do, he's going to put two and two together real fast. And whether he wants anything to do with them or not, he's going to be livid."

Not unlike how he would be when he learned she'd told him a bald-faced lie only yesterday. He would accuse her of purposely keeping the girls from him.

"Of course he'll want something to do with them. That's what parents do." Her mother's cell made a noise and she pulled it out.

"Really?" How the woman could make that statement when her own husband had deserted her and his two kids was a mystery. Not to mention he left his oldest daughter behind with a woman who wasn't even her mother. "It's my experience that's not always the case, Mom."

Her mother waved away her concern, then tapped a message on the keypad of her phone. "He's different than your father. That man had wandering genes. Of course Cody will want something to do with them."

Right, like being a vet who bounced from city to city proved stabilization.

The cell phone chirped again and a line formed between her mother's brows. She then glanced up at Lee Ann. "It's after five."

"Yeah?" *Oh.* The girls weren't home. She looked around as if she could see the school from where she sat. It was up the hill behind the house. "Maybe they came in quietly."

Blue eyes that matched her own showed back at her with a sarcastic gleam. "And you think I'm the one who always believes the ridiculous. Those two couldn't come in without making noise if the peace of the world were on the line."

Lee Ann stood, worry filling her. Her mother was right. Even on days she was in the darkroom and the girls didn't seek her out, she never missed the sound of them coming in the house.

"Where could they be?" she asked. She hurried to the side of the yard and stared up at the school. No girls.

As panic threatened, she reminded herself they lived in a city where only one police officer was needed, and he spent 95 percent of his time playing gin rummy with his wife-receptionist.

Her mother held up her cell phone. "Beatrice says they just went into the back door of Keri's clinic."

Alert signals clanged in her brain. Half-jogging, she hurried to the middle of the road and craned her neck as if she could see to the other end of the road. "Why would they go there? Keri isn't even working now. She's at home waiting for the baby to come."

Her mother's cell signaled again and she read it out loud. "They figured out Dr. Dalton wouldn't have any plans for Thanksgiving so they're going over to invite him to Lee Ann's."

Lee Ann's lunch almost returned. She didn't want him at their house on Thursday. Worse, she had a very bad feeling about this unplanned excursion. "I need to go."

🌸 🌸 🌸

Cody jotted notes from the day's last patient while Kendra and Candy London continued with their steady stream of information. Though the clinic had closed at four thirty, they'd arrived shortly after via the unlocked back door, and had promptly situated themselves in his office, attracting Boss and the clinic cat, Howard, over to them. They'd been talking nonstop ever since, and he had yet to figure out a way to get rid of them.

Not that he wanted to be rude, but he struggled to look at either one of them without jealousy swamping him. At least Lee Ann knew who he'd cheated with. Not that either of the incidents mattered at this point; they'd happened so long ago. He let out a soft sigh and tossed his pen to the desk. He just couldn't seem to let the infidelity go.

He'd almost broken his own code of staying out of people's business and called Holly to ask her who the father was. He'd taken her to the fund-raiser, so she owed him one. Plus they were becoming friends of sorts. When he'd gone to the diner Sunday, she'd taken a break and sat down to have breakfast with him again. He believed her when she said she wasn't looking to date him, but he also wasn't what you would call comfortable eating with her on a regular basis. He preferred his solitude. Regular meals taken together could easily bleed into other parts of his life if he wasn't careful.

That was the reason he'd given himself for skipping breakfast that morning, but he could admit it when he was lying to himself. He'd 100 percent not wanted see Lee Ann.

Yet if he'd gone to the diner, he could have used the time to ask Holly who'd sired the London kids. Even if she didn't know, it would take her less than two minutes to get him the answer. But he didn't like gossip, and he certainly didn't want people thinking that anything around there mattered to him, so he'd stayed home and eaten the leftover macaroni and cheese he'd fixed for dinner the night before. Cold, boxed mac and cheese was not good for a person's mood.

"So Coach Taylor told me that if I keep practicing, I'll be on the first string before the season is over." Candy's words worked their way back into his consciousness, and he looked at her. She wore an earnest expression. "I'll probably take that mean Jenna Hopkins's position."

He didn't think she was expecting a reply, so he sat in silence. What was he supposed to say anyway? He didn't know anything about Candy's athletic skills, nor whether she was any better than Jenna what's-her-name. Too bad there were no more animals to see. The office manager had confirmed that the numbers had already declined in the two days he'd been alone in the office, even though he was doing all he could to let it be known he wasn't the reckless teen he'd once been.

Hadn't he shown up to help put the town's Christmas lights up the moment he'd been asked?

When Kendra jumped from her chair and held her hands out in front of her, Boss lifted his head from where he rested next to her, and Howard gave a sniff before darting out of the room. Cody waited, wondering what she would do next. He hadn't spent a lot of time around kids, and these two had spoken more words in the last ten minutes than he'd heard since his first job out of school. He'd signed on with a small office where one of the assistants often experienced babysitting troubles. She'd brought her two toddlers to work more often than not. But toddlers' energy had nothing on that of preteens.

"Do you know anyone who is double jointed?" Kendra proceeded to twist her thumb back until it lay flush against her wrist. Candy joined her, folding fingertips of one hand down at a perfect ninety-degree angle. "Very few people around here can do this, but me and Candy can. Our mom and Grandma can't, though. I don't know where we get it."

Finally here was something he could relate to. "You know," he said, twisting his own thumb backward, "the medical term is hypermobility. You don't actually have extra joints."

"You have it, too!" Candy's eyes widened as she brought up her second hand, flattening the tips the same as the first. "It freaks people out when we do this."

Cody laughed out loud, then stood and adjusted both knees so they bent backward.

"Wow." Both girls edged closer. "We can't do that one, but we can do our arms."

All three proceeded to hold their arms out, bending their elbows in the wrong direction before collapsing into their chairs, laughing until winded. Cody swiped at his eyes. He couldn't recall the last time he'd laughed enough to bring himself to tears. Maybe he should give these kids a chance. It wasn't their fault their mother wasn't who she'd led him to believe.

Once the laughter calmed, Kendra nudged her sister as if reminding her to do something. Leery of what they were up to, he brought up the subject that had so recently turned his memories upside down. "I understand you two young ladies will soon become official teenagers."

Four brown eyes glowed at him. "We are having the *best* birthday party ever."

Candy cut in. "Better than Sadie Evans's party even. Hers was two months ago. She had a massive sleepover, but it was only girls. Ours is in twenty-five days, and we're having a real *dance*."

"You should come." As soon as the words were out of Kendra's mouth, Candy clamped down on her sister's wrist and shot her a look he thought might mean "I'm the oldest, so let me do it." Candy had already explained how she'd been pulled from her mother's stomach over four minutes before Kendra.

Shrugging off Candy's hand, Kendra ignored whatever silent command had been issued. "We sometimes get a second 'birthday party,'" she air quoted. "If you're still here, maybe you can celebrate with us again. Of course, Mom may not do it this year. It was only started as a joke anyway."

It had been hard keeping up with all the subject changes, but they'd finally lost him. "A second"—he mimicked her air quotes—"'birthday party?'" He rested his forearms on his spread knees. "Why?"

Candy shot her sister a glare he read loud and clear. *Shut up!* "It was my idea, actually. You see, when we found out, uh—"

"Three years ago—"

"Yeah." Candy elbowed her sister back into the chair. "When we found out three years ago that we'd been preemies—you know what preemies are, right?"

Her innocence was priceless. She reminded him of Lee Ann when they'd first met. "Yeah, we learned about preemies in vet school."

"Stupid," Kendra mumbled and made a face to the back of her sister's head.

"Yeah, well, of course. Anyway, when we learned we were preemies, we told Mom that we should get another celebration on the day we were supposed to be born."

Lee Ann hadn't mentioned the girls were born early. How early could they have been if she'd been pregnant when he'd left? He nodded as if their words made perfect sense. "And your mother agreed, huh? So when's the second big day?"

Kendra was finished being quiet. She pushed her sister's arm out of the way and instituted hers firmly in front. "January thirty-first."

The outside world closed in, and Cody suddenly could focus on only a very narrow piece of information. January thirty-first. Lee Ann had found him with Stephanie the last week of April. Maybe she hadn't actually cheated on him until she'd caught him with Stephanie.

But then, why didn't she clear herself instead of letting him believe the worst?

"And so, since you have nowhere else to go"—Cody realized Kendra had rattled onto a different subject but had no idea what he'd missed—"we think you should come to our house Thursday for Thanksgiving. We and Mom and Grandma like to invite anybody who doesn't have family to share it with, and you didn't come with family."

His head spun. Lee Ann possibly had not cheated on him, and now her daughters were giving him the perfect opportunity to get close enough to confront her.

Candy huffed and mumbled under her breath, "I was going to ask him."

"We eat at six and hope you can make it. Everybody deserves a second chance."

"She means everybody deserves to spend Thanksgiving with someone." Big sister shot another one of those looks, and this time Kendra quieted.

Finished, both girls sat back, and he could once again hear the creaks of the house turned office. They waited for an answer, but his mind reeled as he soaked in everything they'd just said. Thanksgiving...a second chance?

He took in their identical innocent expressions, their long brown hair pulled back to accentuate high cheekbones that would one day drive every boy in town crazy, and brown eyes twinkling as if fighting the urge to glow in mischief, and had a feeling they were doing more than thinking of someone who might be alone for the holidays. Were they looking to set their mom up? When he turned the idea over in his head, he knew there were worse people to be set up with. If he was in the market for that sort of thing.

But he was leaving soon. Starting something he couldn't finish might not only hurt Lee Ann again but possibly her daughters as well. He found the idea of hurting these two girls as distasteful as doing the same to their mother. Somehow, in the few minutes they'd spent in his office, they'd burrowed under his heart a little.

"I don't know. I appreciate the offer, but—"

"Wait." Candy held out her hand, palm up, and he stopped talking. Funny how they already seemed to have him under control. Something they'd picked up from their mother, no doubt. No matter what reputation he'd had around town, he'd always found himself unable to say no to Lee Ann and thus did whatever she instructed.

As Candy sat there, Kendra stooped over and dug through her backpack, pulling out books, loose papers, a pen that skittered across the floor. Finally she latched on to a small notebook and flipped the cover open. As she leafed through the pages, two pictures fluttered out to land on the floor in front of him. Bending over, he scooped up the squares, expecting to see some boy she was sweet on, but what he found were two pictures of Stephanie smiling back at him. His mouth dried.

"Got it!" Kendra held up a list. "We were afraid you might say no, so we thought we'd let you know who else is coming."

"You see, we've heard that some people aren't going to bring their pets in if they're sick, because they think you're a hoodlum or something." Candy rolled her eyes in complete mystification. "Anyway, according to the rumors, one of the people who refuses to come—even though his dog has diabetes and Mom says needs his sugar checked again because he hasn't been keeping up the shots—is coming to the house Thursday."

Kendra wore an overly innocent smile. "So don't you want to meet him and show him you aren't a hoodlum so he'll get his dog the help he needs?"

Oh, these girls were good. They figured out what they wanted and didn't just come up with one plan but also a plan B. He liked resourcefulness in people.

"So what do you say?" They both sat back again, angel expressions and blessedly silent.

He raised his chin at the list clutched in Kendra's hand. "Can I see that?"

She passed it over, and she was right. On the list he saw not only the person he'd already heard about whose dog was struggling, but also someone else who was circulating rumors at a fast pace, supposedly in the hope he'd run Cody out of town early. How that would help anyone, when the town would be left without a licensed veterinarian, was a question that hadn't been answered.

Going to a big family dinner with a group of people who'd rather he didn't exist was not his idea of a good time. He held the sheet of paper up for them to see and tapped his finger on the name of the troublemaker, Buddy Sawyer. "You missed some good bait here."

They exchanged glances before Candy spoke up. "We didn't know if you'd heard about him, and we didn't want to hurt your feelings if you hadn't."

Kind, too. They had a lot of Lee Ann in them.

As he struggled with a way to turn them down gently, the pictures in his hand caught his attention, and he held them up. "You carry pictures of Stephanie with you? Lee Ann mentioned she passed away years ago. You probably weren't very old when that happened."

Kendra reached for the snapshots. "She died five days after we were born. I have those today because we're doing a thing in science class about genes. The kind that make up who you are, not the kind you wear."

Lee Ann had just given birth to premature twins with no husband by her side and then had to deal with the death of her sister on top of it? The idea of either happening was bad enough. The two together launched a wave of disgust deep in his gut.

"I have pictures, too." Candy reached for her bag. "Want to see?"

"That's okay. I was just surprised you'd have pictures of your aunt when you've never really known her. I can totally understand needing them for science class, though."

Confusion flitted through the girls' eyes before they cleared, and smiles covered both their faces. Like the first time he'd met them, he was taken aback by their smiles. Something about them seemed so familiar that it made him uncomfortable.

"Of course," Candy said. "You wouldn't know. You weren't here."

The slamming of the back door got his attention and he rose, along with Boss. He stayed where he was when he heard Lee Ann yell for the girls. She sounded frantic. And then, as if in slow motion, everything clicked into place.

He looked back at Candy and had to force the words through dry lips. "Wouldn't know what?"

Lee Ann reached the open door to the office, out of breath, and motioned for the girls. "You two have scared me to death by not coming home after practice. Come on, let's go."

Cody held out a hand toward the girls, and they stayed where they were. "Give them another minute, Lee Ann. They were just about to tell me something of which I seem to be the only person unaware."

Lee Ann's eyes darkened, and she jutted her chin in the air. "They need to come home with me right this minute."

Fear. He saw it in her at the same time as it burned through his body. He wasn't entirely certain he wanted to hear what they had to say. If he heard it, he couldn't hide from it. If he heard it, he'd have to get involved whether he wanted to or not.

He looked at the girls. But if he didn't, what would he be missing out on?

Candy pulled the pictures from her own bag and held them up for all to see, and a soft moan slipped from between Lee Ann's lips.

"What you don't know," Candy said, as she held one picture parallel to her cheek and Kendra leaned in so the picture was positioned between both their faces—and even without the photo, Cody could finally see it. They'd inherited his eyes and smile, and Stephanie's long legs, cheekbones, and thin frame—"is that Stephanie was our *biological* mom, but Mom has been our mom since we were born."

CHAPTER

Lee Ann sagged against the door as she closed it behind her customers. She'd just finished a last-minute, one-hour-turned-three-hour photo shoot for four siblings all between the ages of one and five. Their mother had decided yesterday that new pictures were needed for their Thanksgiving visit with Grandma. Thanksgiving was tomorrow.

Exhausted, she pushed off and headed to her back room. She scrolled through the collection on her docked iPod and chose a playlist that would do its best to wipe her mind of her stress. She cranked up the volume as she went about cleaning up the miscellaneous toys and equipment she'd used during the session.

As she cleaned, she kept shifting to the side of the room where she could see the outside door. Cody should be showing up soon. He'd insisted on talking yesterday afternoon, but she'd refused to in front of the girls. She'd shook her head as he'd glowered at her, trying her best to let him know that she hadn't known, then had barely gotten them out of there without the girls asking too many questions.

Not only had she needed to get the girls away and go to the grocery store, but Cody had needed time to cool down as well. She would guess he hadn't changed completely over the years, and from what she remembered, though he typically took things pretty much in stride, when too much built up, he snapped. At that point he did things such as go on a tear through the town, busting out shop windows and pulling down statues. Not that she thought he was still that immature, but she had to guess that finding out he had two kids he never knew anything about had to be a bit worse than whatever "bad news" he'd discovered the day the kids had been made.

She'd actually expected him earlier in the day, since she knew the clinic closed early today, but thankfully he hadn't shown up while her clients had been there. He hadn't shown up at the diner for breakfast again, either. She couldn't help but wonder if his absence meant he wouldn't show up to talk at all. Maybe he'd already packed up and hit the road. Wouldn't be the first time he'd bolted.

The thought of him leaving instead of owning up to his responsibility irritated her, and she reached out to turn up the volume. Several minutes later, she'd stored the last of the equipment, and she turned to check the door again. Cody had entered without her hearing the chime that would have sounded. He now stood five feet away, wearing the same expression from yesterday afternoon.

The saliva in her throat disappeared.

As they stood there staring at each other, the words to the song playing through the speakers, Dead or Alive's "You Spin Me Round (Like a Record)," registered in her head.

She reached over and pushed a button, and silence fell around them. He definitely spun her round, in more ways than one. Even his furious, ticked-off look set her pulse on a slow gallop. The man—damn him—expelled testosterone like her radiator had blown antifreeze when it busted last winter. It spewed from every possible angle.

Finding out that he hadn't known he'd fathered kids had messed with her mind and had caused a behavior she wasn't proud of. Her brain had been infiltrated by silly thoughts, not unlike those her mother might have. Thoughts along the lines of maybe he'd stay. Maybe he'd be just what the girls needed. Maybe he'd thought about her once or twice over the years.

She fought the urge to roll her eyes at the last one. Didn't matter if he'd thought about her every day of his life. He'd proved years ago he wasn't the man for her. She did not need men who left.

While she continued to stand there staring at him, unable to find words to start the conversation, the studio phone rang.

"Excuse me," she said, coming out of her trancelike state. "I need to take this."

"Let it ring." Cody's deep voice did not come across as a request.

Her heart thumped. "It's business. I can't afford to miss any opportunities that might come up."

She reached toward the phone on the corner of her desk.

"Is there any doubt they're mine?"

His words stopped her hand in midair. She couldn't have ignored the question if her house had literally been going up in flames around her.

She slowly pulled back from the phone and wet her lips. "All you have to do is look at them. They're replicas of you across the eyes, and then when they smile..."

Pausing, she picked up the framed photo she kept on her desk and caught her lip between her teeth. It was a shot she'd made during a Dollywood trip three years before. Both girls had been laughing as they'd come off a roller coaster, and she'd captured them perfectly. The photo was a head-and-shoulders shot, and with the shadow of the trees above them making their hair a shade darker, they'd looked so much like Cody that later that evening she'd caught herself bringing up the Internet to search for him. She'd wanted to scream at him, to make him understand what he was missing out on.

Instead, she'd shut down the computer and cursed him for the decisions he'd made. Not for leaving her to raise the girls alone, but for not being there for them. They deserved a father. But only one who chose to be there.

The phone quit ringing, and she passed the picture over to him. "They look just like you. Also, the timing couldn't be more perfect." She shrugged. "I'd bet my life on it."

He studied the photo in his hands, but she could read nothing in his expression. It remained as tense and angry as it had been when he'd entered the room. Finally, he looked up and caught her gaze. "And you chose to never tell me?"

The phone began to ring again. "I swear, I thought you knew."

His entire body seemed to turn to concrete in front of her. "And what? You thought I'd just walked away? Felt no responsibility at all?"

"I didn't know." His pain hurt her, but she had no idea how to lessen the wound. The phone continued to ring, its shrillness in the thick tension adding to her stress. "I didn't know what to think," she whispered.

"So you thought the worst," he accused. His nostrils flared a bit as his chest rose on a deep breath.

If the guilt wasn't bad enough before, it certainly was now. Why had she ever believed her sister?

As if the phone were a lifeline, she reached out and snatched it up before it went silent once more. She turned her attention to the caller, discussing appointment options, then brought up her calendar to book them into a slot in the coming week. All the while she kept an eye on Cody. He'd moved away from the desk and now edged around the room until he stopped at her back wall, arms crossed tight, broad shoulders taking up way too much space. He stood studying the black and whites arranged there. They were her favorites.

When she was finished with the customer, she quietly hung up the phone and simply watched Cody from across the room. She sensed the aura of protective distance that he'd once been a master at putting between himself and everyone else. It hadn't been there the other times their paths had crossed this last week. At least not as strongly as it was today. It amazed her that it still existed. Probably it had shown up today because he was hurting over all he'd missed out on. The guilt over that ate at her, while at the same time the seventeen-year-old who'd had her heart crushed wanted to stomp her foot and childishly tell him he'd gotten what he deserved.

But he didn't—he hadn't deserved this. She knew that. No matter how they'd ended, he'd had a right to know about his children. If she'd had any real clue he hadn't dismissed them as callously as Stephanie said, she would have continued looking for him.

"This is from Roy and Pearl's." Cody pointed to the shot taken at his foster parents' farm four years ago and glanced back at her. His features weren't friendly, but at least he no longer looked as if he wanted to snap her in two. "I recognize the tree."

She nodded. The unique knot in the side of the elm was the reason she'd wanted that angle. "They purchased the most beautiful mare a few years ago. She wasn't quite as white as the photo makes it seem, but I liked the contrast, so I developed it to come out that way."

She wondered if he realized both of his foster parents had passed away.

"It's impressive." He faced the wall again. "You still develop from film instead of using digital, then?"

"Only the black and whites." They were what she enjoyed most. There was a magic about seeing them come to life beneath her hands that she loved.

She stood and moved closer to him. They'd once been the best of friends, and though she didn't want to be, she was as drawn to the haunting pain clinging to him as much today as she'd been the first day they'd met. He was a man who'd been hurt many times over in his life, and she hated that she'd added to it.

"I'm sorry you had to find out about them the way you did."

His jaw jerked.

She tried again. "When I realized you didn't know—"

"You lied and told me you'd been pregnant before I left town."

Well, there was that. But no, that wasn't quite how it had gone down, either. Discussing all this in the middle of her studio, though, was making her uncomfortable. It felt too personal. This was her private space, and she found she wanted him out of it.

"I know I can never make up for the lost years, Cody, but I promise to do my best to explain everything." She turned away from him and headed across the room. "But we'll do it in the house."

He'd always been able to see too much under the surface when they argued. Having him standing there now, staring at her pictures, made her feel like he was seeing a part of her she didn't share with others. She didn't like it.

"You never wanted to do portraits." The words were spoken quietly behind her just as she reached the door.

She paused, unsure how to reply and unwilling to answer his unspoken question. Yes, she'd settled. She hadn't gone after all she'd wanted. But she hadn't had a choice. Without facing him, she gave him the only answer she could. "I've found I'm quite good at portraits."

Without another word, she entered the house through the connecting door. They were there to discuss their kids. Discussing her or her photography was off-limits.

🌼 🌼 🌼

Cody watched Lee Ann retreat to the house, and for just a second considered turning around and heading back out the door he'd come through. After he'd exhausted both himself and Boss the night before with an arduous run, which had not done the job of lowering his anger at all, he'd spent the better part of the evening stewing. She'd kept the knowledge that he had two kids from him for years. Until he'd walked in there today and started the conversation, though, he hadn't really thought about the fact that *he had two kids*.

How could he have skipped that fact?

He had two kids.

The very idea overwhelmed him to the point that he feared he was about to experience his first panic attack. How had he come to be the guy who had not only *not* been there for his kids, but also had no idea if he even wanted to be there for them now?

Of course he would be. Financially at least. That was the right thing to do. And sure, he'd like to know them. They seemed like good kids.

But do everyday things? Be a dad?

The thought brought a taste of sourness to this throat. He had no idea how to even begin such a thing.

He shook his head as he got his feet moving across the room to follow the perfectly tucked-in pink shirt that had now disappeared from view. He had no idea how to even go about being there for the girls daily. He never lived in the same place for more than a few months. How was he supposed to work two teenagers into that lifestyle?

As he stepped inside the living room, he took in the changes and wondered if Lee Ann still lived there with her mother. He assumed so, given the fact it had been Reba's house when he'd last been there.

The wall color had been updated to a light brown in both this room and the connecting den. The furniture was newer but not new, replacing the older versions he'd grown used to during the months he'd spent hanging out with Lee Ann, and the overall feel was one of calming comfort and order. Either Reba no longer lived there or if she did, Lee Ann ran the household. Because it definitely had more of a feel of Lee Ann now than of her mother.

He inhaled, filling his head with the lemony-clean scent of the room, and slowly blew the breath out. A dull headache began behind his eyes. He'd never wanted kids. Hadn't even given thought to having any. Ever. Yet he had two.

He would have doubted he was their father if he hadn't seen the same things Lee Ann had pointed out. The girls did look like him, exactly as she'd said. And that disturbed him in a whole new way.

There weren't enough similarities for others to have noticed, and they weren't likely to now since he'd only been in Sugar Springs for a year before, and apparently no one else knew of his actions with Stephanie. But the similarities were there nonetheless. He'd seen them before he'd even let himself recognize the fact.

Anger suddenly blazed again, though he couldn't quite pinpoint the root cause. Stephanie? Lee Ann? Him? Any one of the past foster parents in his life who'd helped shape him?

No, not the foster parents. They'd merely given him a valuable education at a young age. Don't rely on the idea of family. It never existed quite like you wanted.

Only Lee Ann had made a family with her kids.

His kids.

And once again he didn't fit in there, either.

He blew out another breath as he fought to get his emotions under control.

Lee Ann continued into the den without saying another word. He closed the door to the studio behind him and followed. She stood with her profile to him, and as he stepped across the threshold, the bottom dropped out of his world. There was a small lifetime of pictures lined up across the front wall of the room.

He scanned the photos marching along each frame before landing on the last one. Candy and Kendra, happy and smiling out at the world, stood slightly behind, and to either side of, Lee Ann. Once again he had the urge to walk out of the house and never look back. They were happy. His being there would mess things up.

Lee Ann waited patiently in front of the first one. He ripped his gaze from the most recent photo and moved closer to her, his jaw clenched so tight he wouldn't have been surprised to feel a tooth break. In front of him now were two tiny babies, with pink blankets and white stocking caps, being held in Lee Ann's arms. Red faces squinted out in utter disgust at the world while Lee Ann smiled as if she'd just been given the best present of her life.

"This was a few days after they were born," she said. "They were so tiny I didn't get to hold them for a couple days, but they were very healthy. We got to bring them home when they were less than a week old."

His pulse pounded in the side of his neck. "Was that before or after Stephanie died?"

She closed her eyes for a moment so brief he wouldn't have noticed if he hadn't been watching her intently. "They came home on Christmas Day, the day before she died."

He waited, wanting to hear more, but not quite sure what to ask.

"She never held them." Her voice was soft, and it sounded so lost. She stared at the portrait. "She'd announced as we went to the hospital the morning they were born that she was heading back to Nashville just as soon as she recovered, and that either Mom or I could keep them, or she would put them up for adoption."

The thought shouldn't have shocked him, but it did. Thank goodness they hadn't had to spend time bouncing from family to family like he had.

"Once they cut her open for delivery, they discovered the cancer," Lee Ann continued. "This made things even more…

uncomfortable between us. She was angry and scared, and to the day she died, I think she hated me."

"Why?" He took a half step closer to her, but stopped himself. He couldn't comfort her. He didn't want to imply that he was there for any reason other than to find out about the girls, no matter how much he found himself wanting to reach out and attempt to take some of the pain from her. She seemed so fragile standing there. "I never understood why she'd done what she had—why she would hate you so much."

She crossed her arms over each other and cupped her elbows. "Because I was the reason our dad left. For the pregnancy, though, she blamed me for having you as a boyfriend to begin with. Stupid, I know, but she claimed she wouldn't have been tempted to have sex with you if you hadn't been around to begin with. Therefore, it was also my fault they didn't find the cancer until it was too late. She said I killed her."

"Wow." And he thought he had issues. But that certainly sounded like something the self-centered girl he'd known for all of sixty minutes would have said.

Tired of fighting the urge to comfort her, he reached out and ran the backs of his fingers down the outside of Lee Ann's arm. She tensed at first but then relaxed. He lingered on her skin for a few seconds longer, then pulled his hand away before being tempted to do more.

"You know that's not the truth, right?" he asked. "I'm not trying to shed any of the blame, but she wasn't a good person, Lee. She was out to hurt you that day. It sounds like she went to her grave wanting nothing but the same."

She nodded. "I know. I never could get her to like me. I know I was too much trouble when I was little, but I was only four when he left. I didn't mean to be so difficult."

Her fragility was almost too much for him to bear. He reached out his hand again, but she shifted away, and he dropped it. The urge to take her in his arms was as strong as the desire to uncover how he'd come to have two kids he knew nothing about.

"To find out that I let her parting shot hurt all of us the way I did..." The words trailed off as she shook her head. All the fight seemed to drain out of her. "I have no idea why I fell for her lies. I feel so bad about that."

Quite likely because it was the easier thing to do, he thought. Her easy acceptance of Stephanie's lies still angered him, but he couldn't say he wouldn't have done the same thing if their situations had been reversed.

"This is when they were one," Lee Ann said as she returned their attention to the photos and shuffled a step down the wall. She brought a hand up and it hovered slightly beside her face, as if it had no idea where it should land. She then turned and looked at a nearby bookshelf. "I have more in albums that I can show you later. Hanging in here, though, I only have pictures taken from each of their birthdays."

Cody scanned each frame again. The anger he'd shown up with had been replaced with something else. It was a pain of a different kind, but this one didn't upset him so much as make him uncomfortable. Every picture other than the first contained three wide smiles and shining eyes. "They're all of the three of you. Yearly family portraits?"

She nodded. "They'd lost their mother and I'd been told their father wanted nothing to do with them. I decided to make certain they could one day look back on their lives and know they had a parent who loved them no matter what."

"That's what she said, then? That I wanted nothing to do with them?"

The blue of her eyes appeared dull as she glanced sideways at him. "Said she called you from the hospital the day they were born and told you all about her sickness and where they were. According to her, you weren't interested."

"And you just believed—"

Lee Ann held up her hand as if to stop his words. "I don't know why I did, but yes, Mother and I both believed her. The way you'd left town…" She gave an apologetic shrug. "It made sense at the time."

"Except you knew me. You knew I wouldn't just walk away from something like that."

"Yet that's exactly what you did." Her voice rose as she turned to face him. "When I came home and found you and Stephanie that day, you didn't even stick around long enough to *try* to explain things to me. You just left. And you never came back again."

As Cody watched her, she turned away and fiddled with a cup of pencils on the corner desk, and he got it. She was right. That is exactly what he'd done. Why would she think he'd come back months later just because there were now kids involved. Hell, for most people that would ensure they *didn't* come back.

He thought back to that day with Stephanie and understood how hard the months following must have been for Lee Ann. It was bad enough that he'd allowed his crappy day along with Stephanie's taunts to let him accept what she offered, but as soon as the physical act had ended, he'd known in an instant that he'd been used. Just as everyone else in his life had used him.

The second he'd pulled away, with Stephanie laughing about how fun it would be to see Lee Ann's face when she told her, he knew he'd made the biggest mistake possible. A mistake that would destroy the only person who'd ever looked deeply enough to see the real him.

Maybe what he and Lee Ann had back then hadn't been perfect, and maybe it wouldn't have worked long-term—who knew?—but he couldn't have loved her more at the time. He'd known this as surely as he'd known he was not the man for her.

She'd deserved better.

So he'd left.

"She told me you said there was a perfectly good foster care system that would take them."

He reared back as if she'd just slammed a two-by-four into his head. "Foster care?"

She faced him, and he couldn't utter another word. Did she think he'd said that? That he would be so unfeeling as to toss his kids to the same system that had placed him in homes he'd continually had to run away from? Not a one had done anything for him. They'd seen him purely as a means to an end. Take care of the other kids, do the household chores, be a punching bag. Whatever they'd wanted, it hadn't been a kid.

Her top lip slid between her teeth, and he shook his head. "No, Lee Ann. Of course I wouldn't—"

"I know," she whispered. "I should have known then, but I was so hurt. Everything somehow just made sense. I'm so sorry."

He finally reached for her and wrapped his arms around her before she could get away.

Surprisingly, she immediately fit herself to him. They stood together, him stroking her short hair, she with her face buried in his chest for several minutes as he thought back over earlier times. The night he'd realized he wanted more than friendship from her, he'd opened his soul for the one and only time and shared the beatings, the desertions, and told her how he'd often been nothing more than hired-out child labor.

He'd told her in the hope she'd someday trust him enough to let him be more. He'd needed her so badly. He'd needed to believe in what the idea of the two of them together offered. Given how much closer they'd grown after that night, she should have known he would never voluntarily send anyone to...

His thoughts froze. Bile rose, continuing until it burned his nostrils, as memories fought to the front of his mind. His breathing picked up.

Stephanie laughing.

Lee Ann walking in and finding him fastening his jeans.

Her destroyed gaze locking on him, her jaw quivering, before she disappeared from the room without a word.

He'd stomped to the front door and yanked it open as Stephanie's taunts hit him like ice water between the shoulder blades.

"What if you just got me pregnant, Cody? You will do the right thing, won't you? Marry me and make an honest woman out of me?"

Pregnant? He faced her, disgust pulling him under. "There is no way you're not on the pill."

Her bottom lip pouted out. "You know times are tough. I'm trying to make it in the country-music business. I can't afford luxuries like the pill."

She was lying. She had to be. No way he could have just gotten her pregnant. He stalked across the room, leaned down into her deceitful face and spit out, "If you managed to just get yourself pregnant, I happen to know firsthand there's a perfectly good foster care system that would be more than willing to take the bastard."

Oh. God.

He released Lee Ann and pressed the back of his hand to his mouth to keep the frustration from boiling out. That was not what he'd meant. He hadn't believed for a second she was stupid enough to seduce him when she wasn't protected.

Lee Ann's gaze flicked questioningly over his face, and he wondered what she saw. He couldn't tell her he'd actually said those words. No way could he let her know that.

Seeming to accept the moment was over, she turned back to the pictures and shuttered her expression, no longer letting him see her vulnerability. No longer letting him see what mattered to her.

"Though I fully believed her words, I had the hardest time accepting you wanted nothing to do with them." A thin finger smoothed over the dark frame of the second picture. "Right around their first birthday I decided to try to find you. And I hated that. The last thing I wanted was to see you. But they were your kids. I just couldn't believe you wouldn't want to be a part of something so wonderful."

About that time he would've been getting his shit together and remembering that Lee Ann had always believed he had the ability to succeed. He'd spent the prior year working at the South Chicago clinic of the veterinarian who'd saved both him and the dog he'd had at the time. He'd saved him from living on the streets and his dog after a hit-and-run that occurred while they'd been somewhere he'd had no business being.

"No doubt there wasn't a lot of information out there on me." Given the effort he'd gone to in order to stay off the radar, he would have been surprised to learn there had been.

One shoulder lifted. "Nothing. It was pretty amazing. I figured there'd be a phone number or something, but I found nothing. It was as if you'd disappeared off the face of the earth."

"Nah, just Chicago. A guy can easily get lost there if he doesn't want to be found." And he didn't. Even when he'd been able to afford a phone he hadn't gotten one. Not until he'd started college.

He'd been existing purely to take care of the dog he'd found while living on the streets. He'd lived in Doc Hutchinson's apartment, gone to work, paid his rent and stayed as far out of trouble as he could get. Eight months of being on the street had taught him a lot about what he did and didn't want out of life. He hadn't had it all figured out yet, but he'd seen enough to know what he didn't want.

"Ah," Lee Ann said, as if unsure what else to say. "Anyway, I couldn't afford to hire anyone to search for you, so I let myself believe what she'd said to be the truth."

He deserved every bad thing she'd ever thought about him.

She moved to the next picture and a sad smile flitted across her face. "They had a really bad case of the terrible twos. I was still living with Mom at the time and she ended up being a big help. Not only with the girls, but with keeping me sane as well. On their birthday, I believe I took close to forty pictures before I could get all three of us smiling together."

"So you had Reba's help, then?" He looked around, needing to not look at the pictures of his kids for a minute. "Does she not live here now?"

Guilt reached for him from every angle. For Lee Ann, for the girls. For the simple fact he'd had anything to do with bringing them into the world in the first place. He inhaled a long breath through his nose and tried to act as if he were interested in what she had to say instead of desperate to get away. He shouldn't be there. He would only turn her world even more upside down.

"She bought the smaller house next door when it went up for sale. I bought this one from her."

"Ah." He nodded, but he didn't know what he was agreeing to. His head was heavy, as if he were spinning too fast to hold it up. With his lunch rapidly rising, he turned toward the door, panic setting in. He stumbled toward it before pulling up short, sweat coating his skin. He couldn't just walk out. His hands clenched. But he couldn't stay.

"I need a minute," he muttered and pushed through the front door, letting it slam closed behind him.

CHAPTER

He made his way from Lee Ann's front porch and up the sidewalk, taking in gulps of cool air until the burning inside his chest calmed to a low simmer. He had no idea what he was doing. He couldn't be a father. Could he?

He'd never once thought about what having kids might entail.

When he reached his car, he stretched his arms across the top, flattening his palms against the cool metal.

But what would happen if he didn't try? He'd walk out on his kids before they even knew about him. That would make him no better than the woman who'd given birth to him. Or any of the homes he'd stayed in afterward. Not a one of his foster parents had been there for him, and he'd sworn to himself years ago that he would never be like them.

He twisted around and stared at the school sitting like a giant behind the row of smaller houses. There had been cars and buses in the school lot as he'd driven by earlier while waiting for Lee Ann's customer to leave. That was where the girls would be at this very moment, in school. Unaware that their father stood there stressing over the fact of their very existence and what he was going to do about it.

He checked his watch, wondering how much time he had before school let out. One thirty. A breath burst from his lungs and he leaned over, his hands resting atop his knees. He had to figure out what to do.

He closed his eyes, already pretty confident of the answer. It was the only thing he could do. He just didn't know how.

"Thirty minutes." Lee Ann's soft voice hit his ears.

She bumped against his car as she settled beside him, and he opened his eyes a slit but remained bent over, so all he saw was her trim, jean-covered calves crossed at the ankles. Her pristine white tennis shoes made his mouth lift in a small smile in the middle of what he believed to be that panic attack he'd feared earlier. His gaze traveled up her legs to find her backside casually resting against his SUV. "What's thirty minutes?"

"When school lets out. They get out early today because of the holiday."

Christ. She had always been able to read his mind.

The fact she'd looked for him about the same time he'd decided to make something of his life proved it. Whatever had connected them years ago hadn't disappeared overnight. And what he'd known about her then was that she was as honest and straightforward as they came. She wouldn't have made the decision to keep his children from him. This mess was Stephanie's doing.

He straightened, scrubbed both hands over his face and held in the growl he wanted to roar at the world. How had everything gotten so messed up?

Reaching into his pocket, he pulled out the folded paper he'd stuffed there earlier, and held out the check to her. "This doesn't cover their first thirteen years, but it's a start."

He knew by the way she reacted with a jolt that he'd caught her off guard.

"I don't need your—"

"Take it," he said, more gruffly than he'd meant. "I may not have known, but that doesn't lessen my accountability."

She stood there for a good fifteen seconds staring at the check, as if taking his money would be akin to accepting charity she didn't need. Finally, he took the choice out of her hands. He leaned down in front of her, stopping dead still to lock his gaze on hers, and tucked the slip of paper into the front pocket of her jeans. A small breath exhaled from between her lips to whisper across his. It smelled like mint.

"I don't need it." Her words came out soft and he couldn't help watching her lips form the words. Being this close to her made him think of things he shouldn't.

"You're working two jobs, Lee," he said. He lifted back up to her blue eyes. "You can use the money. Take it. Learn to relax a little."

"I'm perfectly fine, and I don't need to relax."

He shot her a glare. "You should quit the diner, too. Believe it or not, it'll keep running without you."

Her mouth thinned into a straight line at his last comment, and he almost laughed at the irony. She was still the same girl who liked to control everything, yet just like his life, everything was suddenly all kinds of out of control. He evilly hoped it was causing her as much anxiety as it was him.

He went back to staring at the school and ignored the look she was shooting him. She would either accept his check, or he'd go to the bank and deposit it for her. That would get the gossip going, but likely no more than it would when she took it to the bank herself. Either way, he would never be one of those men who didn't step up to the plate when it was his turn. He'd participated in creating this mess, he would take care of it. And she would not stand in his way.

After several more seconds of directed glaring, she finally crossed her arms over her chest and murmured a tight "Thanks."

The moment she accepted, the pressure in his chest began to let up. He leaned back against the door of his car and tried to relax. "Do they know anything about me?"

"Not really," she said. "The first time they asked, they were four and I simply explained they didn't have a dad."

Cody felt his spine align even closer to the glass of the car window and waited, her words calming him more than the space and air could.

She shrugged. "I couldn't very well tell them you had better things to do than be around them."

"I had no idea."

"I know. And I probably should have tried again to find you. I did, actually, when they were three. I found a phone number for you in Indiana that time. But then I talked myself out of calling."

He studied her, picking up on the fact that there was something more she wasn't saying. He didn't push for it, though. Having privacy of your own thoughts was important to him.

"I was comfortable by that time, so I let it slide. I hadn't started my studio at that point, but I had a decent job at the casket factory outside of town. I was also semiregularly dating a nice man. I convinced myself I was doing the right thing."

Knowing she'd dated shouldn't have bothered him. "How did you date with two small children?"

"Mom is actually a terrific grandmother. She was made for spoiling kids, even though she wasn't perfect at raising them." She lifted her arms and rested her hands palms-up on the top of her head, elbows out, as she stared off into the distance. "She watched them a couple evenings a week and I dated. I wouldn't bring him home to meet them, though, until I knew he might be around for good. Especially after they clearly wanted a man to be their daddy."

"And did you?" He tucked his fingers into the belt loops of his jeans and watched her. "Did you finally bring him home to meet them?"

He almost missed the silent shake of her head as he eyed the jacket she'd donned before following him outside. With her hands positioned above her as they were, he could just about picture what her breasts would look like lifted and pressed to the pale pink shirt underneath. When he realized what he was doing, he jerked his gaze away. He'd walked back into her life bringing nothing but trouble. The least he could do was not add to it by ogling her. It wasn't her fault he was more attracted to her today than he'd been fourteen years ago.

"Any other suitors make it home to meet the family?"

She turned her head and studied him for a minute, her face half-hidden by her raised arm, so that only one eye peeked out. "None ever made it through the front door of that house."

The relief he felt was wrong. He'd wanted her to find someone good enough for her. That was what he'd told himself for years after he'd left. She deserved the best. And he wasn't it.

"So what happened? Did the girls ever ask about me again?"

"Occasionally." Her hands lowered and she tilted her head back, staring up at the sky. "Each time I would tell them a little more, until one day I figured they were old enough to understand. I think they were about ten."

"You told them what Stephanie said?"

"No." She said the word quickly, and a sense of relief poured through him. No one should hear that her parent doesn't want her. "I told them that you had chosen to let me raise them. That you felt I would do a better job than you."

"Ah," he said. "And that was fine with them?"

She chuckled. "Not exactly. They were pretty ticked. Couldn't understand why you wouldn't want to at least see them once in a while." She shrugged. "I had no answers for them. Told them that maybe one day you'd change your mind." She rolled to her side to face him. "But that I wouldn't bet on it."

He shifted to match her position, facing her, and silently acknowledged that he could understand her point of view. She had told him once that her dad had left when she was four and had never come back. Why would she believe any differently? Especially when she believed he was no better than her father to begin with.

She spent the next several minutes filling him in on his children. Sharing stories, telling him what they were like. It was almost as if she was talking about someone else's kids, only…it wasn't. With each milestone she mentioned, he felt his heart grow larger.

How was it that two people you'd only briefly met could already mean so much to you?

The smile that covered Lee Ann's face as she talked told him something he found impossible to doubt. She loved those girls. Very much.

"It's my opinion they're going to be fabulous women when they grow up."

"I've no doubt that'll be because of you, Lee." He reached out and stroked a finger down her cheek, the barriers between them seeming to melt just a little at his touch. "They couldn't have a better mother as far as I'm concerned."

Her smile was small. "I've done what I can, but they need more. They need a dad."

His heart rate sped up. "I don't know how, Lee. I'm afraid I'll make it even worse."

She adjusted her position to lean her rear against the car and set her gaze back on the school. For the few minutes they'd faced each other, he had felt as comfortable with her as he did when they'd been teenagers. "The way I see it," she said. "You have two options."

He agreed. "Either tell them or not."

"Yep."

"And you're good with telling them if that's what I want to do?"

She eyed him. "Don't you think they deserve to at least know who their father is, even if he doesn't stick around?"

The edge creeping around her gaze told him that telling them or not, she would have his balls if he hurt them. The funny thing was, he felt the same way. The last thing he wanted to do was cause them or Lee Ann any more pain than his actions already had.

"And if I don't want to tell them?" he asked. "If I'd rather finish out my contract and leave without them ever knowing who I am?"

The mere idea caused a pain that weighed down everything about him, and his arms became almost too hard to lift.

He didn't know how this was going to pan out, but he knew he didn't want them to never know him. He couldn't imagine not getting to know them, too.

Looks like, he had his answer.

When he peeked at her, her jaw jutted out a bit more than it had, but she nodded. "If you don't want to tell them, then I'll stick by your wishes. They don't need someone around who cares that little."

He nodded. The panic threatened to return at the mere thought of leaving town without getting to know his children. Might as well jump in with both feet.

"Then let's do it. Let's tell them," he urged. "Today. I don't know how to be a dad, Lee, and I have no idea how to make this work after I leave, but I can't just turn my back and walk away. Will they be okay if I'm not very good at this?"

A soft chuckle came from her that relaxed him a hair. It also made him realize how much he'd been rattling. Apparently he talked more when he was nervous.

"They'll be great," she said. "Especially Kendra."

"Why's that?"

She shrugged. "She loves animals. She's said for seven or eight years now that she wants to be a veterinarian."

A strange pressure pushed out from the inside of his chest. She wanted to be like him? He gulped. He'd never thought about what it would be like to have someone follow in your footsteps.

"Can we tell them when they get home today?" A flicker of red caught his attention, and he paused and looked around, trying to figure out what it had been. A set of red curtains in the house to their left shifted, and he narrowed his eyes. Were they being watched?

And then he remembered. "You said your mother lives in the house right there?"

"Mm-hmmm."

"Are you aware she's been watching us?"

"Do you remember Ms. Grayson who lives up there on the corner?" Lee Ann pointed across his body up the street to the small house whose porch railings were in serious need of some tender loving care. He didn't make it back from his run each morning without bumping into the owner of the house. Avoiding the daily gossip she wanted to throw at him was becoming difficult.

He glanced at Lee Ann. "Of course. What's she got to do with your mother watching us? Don't tell me your mother is one of her spies now?"

Lee Ann shook her head, loving weariness filling her expression. "My mother, I do believe, is staging a coup. She's in full-out overthrow mode of Ms. Grayson's town gossip throne."

Her meaning registered immediately. "She's probably been on the phone the entire time we've been standing here, swearing she can read our lips just so she'll have something to spread."

Lee Ann laughed out loud and pushed off the car. He liked the sound of her laugh.

"Come on," she said.

She reached back for him, and he slipped his hand into her warm palm out of long-ago habit. Her instant stiffness let him know she hadn't realized what she'd done until it was too late. Yet she was too polite to pull away after making the initial gesture.

He allowed himself a few seconds, enjoying the feel of her soft skin, but too soon dropped his hand and tucked it in his pocket. He'd do best not to touch her. "What's so funny?"

They strolled side by side to her house and settled in separate chairs on the front porch, almost as they used to do when they were kids, only then they both would have chosen the swing. "Mom recently went to the nearby community college to take a night course in lip reading."

He banged his head against the back of his chair. "You're serious, aren't you?"

"Never been more so, though she won't spread anything more about us than we were seen talking together. Maybe that you touched my cheek and I didn't slap your hand away. There's already the flurry spreading around town that we must be getting back together, since you keep seeking me out." She rolled her eyes. "I'm apparently playing hard to get."

Lightness filled him for the first time since yesterday afternoon, and he couldn't help a bit of teasing. He shot her a wink. "Want to give them something to talk about?"

Laughter shook her small shoulders, and as he watched the tension lift from her face, he realized the idea wasn't a bad one. He wanted to wrap his arms around her and kiss her the way she was made for. The way he used to do.

And it wasn't purely from loneliness, either. At least, he didn't think so.

Granted, it had been a while since he'd been with a woman. He didn't make a habit of sleeping with women on assignments, but that didn't mean it never happened, either. But as he watched Lee Ann's easy laughter and the way her lips curved, he cursed the immaturity that had sent him packing all those years ago. More accurately, he cursed himself for being so weak he fell for Stephanie's manipulations in the first place.

Perhaps he and Lee Ann would have burned out over the summer, but he sure would have liked the chance to find out.

Her laughter died as he continued staring at her, and anxiety of a different kind slowly oozed down around them. Clearing his throat, he glanced away and kicked out at the swing, sending it on a lopsided back-and-forth journey. One of the outdoor pillows tipped and rolled down to the porch. As he bent over to retrieve it, he peeked back at Lee Ann and caught her watching him in a way that made his breath hitch.

She had the same look in her eyes that matched the thought running through his mind. What would it be like between them now?

Dang, he did not need to go there. But he would need her to not want to go there with him or he would lose that battle. Because one thing he knew for certain...he had never been able to keep his distance from a warm and willing Lee Ann.

🌼 🌼 🌼

Her chest quit moving up and down, and Lee Ann figured out that was because she'd quit breathing.

With a jerk, she wrenched her gaze from Cody's and studied the chrysanthemums lining the porch steps. What had she been thinking? That she wanted to kiss Cody?

Noooo.

Surely not. What would kissing him accomplish? Besides confusing the whole situation even more?

She shook her head. No. Definitely no kissing could go on between them. Maybe their past had been left without any real closure, but that did not mean she had to do anything about it. Too many years were spread between then and now for it to matter at this point in her life. Especially not now with them about to tell the girls who he was.

The thought brought her quickly back to the present. No kissing, only parenting. Got it.

No matter how hot he looked every time she saw him.

She glanced at her watch, then shot to her feet. "They'll be home any minute."

Wary eyes looked up at her from the white rocker she and the girls had painted last spring. When they'd been redecorating the porch, she'd never pictured anyone like him taking up space there.

"Are you ready?" she asked. She wasn't sure if she was herself. This was all happening so fast, but since he'd already been there almost a week, they didn't need to put off telling them much longer. The girls needed time to get to know him, and she needed time to figure out just what kind of father he was going to be.

If he was going to be the kind to leave at the end of the year and never look back, she would prepare her girls as best she could, but she would also keep her fingers crossed that he would make it a priority to stop by and visit at least a couple of times a year. Surely he had changed enough that he could be that person. Given the fact he'd handed over a check to help with their expenses, she had to believe he'd grown up in more ways than just physically.

Slowly, he stood and gave her an uncertain lift of his shoulders. "As close as I'll ever be, I suppose."

She nodded. He was nervous, but there was nothing she could do about that. The next few minutes had to play out however they would. She only hoped she was doing the right thing and he didn't totally crush the girls when he left. The idea, however, of him being right there and her never introducing the three of them to one another had suddenly been unimaginable. No matter what kind of father he was, they deserved to at least know him, didn't they? Deserved the chance to make their own decisions about him.

She held in a groan. When had she turned into her mother? Until these last few minutes, she would have bet good money that she'd make the man jump through hoops to prove himself before she would so much as let him in the same room as her girls. Yet something had changed as they'd stood out at his car and talked.

Part of it had been the look of awe that had crossed his face as she'd told him about them, but part had been her, too. She wanted to believe in the goodness of him. She wanted her girls to have a dad, even if only a long-distance one, and she wanted him to be the man she'd once believed he would someday be.

She only hoped she wasn't making the biggest mistake of her life.

"We should probably do this inside." She almost reached her hand out for him again but stopped, reminding herself they were not teenagers again, no matter how close to him she'd felt as they'd been talking. "Everybody will find out soon enough, but no need to instantly share everything going on here with the whole town."

Rising, he followed her. "Good idea."

When they got to the kitchen, she stopped at the island in the middle of the floor and watched him take in the room. She always wondered what people thought when they saw her home for the first time. For some reason, wondering what was running through his mind made her nervous. He'd seen it the way her mother had once decorated it, which had been loud and chaotic. Lee Ann preferred things a bit more subdued. Clean lines and order yet comfort at the same time.

"I like what you've done with the place, Lee. It looks like you."

Every time he called her by the shortened name he'd once used she felt a bit more of her defenses chip away. Without trying, the man was sliding under her walls.

She needed reinforcements.

Footsteps outside the house pulled both their gazes to the door. His shoulders hardened, but she had to give him credit for staying put. It had to be nerve-racking for him knowing he was about to stand in front of those two and tell them he was the man they'd been wondering about for years.

Two seconds later the back door swung open.

"Mom!" Candy shouted as she entered. "Coach said we could stay later today and practice, but I told him we had to get home to..."

The girls stopped in the middle of the room and stared.

After taking in Cody, Kendra glanced at her mother and asked, "What's he doing here?"

❀ ❀ ❀

Both girls stood immobile just inside the door, their brown eyes identical to the ones Cody saw in the mirror each morning blinking back at him. One of them had a basketball, slick with use, tucked under an arm and a backpack slung over her shoulder, her coat buttoned up the front. The other carried no books but had several notebooks in her hands with papers sticking out at every angle, and her coat tied around her waist. From his short time with them the afternoon before, he already knew which was which, even though they looked exactly the same.

His throat tightened, nerves closing off his airway. They were not going to take this well. Who would? He was about to mess up their world.

A cold sweat began at the back of his neck, but he fought off the panic. They were just two young girls. He could handle this.

"Mom?" Candy shuffled closer to her mother. She dropped her backpack to the floor and wore a mix of curiosity and worry on her face. "What's going on?"

He looked at Lee Ann then, uncertain if he was supposed to just blurt it out or if she was going to tell them. They hadn't had time to think this through. Maybe they should wait and save it for another day.

Before he could back out of the decision to tell them now, Lee Ann stepped over between the girls and wrapped an arm around the waist of each. Though her stance said relaxed and her mouth wore a curve, she looked like a mother bear ready to protect her cubs. "We have something to tell you."

Lee Ann glanced at each girl, both of whom surpassed her in height, and he couldn't miss seeing Stephanie in them. She'd been half a foot taller than Lee Ann. Tall and lithe, while Lee Ann was petite and more curvy. Candy and Kendra would have a body shape like their biological mother when they grew up.

"Lee Ann, wait." It seemed wrong to so bluntly explain that Stephanie had been a bald-faced liar and that he was their father. The one who'd never known anything about them.

A perfectly shaped eyebrow arched before him.

"Maybe we shouldn't," he said.

"Shouldn't what?" This came from Kendra. She tossed her papers on the kitchen table and inched closer to her mother.

Lee Ann shook her head. "I don't hide things from them, Cody. Not without a really good reason." She nodded. "It's time. It'll be okay."

She squeezed both girls tight to her side and kept her fingertips dug slightly into their waists. He couldn't tell if the act was from nerves or maybe a fear that they'd attempt to run out of the room the minute they knew.

"The fact is..." she began, then paused, clearly without a clue of the best way to proceed, either. She lifted one shoulder at him and shot him a questioning look. All he could think was to just blurt it out. Like ripping off a Band-Aid. Then they could deal with it.

With the slightest nod of her head, as if she understood his thoughts, she did exactly that. "Cody is your father."

The sound of the clock ticking in the room was all he heard for several long seconds as what their mother had said registered with the girls. Then two sets of feminine eyes fastened on him. The girls were looking at him as if he'd come to the house specifically to screw with their existence. For five seconds more he stood in utter silence, and then the room of estrogen became too much for him to form a single cohesive thought.

"And what?" Candy finally asked. Her tone was not accepting. "You didn't want anything to do with us before, but we're supposed to jump with joy that you do now? Oh, yay. Or do you still want nothing to do with us? Maybe you just wanted to drop in and say hi then be gone again. Just like you have the first thirteen years of our lives."

Lee Ann had warned him that they were tough. He licked his dry lips.

"It wasn't like that," he began. How was he supposed to explain this without making Stephanie look worse than she was? He shot Lee Ann a pleading look, hoping for a little help. He had no idea what to say.

She cleared her throat. "They know Steph was a good person in her own way," she said, "but too many stories are known around here for them to think she was an angel." She looked at both girls. "This is one time she truly wasn't."

"What do you mean?" Kendra asked. Her voice was more childlike than it had been before. He curled his fingers into his palms with frustration. There had to have been a much better way they could have handled this.

"I have no idea why," Lee Ann said. "But your biological mother...apparently never told Cody about you."

Hurt eyes turned to Lee Ann. "But you said—"

"Yes," she said, nodding. "Because that's what Steph told both me and your grandmother. She swore she'd told him." Slim shoulders he'd once had the right to pull close lifted and settled back into place. She looked so lost trying to explain this to them. "I have no idea why she lied, but she did."

"No way," Kendra muttered.

"I swear," he jumped in. "I had no idea until you told me about Stephanie being your mother."

"If that's the case, then why hadn't you told him already, Mom? And why didn't you tell us? He's been here for days. We had the right to know." Candy was laying into Lee Ann now, and he wanted to reach out to her. Protect her. But it likely would help nothing if his daughters saw him touching their mother. Not to mention the mother might just slap him right out of her house.

"I thought he knew," Lee Ann whispered. "I didn't want to say anything until I knew what he was back for. If he didn't want anything to do with you..."

Her words trailed off, and she gave her daughters an apologetic look. She finished with, "It's not easy knowing the best thing to do all the time."

"And you believe him?" Candy asked. "Just like that? Why not believe Stephanie instead?"

Pain flickered across Lee Ann's features. "Your biological mother rarely told me the truth about anything. I should have known better when it happened, but I wanted to believe she'd contacted him. I wanted your mother to care that much."

"But then that meant *he* didn't care," Candy rebutted.

"Yes," Lee Ann agreed. "But since he was gone, and Stephanie was family, it was easier to believe her. But Cody's explained it to me. He never talked to her. I believe him."

Kendra matched her sister's glare as they both stood silently beside their mother. She then lowered her eyes and leaned forward to made eye contact with her sister. Time stood still as the two communicated with a look before Kendra settled back in place. Nothing had been spoken, but it was clear they'd come to some agreement. He only hoped it was to believe him instead of tell him to hit the road.

Relaxing his features, he smiled at the two young ladies he may not have known what to do with but did know he wanted to get to know. Desperately. He also recognized the odd desire of hoping they felt the same way. "I truly am happy to meet you."

They shrugged out from under their mother's grasp and stepped forward together, both crossing their arms over their narrow chests, matching a stance he'd seen many times on Lee Ann.

"We need some time to adjust to this," Candy said, and his heart fell. He silently prayed that at the end of their adjustment, he would come out on the good end of things.

He nodded. "I understand. It's a pretty big shock. For all of us."

At his last words, Kendra's face crinkled up in concentration. "That's right. We didn't think about that. You just found out about us, too."

That meant that they believed him. Pressure lifted from his shoulders as a breath whooshed from his chest. He nodded anxiously. "That's right. I'm as blown away as you are."

"Hmmm," she said. She seemed to be more willing than her sister to give him a chance, as her shoulders had softened a bit. Candy remained motionless and a bit squinty-eyed.

Her distrust didn't keep her from jumping back into the conversation, though. "We still need time to think about it."

He nodded again. "Absolutely. You know where I live. I'll give you all the time you need. You just let me or your mom know when I can come back and visit with you and I'll be right here." He smiled then, and it came out feeling normal. "I really do want to get to know you both. I hope you decide that you want that, too."

He gave Lee Ann a quick look, then began backing toward the door. Seemed the best thing was to get out of there before any of them changed their minds completely and told him never to come back.

"Wait." Kendra took a step toward him. "You can't just go. You're still coming for Thanksgiving tomorrow, right?"

He blinked. Was he still invited? He looked at Lee Ann and she gave a single nod. He looked at Candy. She seemed to be the one with the most concern about the whole situation.

"What do you think, Candy?" He couldn't believe he was considering begging to come to Thanksgiving dinner. "Should I come on down or wait for you to call me?"

Her face read bullheaded and stubborn, but Kendra turned pleading eyes to her. "He's got to come, Can. Then he can also dance with us at our birthday party, and it'll be so much better than Sadie's."

She turned to him. "You will come to our party and dance with us, right? A father-daughter dance."

It was almost too much to take in at once, but the sight of those gazes staring up at him—one hopeful and excited, the other uncertain and not quite trusting—did something to his insides. Something squishy yet nice.

These were his daughters, and he wanted to do whatever they'd possibly allow him to while he was in town. He nodded. He wanted to dance with them at their party. "If you both agree that you'd like me there, then yes, I would love to come dance with you at your party. I would be honored to, in fact."

Afraid Lee Ann would be able to read every emotion currently running through him, he kept his gaze averted and focused on his daughters. He needed to get out of there and think. What he needed was to get Boss and go for a *really* long run.

He had two girls. The idea still blew him away.

Yet one of them also seemed to want little to do with him. That could be a problem. He could only hope she came around, because he couldn't imagine not having them both in his life at this point.

❀ ❀ ❀

Lee Ann watched the man in front of her and alternated between wanting to turn back time to keep him from showing up in their lives and wanting to rush forward and welcome him into the family. Whether he wanted her to see or not, she could tell this meant something to him. Just as it meant something to the girls.

And whether they were both ready to admit it or not, it meant the world to them. They now had a dad.

What remained to be seen was how active a dad he would be. They had time, though, to figure out the logistics.

"Candy?" she asked. "You're good with him coming over tomorrow, right?"

At her daughter's snarled look, Lee Ann reminded her that they didn't like people to have to be alone on the holiday and Candy grudgingly nodded.

"It's settled then." Lee Ann forced a smile. She couldn't believe she'd just been the one to convince her daughter that Cody needed to be at their house tomorrow. What she personally needed was some breathing space and for the man not to show up anywhere near her house for a good long while. But that wasn't reality. "We have a lot of preparations to do tonight, and I'm sure all of you need some time to adjust." She knew she did. "We eat dinner tomorrow night at six, Cody. We'll see you then?"

He nodded, the movement not quite smooth. "Tomorrow it is."

If she had to guess, she would say his dog was about to get a really good workout. She'd caught the two of them running most mornings as she'd headed to the diner, and understood they did the same every afternoon.

As he started to step away, he took one last look at the girls, and then his gaze locked on hers. What she read in their depths was thankfulness, and suddenly his dark eyes reminded her of melted chocolate and the hot kisses they'd once shared. Parts of her she hadn't thought about in years roared to life at the memory.

Oh, boy, what had she invited into their lives?

CHAPTER

8

The street in front of Lee Ann's house had cars along both sides as Cody neared it on foot. Some of the visitors were likely at neighboring houses, but knowing Lee Ann and given the list the kids had shown him, the majority would be at hers. He crossed to her side of the road and headed toward the front sidewalk. Stopping at the base of it, he stared at the two-story bungalow sitting there as if waiting for him. As if it had known all along that he'd one day be back.

He was about to join a big, happy Thanksgiving dinner with people from all over town, and he'd once thought it the last place he wanted to be. Only, now that he was here, he couldn't wait to get inside. He had two kids in there waiting for him.

And Lee Ann.

He started slowly up the sidewalk, thinking about the afternoon before when they'd told the girls. The thought that they might resolutely refuse to have anything to do with him had scared him in a way he hadn't known before.

It had been terrifying standing there waiting for them to decide. Until that moment he'd thought he was merely doing the "right thing." But at the thought that they might say "No thanks" and send him packing, he'd figured out real quick that he was there as much for himself as for anyone. Not because he'd ever wanted fatherhood. He still didn't know how to reconcile his lifelong thoughts of a life of solitude with who he now found himself to be. But something about those two had gotten to him the instant he'd met them, and he was unable to walk away.

The door opened before he reached it, and Lee Ann's mother stepped out, fake blue-green eyelashes glittering as she gave him a once-over. When finished, she lifted her gaze to his and greeted him with a genuine smile. "Welcome home, Cody."

He pulled up short. Did she mean this house or Sugar Springs? Neither was home. Not exactly. It had been for a year, but that had always been temporary.

He nodded, unwilling to correct one of the few residents he'd once enjoyed being around. With her happy-go-lucky ways, she'd often been a frustration for Lee Ann, but he'd found her refreshing and fun. "Good to see you, Reba."

Reba London had never gone anywhere unnoticed, and today was no exception. A handful of silver and turquoise bracelets jingled from her wrist, and a matching ring covered half of one finger. A gypsy-style skirt floated around her legs as she shifted and motioned for him to finish his walk up the steps.

"You must have been watching for me."

She held up a cell phone. "Actually, I got a text. I knew you were heading down the street the minute you put Boss back in the apartment after he did his business."

His feet stalled. She even knew his dog's name? He smiled, the grin growing larger than he would have thought. Of course she knew his dog's name. She also probably knew Boss's feeding schedule and the brand of food he ate. He shook his head slightly, amazed that didn't bother him the way he thought it would have, but it was hard to be annoyed with someone like Reba.

"Come on." She motioned him inside. "Everyone moved to the dining room when I told them you were heading this way. We eat at six, you know. Lee Ann has been fretting because you were already five minutes late."

Cody followed Reba through the room, trepidation clawing at him. He would much rather get to know the girls without a crowd, but he only had a few weeks, so he'd take whatever he could get. When he entered the dining room, however, Lee Ann was the one who immediately caught his attention.

She entered from the kitchen, a bowl of mashed potatoes in her hands, and looked as good as she had the day before. Better.

He scanned his gaze down her body. A dress the colors of the earth and fall leaves hugged every curve, and a bright swath of orange with lace at the top poked out from between the open buttons marching down her chest. As a teenager, she'd had the kind of chest that made the tight shirts other girls wore inappropriate, but he'd never complained. Nor did he now.

The room grew silent, and he realized that everyone at the table sat watching him take in Lee Ann. Aside from the kids, she would be the other reason he was glad to be here. He shouldn't care, but since he'd teased her the day before about giving the neighbors something to talk about, he'd been able to think of little else. Clearing his throat, he swept a quick look around and caught Kendra's shy smile. He knew it came from Kendra because she dressed more like her grandmother, whereas Candy was wearing a scowl and had on more conservative clothes that mimicked something Lee Ann would wear.

Kendra pointed out a vacant chair at the end of the table, and his heart flipped over in his chest. At least she hadn't changed her mind about him overnight; she still wanted him here. He would work on Candy and get her there, too. Somehow.

Once everyone was settled and the conversation resumed, the food began making its way around the table. Cody passed a platter of rolls to the man on his right, Sam Jenkins, and Sam grunted.

"Saw you at the diner the other day," Sam said. He took a roll and kept the plate moving. "I remember you. Not exactly a saint."

"No, sir. I wasn't." Out of the corner of his eye, Cody saw Kendra perk up as if hopeful to hear some dirt. Candy seemed to grow still as if listening, too, but she had yet to make eye contact with him. Sam had been a longtime friend of Roy and Pearl Monroe, and Cody had no doubt he would relay how this evening went back to them. He was also the owner of the infamous diabetic dog.

From the other direction a bowl of green beans was thrust in front of Cody by Lee Ann's friend Joanie.

"How are you today, Cody?" She wore a fake smile for the rest of the table, but her eyes speared him. "Not having another bad day are you?"

Bad day? He started to ask what she was talking about and then he got it. A glance at the glare Lee Ann shot at her friend confirmed his suspicions. She had told Joanie about him saying he'd gotten some bad news the day he'd slept with Stephanie. Clearly, Joanie wasn't taking it any better than Lee Ann had.

He might have to eventually do a better job of explaining that.

Ignoring Joanie for the moment, he scanned over the rest of the guests. There was Keri—still bursting at the seams, as that baby had yet to come—three people he didn't recognize, and Buddy Sawyer, the one who'd been spreading any and every rumor he could think of about Cody. Given the fact Cody had busted out his hardware store window on his way out of town before, he probably deserved the animosity. He'd anonymously sent the man a few thousand in product a few years back when he'd finally been able to do something to make up for it. The contribution had soothed his conscience but of course did nothing for the man who, as the girls had informed him, apparently still felt Cody was a "hoodlum."

The rest of the table consisted of Sam, the girls, Reba, and of course Lee Ann. She sat at the opposite end, separated from him by all the traditional Thanksgiving dishes.

He returned his attention to Joanie and gave her as fake a smile as she wore. "So far so good today, Jo." He shot her a wink meant to irritate. It probably wasn't the wisest move to piss off Lee Ann's confidant, but he didn't appreciate the attack at the dining room table. He'd quit letting people take advantage of him the day after he'd met Stephanie. "If anyone comes at me with bad news, though, I'll sic Boss on them. He thinks he's my protector these days."

She snorted. "From what I've seen, he's a big baby. Every woman you come into contact with has to stop and pet him while he just sits there lapping it up."

Some wanted to pet other things, too, but he wasn't about to tell her that. Nor had he let them. He was in town to do a job...and now to get to know his kids...and that was all. He glanced down the table at Lee Ann and wondered if that would, in fact, be all. Or if he and Lee might have a bit of unfinished business as well. He couldn't help but feel like there was still something there.

He took the next dish from Sam and turned his attention away from his libido. "How about you bring Josie in next week, Sam? I'd love to get a look at her. Let her spend the day with me so I can monitor her sugar level and get her the right dosage of insulin."

He'd learned the sick dog's name from Keri. The dog had been on shots at one point, but Sam had run out and by the time Keri found out, the dog's glucose level had risen sharply. They needed to get it back under control before it led to blindness or worse.

"I don't know," Sam hedged. Cody wondered if Sam's hesitation was purely because of him, or if the man was running low on funds. From everything he'd heard, the man loved his dog. Surely he couldn't stand to see her suffer.

Cody motioned to the other end of the table. "You trust Lee Ann, don't you? She wouldn't have invited me over if she didn't believe I'd changed, grown up. Plus, I could use some help at the clinic. You hang around and keep Josie and my dog, Boss, company between blood tests, and I'll give you a deal of half price."

Keri's eyebrows rose, then she tilted her head slightly in acknowledgment that he'd made the right choice. Cody would ensure the other half of the man's charge was paid himself—he had no intention of shorting the clinic—but clearly Keri agreed that he'd keyed in on part of the issue with Sam.

Sam leaned forward and squinted down the table at Lee Ann before plopping back in his chair. He gave a half shrug. "Josie has been feeling pretty rough lately. I guess I could give it a shot." He pointed his work-roughened finger at Cody. "But I'll know if you ain't doing a good job."

Cody held his hand out. "You'll see I *am* doing a good job. I'm glad you're giving me a chance, Sam. Come on by any day next week."

Sam grudgingly shook his hand, before promptly shoving a bite of roll between his dentures. Buddy Sawyer made an irritated sound. Then silence fell as everyone finished filling their plates and began to eat.

More and more, curious looks were shot in Cody's direction. Lee Ann tried to start a conversation a couple times, but each one soon died out as those around the table returned to sneaking peeks at the troublemaker they'd found themselves seated with.

"Tell us about your work in LA, Cody," Keri insisted. "I've never known anyone who does doggy plastic surgery."

His teeth cracked together as everyone swiveled their head in his direction.

"You do plastic surgery on dogs?" Candy asked. At least something had gotten her to speak to him.

"Sometimes." But it wasn't as bad as the look on the faces gaping at him indicated. He earned good money and he did a surgery only if the animal truly needed it. "There are instances where a pet's quality of life would be better with a certain lift or adjustment."

Keri leaned in as far as her belly would allow and peered over the dishes at him. "How did a general practitioner get involved with doggy face-lifts and nose jobs?"

"It's all who you know, I guess." He gave her a genuine smile. They'd already talked about this in the office when she'd asked, but clearly she was trying to help him out instead of just having everyone sit and gawk at him. He appreciated it. Having something to talk about was always better than being the freak show in center stage.

"A friend from school went into orthopedic veterinary medicine and ended up in Los Angeles with one of the more renowned clinics. As they took on more clients who insisted on less scarring, Crocker, my buddy, remembered that particular talent of mine. The practice eventually grew to handle more than just orthopedics, and I'm one of the surgeons they call on when they need extra hands." He winked. "I can sew up an animal more precisely than ladies' maids once tied up corsets."

Soft chuckles bounced around the table from the men.

Candy scrunched her nose in disgust. "I don't understand why someone would spend money to make their dog prettier."

"They have more money than brains," Lee Ann muttered. The women murmured agreements.

"If I had a dog I would love him just like he was," Candy declared. "I—"

"I've read about it, though," Kendra piped in. With the interruption, Candy shoved a bite of potatoes in her mouth and Kendra continued. "Sometimes they have so many folds of skin, it's healthier to have plastic surgery."

"Exactly." His daughter might be seriously interested in veterinary medicine if she'd read about plastics.

"Then I wouldn't—"

"I want to be a vet, too, did you know that?" Kendra interrupted her sister again. "Just like you and Dr. Wright. And I'm already learning. Dr. Wright lets me come to her office sometimes and help out."

"Is that right?" Cody was impressed. He hadn't known she'd been helping up at the clinic. He took another look at the lady vet, noticed her exhaustion, evidenced by the dark circles under her eyes, and couldn't help but wonder where the father of her child was. Then he got it. Everyone at the table was there because they had no family to share the holiday with.

Everyone except Lee Ann, Candy, Kendra, and Reba. They were the surrogate family for all of these people.

Dr. Wright smiled. "Kendra is a very bright student. I've no doubt she'll make you proud someday."

He stiffened. That was the first indication that someone other than Lee Ann and Reba knew he was the girls' father. He glanced around the table, but no one made a big deal of the comment or what it implied. They also had all found something more interesting to look at than him all of a sudden. The Sugar Springs grapevine was seriously amazing.

Kendra glowed at him from her seat. "I want to be a specialist. A neurosurgeon. I've read all about it."

Pride bumped inside his chest. He'd never been proud of anything but his own accomplishments before. "That sounds like a good plan, but don't stop working with Dr. Wright. You don't always know what you'll love best until you've gotten some experience."

"Oh, I don't intend to let her back out on our agreement." Keri smiled at Kendra. "As soon as I'm back to work, she promised to come in for two hours a week until school was out, on Saturdays. Then I have her for six hours a week next summer."

"I'm sure she'll make a terrific assistant. I might let her help me out as well while you're out, if you're okay with that."

He caught Candy's sullen expression as she stared down at her plate. Did she want to help out, too?

"That sounds perfect to me," Keri said. "Now, tell us more about some of the jobs you've taken. And how you came to be someone who travels to different locations instead of working in the same office year-round." She looked around. "If the others don't mind, of course."

After general agreement for him to continue, and another glance at a withdrawn Candy, he detailed several of the locations he'd been to in the last couple of years. "But how I got started in all of this was because of Dr. Hutchinson in Chicago. He passed away before I earned my degree. If it hadn't been for him, I might never have gone to school." As well as for Lee Ann, but he would keep that to himself. The group didn't need to know what she'd meant to him back then. "When I worked for Dr. Hutchinson, I always liked how he would keep an eye out, as he was out driving around, for animals that might need a little help."

As well as stupid humans like him who had no more sense than to live on the street in the dead of winter.

"After I spent the first year after graduation in a clinic in Baltimore, I decided that I'd do my own version of traveling around looking to help. There are always communities like yours that would be in bad shape if no one were there to care for the animals." He shrugged. "I like being there for a bit, and then I move on. It's always suited my lifestyle."

Only he wasn't sure how it would suit fatherhood.

One day he'd do more to honor his mentor, too. Specifically in the area of a scholarship. Exactly as Doc had done for him. Cody was convinced that if that man hadn't come along, not only would his dog have died instead of living to a respectable age, but he would have as well.

Though it had taken him years to accept his living through that night as a good thing, he now believed wholeheartedly that it was. He may not be the ideal person in all ways, but he did his due diligence to do the right thing these days.

He caught sight of Lee Ann, and his chest swelled. She was watching him across the table with a look of admiration he'd once only dreamed of seeing coming from her. It made him feel like he hadn't turned out so bad after all.

"I see," Joanie said, rejoining the conversation, her tone still what he'd call snarky. She pointed her fork at him, eyes glinting. "Not quite the loser you tried to pretend you were in high school, huh? At least not in the education field."

"Joanie." Lee Ann spoke softly, clearly trying to keep her friend and the father of her children from sparring. She glanced around at her guests. "Let's change the subject. Candy, why don't you ask our guests what they're thankful for? Start with Sam."

Cody lowered his silverware and sat back in his chair as Sam Jenkins began listing off his many reasons for being a part of this celebration. A big holiday dinner was not Cody's idea of a good time, but good time or not, he was glad he was here. The looks the girls kept passing him—even though Candy's were few and far between, and mostly hostile—along with what little conversation they'd exchanged, had sealed his fate. He had to be in their lives.

And then there was Lee Ann.

He glanced her way, and a gush of heat swirled through him at the sight of her. He was glad he'd come. Something about the homey atmosphere she'd created, which should have scared the devil out of him, made him desire to be closer to her instead. To push and prod and see what was there. Her enthusiasm to give everyone a special day, along with her honest warmth toward her guests, would charm anyone.

Add to that the calm way she'd heralded Buddy back to the table once he'd laid eyes on Cody, and she was one special lady. It reminded him why he'd once fallen so hard for her.

Low giggles pulled his attention to the girls. The laugh had come from Kendra, but Candy was finally looking a little like she was actually enjoying herself. They sat with their heads together, sharing a secret as guests continued extolling the many things they were thankful for, and he couldn't help being thankful for them. Lee Ann shot the girls a look and they went silent but peeked at their grandmother from under their lashes.

Time with them would be limited once this job was over, but there was always the phone and e-mail. He wondered if staying in touch in either of those fashions would interest them. If asked only last week, he would've vehemently denied a desire for anyone to ever get to know him enough to care. Today he knew that to be a lie. Another soft giggle made him try to figure out what was so funny.

He glanced at Reba and caught her wiggling her eyebrows at the girls before giving the slightest of nods toward Lee Ann. Both girls glanced in Lee Ann's direction, and he followed their gaze. Lee Ann looked down at her plate the instant he made eye contact. She'd been staring at him.

He grinned. She couldn't keep her eyes off him any more than he could her.

He studied the orange material peeking out between the open buttons over her chest. He had no real place in her family, though, and that's what she needed. A husband for herself and a father for her kids.

The roll he'd just taken a bite of stuck in his throat. Her kids? *He* was their father. He glanced at them, their smiles so much like his, and coughed into his hand to clear the bread. He didn't want some other man being their father.

"What about you...Dad?"

"What?" He jerked his head up and saw that it was Kendra who'd spoken. His heart pounded. Had she called him "Dad"?

"What are you thankful for this year?" This came from Candy.

The entire table grew silent as they waited for his answer. Even though he didn't know all of them, it was clear from the sparkle in every set of eyes facing him that he should be grateful he'd just learned he had two children.

His gaze shifted back to Candy and Kendra, and he knew he was. Really grateful. He was also terrified out of his mind. "I'm grateful it wasn't another thirteen years before I learned I fathered two girls."

Both girls grinned at the same time, and he got the oddest glimpse of a different life. A life that included coming home to them every night.

Yet he loved his life exactly as it was.

Sam Jenkins's fingernails scraped over his sandpaper jaw, grabbing Cody's attention. "Seems you've done some growing up since you left, then."

"Yes, sir."

"Humph. Roy and Pearl might like to have known that before they died."

Cody stared at the man, completely taken off guard. Granted, he hadn't intended to visit his foster parents while here—they'd been decent people, but no love had been lost between them when he'd left—but he hadn't realized they'd both passed away. Now he couldn't go see them even if he wanted to. His throat burned as he sat there staring at Sam, unsure what he could possibly say in reply to the man.

Lee Ann rose, saving Cody from having to answer. "Dessert will be served in a few minutes, everyone."

She nodded to Kendra and Candy, and they sighed simultaneously before pushing their chairs back. Needing the escape, Cody stood. "They can stay. I'll help you."

Lee Ann eyed him before glancing back at the twins. They half-stood and half-sat, waiting for their mother's decision. Cody didn't hang around for the outcome.

Once in the kitchen, he stopped at the sink and stared out into the darkened night. A slight sigh followed him into the room seconds later. The twins must have come after all. Then the flowery scent that he equated so strongly with Lee Ann surrounded him, and electricity zapped him in the back of the knees.

Turning, he leaned against the counter to find her the only other person in the room. She knelt at the refrigerator to dig out pies, then handed them up to him. He placed them beside the waiting stack of plates. "Thanks for convincing Candy to let me come today."

She straightened, then began slicing and scooping portions onto the plates he held out for her, remaining silent for so long that he began to think she wasn't going to reply.

"She wanted you here as much as her sister did," Lee Ann finally said. "Even if she couldn't admit it yet."

Was that true? He hoped so. When he didn't answer, she locked her clear gaze on his.

After a long breath, she broke eye contact, and he immediately missed the connection. The muffled sounds of guests filtered through the swinging door.

"Maybe you did it for us, too." Where the heck had that come from? "Maybe you wanted me here."

A soft breath parted her lips, slowing the motions of her hands, before she picked up speed and renewed her efforts. "You're here for the girls, Cody. Don't let memories of the past fool you into thinking otherwise."

He shouldn't have let the words out. She was right. He was simply remembering the past. Only there was something still there.

Attraction. Electricity. He knew she felt it, too. He could tell by the nervous shift of her eyes every time he glanced her way. Cody placed an empty plate back on a tray and wrapped his fingers around Lee Ann's wrist, halting her movements. The knife clattered to the countertop.

"Look at me, Lee."

Tension spiked. "I've got to finish."

"There are twelve people here. You've already cut fifteen pieces." He squeezed her wrist lightly and lowered his voice. "Look at me."

When she turned her head and tilted it up to his, it took everything he had not to lean in and press his lips to hers. He wanted just one taste, no matter how wrong.

"Thank you." His voice was low and sounded far more sensual than he'd intended. "I mean that. I know everything about me being here upsets you and messes up the order of your world, but there isn't another place on this earth I would rather be today."

She stared at him, a mixture of doubt, hope, and fear fighting through the blue gaze. "Everything about it doesn't upset me. I told you, the girls need a dad. I can only be so much to them. I grew up without a father, so I know what it's like. I just hope you get that and don't hurt them. They're going to fall hard for you, you know?"

He found himself wishing she'd fall just as hard. Though that made little sense. He didn't need to get entangled with more here than he already was.

As they watched each other almost suspiciously, the pulse in her wrist thumped against his thumb. He smoothed over her tender skin and felt her heart rate speeding up. "I may not be perfect, but I'll do my best to make sure I never cause them any pain. I promise."

Lee Ann scanned over his face before she disentangled herself from his grip. "I hope you mean that. But also keep in mind that the only thing going on here is between you and them. There's nothing between us."

He arched an eyebrow. She was wrong. But tonight wasn't the time to prove it. They would have plenty of opportunities in the upcoming days to work through their issues. And one of the issues was that he needed to tell her what he'd learned the day he'd slept with Stephanie. He hadn't wanted to bring it up before, but as he'd sat at the table earlier tonight, being blatantly reminded of what a good person Lee Ann was, he knew she deserved to hear all of it.

It still wasn't a good enough excuse for what he'd done, but she did have the right to understand the full reason that had driven his actions.

"I need to tell you more about that day, Lee."

Her eyes rounded for a second, then slit into nervous lines. "We've already talked about it all we need to."

"But I didn't tell you everything. You need—"

"This is about the kids," she said, shaking her head. She lifted one of the trays and held it high in one hand. "That's all. If you want to talk, we talk about them."

Again, she was wrong, but he'd bide his time on that one, too. "Fine," he said. "We'll start tomorrow."

A frown marred her gorgeous face. "Start what? I have plans—"

"Are you working in the morning?"

"No, the girls and I—"

"Then I'll be here bright and early." He balanced the other tray on his open palm and gave her a steady look. He wouldn't be put off when it came to getting to know his kids, nor would he let time with Lee Ann slip away without at least trying to figure out what this thing was still between them. "We can all do something together."

"Like what?"

"I don't know. What do they like? I don't have the first idea."

When she didn't look as if she wanted to help him out, he stroked a finger along the inside of the forearm supporting her tray and the plates rattled above her head. "I need your help on this, Lee. Tell me what they like to do."

Her blue gaze narrowed on him, and then with a soft sigh her shoulders drooped. "Fine. We were planning to go into Knoxville tomorrow, to the mall. I suppose you can go with us."

"Shopping?" A quick vision of him shopping with three females was almost too much.

Lee Ann shot him a look, both eyebrows aiming for her hairline. "I thought you wanted to get to know them? They like going to the mall."

He gulped. "Then to the mall we shall go."

She pressed her shoulder into the door, turning her back to him, but he stopped her with a low voice, suddenly unable to let her walk away with the upper hand. "One other thing."

She peered over her shoulder, wariness in her eyes, and he very purposefully roamed his gaze down her curvy backside and back up before leaning into her space. He smelled a hint of corn bread dressing on her breath.

"You look amazing tonight," he whispered.

CHAPTER

9

Lee Ann exhaled and dropped into the bright yellow chair, settling her oversized bag on the top of the food court table and her packages of newly purchased items on the floor beside her. They'd been at the mall for hours in the middle of the biggest shopping day of the year, and because she had a perverse streak, she'd encouraged the girls to keep going just to force Cody to endure the day even longer.

The poor man had looked far more than overwhelmed when they'd shown up at the mall and had to elbow their way into the first store, and after five hours of the same, she was starting to feel sorry for him.

Almost.

"How about I grab some milkshakes?" Cody said. "You girls want anything?"

Neither paid him any attention, exactly as they'd done most of the day, and Lee Ann really felt bad for not warning Cody they would try their best to pretend neither he nor Lee Ann existed. They were, after all, almost teenagers. And they were in public!

He focused on Lee Ann. "Chocolate?"

God, yes, chocolate.

She nodded and dug her camera out of the bag. It both thrilled her and annoyed her that he remembered her preferences. "Get them both one, too, please. But make one strawberry."

Before heading off in the other direction, Cody set the bags he carried on the floor beside hers and propped his hands on the table. He leaned in. He was so close to her that she saw the dark specks in his brown eyes. "I'm going to get you back for this, you know."

She blinked. He knew she was dragging this trip out just to get to him.

His eyes crinkled. "Be right back."

Lee Ann watched his backside make quick work of the distance to the burger counter, admiring the fact there wasn't an extra ounce anywhere to be found. Geez, she had to get herself under control. Since he'd shown up early that morning bearing breakfast from the diner, she'd barely been able to keep from drooling. And not over the smells wafting from the bags.

He was hot when he wandered around town with his cap pulled low over his head and day-old whiskers shadowing his jaw, but when the man cleaned up?

Oh, God. When the man cleaned up she had a hard time sitting like a lady.

His jeans showcased the body of a god, his pullover was just the right amount of tight, and then there was his face. Sweet mama, the man had both shaved and combed his hair back off his forehead. With all that hot masculinity facing her every time she glanced his way, she'd been short-circuiting for hours.

Snickering caught her attention, and she glanced toward Kendra and Candy. They rolled their eyes as they looked from her to Cody. Fantastic. Now her kids thought there was something going on between her and Cody. Just what she needed.

It was bad enough that they'd caught her staring at him last night across the table. If she weren't careful, they'd get the wrong impression and get their hopes up that they were going to have something more than merely a part-time father.

She'd had a long talk with them yesterday before everyone had arrived to see how they were handling this new thing of having a father. Though Candy was still hesitant to let him in all the way, both girls were in heaven over the thought that they not only had a dad, but he was also the town heartthrob. Apparently it was cool that all the girls went gooey-eyed over him. Who would have guessed?

The men around town still thought he was the wild boy he'd been years ago, and the women only hoped he was. Bad boys fueled fantasies.

As for her, she was beginning to wonder if he might have actually grown up some. Though she knew he'd been uncomfortable the night before, he had handled the evening like a pro. He'd replied to the many questions with all the right answers and couldn't have come across as more upstanding, even when it became clear that everyone at the table was aware he was the girls' father.

That had been the key in her figuring out the girls were really okay with everything. They'd called their friends the night before to share the news.

All day Thursday Lee Ann had fielded calls to confirm what the townspeople had heard. Cody himself had also been the main topic of the evening's predinner conversations.

This was before Cody had arrived. She had wondered if they would bombard him with questions when he showed up, but amazingly, once she'd gotten Buddy to calm down when he'd first seen the man, everyone had been civilized, and dinner had been enjoyable.

She caught sight of Cody again as he cocked a hip against the counter and waited for the server to come back with the shakes. The best darn pair of jeans she'd ever seen on a man. She rolled her eyes. If she weren't careful, *she'd* begin to wonder if he couldn't be more than a part-time father.

Closing her eyes, she concentrated on breathing techniques to calm herself. They were at the mall for him to get to know the girls. That was all. It didn't matter that it had been years since she'd seen the naked side of the male anatomy.

Not that she'd ever seen many with twin girls underfoot, but with them being involved in so many activities the last few years, Lee Ann could barely remember her last date.

"Mom!"

She quit imagining what Cody's behind might look like naked and opened her eyes. "What?"

Kendra bounced in place. "Can we buy something from Victoria's Secret today?"

"What?" They were only twelve! Did normal twelve-year-olds actually want sexy underwear? And *why*?

"You promised last year we could get something for our birthday, Mom," Kendra pleaded. "Please."

"But your birthday—"

"Is only three weeks away," Candy interrupted. "You know we won't be back here before then. Say yes."

"But..." Lee Ann looked toward Cody, envisioning what would happen if she said yes. Though the girls had done their best to ignore the fact they had parents tagging along today, he'd held fast, insisting he was more than thrilled to go into each and every store they'd visited. Victoria's Secret was within sight on the other side of the food court. If she said yes, either she let Cody follow them in, which was out of the question, or she sat out here with him while the girls shopped alone. And that meant she and Cody would be alone.

She turned to the girls, almost pleading with her eyes for them to understand the dilemma they were putting her in.

"Tell me something first," she began.

"What?" Candy asked while Kendra sighed and rolled her eyes.

"It's been a couple days now since you learned about Cody. Are you still okay with it?"

Candy shrugged nonchalantly, trying for unaffected. "Yeah, it's cool. Just...weird, you know?"

Lee Ann looked at Kendra for her opinion on the matter.

"I'm not weirded out at all," her other daughter stated. "I love it."

"And you'll be okay when he leaves in a few weeks?"

The question took a bit of the air out of Kendra, and both girls glanced in Cody's direction, as did Lee Ann.

"He'll come back and see us sometime though, right?" Candy asked, her tone sounding both scared and confused, very much how Lee Ann often felt about the whole situation.

She nodded, praying she was giving the right answer and silently swearing that if he didn't, she would hunt him up and personally beat some sense into him. "He cares about you. I can tell. So I can't see why he wouldn't come back to see you on occasion."

Except, not all men remembered their kids once they left.

As they all watched him, each of them fell into her own sort of trance. The girls were dreaming about a father who stuck, but Lee Ann couldn't help but dream of a little more. She had once believed in him so much. She found her hopes sliding in that same direction again, and in more ways than simply fatherhood.

Her danged pulse had forgotten how to behave when he was around.

Candy stepped closer and pressed a hand lightly to Lee Ann's. "We're happy you two like each other, Mom. Joanie told us how she didn't think you'd ever gotten over him."

"Excuse me?" The words jerked her out of her silly fantasy. Her best friend, the one who'd been giving Cody the evil eye and grilling him all night at the dinner table, had told these two that she still had feelings for him?

Kendra nodded. "We can tell, too."

Lee Ann narrowed her eyes. "What can you tell?"

"We're almost thirteen, Mom." Kendra propped her hands on her hips. "We can tell when two people really like each other."

Candy peeked at Cody as he made his way back toward them. "He's checked out your butt, too, like you just did his."

Oh, crap. Knowing the two of them, they'd probably share that same information with Cody if she didn't get them away from there. She glanced over at the store they wanted to go into. There were some cute tanks and robes in there. Surely they could find something appropriate for someone their age.

"Fine," she said. "You can go buy something for your birthday, but we're dropping this other conversation. You can each buy *one* item. But nothing too grown-up, or I'll return it myself."

Both girls grinned with happiness, and the air whooshed from her lungs. She'd swear they were looking more and more like their father every day.

"Here you go." Cody stopped at the table and handed Lee Ann her shake. He narrowed his eyes at the girls' bright faces. "What did I miss?"

Kendra opened her mouth.

"Nothing," Lee Ann interjected.

Kendra laughed out loud as she reached for one of the chocolate shakes.

Candy grabbed hers and they both scampered away, each competing to be first to the store. Candy won, but then Kendra kicked her in the back of the knees, knocking her to the floor, and hurried around her.

Cody shook his head. "It's bad enough I don't understand women, but teenagers? Not sure I should even try."

A smile stretched across Lee Ann's face when the girls both suddenly straightened as if realizing they were going into a grown-up store and needed to act the part. She was so lucky to have them. She turned to Cody and discovered he was smiling as well, as he watched them, too. "Don't waste your time trying. If they catch on you're on to them, they'll immediately change. It's an inner sensor."

He lowered himself to the seat at a ninety-degree angle to hers, groaning with the movement, his arm brushing over hers as he settled into place. The unpredictable weather of Tennessee had heated the day to a balmy seventy-five, calling for short sleeves, but with his touch she found herself wishing for a sweater to keep his skin from hers. She also wished she couldn't see the tattoo he had peeking out from below his sleeve. It was bad enough at his neck.

She had a hard time stopping herself from rolling up the material to see what he'd marked his body with underneath.

Dipping her head to the straw, she peeked through her lashes, catching Cody studying her. She still had reservations about everything, but the day had been so casual and easy, she couldn't help but relax. Around a mouthful of ice cream, she asked, "What?"

"Just wondering if you're enjoying yourself." He took a sip of his own shake. Strawberry if she had to guess. "You think the girls are?"

She saw the uncertainty in his eyes and guessed he wasn't aware she could read him so easily. He was worried the girls would rather he wasn't there. Their habit of ignoring the two of them couldn't have helped allay his misgivings. Strangely, this made her want to reach out and touch him the way he kept finding excuses to touch her.

"They're having a blast." She didn't comment on her own enjoyment. "They're glad you're here even though it's not cool to act like it."

He drank quietly as they both watched the girls flip through a rack of conservative robes, she and he both lost in their own thoughts. When he spoke, his voice was low but determined. "I don't know how exactly this is going to work yet, but I won't just walk away."

Like her father had done to her? "You'll leave at the end of the year."

"Yes, but it doesn't end there. I'm their father, though Lord knows I have no idea what that fully means yet. But I do know I'll keep in touch, be there for them as much as possible. And I'll stop in when I can. They can also travel with me some when they're out of school."

Panic yanked Lee Ann to her feet. For some reason, she hadn't even considered he'd want them to go with him. She glared down at him. "Their home is here, Cody."

"I'm not suggesting anything permanent. Simply the occasional trip. They'll get to see part of the country and have new experiences."

The milkshake sat heavily in her stomach all of a sudden. "And who will take care of them while you work? No, it's not possible. They need the stability I've provided for them. You'll have to visit them here."

Brown eyes burned into hers. He stared at her for several long seconds, his jaw tight, before he blinked and dropped his gaze to the table. "This isn't about you and me."

"I know that!" Her raised voice got the attention of the family at the next table, and she brought it back under control. "I'm the one who's raised them all their life. I know what's good for them. I know what they need."

"Do you? Or do you just know what would be easiest for you?"

"Easiest for me?" Anger quickly rose to the surface as her pulse pounded behind her ears. She pasted on a small smile and nodded at a passing couple, then continued talking through gritted teeth. "Don't talk to me about easy for me. I'm the one who was left here. *Alone.* No help with the bills, while raising my sister's children. Your children. While you were out making a life for yourself."

He closed his eyes. "I knew nothing about it, Lee Ann. We've covered this."

"I know."

He cut his eyes up at her, a skeptical crease covering his forehead from one side to the other.

"I do, I know," she continued. "I believe you. No matter how much easier it would be to believe Steph and tell you to get the heck out—"

"You couldn't do that even if you wanted to."

She paused. "Couldn't do what? Tell you to get out of their lives?"

"*Make* me get out of their lives."

They stared at each other, him sitting calmly in his seat, her still standing, fear trickling through her, until she finally broke eye contact. She turned and watched the girls and crossed her arms over her chest as she took several deep gulps of air. This whole thing scared her to death.

"Don't hurt them," she finally whispered, almost pleading. "Please don't hurt them."

He waited for her to look back at him before he answered, and when he did, his voice was clear, his gaze unwavering. "I swear I won't."

But he might. She could still remember the night her father had left. That was a pain she would do anything to keep her kids from ever feeling. Words died out as they sat there; she didn't know what else to say. The situation with him and the girls would play out however it was going to, and all she could do was be there to pick up the pieces when needed.

"I won't hurt you again, either, Lee."

Her eyes watered, upsetting her even more. The last thing she wanted was to cry in front of the man. She didn't want his pity, and she certainly didn't want him realizing just how hard her life had been those first few years. They were all fine now. As long as he didn't mess it up too much.

He patted the seat she'd vacated. "Sit back down. Let's talk, get to know each other again. It's been a long time."

She shook her head. "You don't need to know me."

"Wouldn't it be best for them," he said, nodding toward the store that the girls had disappeared into, "if we got along?"

Yes, but that was such a grown-up, parent thing to say that she refused to answer him.

While she continued standing there brooding, a hand reached out and wrapped around her wrist and tugged until she finally gave in and lowered to her seat. She probably looked silly standing, anyway. Especially with him still sitting.

"Tell me about college," he said, his voice low and deep, and she couldn't help but want to answer just to keep him talking. "Did you get to go at all?"

She nodded. "I finished my first semester right before the kids were born. I didn't go back in January."

"And your scholarship?"

Lee Ann glanced over at him but then just as quickly lowered her gaze. Unintentionally, she fastened on to his lips. She couldn't let him see into her soul at that moment. He was fully aware how hard she'd worked for that scholarship. He would know what it had meant to give it up. "Was no good to a single mother of twins."

The sound of strangers talking and kids squealing was the only thing she heard for what seemed like a full minute. She had the strongest urge to lift her eyes to Cody's so she could see what he was thinking, but it was best not to look. She did not want him seeing how dropping out of college had crushed her.

"Your mom may not have been the best mother in the world, but she raised you okay." His lips, as they moved, were mesmerizing. "You could've asked her to take them. You could've given them up as Steph had originally planned."

"I couldn't." She moved her straw up and down in the lid. The squeaking of plastic against plastic finally allowed her to break free from his pull and slide her gaze away from him. How could she make him understand? "No matter what, she had been my sister. This was my chance to be close to her."

And my last chance to be close to you.

It hadn't mattered how often she'd tried, how much she'd attempted to attain perfection; she'd never been good enough. Not for either of them.

Cody leaned toward her until their arms brushed. "You'd never told me just how bad it was between the two of you. I knew there were problems, but..."

But not so much that her sister would seduce him just to hurt her?

"I know." She stretched her hands flat over the table and shrugged. What did it hurt to admit the truth? Facts were facts. "She hated me from the day I was born."

He touched a finger to the side of her chin and turned her face to his, sliding his warm touch along her jawbone. His dark eyes roamed over her face before locking on to her eyes. "I'm sorry your sister wasn't worthy of you, and I'm sorry you had to postpone your dreams. But thank you for taking care of my girls. I would hate myself even more if they'd ended up in the system like I was."

She gulped. "I couldn't have lived with myself if I'd done it any other way."

And that was the truth. Knowing the childhood Cody had experienced and the unhappiness that had come with it, she could not have risked that happening to his girls, no matter what she'd had to give up because of it.

The moment was suddenly way too serious. She moved back out of his reach and glanced toward the store. "I heard

Keri gave birth early this morning. Word is it was a quick labor, and they're both doing well."

A low chuckle hit her ears. "Changing subjects on me, Lee?"

She shivered with the easy way he said her name. "You bet. We should focus on having fun. Not dwelling on what can't be changed."

That chuckle sounded again, and she couldn't fight the urge to look over at him. But when she did, she knew it had been a mistake. The heat twinkling back at her indicated that his idea of fun just might not be the same as hers.

Then again...She glanced at his mouth, noticing the tiny pink drop of milkshake now clinging to his upper lip...Maybe they both knew exactly what fun could be.

Crap! She'd gone there again. She had to stop doing that.

She returned her gaze to the girls and decided to bring up another subject that, though it might not be fun, did need to be discussed. Reaching into her bag, she pulled out the check he'd given her two days before and slid it across the table to him. "I can't accept this. It's too much."

He didn't pick up the check.

She nudged it closer. "Come on, Cody. Take it. I can't accept more money from you than I make in a year. Keep it for a college fund if you insist on using it on them, but I don't need it."

"I don't recall asking if you needed it."

"Well, I don't." She pushed it to the edge of the table, directly in front of him. "Take it."

His hand finally moved, but instead of picking up the check he simply pushed it back across the table to her. "How about you quit the diner instead? Pursue the career you put on hold."

"Nothing was put on hold. I changed my path. People do that all the time." Again, she pushed the check back in his direction. The thought of depositing that much money in her account gave her a vicious thrill. She could do a lot for the girls with that, and he was right, she could quit the diner. But it didn't feel right. It felt as if accepting it would tie the two of them together in a way she wasn't comfortable with. "I've been making it just fine on my own."

"And now you don't have to. I've already arranged for a monthly check to come to you."

"Cody." Exasperation had her voice tightening. "I'm making it fine."

"Quit the diner, Lee. Pursue your photography."

She shook her head. "You can't just come back and start directing things."

"No?" His voice had sharpened in a similar manner to hers, indicating he was equally annoyed. He picked the check up, grabbed her bag and shoved it back inside. "Watch me."

"You can't—"

"Try and stop me," he gritted out. "They're my kids. I will make sure they have everything they need, and I will not sit around watching you work yourself to death anymore when I can do something about it."

"*I* am not your priority."

"Yet...you are." His tone changed, and she sensed that he'd gone away from thinking solely about the girls. Suddenly, she didn't want to hear whatever else he was about to say. Her breathing grew deeper and she pushed to her feet again. She felt more comfortable around him when she was standing up.

"Fine," she said. "I'll accept the check. But I, personally, am nothing to you. The only things between us are those two girls."

She moved to the other side of the table, putting it between them while at the same time mentally reconstructing her wall.

She silently watched her children move through the store and wished Cody would just walk away. He used to be good at that. There could not be anything more between them. He'd hurt her too much the first time.

"You're lying," he said.

She jerked around to glare at him, but he'd risen, his height now taking the sting out of her look. "I am not," she muttered.

"There's something there. You feel it just like I do."

She turned her back to him. "Whatever we had ended the day you dropped your pants for my sister."

"Or maybe it was only put on pause." His deep voice came from right behind her now, sparking goose bumps across the base of her neck.

"There's nothing left, Cody. You might as well give that thought up." How had they gotten back here?

"I can't. I feel it." He pressed his fingers to the small of her back and her traitorous body shivered. "You feel it, too. The question is, what do we do about it?"

"I don't feel a thing." If ever she needed strength, it was now. She bit down on the inside of her lip and forced herself to remain stiff against his touch. Why did it have to still be him who had this effect on her? She did not need this in her life.

He pressed his hand fully to her back, spreading his palm wide until every inch of it burned through her lightweight top. She fought the urge to close her eyes and lean into him. "You always were the worst liar," he murmured.

With a gentle caress of his thumb directly beneath the back strap of her bra, her knees locked in place to keep her from collapsing at his feet. His hand felt so perfectly right on her body. She curled her fingernails into her palms and reminded herself that they were there for the girls, not for the two of them. The two of them had ended. Years ago.

As the girls crossed her mind, they burst from the store and raced for the table. Cody removed his hand from her body.

Sliding to a stop, Kendra spoke. "We're ready to check out, Mom. Can we use your debit card?"

"I'll get it." Cody's voice was deeper than normal, and Lee Ann shivered again, but this time he wasn't looking at her. He pulled out a credit card, and the girls' eyes widened.

"Will the store let us use your card?"

He shrugged. "No problem. I'll come with you."

"No!" both girls shouted, causing several people to look at them. They ducked their heads in embarrassment, pink tinting their cheeks.

Cody looked to Lee Ann for help, clearly not grasping the severity of the issue. If he paid, he would have to go into a sexy underwear store with his daughters. But she refused to help him out. After all, he'd just made her admit to herself that she not only wanted to see his butt *out* of those sexy jeans, but she also wanted his lips all over her as well. She shrugged as if she wasn't standing there with only half a functioning brain.

He looked from the girls to the store and back, still not getting it. Then his neck almost snapped as it twisted quickly back in the direction of the store. "You want something from there?"

The girls both groaned. "Never mind."

They put several feet between themselves and the grown-ups, clearly hoping no additional embarrassment would befall them, and Lee Ann finally felt bad for everyone. She picked up her bag and eyed Cody. "You stay here. I'll handle this."

"But that's a store for adult women, Lee Ann." His whisper wasn't nearly quiet enough. "Not kids."

Nearby laughter turned the girls two deeper shades of red, and guilt ate at Lee Ann for letting her pettiness with Cody cause them embarrassment in the first place. How he'd missed what store they'd been in all this time, she had no idea. Maybe because he'd been too busy trying to make time with her.

She shot him a harsh look. "Take the packages and we'll meet you back at the car."

He opened his mouth as if to argue, but she shut him up with a look.

"At. The. Car." She marched off to take care of her girls. Without Cody. As it should be.

They didn't need anyone else. Only they did. And she feared it was all of them who did.

CHAPTER

Twelve-year-olds could pack away some food.

That was the theory Cody had come up with as he'd watched his daughters put down pizza that night. Following the mostly successful day they'd had at the mall the day before, he'd talked Lee Ann into letting him hang with them after the clinic had closed today. With a low fire now burning in the patio fireplace, they all lingered in the rapidly growing dusk. November or not, when it hit almost eighty during the day you took advantage of the heat.

He'd offered to pick up dinner, and from the looks of the single, remaining piece of pizza, he'd chosen well.

"Mom, did Dad tell you about the procedure he let me watch at the clinic this morning?" Kendra had moved to sit on the back steps with her grandmother, and the two of them were playing a card game. Reba had shown up when the pizza did and had yet to leave. Cody suspected she was there as much to pick up something juicy to share with her friends as to simply hang with her family.

Boss had settled down on the other side of Kendra. The kids had chased him all over the yard as they'd waited for dinner, and now the dog seemed perfectly content with the occasional pat Kendra tossed his way. If Cody wasn't careful, his dog would want to stay there when it was time to go.

"He did," Lee Ann said, answering her daughter's question.

Cody cut his eyes over to Candy, who'd picked up her basketball and stood several feet away, dribbling. Occasionally she tried a move through her legs, but given her height, her main skill was shooting. Still, she wasn't bad.

As Kendra proceeded to tell her grandmother about the procedure he'd done that morning, he headed over to Candy. He scouted out the area, then pointed to a level spot in the corner of the yard. "How about I put up a basketball goal there?"

Dark eyes glowed up at him for a second before Candy frowned and scrunched up her nose. She shook her head. "It's in the yard. Mom wouldn't like it."

"What?" He looked around to ask why not, but Lee Ann hadn't heard the comment. She was busy picking up paper plates, empty cups, and the three beer bottles the adults had drained. She dumped everything in the proper receptacles as he turned back to his daughter. "Why wouldn't she like it?"

"It'll kill the grass if we play in one spot like that."

"So?" That was the most ridiculous thing he'd heard. Kids needed a place to play. "Then we find another spot. Or we pour concrete on top of the grass and take away that argument."

Candy grinned at him then, giving him one of the few honest smiles she'd turned his way since learning who he was, and he went a little weak at the knees. She was a tougher nut to crack than her sister, but he hoped to eventually win her over. The thought of one of his daughters not liking him was not pleasant.

He nudged his chin toward the ball. "Pass that over. Let's see if I still remember how to dribble."

Not that he'd ever played on a team; he'd rarely gone to the same school for more than a year. But he had played in enough pickup games over the years to know his way around a ball.

She bounced it to him, and they proceeded to get into a heated battle of keep-away. She was quite good.

"So tell me more about the birthday party coming up." He'd wanted to bring the subject up for the last couple of days, the thought of dancing with each of them on their big day meaning more to him than he'd ever imagined, but fear had made him keep his mouth shut. What if Candy refused to let him attend? He'd said he wouldn't go unless both of them wanted him there.

She took the ball away from him and went into a protective dribble. "It's just a party."

"You said before that it was a dance."

"Yeah, a boy-girl dance. Not like Sadie's party."

Apparently Sadie's party had been a big deal. *But theirs was better.* He grinned with the thought. Lee Ann was sweet and polite and took care of whoever needed it, but she was also subtle, and she liked to win. Throwing the girls a party that would be better than their friend's bash had made him realize that it really was the Lee Ann he'd once known who was still driving matters these days. He'd thought she'd changed a lot, but the more he got to know her again, the more he saw he'd been wrong. She was still the strong, independent yet attractively vulnerable woman he'd once fallen in love with. She'd merely adapted to changed circumstances.

He and Candy played through a few more minutes of silence before he got up the courage to ask, "Would you let me come to the party? I'd really like to."

Candy stopped bouncing the basketball and looked at him. He felt like an insect trapped under a microscope. She studied him as thoroughly as he'd ever seen Lee Ann do. She may have been another woman's biological child, but Lee Ann ran through her with clarity.

Finally, she lowered her gaze and nodded. She went back to dribbling. "You can come."

Relief washed over him, and he took a step toward her, wanting to hug her. He stopped before allowing himself the luxury. No need scaring her off when he'd just taken a giant step forward.

"Thank you," he said, sincerity filling his voice. "I'm very much looking forward to it. I'd love to dance with you, too, if you'd like that."

She nodded but didn't say anything else, only dribbled some more.

They played a few more minutes, and then he yelled over for her sister. He wanted both his girls around him. "Want to join us? Your sister is kicking my butt over here."

Kendra looked up from her game but then glanced down at her watch. "Uh...actually, I have some homework to do."

"Oh," Candy said, then stood straight and shot a look at her mother. "Yeah. Homework."

Within minutes, she and Kendra had disappeared inside with Boss, Reba had made her way across the yard to her own house, and he found himself alone on the patio with the woman he hadn't managed to stop thinking about since seeing her again.

It wasn't that he minded being alone with Lee Ann in the growing darkness—hell, he loved it, especially given the conversation they'd started at the mall the day before, before he'd freaked about the girls buying something at Victoria's Secret. He shook his head at the thought, still uncertain why he was the one wrong over the whole matter. He couldn't help feeling like right now he'd done something else to send them scurrying.

He straddled the bench Lee Ann had settled down on and faced her, pleased when she didn't get up and move to the other side. Fresh beers appeared from out of nowhere and she passed one over to him. Grateful, he opened it and touched the neck to hers.

"Thanks," he murmured. "When did you sneak these out?"

She smiled. "I grabbed them when I took the extra slice of pizza into the house."

The sounds of the night started up around them, adding to the ambience of the candles in the middle of the stained wood table and the lazy evening, and he couldn't help but want more out of the night than what he suspected she was willing to offer.

"What exactly just happened here?" He motioned with his bottle to the emptiness around them. "One minute everyone was content, hanging out, and then as if a bell rang, they all scattered. And you can't convince me they're really going in to do homework on a Saturday night."

Soft laughter made its way out of Lee Ann, and he leaned in closer to hear it better. He loved making her laugh. He feared there had been too few moments of laughter during the last thirteen years. He would make that up to her if she'd let him.

The thought gave him pause, but he realized it was the truth. He wanted to make her laugh on a regular basis. That meant he wanted to be around her the same.

She tilted up her beer instead of answering. After taking several long pulls, she remained silent.

"Did I do something else wrong?" he asked. "Just tell me and I'll try to fix it. I swear, girls should come with owner's manuals."

One more long drink and she turned to him, her face mere inches away. "They think we want some alone time," she stated blandly.

Oh. He had smart kids. "They might be right."

She shook her head, the movement a bit off, and he realized it didn't take much to make her tipsy. "No, they aren't right. You're here only for them." She took another drink. "In fact, since they've gone in, you should probably go, too."

"And what if I don't want to go?" he asked. He lifted a hand and touched the backs of his fingers to the soft underside of her chin. Her face tilted up. "What if I want more than to be here only for them?"

God, he wanted to kiss her. He'd wanted to since the moment he'd seen her glaring at him from behind the diner's grill. The desire was only getting worse. He just wasn't sure if he would be able to stop with a kiss.

Her head shook back and forth with the slightest movement. "You've got to stop the full-court press, Cody. It's not going anywhere."

A ringing phone broke through the night, but it stopped almost as suddenly as it had started. All he could think as he sat there looking at her was that he could not make it through another night if he didn't get his lips on her in some fashion.

He tilted his head and leaned in closer, within striking distance of the curve of her neck. "If our daughters are playing matchmaker now, you know that means I'm not the only one who sees it. There's something burning here, Lee. Something strong."

Whatever it was, it sucked him in like a magnet every time he got near her. And she was probably right. Maybe it shouldn't go anywhere. They had the kids to think about after all. But how was he supposed to not poke at it and see what it was? This was Lee Ann after all.

She shook her head again, but didn't pull away.

"You do realize," she started, then waved one hand out toward her mother's house, "that my mother is probably watching us right now, and if that wasn't her calling back over to report that you're out here trying to put the moves on me, then it was likely someone else she's already called now calling here to try to find out what's going on."

The words stood a very good chance of being fact. And though the gossiping should have bothered him, it didn't nearly as much as it once would have. Most likely because he was a mere breath away from finally touching her.

"You're trying to scare me away." He pressed forward another inch before he could change his mind, and his lips grazed her neck. She trembled, and he was pretty sure she moaned, but the sound from his own throat overshadowed it. That brief touch had done more for him than any touch had in years.

"Cody." The word barely made it out into the night.

It was time to head higher. As he inched his way nearer her ear, never fully landing in any one spot, she groaned and leaned toward him.

With his last sane thought being that this could only go so far with kids in the house, he nipped just below her ear, as he gripped one thigh and pulled her closer into the vee of his legs.

"Mom!" The back door slammed open.

He jumped away, embarrassment heating his face. He only hoped that in the low light no one could tell. He was supposed to be there to see the girls, and they'd just caught him in a near crawl into their mother's lap.

Lee Ann snatched up the beer she'd set down at some point and turned her back to him. "Yes?"

Candy gaped, her eyes shifting from Cody back to Lee Ann. "Never mind," she mumbled and edged toward the door.

Kendra remained where she stood, wearing a wide grin. "Were you two kissing?"

"No!" Lee Ann gasped. "Of course not. Now, what did you want?"

Kendra eyed them both for another few seconds before finally answering, "I forgot to tell you that Sadie asked if we could spend the night." She held up the cordless phone. "Her mom is on her way to pick us up."

"Right now?"

"You always let us spend the night on the weekends," Candy replied. "We thought it would be okay."

Lee Ann sat there and blinked at them as if not fully registering the question yet. Cody would have given an answer himself but suspected that wouldn't be wise when he'd already overstepped what he suspected she would deem "his bounds." It probably hadn't been right to take advantage of her relaxed state and push for more, but he couldn't regret what he'd done. A few seconds longer and he would have made it to her mouth.

"So is it okay?"

Kendra's repeated question reminded him that Lee Ann hadn't answered. He glanced at her and saw the worry in her eyes and suspected it wasn't worry over the girls spending the night with their friend. It was over the fact that the two of them would be alone together after they left.

Lee Ann's throat moved with her gulp, and she plastered on a fake smile. "Of course."

A horn beeped, and the girls quickly hurried into the house to grab their bags. On their way back out, they gave Lee Ann a hug before turning to him and doing the same. His mouth dried with the action. He hugged them both, then waved as they hurried around the side of the house. He and Lee Ann followed, him holding Boss to his side even though the dog whined, wanting to go with his newest friends.

As the car pulled away, Cody decided he would at least get Lee Ann to admit she still felt something for him before he left for the night. How could she refuse to after the moment they'd just had? He turned to head around to the back of the house without waiting for her, hoping to pick up where they'd left off, but she remained where she stood.

"It's time for you to go, too," she said, immediately shutting down his fantasies of a lengthy good-night kiss. He rotated back in her direction.

"I thought I'd stay a while." He studied her unreadable eyes. "Discuss a couple things."

She shook her head and pointed up the road toward his apartment. She wore a too-polite smile. "The girls are gone, so there's no reason for you to stick around any longer. And they'll be at Sadie's most of tomorrow. They go to church with her family when they spend the night. Why don't we all take a day off tomorrow? Having a little break would be good for everyone. The girls need time to adjust to all these changes."

Anger unexpectedly tickled his vision with her prattled-off words. The girls, from what he could tell, were adjusting just fine, but she was tossing him out on his rear because she was afraid to admit that she still felt something for him.

"We should talk about this, Lee."

She shook her head, her expression locked down tight. "Nothing to discuss. Thank you for dinner."

She turned away before he could say anything else, and frustration made him do the same. If she could continue pretending there was nothing there, he could go along with it, too. Who needed a woman so damn frustrating, anyway? He had the kids to get to know. He would do best to keep that goal in mind. It was the important one.

With a low growl, he started off up the road, glancing at the red curtains in Reba's windows as he went past.

They were swinging again.

Great. The whole town would know within seconds that he'd struck out with Lee Ann, the woman who had "hard to get" down to an art form.

✿ ✿ ✿

Cody moved the gearshift into park, then slumped down in his seat, exhaustion filling him through and through. He looked over at Boss, who sat beside him, as worn out as he. They'd gotten up early that morning and driven into the mountains for their daily run. After leaving Lee Ann's the night before, he'd been too wired, his mind going in too many directions of "What if?" to get a decent night's sleep. Seemed like wearing himself out on the hills would be a good idea.

Only...the arduous run had settled nothing. All it had accomplished had been to exhaust both him and his dog.

He reached over and patted Boss on the head. "Hang on, bud. This won't take long. Then we'll get you home and you'll be able to take your morning nap. A good long one today. I might even take one with you."

Seemed a good thing to do on a Sunday when you had nothing else going on. Which he apparently didn't. He clenched his jaw at the memory of how the night before had ended. Didn't do to dwell on things he couldn't change, though.

His stomach rumbled, and he rubbed a hand over his damp tee. He'd called in breakfast as he'd headed back to town, not in the mood for company, but definitely ready for a meal. But now, looking down at himself, sweaty and ripe, he wished he'd taken the time to run by the apartment and grab a quick shower before running in to grab his food.

If he were to believe Ms. G, people were beginning to come around to the thought of him not being so bad. Apparently word had gotten around that he hadn't been a brute at Lee Ann's over Thanksgiving, and for some reason, it seemed to be a positive that he was the girls' father. Whenever he ventured out, he now got words of encouragement and small talk about the kids, as opposed to the snide comments he'd gotten used to overhearing as people passed. It was...odd. Yet strangely comforting.

He also found himself wondering what the Monroes would have thought about it all. Swiping a hand down his face, he pushed that thought from his mind. He would never know. He also would never be able to apologize to their faces for the way he'd left. That was tough to take, especially when he hadn't realized he'd wanted to apologize until Sam had told him they were gone. Again, nothing he could do about that now. No need to dwell.

He opened the door and stepped from the car. Showing up in public looking like the derelict he'd been when he'd first left probably wasn't the best idea in the world, but that was just going to have to be too bad today. He was starving, and people would have to get over it.

Before he could grab for the restaurant door and go in, it swung out toward him and Holly stood there. Tight skirt, makeup too much for a Sunday morning in the Bible Belt, and pink high-top Chucks, which once again seemed to have nothing whatsoever to do with the outfit.

She held a bag of food out to him. "Here's your breakfast."

Before he could reply, she disappeared back behind the door, then reemerged seconds later with two covered trays of food.

"Carry these and I'll get the rest," she said as she thrust them into his arms.

"What's going on?" But he was once again talking to a closed door.

The third time she emerged, she held a gallon of tea in one hand and a bulging bag in the other. "Let's go."

Cody turned with her toward his car before he realized what he was doing. He stopped in the middle of the sidewalk. "What are you doing, Holly? What is all this?"

She stopped by his passenger door and sighed when she found the door locked. "I can't believe you lock your car here. What do you think someone's going to take? Your dog?"

"They'd better not," he muttered. Unsure what else to do, he set the food on the hood and reached into his pocket for his key fob. He pressed a button and the locks flipped. "What's all this food? And where do you think I'm taking you?"

She opened his passenger door, scratched Boss between the ears, and the traitor got up and climbed over the seat to give her his spot. "It's food for Keri. She came home from the hospital this morning, so I want to take this over."

He remained standing by the hood. "Then take it."

"I am," she said. She reached over and opened his door. "Get in. People are staring."

Setting his jaw, he tried giving her the look that normally got people to back off. She merely ignored him and turned to love on his dog some more.

"I'm serious," he said, though he hadn't yet told her what he was serious about. "I can't take you this morning. You'll have to find someone else."

"Come on," she begged. "My car is in for maintenance, and they didn't get it back to me yesterday. I need to get this stuff to Keri so she can concentrate on the baby and not have to worry about anything else."

"Holly," he said, dragging the word out. He moved to stand in his open door, and put the food down on his seat. "Look at me. I'm covered in sweat, and you can probably smell me fifty feet away. Plus, Boss wants a nap. I promised him we were going home."

She merely gave him a look before scooping the trays off his seat and holding them in her lap. "Fine. We'll run by your house. Boss can sleep, you can take a five-minute shower, and then we'll be off. No biggie. Now, let's go. I have a breakfast casserole in here getting cold."

"Don't you have to work?" he asked, but found himself climbing behind the wheel anyway. He had to get to that shower or he soon wouldn't be able to stand being around himself.

"I'm not needed back until the churches let out. But I want to hold that new baby for a few minutes, so quit wasting time and let's go."

With a final look at the woman who'd planted herself in his dog's spot in the car, he shook his head and headed off down the street. How was it that he kept getting pulled into things he didn't want to be a part of?

Ten minutes later, he emerged clean from the shower and saw that Boss had downed most of his water and was now asleep in his spot in the corner. Holly was busy flipping kitchen cabinets open and closed. The instant she saw him, she headed for the door.

"Come on," she said.

"What were you looking for?"

"Huh?" She looked back, then over at the small kitchen space. "Oh, nothing. Just bored. I get that way in this town, and since the apartment is no bigger than a matchbox, it was starting to get to me, too."

"In the five minutes I was gone?" he asked. He grabbed his keys off the table.

She shrugged. "What can I say? Nothing to do around here."

"So you just go through strangers' cabinets?" His life had turned into something he didn't recognize, with people that befuddled him, yet he kept going along with it. Very strange. He followed Holly out the door.

"You aren't a stranger," she said. "And it's not like you have anything of yours in there anyway. That was all Keri's stuff."

That was true. He traveled with his clothes, dog, and the few medical essentials he always kept on him.

As they made their way down the stairs, he tossed a wave to Ms. Grayson, who stood on her porch, sweeping, but mostly keeping an eye on him. He almost hated to miss their morning chat, but apparently there were eggs in his car getting cold.

"Talk to you later, Ms. G," he shouted out as he slid behind the wheel.

Holly's shoes caught his attention again, and as he headed out onto the road, he asked, "What's with the shoes? You always have on quite a unique pair, and though I admit I know little about women's style, I swear they never seem to match your clothes."

She held her feet up in front of her and wiggled them back and forth. "Don't you just love these? They're some of my favorites. At least in my top five."

"But—"

"I know. My shoes never seem to go with whatever I'm wearing. Yeah, I do that on purpose."

"Okay," he said. "But why?"

She gave a flippant shrug. "Because I like it. It also plays into my snap decisions about people. Some immediately turn their noses up when they see them. Others don't even notice. Quite a few are mildly amused, like you. And the last group, they love it."

"And what, exactly, does that tell you about people?"

She smiled, the look so brilliant that it filled the car and made him wish he was the type of person who was as genuinely happy as she always seemed to be. "It tells me who my friends are." She reached over and squeezed his hand where it curled around the steering wheel. "Thanks for noticing my shoes, Cody."

The girl was weird, but it didn't mean her sincerity didn't choke him up a little. "Did you just tell me your secret for your snap decisions?"

She laughed again. "Oh, honey, that's only one tiny factor in my decisions. But rest assured, I had you pegged the moment I saw you. Your interest in my shoes only sealed the deal."

"You are one odd creature, you know. Very strange."

"Yep." Her eyes twinkled with the word, then she changed the subject and kept up a running stream of comments seemingly about anything and everything as she directed his turns through the two-lane roads.

Ten minutes later they were pulling into Keri's subdivision, a newer one on the outskirts of town. Holly had filled him in on the fact that Keri had purchased the house one year before. She'd apparently lived in the apartment where he now lived during her first two years in town, then had upped and bought a three-bedroom, two-bath last year. Next thing everyone had known, she was pregnant and there was no father in sight. Word was that she had used a sperm donor.

And he wondered why he even cared.

"Oh," Holly piped up as she directed him through the maze of streets. "First chance we've had to really talk since the news broke. I almost forgot to ask."

"News? What?"

He caught a sly smile out of his peripheral vision and it dawned on him what she was about to bring up. He groaned.

"You're a daddy," she stated. She seemed to take some wild amount of pleasure from making that statement. "And you never had any idea?"

It was a question, but he didn't sense that she was really asking it. With a shake of his head, he answered. "Never a clue. Had this job opportunity not come up..."

He went silent. Had the opportunity not come up, would he have missed out on everything with them? Never even known them? He wanted to say no, but given the fact he'd avoided Lee Ann all these years, there was nothing to indicate he might have ever made a pit stop in town just for a chat.

And in that case, then yes, he would have missed out on everything with his daughters.

"Wow," she said softly. "I think whatever just crossed your mind was big. They're pretty special, huh?"

He nodded and made another turn. "They are pretty special."

She pointed to a cute two-story with a small covered porch and a large backyard, and he pulled into the driveway. "Tell me about Lee Ann, then," she urged.

"What about her?" He wasn't about to tell anyone that the woman from his past was constantly in his mind, begging to become the woman of his present. "She's a terrific mother. I imagine far better than the girls' real mother would have ever been."

He stopped and put the car in park, but neither of them made a move to get out.

"Of course she's a great mother," Holly stated. "Everyone has known that for years. But what I'm wondering is, what about her? You and her. Seems this was what really broke her heart when you left, instead of you simply not telling her good-bye, huh? Had to have been, given the timing of everything."

Yes. And everyone now knew it.

He wouldn't say too much about any of it for fear of making Lee Ann look bad in ways he wasn't even aware were possible, but he did sense Holly was asking more as a friend than a town mouth. And yeah, he would call her his friend, too, even though he would have sworn he didn't need one. He sensed the bond they'd formed came about because they had things in common.

She wanted to go. Anywhere but Sugar Springs if he were to guess, but to hear her tell it, she thought she was big city stuck in a small town. He'd been going his whole life. He often felt the same way as her during some of his contracts—big city in a small town. Only difference, he always had a plan to move on.

So far, though, he hadn't gotten a sense of needing to flee from Sugar Springs at all. Of course, he also had a short contract, and he had been aware of the terms of the agreement since day one. Less than five weeks and he'd be gone.

He paused. That thought didn't sit the same way with him as it once had.

Finally, he turned in his seat and propped his forearm across the steering wheel. He nodded, chagrin covering his face. "Yes, that's exactly what happened. She was the greatest person I'd ever known, and I did the worst thing ever. I don't deserve the time of day from her."

Holly studied him quietly. When she was pensive as she was now, Cody sensed a whole deeper level to her than the one she presented on a daily basis. He had a feeling she might have been hurt a time or two as well.

"Must have been a heck of a reason for you to do that," she guessed.

He'd once thought it was a good reason—not to cheat on her, but for getting so upset that it had led to that. Now that he was back and remembering just what he'd had, he was giving serious doubt to his prior thinking. With a shrug, he nodded. "Thought so at the time, anyway."

She gave a small chuckle. "Don't we all wish we could go back and have a redo?"

Ah, there was more to her. He didn't ask, and didn't sense that she wanted him to. It was merely one of those things.

"Funny thing is," she said, "she is giving you the time of day, isn't she?"

When he started to deny it, Holly went on, "And you're thankful every time she does. I see it, you know. Most people think you're just chasing her because it's convenient. They want to see her with a 'happily ever after' and are pretending you're stepping up to the plate. But I watch people more than most. I don't just listen. And I see something different."

His blood seemed to grow thicker. Fear almost kept him from asking, "And what is it that you see?"

She gave a small nod. "She's scared of letting you in, but at the same time that's what she's doing. Shopping, basketball practice, dinner...almost kissing."

"Geez, is nothing secret in this town?" he muttered. But it was a stupid question. Of course nothing was, he knew that.

"It's as if she can't help herself any more than you can," Holly finished, ignoring the question.

"We're just—"

"I get it. You're just parents to the same kids, and you're trying to get along and be friends for the girls' sake. Only, I think you want more. You both want more, if you ask me. And just maybe something stronger than both of you is at work here."

It was merely old chemistry reigniting—something they didn't get out of the way the first time flaring back to life, wasn't it? Hell, he had no idea what it was or what he was doing. But he also couldn't turn back at this point.

Holly put a bright smile on her face and pushed her pensiveness aside to return to being the fun girl he'd first met at the diner. "But you didn't ask me, now, did you?" She winked. "I'll shut my mouth. Just wanted to see if my accuracy percentage was going to hold up in this one or not."

"And what did you decide?" He opened his door. They'd been sitting in Keri's driveway for several minutes. No doubt someone on the street around them was curious as to just what was going on inside the car.

She grinned and winked again. "I think I'll keep this one to myself. It'll be more fun watching it play out."

She got out of the car and gave him commands on what to carry. He did as ordered. Something about the women of this town...He constantly found himself doing whatever they said. The notion made him think of Lee Ann again. He'd wanted to spend the day with her and the girls, but she'd said they needed a day off so that was apparently what they were having. And now he was here with two other women and a baby.

His life had definitely turned weird.

Holly didn't knock. Instead, she used her own key and let them in.

"It's me, Keri," she called out as they entered through the kitchen door. "And I have Cody. He's got the food."

Keri appeared in the opening to the living room with a very small baby held snugly in her arms and an exhausted glow shining from her face, and Cody instantly had another one of those visions he'd been getting lately. He wondered if Lee Ann had looked that happy when she'd held Candy and Kendra in her arms after they'd been born.

Probably it hadn't been quite the same given the circumstances at the time, but he could imagine her looking just like that today. Only with a baby the two of them had made.

Whoa. Where had that come from?

"Thanks for bringing all that food over, Hol." Keri gave her friend a smile. "Want to hold Eli while I see what I've got?"

Holly laughed and held out her arms. "I want to hold Eli no matter what you do. You don't think we brought all this over just because of you, do you?"

Both women went on about their business as Cody stood rooted to the spot, pans of food still warm in his hands. He wanted to make a baby with Lee Ann?

No. His head moved slightly in a negative shake. That made no sense.

He *didn't* want to make a baby. With anyone. It was just seeing this baby, and having recently discovered kids of his own...and Lee Ann again...It was understandable to mix them all up together like that.

But no, he didn't want a baby. Definitely not. And he didn't want that kind of relationship with Lee Ann, either. That would mean he'd have to change his life and possibly stick to one place all the time. A new mother wouldn't want to be constantly moving to a new city.

No, he didn't want—*couldn't have*—that kind of relationship with her. Or anyone.

His blood began to flow again, and he realized that somehow he was going to have to figure out how to have some sort of relationship with his kids, though, if with no one else. Because he felt the same way as the woman he was now watching—the one who'd given birth only two days before—looked like she felt.

Like there was no way anyone was going to take his family from him. Not if he could help it.

CHAPTER

"He won't stop flirting with me." Lee Ann collapsed into the pedicure chair and groaned. She fiddled with the controls to get the chair's massage rollers going but didn't bother with letting water into the footbath.

"I assume you mean Cody?" Joanie asked. She looked up from the paperwork she had scattered on the back floor of the salon, her hair blonde and red this week instead of black and red. Same cut, just a different base color. Lee Ann liked it. It wasn't quite as harsh.

"Of course I mean Cody. Who else around here would be flirting with me?"

A snort came from across the room. "Any number of men if only you'd take down the walls every once in a while."

"Well, I didn't remove any walls for Cody, yet that didn't stop him, did it?"

She wondered why that was. She hadn't put out signals that she wanted more than for him to be the girls' father, had she? When Joanie grabbed a bottle of bright green polish with glittery specks and held it up in question, Lee Ann waved her offer away. "I don't need a pedi, I just need Cody to leave me alone. He's been hanging around every day since he found out. Well, not yesterday. I told him not to come around yesterday."

"Ah, so that's why he hung out with Holly instead of you. I guess he hasn't changed as much as I thought. He still lets you control the situation, just like you used to."

"What are you talking about? I don't *control* the situation." And what did she mean he'd hung out with Holly? Doing what?

"I know, sweetie." Joanie pacified her as she flipped through papers, seeming to be accomplishing nothing but making a mess. "Of course you don't. You simply don't allow anything to be done concerning you or the kids without it being done your way. It was unfair of me to suggest that's controlling."

"Hmmm…" There was probably some truth to the statement. But that was only so the girls didn't experience hurt the way Lee Ann had. There was nothing wrong with watching out for your kids. "This kind of abuse isn't why I stopped by here, you know," she grumbled.

Joanie grinned. "Then tell me about this flirting business." She waggled her eyebrows up and down. "You like it, right? Is that what you wanted to talk about?"

"What? Come on, Joanie, of course I don't like it." She narrowed her gaze on her friend. "You're supposed to point out that he's a pig for even thinking about coming on to me. He's supposed to be concentrating on the girls, not on whether there's something sparking between the two of us."

"Is that what he said? Because I have to say—"

"Stop! I already heard about what you had to say, and I can't believe you told Candy and Kendra you thought Cody and I still had feelings for each other. Of course we don't."

"Honey, this is me." Joanie wadded up a piece of paper and tossed it toward a wastebasket. She missed. "I know how completely crushed you were when he hooked up with Steph. You loved him more than your life back then. And you didn't get any real closure from it."

"That was back then," Lee Ann grumbled. "I got over it years ago, so there's no closure needed." Only, it sometimes felt like there was. She'd even gone so far as to wonder if "getting him out of her system" would help her move on. But then, that was an immature and irresponsible thought. And she was neither of those things.

"Then why are we talking about it now?" Joanie asked.

Lee Ann didn't answer immediately. Probably because he'd gotten within a hair's breadth of kissing her senseless Saturday night, and she'd been more upset than relieved when the girls had interrupted them. She wasn't supposed to want to kiss him.

She readjusted the rollers to focus on her shoulders. "I just don't understand why he's trying so hard with me."

Joanie pushed a stack of papers to the side and stretched out her legs in front of her. Her green-and-black zombie socks flashed beneath her jeans. "And?" she asked.

"And what?"

Her reply was a subtle tilting of her head and arching of a single brow, and Lee Ann followed it up with a heavy sigh.

"And I don't understand why I want to flirt in return! Is that what you want to hear? His flirting thrills me and makes me want to retaliate. It makes me feel excited and alive and wanting to see how much fourteen years has improved his kissing skills."

Low laughter was Joanie's only response.

"But I don't want to feel this way, Jo. I'm not interested in him. He's my kids' father. That's all. I just want to see the girls happy."

"And how is he doing with that? Is he serious about trying?"

"He is. Strangely." She wouldn't have ever expected him to be so caring with the girls. "He's attentive. He asks lots of questions and really listens when they talk. And he seems to want to be around them all the time. He's going to dance with them at their party, just like they want."

The bell over the door tinkled as someone came in.

"Sorry, Jo," Linda Sue, one of the manicurists, called out. "We won't be long. I told Gina I'd touch up a couple nails real quick. She has a hot date tonight."

Gina Gregory, the loudest mouth of the county, strolled in behind her. "Hi, girls."

Joanie rose from the floor as both she and Lee Ann returned the greetings, then headed over to Lee Ann so that they could continue their conversation in private. She flipped on the music as she crossed the room.

"And the girls?" Joanie asked after she'd settled down in the seat next to Lee Ann, her own rollers rotating up her back and making her voice vibrate as she talked. "Are they happy?"

Lee Ann pressed the heels of her hands into her eyes and groaned. "Yes," she whispered. "They're thrilled. Kendra more than Candy, but Candy is coming around. She just sometimes spends more time listening to her sister and father talk than she gets to actually join in. He doesn't exclude her intentionally, but the two of them simply don't have as much in common."

Joanie nodded, then reached down to turn on the water in Lee Ann's basin and toss in some salts. "Might as well enjoy the soak while you're here." While she was leaning over in front of Lee Ann, she looked up. "What else?" she asked. "What aren't you telling me?"

"It's nothing." Lee Ann smiled. She loved having a friend who was so close that she knew her better than anyone. Joanie would never let her get away with anything. "It's just that he keeps bungling things, and it's almost funny to watch. But then I feel bad for him, because he's trying so hard."

"Like what?" She turned off the water in Lee Ann's tub.

"You know...things like offering to go into the store and pay for their unmentionables, or asking whether they've got boyfriends. *When boys their age are in earshot.* Embarrassing things. After they recover, they simply roll their eyes, but he really seems to worry about it."

"And you think it's cute?"

Lee Ann sighed. "And I think it's cute."

"And it makes him even more attractive?"

"Yes," she whispered. Everything he'd done since she'd let him into their lives had made him more attractive. "And I really don't want to be attracted to him after all this time."

Joanie turned to face her. "You mean after what he did?"

"Okay, yes. After what he did. I'm over it, but...well..." She shrugged. "Maybe I'm not *fully* over it, you know? I'm not angry anymore, at least. Haven't been for a long time. But he hurt me, Jo. I don't want to give him that chance again." Lee Ann leaned to the right and peered around the half wall partially separating the two rooms. Gina and Linda Sue were in the far corner and neither of them seemed to be paying attention to them, but chances were they had their hearing attuned to pick up whatever they could manage.

Lowering her voice to a near-silent whisper, she continued, "I should hate him forever. So why don't I? Why am I secretly thrilled that he's in the kids' life, and stupidly thrilled he's still attracted to me?"

Joanie propped her feet up on the edge of the footbath and stretched her legs out in front of her, the green toes of her socks practically glowing. "I can't explain attraction, sweetie. Nor why some people have the urge to be together forever. I guess it comes back to the age-old desire most people have to ensure they don't grow old alone."

"You think that's it? Some secret fear I'll be alone forever, so I'm jumping at the first chance to be with a man that I've had in years?"

"That would imply you see him as a forever kind of guy." She shot Lee Ann a sharp look. "You think he might stay?"

Lee Ann sighed. "No. I don't see Cody as someone who would even consider settling down. He likes his life. He goes where he wants when he wants. Seems to be responsible enough, but just not your stay-put kind of guy. Plus, why me?"

"Are you kidding me? Aside from the fact that you're the one who got away—"

"He pushed me away. He left."

"Regardless, honey, you're the best thing that ever happened to him. You have the biggest heart of anyone I know. And whether that man realizes it or not, he wants a woman who can love him just the way he is. Stupid mistakes and all."

Lee Ann dropped her head to the seat back and closed her eyes. Stupid mistakes and all. She didn't know if she could ever really overcome some stupid mistakes.

"Has he said anything more about that day? What set him off to begin with?"

Lee Ann shook her head, the lump in her throat making her words come out tight. "He brought it up the other night, but I deflected the conversation. I wasn't in the mood to hear it."

Joanie reached over and patted her leg. "Maybe you should hear him out, Lee. You were both pretty heated in here last week. I'm sure there were many things that should have been said that weren't. He probably needs to talk about it as much as you need to hear it."

"I don't want to hear it."

"Why? Because you're afraid he'll see you still care?"

"I don't want to care, Jo." She shook her head. "I don't."

"I know you don't want to, sweetie, but maybe you should just let it happen. See what's still there."

"And get my heart broken again?"

Shrill laughter caught their attention, and they quieted to do some eavesdropping of their own. The other women had moved to one of the nearby hair stations.

Gina primped in the mirror, plumping her hair with her good hand and holding two fingers of the other out to dry. "I was in Saturday morning with my nephew and his puppy, and I think I'm going to pay another quick visit. I'm considering my own pet and need some pointers, you know." She applied fresh lipstick and rolled her lips, puckering them as if planning to kiss her own reflection. They looked like two giant red slugs.

Linda Sue gave her a wide smile. "You'd better hurry, girl. I hear he's already got half the women in town lusting after him. He eats with Holly over at the diner nearly every day, and rumor is that isn't all. She was at his place yesterday. Arrived with him, and then they drove off together a few minutes later. And then there's..." Her voice chopped off, and Lee Ann saw her toss a quick glance toward the back of the building.

When Linda resumed the conversation in a whisper—though not nearly quiet enough not to be heard—Lee Ann and Joanie both leaned forward in their seats.

"You heard about Lee Ann, didn't you? He cheated on her with her sister back in the day. Had to have done. Those kids were born less than nine months after he left town. But word is, he's still out to get her, too." Linda Sue brought her voice back to a normal level, and Lee Ann and Joanie both leaned back. "So all I'm saying is, it might be too late to catch him."

Gina straightened from the mirror, smoothed her thin sweater over her hips, and readjusted her bra. Her breasts were like beacons, pointing her way to the nearest available man. "Honey," she drawled. "I just need to catch him for a night or two."

Joanie snorted as they watched the action.

Gina swished her hips toward the door with way more jiggling than she probably realized. As she touched the handle, the door swung outward from the other side, the movement propelling her into the chest of none other than the topic at hand. A shocked Cody automatically thrust his arms out as Gina plowed into his chest and hung on for dear life.

"Looks like she's already caught him," Joanie snickered.

The sight irritated Lee Ann, but only because Gina was so obvious. Some women needed to learn subtlety.

"You don't think he's really dating Holly, do you?" Lee Ann asked.

Joanie shook her head. "They're just friends. Linda just likes to spread rumors."

After more wiggling on Gina's part, Cody pulled her arms from around his neck and helped her on her way. With Candy following, he finally entered the store wearing a dazed expression.

Facing Linda Sue's wide-eyed stare, he stated flatly, "I need Lee Ann."

Candy pushed past him and hurried to the back chairs. "Mom, can I stay here with you?"

"Sure." Lee Ann reached for her daughter's hand and squeezed. "What's the matter?"

"Nothing." Candy shook her head, wearing a forced happy expression. "I just want to stay here while Kendra and Cody go to Dr. Wright's office."

"She said it was okay to stay at the house by herself, but I didn't know if you'd be all right with that." Cody stopped in front of her, and she craned her neck to take all of him in. "I convinced her to come up here."

Lee Ann nodded. "No problem. I thought you were taking them out for dinner, though?"

Cody had offered to hang with them after school today— basketball and cheerleading practice had been canceled, and he hadn't had any appointments after three—and then take them out to dinner. He'd invited Lee Ann, but she'd suggested that maybe it would be good for him to spend an evening with the girls only.

"I am. I just need to run back over to the office for a few minutes. There's a dog there overnight who's due some medicine in about thirty minutes. It won't take long."

"I told him I didn't want to go, Mom," Candy said. "He and Kendra can get something when they're finished. I'll just eat at home."

Lee Ann glanced at Cody's face and saw that he recognized the fact that his daughter didn't want to be with him tonight. She lifted her eyebrows at him in question. "That okay with you?"

"Sure. Whatever she wants." But his eyes said something different. He was hurt and worried at the same time, probably

just now beginning to realize how different his daughters were
from each other. He and Kendra had so much in common that
their connection was easy, but Lee Ann suspected Cody had no
idea how to reach Candy. She'd have to figure out what would
work and talk to him about it.

She winked at Candy. "Sounds like a good deal, only we
aren't eating at home. You and I will have a girls' night. How
about that?"

Candy scooted in beside her and hugged her tight. "Sounds
perfect, Mom."

❀ ❀ ❀

"Your dad's car just pulled up," Lee Ann yelled up the staircase
to Candy as she lowered the load of laundry to the bottom step.

Within seconds, her daughter hurried down the stairs. "Is
he coming in?"

"I don't know. Let's go see."

She and Candy had enjoyed a fun afternoon. After leaving
the salon they'd gone to Candy's favorite restaurant before
stopping for ice cream. Though Candy had enjoyed herself, Lee
Ann had been aware she wished she'd stayed with her dad, even
if he and her sister had been doing only what Kendra liked.

They stepped to the door and watched as Cody turned
around at the end of the dead-end street, then pulled to a stop
in front of the house.

"You know that just because they did Kendra's thing this
afternoon, doesn't mean he didn't want you around, right?" Lee
Ann dropped one arm around her daughter's waist.

"Yeah, I know. I just wanted to do something else. All
they do is talk about animals."

"It's hard not to talk about things you love, sweetheart. Especially if you're around someone who loves the same." But she would make sure he remembered to do something just for Candy in the future.

"I know," Candy said. Her voice grew even fainter as they watched Kendra jump from the SUV and wave, before the car sped off. "He didn't even say hi to me."

Nor me. "He probably didn't see us standing here."

Stepping onto the porch, Lee Ann reached back to keep the screen door from slamming but was shocked to find it slowly closing.

"Cody did that this afternoon," Candy informed her.

"Really?"

She gave a short nod. "Yeah. He also painted Ms. Grayson's porch rails yesterday afternoon. Kids were talking about it at school today. I think he's getting bored."

No. He fixed things that needed to be fixed. That was one of the qualities she'd always admired most about him.

Lee Ann hugged Kendra as she came up the steps. "Have a good time?"

Her daughter's face glowed. "The best! We ended up getting takeout and going back to the clinic. I looked after the animals that had to stay there overnight, then helped Dad prep for another procedure he's doing tomorrow."

"Wow, that's pretty exciting. You're going to know everything about being a veterinarian before you go to school for it."

"I know." She practically swooned with happiness. The excitement on Kendra's face thrilled Lee Ann as much as the dejected look on Candy's hurt her. She definitely had to talk to Cody. He may not have been excluding Candy intentionally, but he had to understand how bad it could get if he wasn't careful. Hurting even one of his kids was not allowed.

☙ ☙ ☙

The sound of the V-8 filled Cody's head as he sped away. Everything had been going along perfectly the last few days, and he'd just had one of the more fun evenings of his life... until he'd seen Lee Ann and Candy standing in the doorway. He needed to deal with issues with both of them but had no idea how to go about it.

The last thing he'd intended to do was hurt Candy's feelings, but he'd been able to tell by the way she'd run to her mother's side that that was exactly what he'd done. It had never occurred to him she wouldn't want to go to the office. Kendra had asked questions nonstop about the place since he'd met her. Since they were twins, he'd just assumed they would both be interested.

One hard lesson learned. Next time he would do something special for Candy.

He smiled as he passed his apartment and the office beneath. A week ago he couldn't have begun to imagine the pride he'd felt tonight as he'd watched Kendra studiously helping him out. The girl was going to make a fine veterinarian someday. And he'd be right there rooting her on.

The smile left his face as Lee Ann floated back to mind. She would let him in the girls' lives as much as he wanted, he was sure of that. He was equally positive he could convince her that it would be in their best interests to travel with him throughout parts of the year. But the thought of leaving Lee Ann here by herself left a strange feeling in his gut.

It would give her more time to pursue her photography the way she should have been allowed to do years ago. That could be good. Yet he couldn't imagine driving away and leaving her here alone. Not for any length of time. The girls were as much a part of her as was her constant need to structure the world around her.

He also didn't know if he could do anything else. First thing he had to figure out, though, was if what was going on between them was lust or something else.

Lust he could deal with. He suspected she could as well. They could sneak off for a few hours, get it out of their system and move on. But it could be more.

And if it was, he needed to know. Then he would figure out what to do about it.

He checked for oncoming cars and shot out onto the open road, glancing in his rearview mirror to make sure there was no sign of cops. He didn't need Barney Fife pulling him over tonight. He just needed to get out and go. Although he'd found Sugar Springs to be more tolerable than he remembered, he was not a small-town guy at heart. He needed to feel like himself again.

The needle inched close to eighty before he let off the pedal. A large part of him would always be the guy who didn't form attachments. To people or places. He liked to go. He'd been doing it since he'd been a kid. But what he'd discovered as he'd sat in the car pretending not to see Lee Ann and Candy was that there was currently only one place he cared to be. And one woman he cared to be with.

And that concerned him.

CHAPTER

12

"I'm going to be a few minutes late this morning, Holly," Lee Ann said into her cell phone as her mom came in through the back door. She came over on school mornings to see the girls off, since Lee Ann had to be at the diner when it opened. Tossing out a little wave to her mom, she returned to her task of filling her Crock-Pot for the evening's dinner.

"Only ten minutes," she added. "I'll still be there before we open."

She listened to Holly tell her to take her time, then said good-bye and disconnected. She'd come up with a plan after leaving the salon the night before, and she needed to talk to Cody to make sure he agreed. If he did, it would go a long way toward making Candy feel special. And the best time to catch him without the girls around was right after his morning run.

Since she routinely caught sight of him and Boss on her early morning walks to the restaurant, and since everyone made a habit of talking about how he finished his run at the same time every morning—which happened to be within minutes of her passing by his place—she'd decided to delay for a few minutes so she could catch him as soon as he finished.

"What's going on?" her mom asked. She moved to the counter and peered into the ceramic bowl to look at the potatoes and carrots Lee Ann had dumped in. "Beef stew?"

"Yeah. The temperature is dropping again, feeling more like it should be, so it'll be a nice night for it."

She was going to suggest Cody spend more time with the girls this week—just him and them—thus the stew. She would not be there for dinner, also ensuring the two of them wouldn't end up outside with a fire, darkness, and the setting for a mood that she did not want to feel.

Opening the door to the freezer, she studied the bread she'd prepared a few weeks back. It would be perfect with the stew, but Cody probably wouldn't want to mess with it.

"Looks like you're about finished," her mom said, not offering to help, but then she never had been much of a cook. "You're running late today."

She eyed her mother over her shoulder, hearing the question behind the words. If she told her she was stopping to talk to Cody, the whole town would know about it before she even got there. But then, if Ms. Grayson reported this one in before her mother did, that would also look bad for her mom. She did a mental eye roll, unable to believe that she was playing into the game.

"I need to talk to Cody without the girls around. Going to suggest he take Candy shopping for a birthday gift for her sister. I also plan to see if he'll watch them the next few evenings. Go through the daily routine with them. That'll give me some time to get up into the mountains before sunset and see if I can catch any good shots this week to go with the winter series I started last year. It snowed a bit on the higher elevations already."

It had been a while since she'd had any time just for herself.

"You're also thinking it'll give him a taste of fatherhood, I suspect." Her mother tapped the list Lee Ann had stuck to the refrigerator door. It contained the afternoon schedule for dinner, homework, and chores, along with the rules about what the girls were and were not allowed to do on a school night.

And yes, she wanted Cody to see that fatherhood was more than just handing over a check and showing up to play. Not that he'd given the impression he thought that, but so far it was all he'd had to do.

She nodded. "Something like that."

Her mom studied her, more serious than she normally was. "It'll also let you avoid being around him, I suspect."

Yeah, there was that, too.

The questions were definitely moving into gossip territory, so she put the lid on the stew, picked up her purse, and kissed her mom on the cheek. "There's no reason I'd want that, Mom. I'm perfectly fine being around him. Quit trying to make something more out of it than it is."

She headed out the door and up the street, then finally let herself breathe normally again.

Of course she wanted to distance herself from the man. His mere presence had become the only thing she could think about. Whether he was there in front of her or off doing who knew what, she couldn't stop thinking about the near kiss on her patio, nor about the fact she wondered what that kiss would have been like probably as much as he did.

As she neared his place, she slowed, suddenly nervous. He didn't know she was coming. She checked her watch. If she'd timed things correctly, he should have returned less than two minutes before. Hopefully she'd catch him before he hit the shower.

She climbed the stairs and rudely peeked through the storm door before knocking. He hadn't pushed the main door closed, and from where she stood, she could see Boss in the corner of the living room. He lifted his tail briefly and looked at her but didn't get up. Then she caught sight of Cody.

And her mouth turned as dry as the grass in a long, hot summer. With no rain.

He was in the middle of the living room floor, earbuds in place, no shirt on, and doing push-ups. Wow.

She couldn't help but watch. The man was a work of art. He also had a work of art. The tattoo scrolled over his upper arm that had been tempting her since he'd first shown up stretched and moved with each up and down motion.

Oh, God. She shouldn't have shown up there unannounced. She should leave.

Or she could watch just a tad more.

No...leave. She gave a short nod. Definitely leave.

Before she could force herself to turn to go, his gaze shifted and snagged with hers, and she was stuck. He didn't stop with his push-ups. And she didn't stop watching.

The man's body should be illegal.

Ten more and he shoved to his feet in one powerful move, never taking his gaze from hers. He removed the earbuds and wrapped the cord to dangle around his neck.

"You do know I'm currently Ms. G's favorite pastime, right?" He gave a nod to the door, and she realized what he meant. She was standing outside his apartment, peering in like a stalker. And Ms. Grayson was no doubt watching.

With quick moves, she opened the door, entered, then closed not only the storm door but also the wood one behind her. The instant she stilled, she felt like she'd just walked into a trap, yet she wasn't at all sure how to get out of it. Or if she wanted to.

Cody picked up a towel and studied her as he crossed the room, his jaw-dropping body moving with an easy grace she wasn't sure she had completely appreciated before. He stopped directly in front of her.

"Morning, Lee," he said, his voice rich and thick and tickling all her girl parts. "What are you doing at my house?"

She gulped. That tattoo caught her attention again. It was one of the tribal type that had been popular a decade or so before. She squinted, trying to make out the design in the middle. It was also done in the tribal markings but was something more than a mere pattern. She tilted her head and leaned forward. An animal maybe?

"Lee?"

"Oh." She jerked back and looked up at him. She'd forgotten to reply. "I needed to talk to you," she blurted out.

His bicep flexed and her thighs grew warm. He finally made use of the towel, but the slow swipes across his chest and shoulders only managed to capture her attention again.

What had she wanted to talk to him about?

Before she could do anything about remembering, she found herself pressed against the door, up on her tiptoes, with his mouth melded to hers. It was hot and gentle and feral and delicious all at the same time, and her heart pounded in her ears and her blood roared through her veins and every tiny last speck of her insides heated as if set to a torch.

He tasted like man, toothpaste, and a hard workout. He tasted like heaven.

Too soon, he pulled back, and she stood there winded. Instead of speaking, he merely gave a jerky nod. His jaw twitched. Then she clued into the fact that her arms had wound their way around his neck. She was clinging to him as if she would sink to the floor without his support.

With less than stellar grace, she lowered her arms to her sides and attempted to put a look on her face that didn't show everything she was feeling.

"What was that for?" she asked, the lack of strength in her voice giving away how much the kiss had affected her. She had yet to figure out whether she liked that he'd taken a kiss, but she was not unsure as to whether she had liked it. The man did know what to do with his mouth.

He tossed the towel toward a chair and grabbed a crumpled T-shirt off the floor. It was damp when he pulled it over his head—clearly the one he'd discarded immediately after his run—and it didn't help the matter of her still-discombobulated brain that it clung to every dip and valley across the broad expanse of his chest.

"For two reasons," he answered. It amazed her how steady his voice was, but she did pick up on the undertones of heat. If she had to guess, he had liked that kiss as much as she. "One, it was time. We both knew it was coming, so I figured we needed to get it out of the way."

His pause had her clueing into the fact that he was waiting on a response from her. She nodded, agreeing. When his eyes twinkled and his mouth quirked up, she realized that she'd just agreed that yes, they would have kissed eventually.

She narrowed her gaze. Did he have to be so smug? "Hope you got it out of your system."

He winked. "The first one, yes. But back to the reasons for it. Two, I figured that since we'll be the hot topic of the day anyway, I should at least get a taste of what we'll be accused of doing."

"What?" This finally broke her mind free of his way-too-impressive body, which was still standing in front of her...and that insane kiss. "What do you mean?"

His brown eyes smiled. "You came in and closed the door, babe. What do you suppose Ms. G thinks is going on?"

"Oh!" She jumped, stepping farther into the room and glancing at the door as if it had done her wrong. With a quick jerk, she opened it. "I didn't think about that."

He smiled again. "Then what *were* you thinking about, Lee?"

He was evil—there was no other word for it. Let a man kiss you until your toes pop and he thinks he's a God.

Of course, her behavior wasn't helping any—standing there gaping and tongue-tied. Forcing her mind to clear, she decided to forget about the kiss for the moment—and the fact he'd implied there would be more—and bring up the topic she'd come to discuss. It was much safer. Plus, she still wasn't sure what she thought about the kiss. Or the thought of future ones. She needed to think about both of those things more when she was alone and didn't have the distraction of him around.

She took a small step away, unsure if he'd gotten closer or if she'd done it herself. Either way, she needed distance.

"I wanted to talk to you about Candy."

This made *him* step back, and his shoulders drooped. Not a lot but enough to notice. "I did not mean to make her feel excluded, I swear," he said. "I had no idea. I thought she'd like coming to the clinic as much as Kendra."

"They're two different people, Cody. You have to remember that."

"I know," he responded quickly. "I know. I swear. I just..." He shook his head. "It didn't occur to me she'd hate it that much."

She wanted to reach out and squeeze his hand to offer comfort, but touching him at the moment seemed like it would be a bad idea. Instead she relied on her softened tone to give the same message. "She didn't hate it. She was merely tired of listening to you two talk about animals. It seems to be the main topic of conversation with you and Kendra most of the time."

He nodded, moving to the other side of the table and pulling down an oversized coffee mug. He held it up to her in question.

"No thanks. I'll get some at the diner." Which reminded her that she needed to hurry. Kissing hadn't been in her ten-minute schedule. "I had an idea last night that I thought might help with Candy."

"I had one, too," he said and put the cup under the one-cup coffeemaker, then pushed a button. It started dripping almost immediately. "While I was out running this morning."

She was impressed he'd already been thinking about it. "Yeah?"

"I'm going to call a concrete company and have a slab poured in the corner of your yard. For basketball."

Her eyes widened. "You're going to what? I don't want concrete in my yard."

But why she'd never thought to get a basketball goal put down in the driveway she didn't know. Candy always just went up to the school to play. "You can get her a goal if you want," she said. "We can put it in the back drive."

"That won't work unless we concrete the drive, too. Or put down blacktop."

She shook her head. "That's too expensive. I can't afford it, but the goal alone will be fine. And she'll love it."

"No it won't, Lee. It needs to be done right or not at all." His tone was belligerent, and she could see he had no intention of backing down. "If you insist it be in the driveway, then I'll pay to have it paved."

Irritation swelled in her. He didn't have the right to make decisions like that. It was her yard.

Trying to stave off an argument, she went with her plan. "How about we do something else, instead? She loves to shop for gifts for others, and with their birthday coming up she needs something for Kendra. I thought you could take her. There are several stores in town she could find something nice in."

She nodded her head encouragingly and smiled as she finished, trying to sell him on the idea, but he only sipped the coffee he'd pulled from the machine and eyed her over the top of the steam. Finally, he put the cup down and leaned back against the counter. He crossed his arms over his chest, drawing her attention to it again.

"You think shopping for one afternoon, something she'll be doing anyway even if it's not with me, is better than a basketball goal?"

"Well it's better than pouring concrete in my yard."

"For who?"

"For everyone."

He lifted a brow, and she was smart enough to know when she'd lost an argument. Candy would *love* a basketball goal, and she would also love for it to be done right. She took several deep breaths as she watched him. He returned to drinking his coffee, highly unconcerned, as if he already knew he'd won.

She let out an unladylike noise. "You're not paying to pave my drive."

Another brow lift.

"Fine!" she shot out, flinging her arms in the air. "Pour it in the yard. But you make sure they don't tear up any more than is absolutely necessary."

He nodded, his mouth remaining neutral, but she saw that the laughter had returned to his eyes. "Will do, babe."

"And quit calling me 'babe.' Why'd you start that anyway?"

He put the cup down and pushed off from the counter, and she began edging away. Her pulse took off at a run as he crossed the room and stopped in front of her. She didn't want to look up at him, but if she didn't she'd be standing there staring at his still-damp chest.

She lifted her gaze.

"Because you showed up at my apartment," he started, his dark eyes intense as they bored into hers. "And looked me over like you wanted to have me for breakfast."

He slid his fingers into her hand, which hung loosely by her side, and brushed his fingertips over the center of her palm. Her fingers curled inward, and her traitorous body shook.

"It's always on the menu, babe." He winked. "All you have to do is place an order."

She could not believe the audacity of the man. And she couldn't believe she actually gave brief consideration to the idea. It's not like them getting together in that way would really hurt anything. Just two people with some unfinished business they were working through.

Only, everyone in town would figure it out.

And she wouldn't be able to simply do it and move on if everyone was constantly looking at her as if they thought she wanted more. Because that's exactly what they'd do.

Stupid idea, anyway. She shot him a hard look.

"I am not hungry," she said, a little too emphatically. She decided it best to put the idea of the two of them naked together out of her mind and finish what she'd come for. If she didn't, she might find herself agreeing to a tasty meal as easily as her arms had twined themselves around his neck.

"I also thought it would be good for you to hang out with the girls after they get home the next few days. By yourself." She dug into her coat pocket and pulled out a house key. "I have dinner in the Crock-Pot and a list on the fridge of their evening schedule. I'll be home before they go to bed."

A small smile played with his mouth, but he didn't say anything. He simply reached for the key and plucked it out of her hand.

When it disappeared behind his fingers, she almost reached out to snatch it back. He wouldn't use it inappropriately—she wasn't worried about that—but knowing he could walk into her house at any moment made something inside her feel oozy and warm. And totally exhilarated.

❀ ❀ ❀

Cody directed the workers to the area where he wanted the concrete poured, then moved back to the patio as they began marking off and preparing the spot. He'd been lucky to find a crew that morning, after he'd gotten Lee Ann's approval, and to get them to her house before the girls got home from practice. The company had also agreed, for a small sum, to stay late and get the area prepped tonight.

Tomorrow they would pour, and then Friday Candy could play on it. He was almost as nervous for her to see what he was doing as he had been when he'd first met them. He might be completely wrong in his assessment, but he felt like this was spot-on what he needed to do to start winning her over.

And he had to win her over. He couldn't have one daughter thinking he liked the other better.

"What about this?" one of the workers called out. "You want to save it or just rip it out?"

It was a bush, and not a very pretty one at that. He started to tell the man to toss it, but then thought about the fact it was Lee Ann they were talking about. Likely the bush had a purpose. A reason she'd put it in the yard.

"You'd better save it, I suppose."

He glanced around the nearby area, trying to figure out where she might want it replanted, and caught sight of the Christmas lights and decorations that had been strung up along the front porch. He'd noticed them the afternoon before, along with a tree sitting inside the wide front window, and his first reaction had been annoyance that the three of them hadn't asked him to help. They'd apparently done the decorating when he hadn't been around on Sunday.

But then it had occurred to him that his coming back had been a lot of change for Lee Ann in a very short amount of time as well. She might have needed to have her normal traditions just to feel like she wasn't completely losing control. He could give her that. For now.

All in all, she'd been a trouper with the changes, letting him tag along and be a part of so much, so—yeah—he could give her the lights. Things would be different, though, next year. He wasn't sure quite how yet, but he did know he wouldn't be as easily pushed aside.

Reba came out of her house and crossed the yard. She wore boots up to her knees and a skirt that looked like a patchwork quilt, and he couldn't help but smile at the picture she made. He was never let down with her attire.

"Afternoon, Cody," she greeted him. "You've got quite the project going on here."

He gave a quick nod. "It's for Candy."

A curve lit her lips, and he couldn't help thinking that Lee Ann would age well. She and her mother were both beautiful women.

"Candy will love it." She motioned to the shallow, square hole the men were digging. "Sure hope you talked about this with my daughter first, though it would be highly fun to watch if you didn't."

Laughter rolled from his gut. "Yes, Ma'am. Talked to her just this morning. It was either this or pave her drive. The woman's too stubborn to let me pay for that, though."

"That sounds about right."

They stood in companionable silence for a moment before he pointed to the ugly bush the man had just carefully pulled from the ground. "You know anything about that?"

She nodded. "The girls brought it home from school in kindergarten. Each kid got a plant during conservation week. Candy's died, so they all threw their energy into making this one live."

Uh-oh.

"Lee Ann has far from a green thumb, but she worked hard to keep this thing alive." She cocked her head, studying it. "It's done well until now."

"I'm a dead man."

"Nah." She reached out and patted him on the arm. "You're giving her girl a basketball court. You'll be okay."

He eyed her, trying to figure out if she was pacifying him or not. "You think so?"

Blue eyes matching Lee Ann's glowed back at him as she nodded. "I think so. The fact you had him dig it up and save it is all that will matter."

"I would replant it if I knew where she'd want it, but she won't be home until later tonight, and chances are good I wouldn't choose the right spot on my own." When Lee Ann had told him she planned to spend the afternoons this week away from the house, it had bothered him more than he'd imagined it would. He was thrilled to have the time with the girls, but he'd discovered that he wanted that time with Lee Ann as well.

Planting a kiss on her had done nothing to change her mind about sticking around in the afternoons, either. Though if he had to guess, it would ensure she stayed out even later each evening.

As the kiss replayed in his mind—as he thought about how her lips had moved under his, about how she'd moaned and instantly curled her body into him—he couldn't be sorry. Even if it did make her try for more distance. He only wished he'd gotten his hands on her as well.

But he'd intended solely to get a taste. He'd needed to see if what he was feeling was only old high school fantasies or if there was more to it—if the chemistry was what he suspected. And he'd needed that with the force of nature after he'd gotten a glimpse of her watching him.

He'd been shocked to find her at his door as he'd finished his morning routine, and even more shocked that she hadn't turned tail and run when he'd caught her looking. When she'd stayed, the timing had struck him as perfect. He'd been thinking about her. Wanting her. And then she was there.

And now he knew there would be more kisses.

"Heard she stopped by your place this morning," Reba stated. The woman was not subtle in her probing. "Had the door closed tight. For a few minutes anyway."

He chuckled as he tucked the memory of the kiss back into his mind for additional scrutiny later. "You're getting nothing out of me, Reba. Whatever you and Ms. G have dreamed up will likely be better than what actually happened anyway."

"Hmmm...So something did happen?"

He didn't mean to, but he shot her a quick glance. Apparently she read the truth, because she clapped her hands and laughed out loud. "I knew it," she yelled.

"You know nothing."

"Au contraire, good man, I know my daughter, and I know a look of guilt when I see it. All I need to figure out now is if you instigated it or she did."

He was saved from additional embarrassment and possibly inadvertently giving away even more details when Candy and Kendra appeared around the corner of the school. They were talking, not paying attention to anything but their own conversation, and Boss saw them and took off at a run.

At the sound of the dog bearing down on them, both girls looked up and smiled broadly. They greeted Boss with hugs and loving scratches between the ears, letting him kiss them across their faces. Boss ate it up. Candy may not have been the animal lover her sister was, but she did like his dog. And that warmed his heart.

"Hey, Dad," Kendra shouted as she hurried the rest of the way to where he stood. Candy followed along a bit more slowly, scrutinizing the area where the grass was being scraped from the soil.

"Hey, kid." He hugged Kendra. "How was school?"

She rolled her eyes. "Bor-ing," she said, dragging the word out to express her point.

"Yeah," he agreed. "I remember those days." He turned his gaze to his other daughter and held his breath with anticipation. She didn't stop close enough that he could hug her, so he didn't make the move to close the distance. "How was your day, Candy?"

"Fine," she mumbled as she continued to eye the spot in front of them.

"What are you doing with our bush?" Kendra asked. She sounded more curious than upset. She really was very much like her grandmother. "We planted that right after we started school."

"I know," he began. "And I'm sorry. I didn't realize—"

"He's pouring concrete for a basketball goal." This came from Candy, said with a slight air of awe. She looked up at him. "That's what you're doing, isn't it? Putting up a basketball goal?"

He nodded. The look on her face said this was a good thing, but he waited, needing confirmation.

"And Mom said you could?" she asked.

"Mom said I could," he stated. "It'll be ready to play on by Friday."

Her eyes began to brighten then, and a smile stretched across what seemed like the entire width of her face. The unbridled happiness glowing from her loosened another part of his heart, and it took everything he had not to scoop her up in his arms.

He soon found he didn't have to, as she flung herself at him, thin arms wrapping tight around his waist.

"Thank you," she said, breathing the words. "Thank you. I love it."

Emotion stuck in his throat as he stood in the middle of the yard on the crisp late-fall afternoon and held his daughter close. The two of them may not have been perfect yet, but he had broken through. He'd taken a giant leap forward.

Kendra scooted over and accepted a kiss on the cheek from her grandmother, then smiled sweetly over at him as he stood there holding Candy close. It was a big moment.

"You're welcome," he said. Gratitude filled him for the life he'd found since coming back. He had two wonderful daughters and a woman he was about to chase with a very directed purpose. He wanted them. He wanted them all.

"It'll be okay if we replant the bush somewhere else?" he asked Kendra.

She nodded, her face glowing as much as Candy's. It was as if she, too, realized what it was she was witnessing. He wasn't taking no for an answer anymore from any of them. He was a man with a purpose, and he had three females to win over.

CHAPTER

13

"When's Dad coming over?" Candy dropped her backpack and basketball to the kitchen floor and headed for the pantry. Lee Ann's jaw unhinged as her daughter disappeared into the connecting space. She stared after her. When had she started calling her father "Dad"? Geez, what had she missed during the week?

It was Friday afternoon, the girls were just getting home from school, and they were all expecting Cody any minute. The basketball goal was supposed to be ready for use today, but everyone had agreed not to go near it until he arrived and checked it out.

Lee Ann eyed the backpack on the floor but didn't have the energy to point out that Candy needed to put it where it belonged. Her daughters would be teenagers in a week. That meant they wouldn't always do what she wanted, right?

She had to get used to that.

Just like she had to get used to Cody disturbing her life. She glanced out the kitchen window to the patch of concrete in her yard and shook her head with amazement. He had a way of talking her into things she would swear she didn't want.

Only, when she'd seen the excitement on Candy's face Tuesday night, she'd realized that putting up the goal had been the exact right thing to do.

She returned to putting away the dishes and answered her daughter's question. "I haven't heard from him today."

Except at the diner that morning. He'd made it a point to sit in her section every morning that week and had come up with one question after another, as if seeking excuses to keep her at his table. And everyone had noticed. The amount of speculation concerning them had reached a new high, as had the whispered comments saying that Cody was dating Holly at the same time.

She didn't think he was. They talked like easy friends when she saw them together, but then, she had been fooled before. She'd once thought he'd loved her and would do nothing to hurt her. That had certainly proved to be a mistaken belief.

Candy poked her head out of the closet, a box of animal crackers in her hand. "If he doesn't show up soon, can I go up to his apartment and get him?"

Lee Ann smiled, so proud of her daughter. Candy may have been more hesitant than Kendra to step in and take what she wanted, but when she made up her mind, apparently she wasn't going to sit around and wait.

"Absolutely." Lee Ann glanced back out the kitchen window. "Where's your sister?"

"She was talking to some boy and I didn't want to wait for her." Candy rolled her eyes. *"Derrick."*

"Your sister likes a boy?"

Candy shrugged. "Yeah. She's been writing his name on her notebook all week. I think he might be more into Jenna Hopkins, though. Jenna thinks he is."

"Oh." Lee Ann's heart thudded. She didn't want Kendra to get her hopes up and be crushed. Not so soon in her life. "Maybe I'll talk to her."

"*Mo-om.*" Candy made the word two syllables as if to get her point across better. "It won't help. She's got it bad."

A soft rap came from the front door, and Candy tossed the box of cookies to the counter. "That'll be Dad."

She was gone before Lee Ann could remind her to put the box back in the pantry. Instead of calling her back, Lee Ann put away the cookies herself. Next she grabbed the backpack off the floor and hung it on the stairwell pedestal as she made her way toward the sexy rumble of Cody's voice.

Catching the tail end of a hug, she hung back and watched two of the most important people in her life and wondered when Cody had once again become so vital to her. And why. Was it simply because he'd kissed her stupid?

No. She shook her head a fraction. He'd merely wheedled his way back into her life and back into her heart. He meant something to her again. And if she weren't careful, he would crush her once again on his way out. This time could even be worse.

Candy spun around. "Dad says I can try it out," she said. "Can I go now?"

She met Cody's eyes and saw by the shock in them that he'd picked up on the fact she'd just called him "Dad." The emotion on his face almost stopped her heart. The man did seem to want to be a dad to his girls. At least something good would come of all of this. He might not be around full time in the future, but Kendra and Candy now had a father they could talk to and share things with.

"Sure, hon," she said, then peeked back at Cody. They were about to be alone, something she'd avoided since he'd laid that wow of a kiss on her Tuesday morning.

"Woot!" Candy shouted as she raced back through the house. Within seconds, the back door slammed shut, and Lee Ann and Cody stood facing one another. The house creaked as if pointing out what a bad idea their being alone together was.

"Let's sit on the porch so we can watch."

Cody nodded and followed her out to the repetitive thumping of the basketball on the new concrete. She sat on the swing, realizing too late that she should have chosen a chair. Cody followed her down, his weight tugging against the chains as he sat, making her want to scoot in close, as she once had so willingly done. Moving in the other direction instead, she put a few inches between them.

Kendra came down from the school, saw Boss and Candy at the goal, then dropped her stuff to the grass and joined them with a squeal.

"Looks like you did good," Lee Ann said.

Cody smiled, a totally relaxed and happy look, as he leaned back and pushed off on the floor. "*We* did good."

The swing set off in motion, and she couldn't help studying his posture. She'd noticed a similar contentment in him throughout the last few days—one that hadn't been there before.

"We missed you this week," he said, his voice quiet and deep. It made the back of her neck tingle.

"You saw me every night. And every morning."

He eyed her, letting her know that neither had been what he'd wanted. "Only long enough for you to kick me out the door and shoo me home."

She couldn't help laughing, the sound light. It was easy sitting out there with him like that. "I beg your pardon," she teased. "My foot never lifted from the ground."

"Hmmm…good idea." He reached down and grabbed her ankles, lifting her feet to his lap and trapping them there before she had the sense to stop him. "The proverbial kick in the rear, then, but it was there nonetheless." He stroked the skin beneath the hem of her jeans. "I missed you. I missed talking to you."

She licked her lips and glanced back at the girls. She wanted to tell him that she'd missed him, too, but that would only wind up hurting her worse in the long run. Some things a girl just had to keep to herself. But she did leave her legs in his lap, because also, some things a girl just had to take. And she liked sitting there like that.

As they both watched the activities in the yard, Kendra moved to the edge of the grass to begin practicing a cheer, Candy dribbled and shot in a continuous pattern, and Boss loped back and forth between the two, tongue lolling out, looking as happy and content as did the rest of them.

Lee Ann caught her mom peeking out her kitchen window and tossed her a little wave, but appreciated it when she didn't come out to join them. It seemed like an evening for only the four of them…and Boss.

"You should have been here Tuesday afternoon," Cody said. "I'd been so worried I wouldn't ever win her over, but when she realized what the workers were doing, and that you weren't going to scalp the both of us for tearing up the yard…" He paused, shook his head in amazement and gazed out at his girls. "I swear, Lee, I thought her wrapping her arms around me that afternoon was the best thing ever, but she called me 'Dad' today."

Goose bumps lit her arms. "I saw."

She didn't say "heard" because it had been more than that. She'd seen what it had meant to him. And she'd loved it for him.

"Just remember," she said. "You don't need to give her things to make her love you. You can't buy it, Cody."

He cut his gaze back to hers. "You saying I still screwed up?"

"No." She gave him a gentle smile and reached to lightly touch his jaw. She liked feeling the roughness of the day's stubble under her softer skin. "Not at all. The basketball goal, and the concrete, were perfect. Both of them. I'm just saying don't make a habit of it, okay? Otherwise...well, they're kids; they'll take advantage. That's what kids do."

Without warning, the past crowded into her head. Her. Cody. Stephanie. They'd all been barely more than kids themselves.

As if his thoughts had followed the same path, tension became a thick cloud surrounding them. He snagged her hands and held them between both of his. "I made a lot of mistakes in the past, Lee, and hurting you..."

She shook her head and shifted to move her legs off of his lap, but he put a hand on her shin to keep her in place. "Don't," he urged. "We can't go forward without talking about it."

"We can't go forward, period."

His eyes hardened. "Why not?"

Why not? Wasn't it obvious? "We're two different people now, Cody. You have your life and I have mine. There's nothing left between us."

What a lie, and they both knew it. There was a lot left between them.

She ducked her head, hoping he wouldn't call her on it. He twined their fingers together and brought their hands to his chest, tucking them inside the open zipper of his jacket.

"You're wrong," he said. "We have two kids. Chemistry. A past and a future." He spread her fingers flat against his chest and held her hand there, his heart thudding strongly under it. "And we have this. My heart goes wild just being near you."

Her brain screamed at her to remove her hand. Instead she rubbed her thumb back and forth over the cotton of his shirt. She shook her head. "That doesn't mean anything."

"Yours goes wild, too."

"No, it does—"

Cody put a finger to the pulse hammering in her neck, cutting off her words, and whispered, "Every time, baby."

She concentrated on taking steady breaths. "We're too different. It would never work even if we did want it to."

"I do want it to."

The words were spoken urgently, forcefully. He put her hand back in his and curled her fingers over the top, then kissed the tip of each one. She could feel herself being pulled under.

"I don—"

"Don't lie." His entire body grew taut. "Don't lie about it. You know it's still there. After all these years, we'd be fools to let it go again without even seeing what it is."

"I didn't let it go the first time." She hated the whiny sound of her voice.

"I know." He forced her to look at him. "I did. I was weak. I was an idiot. And up until those two girls barged their way into my office last week, I've regretted those actions every day of my life."

"You no longer regret them then? Hurting me?" The words didn't cause the pain they once would have because she knew what mattered now was the kids, not the past.

He pressed a kiss to her palm. "I'll never quit regretting the pain I caused you," he stated. "Never. You deserved so much better than that. But I also can't regret the action that gave me those two daughters."

Her heart exploded at the quiet admission. His love for them shined bright. She nodded, letting him know she understood, and looked away.

"I need to ask you for something, Lee. Three things."

She was terrified to ask. Everything suddenly felt too intense. "What?" Her heart thudded.

"The girls." That was all he said for a moment, and she glanced back at him. The intensity in him trapped her. "Don't let me mess up. Nothing big. I know I will with little things, but stop me before I do anything major. Will you do that for me?"

She nodded. The darn man was going to bring her to tears if he didn't quit saying all the right things. "You do great already without any help from me, but yes, I will do my best not to let you go too off course."

She pushed out of his grasp and off of the swing. She needed space to breathe. He followed.

They ended up on the other side of the porch, standing near the trellis where her Don Juan rosebush bloomed late into the summer. They now stood where neither their children nor her mother could see them, and an itchy feeling began inside her. She should have stayed on the swing. It was safer than being tucked away in the corner with him.

He leaned against the house and looked out over her yard. "I also need your forgiveness," he stated flatly.

The tone had gone hard, causing her to tense. She was unsure if he was referring to the past and his sleeping with Steph, or to something else.

"It was purely innocent, I swear, but I did actually tell Stephanie there was a perfectly good foster care system if she was pregnant."

"*What?*" Lee Ann jerked around to face him, but her vision was as blurry as her brain.

He continued before she could reconcile his statement with the man she was learning him to be. "She was taunting me. Asking if I planned to marry her if I'd just gotten her pregnant."

She took a step back, but Cody's hand closed around her forearm to keep her from going farther. She didn't know if she wanted to get away from Cody, the memory of what he did, or simply the hurt of all of it.

"No excuse on my part—I know I did wrong—but she pushed everything that day. And I didn't for one second believe she would have had sex with me without being protected."

"And would you?" Lee Ann gulped in a deep breath, eyes burning from unshed tears. "Would you have married her had you known? Would you have said the same thing about the pregnancy?"

"No way would I ever have said that about the pregnancy. Absolutely not."

She wanted to shove him away from her, tell him he didn't deserve those girls after what he'd just said, but his recent actions told the truth. He was a natural father and likely would have been even then.

"What about her? Would you have married her?" She had to know. Somehow, she suspected that hearing that he would have would hurt more than catching them together in the first place.

Cody pulled her against him, wrapping an arm around her to keep her in place when she pushed against his chest.

He pressed his mouth to the side of her head, his warm breaths ruffling the hair at his mouth, and she stilled. Fear held her immobile.

Finally, he lifted away from her enough to speak, and his voice came out scratchy. "I honestly don't know what I would've done concerning the girls. Not foster care, but looking back at who I was then, I have no idea how exactly I would have handled it. But there's no way in hell that marrying Stephanie would have ever crossed my mind."

Her body was so rigid as it pressed up against his that it was beginning to hurt. She forced herself to relax. He was not a bad man. He'd proven that many times over since he'd been back. But he had made bad decisions in the past. "How can you be so sure?" she asked.

His silence went on for so long that waiting to hear what he had to say became painful. Finally, he wrapped his other arm around her, as if the first one didn't have her locked tight enough. "I couldn't have, Lee. I couldn't have done that to you. Ever."

A car drove down the road, and she gave a halfhearted tug back against his arms. "Let me go. People are going to see."

"No." The simple statement left no room for argument. "We aren't finished. Will you forgive me for that, Lee? And will you help me be a good dad? I want to share things with them, teach them things." He lowered his voice. "I want them to be as proud of me as I am of them."

Her heart melted. How could she say no to that? While staring at his chest—she couldn't stand to see the honesty in him at that moment—she nodded. "Of course. To both questions."

"Thank you." The words were full of emotion as he pressed another kiss to the side of her head, and she melted into him.

She laid her head on his chest as if it had suddenly grown too heavy to hold up. It would be so nice if the past wasn't in the way.

Silence permeated the air as they stood there, both thinking about the past and all it might have been, and she couldn't help but wonder if things could be different now. If they could somehow make something work. But it felt like too much time had passed. There were too many hurts between them. She would do best to put an end to the moment and move on.

"There was one other thing I wanted to ask from you."

"What's that? Birthday gifts for the girls?" She hoped to lighten the mood with the suggestion, but his body tensed against hers.

"Dang. I haven't even thought about buying gifts."

She laughed, unable to help herself. He sounded like such a boy.

"I love that sound," he murmured, as if talking to himself. He lowered his head, and his next words vibrated against her ear. "I want you to give us a chance, Lee. To see what we have."

Hair stood at attention down her arms, but not because of the words so much as the brush of his lips against her ear. "It's a bad idea." It was a token argument, and they both knew it. She had no real protest left in her.

"And I don't want to hide our feelings from the girls."

She stiffened. "They can't get their hopes up for something with so many odds against it."

"Why can't it work?" He slid the fingers of one hand along the curve of her throat. "We have chemistry, Lee. We care for each other. We have kids together. What doesn't work?"

It sounded so easy.

Fighting the urge to turn her head and reach for the lips still hovering near her ear, she silently counted to ten to get herself under control. When she succeeded, she spoke normally, trying to break the seductive spell he was weaving. "The girls and I live here. And you don't live anywhere."

"That's purely logistics. We can figure it out. I'll be here another four weeks, and then I have a three-month contract in Florida. While I'm there, we could see each other every other weekend or so. I'll have to see the girls anyway. I want to know that you'll be there for me, too. I want to try."

"But what if it doesn't work?" she asked. "I don't want to hurt the girls." Or herself.

"But what if it does?"

She struggled with that question because she knew the answer. If it worked, she could have everything she'd ever dreamed.

But if it didn't...she'd have another heartbreak. A grown-up one this time. Her chest ripped down the middle at the thought.

Attempting to keep a sensible head, she compromised. "We make no promises to each other or the kids. Not yet. Nothing but that you won't disappear for good out of their lives."

He didn't immediately answer, then gave a single nod. "Agreed."

His lips moved in, and she shut down her brain and lit on fire. With a moan, she leaned into the kiss, reaching for what she wanted, and let him show her with actions what his words had yet to completely convince her heart. He cared for her. A lot.

Wanting more, she opened wider, and he touched her with reverence. His groan reverberated through her as he held her against him, trapping her arms against his chest, and loved her mouth with a touch so heartfelt she wanted to cry. He was perfect—hard and taut and strong enough to protect her forever, if only she could be certain that he would.

She strained for more, wanting the kiss to never end. This was the most poignant moment of her life, and she didn't ever want to let it go.

Too soon, Cody's lips pulled back, clinging until the last second, but he didn't remove his arms from around her body. She couldn't bring herself to open her eyes and let him see inside her at that moment. Instead, a row of tears slipped from beneath the outer corners of her lashes and tracked toward her chin.

He released one arm from around her, and long fingers lifted to caress along the path of each tear, breaking her heart as much as making it soar. She was so scared.

"Say yes, Lee. Tell me you'll give us a chance."

She shook in his hands. Opening her eyes, she studied his serious face, wanting nothing more than to accept everything he seemed to be offering.

"There are rumors you're dating Holly," she stated. She didn't believe them, but she also couldn't let herself totally ignore them.

The corners of his mouth lifted. "And there are rumors I've already had you in my bed. More than once. Apparently you sneak out of your house at night, babe. People like to talk. You know that. But you also know I would never date someone else when it's your heart that I want."

That was a bold statement considering his past. But then... She blinked. Had that been the problem? Had he not been ready for her heart back then? Even though she'd already given it to him?

She met his gaze, and the brown of his eyes burned steadily into hers. "Say yes," he whispered.

She took in a deep breath. "We agree to nothing long-term? We'll see where this goes, then if the time comes, we'll reassess?"

His eyes softened, and he pressed warm lips to her forehead. "However you want to do it, babe. Just say yes."

She couldn't overlook the fact that as she stood there in his arms, kissed senseless, she was happier and more optimistic than she'd been since that day when she'd headed home as a teenager thinking her world lay happy and perfect before her. The irony was that he was making her see the very same sight, all over again. And it terrified her. But what was life if you didn't go for it once in a while?

She nodded, jumping off the ledge in a giant leap of faith.

"Yes," she whispered. "Yes." She then reached up and kissed the man, who now had complete power to break her heart into a million shattered pieces.

CHAPTER

14

Cody climbed the steps to Lee Ann's house early the next morning with two bags in hand and knocked on the door. She wasn't expecting him until after he got off work at noon, but he'd been unable to wait. They were going to tell the girls that they were dating. And then he had to actually wrangle a promise of a date out of her. He wanted to get her alone. The sooner the better.

When she didn't answer, he pounded on the door again and glanced at his watch. It was only six thirty in the morning, but as she was someone who was at work by six every day during the week, he'd expected her to be up. It had never occurred to him that her schedule would allow her to sleep in on a weekend morning.

When there was still no answer, he dug out the key he'd been using during the week, knowing it would tick her off when she found him inside her house, then quietly let himself in.

All was still, with filtered light just barely starting to make it through the windows into the rooms. He held the door and let Boss in, then pointed him to a spot by the couch and told him to stay. No need to wake anyone just yet. He'd get breakfast set out and then call them.

As he passed through the living room and turned left to head to the kitchen, he couldn't help but look back over his shoulder, hoping to catch sight of Lee Ann in her bed, rumpled in sleep. Instead he found the bedroom door open to a perfectly made bed, and no one in sight.

Well, dang.

He set the diner bags on the kitchen counter and went back to peek into her room. The adjoining bathroom was just as empty and spotless as the bedroom. He retreated and glanced up the stairs. The kids' bedrooms were up there, but would Lee Ann have also slept upstairs for some reason?

And then it occurred to him where she would be.

Of course she wouldn't have slept in. He'd known that wasn't like her. She would be in her darkroom, and chances were good she'd been there for a couple hours.

Breakfast could wait. They used to have some good times in her darkroom. He wanted to see if that option was still open to him today. Making his way back through the living room, he closed and locked the front door, then went into her studio. Sure enough, the lights were on, and the darkroom was locked tight. He rapped softly on the door and waited. If she was in the middle of some-thing, she wouldn't be able to let him in, but he had to at least try.

"I'll open the door in a just a minute" came through the door. "Is something wrong?"

Only that he wanted to put his hands on her and get a few more minutes like they'd had the night before on the porch.

"Can I come in?" he asked.

There was a charged pause from the other side, and then a slight noise as if she'd put her hand to the door. "Cody?"

"Uh-huh. Let me in. I want to give you a 'Good morning' kiss."

The thought was almost enough to make him forget breakfast. If he'd been thinking straight, he would have known this was where he'd find her early on a Saturday morning. He would have skipped the food altogether and come down solely to "help her out."

"I can't until I pull this last picture out. Did you use your key and let yourself into my house?"

And here it came. "I did." He paused. "But I brought you breakfast. Should I turn around and leave?"

He could hear her breathing. He couldn't help wondering if she was having the same illicit thoughts as he.

"Are you okay in there?" he asked. "You sound a little... winded. Not thinking naughty thoughts are you, Lee?"

Light laughter filtered through the door, and his shoulders relaxed. She wasn't going to send him packing just yet. "What makes you think I'd be doing any such thing?" she asked.

He pressed the side of his face against the door and imagined her on the other side doing the same. He needed to touch her. "I saw the way you watched me in my apartment the other day, babe. I know exactly what kind of naughty thoughts run through your head these days."

Her laughter sounded again, but this time it came out tight. "Give me a few seconds and I'll be right out."

"I'll be here."

While waiting, he shrugged out of his jacket and tossed it over the seat at her desk, and the photo on her computer screen caught his eye.

"Wow," he murmured to himself. He stepped behind her desk to get a better look as she came out of the adjoining room. He glanced up at her and pointed to the monitor. "This is amazing."

She stood beside him. "Thank you."

It was a shot of a mother dog licking the head of a newborn while at the same time eyeing the camera. Lee Ann had captured the pure exhaustion of the dog, along with the maternal instinct most females seemed born with. No one had better come near her puppies. "I want that."

"What?" Her eyes widened with surprise but then she shrugged. "Okay. I'll give you a copy."

He turned to look at her then and like always, she took his breath away. With one long step, he closed the distance between them and slid a hand along each side of her face. He leaned down and gave her a proper hello. Loving the fact she didn't discourage the kiss, he took more, roaming slowly over her lips until both of them were more out of breath than two people with kids in the house should have been.

"Good morning, babe." His voice was husky and that made him chuckle. He liked what she did to him. He'd forgotten how much fun it was to get up every morning knowing he had the right to hold her in his arms. "I missed you."

Rosy-kissed lips smiled back at him. "You were only here last night."

"Yes, but you kicked me out too early." He pressed another quick kiss to her mouth, fighting the urge to linger. "So I came back."

"I noticed." She giggled, then turned a serious eye on him. "Though I'm pretty sure you can guess that I didn't give you that key to let yourself in while I'm at home."

He held his breath, praying they weren't about to argue. It was too good a day to do anything but enjoy being with her.

Seeing her before he had to go to work was the way it should be. "I did knock first," he said. "A lot."

After several long seconds and another squinty-eyed look, her face cleared and a smile bloomed across it. She was beautiful. "I'm glad you came on in."

She rose up on tiptoes, her mouth seeking out his, and he kissed her again. He could do that all day. When she pulled back—far too soon for his taste—he remembered what he'd been looking at and pointed to the screen.

"Seriously, this is amazing, Lee. Why aren't you out there selling these?" And then he remembered the site he'd perused before coming back to town. "Or do you? Was there a page on your website where you have photos up for sale?"

"I have some old ones up. I haven't had the time to really pursue selling anything but portraits over the last few years." She leaned down and pulled the computer mouse to her. "I'll print you a copy."

"No." He reached to stop her, resting his hand atop hers. "Get me an eighteen by twenty framed and let me know what I owe you. I want to put it in Dr. Wright's office."

She frowned up at him. "I imagine Keri already has all the art she needs in the office."

"She'll love this," he stressed. His thumb caressed the soft skin covering the back of her fingers, and he wondered if she realized just how talented she was. She was a smart girl, so how could she not know? Or was it merely, like she said, a lack of time? Possibly a lack of connections. "I have a friend in Nashville who owns a studio," he told her. "I've no doubt she'd be interested in taking a look at your work."

She pulled her hand out from under his and stood up straight. "I'm not your charity case, Cody. I'll get you a copy made, but other than that, let's drop it, okay? Someday when I have more time, I'll do more with these photos."

"But I want you to do more now," he insisted. He grabbed her hand as she headed back to the darkroom and gave it a little squeeze. "You can do it now."

She turned to him, then lowered her gaze to his mouth. "Are you about finished lecturing me? I have a couple more photos I want to finish this morning. You can either come in while I finish or go away."

He wasn't going away.

🌼 🌼 🌼

Lee Ann didn't wait for Cody to follow but knew he would. They'd shared good times in this room. She flipped on the red light and went back to the chemicals with which she'd been working before he arrived.

"This used to be one of the places I could always find you. Either here or on the softball field."

He moved to stand beside her, and she caught his eye in the darkened room. She pictured the younger version of him watching her third-base plays from the fence. He'd rarely joined the others on the bleachers. "Not much has changed, though in the summer instead of softball I can now be found watching a mean game of street hockey."

Shock registered on his face and then he laughed out loud. "My girls are tough, aren't they?"

"That they are." She grinned at him, happy he'd shown up at her house that morning. She had missed him last night, too. He'd stayed for dinner, watched a movie with all three of them and then lingered only long enough to sneak in a quick kiss before he'd left.

Though she'd agreed to let the kids in on the fact they were going to give this a try, she'd been wary to do it last night, so had kept him at a distance. But she had agreed that they would have the discussion today. And then they were going to spend some time together, just the two of them. She wanted to get her hands on him. In a very bad way.

It hadn't occurred to her until she'd seen his handsome face on the other side of her door that they could sneak into the darkroom any time they wanted. Though Candy sometimes came in with her, it was mostly her sanctuary.

Before she went after what she *really* wanted for breakfast, though, she did have a few prints she needed to finish. She nudged him in the stomach to move him out of the way. "Scoot. I need to finish."

He took a step to his right, but not before Lee Ann acknowledged to herself how the light touch of him burned through her sleeve. Oh, she had it bad.

"Knocking you off schedule, am I?" he teased.

She gave him a smirk. "There is nothing wrong with adhering to a plan."

Though she was learning that she did like him occasionally messing with her schedule. Like this morning. It brought a feeling of excitement to her life that she hadn't experienced in a long time.

She went back to work. Cody scooted in beside her to watch as she dipped a picture in the chemicals. It was one she'd taken of the girls, their faces turned up and laughing while Cody had proudly held up one hand indicating where a fake bird should have been. He'd been telling them a story about his short foray into the world of magic.

"You took that at the mall."

"Yes." She'd taken many more with her digital camera, but had hoped these black and whites would turn out well.

"It's great." He reached toward the picture as she moved it to the next tray, but stopped. It couldn't be touched until washed. "Roy taught me that trick my senior year."

His foster parents had been some of the best people Lee Ann had ever met. The way Cody had left town had hurt them as much as it did her. She dipped another picture. When she had the photo hung, she said softly, "They were hurt, you know. When you left town."

"Nah." His tone was easy and casual, but Lee Ann saw the tightness in his expression from the corner of her eye. "They might have missed me working on the farm, but they were happier to see me go than to have to worry about me sticking around after graduation."

She turned to him then, and propped her hands on her hips. She waited until he squared up with her. "You do not believe that for one second. They were the sweetest people I've ever met."

He started to look away, but she reached up and put a hand to his jaw. The movement was enough to keep him in place. "They worked me like a slave," he said, sounding a bit childish.

"You tried to pretend that's all it was then, too, but even as a dumb kid you didn't believe it." She smoothed her hand over his jaw, loving the strength she found there. "They worked you to give you a sense of responsibility. And to keep you out of trouble." She lowered her voice until she was almost whispering. "And you were a jerk for leaving and never even saying good-bye."

Sad eyes roamed over her face before he gripped her hand, almost desperately, and pressed a kiss to her palm. "I was a total jerk to all of you."

She closed her eyes briefly, the past and the pain all rolling into one, as she remembered her own hurt. They needed to have another conversation about it before she could completely move on, but she didn't want to do it right then. She just wanted to feel. It had been too long.

She tilted her face up to his. "Kiss me, Cody."

He hesitated only long enough to decide how to start.

Large hands settled down over her shoulders, and he lowered his lips to hers. At first he just set them there. He touched her lightly—a nip on each corner of her mouth—and intense pleasure exploded behind her breastbone. She felt like she was home.

And she felt love.

Oh, no...She almost dropped back out of his reach. She still loved him? Oh, crap. It was going to kill her if he left again.

She vibrated in his hands when a low animal growl came from his throat, and he shifted his head for better coverage. He kissed her then, like a man barely hanging on to his control, and for once the past didn't come crashing back but the possibilities of the future. She wanted this with him. She wanted to wake up to a kiss every morning, go to sleep with the same at night—and have it all during the days.

She wanted forever.

And she wanted it to start now.

Her groan mimicked his and she stretched, reaching higher, wanting more. She wrapped her arms around his neck as his tongue played over hers, lighting her on fire and making her think of other places he could use that particular body part.

"Cody," she whispered. She tunneled her fingers into his hair. His hands slid along the curves of her rear, and he pulled her into him. He wanted her; there was zero doubt.

He backed against a counter and lifted his head. Dark eyes seared into hers. "I've missed you forever, Lee."

Pressure squeezed her from the inside. No—she shook her head. She didn't want to think about the past this morning, she just wanted to feel. With another quick shake of her head, she brought his mouth back to hers. "Kiss me," she begged. "We'll talk about everything else later. Right now just kiss me."

That did the trick.

In the next instant, his hands were everywhere, his mouth hot. He scraped his teeth over her lips before roaming down to her throat, his fingers leading the trail along the way, and she came to life in his arms.

Wanting more, she gripped the bottom of his shirt and shoved at it. Her fingers landed on hot skin and she had the brief idea of shoving chemicals and pans aside and making room up on the counter. He yanked his shirt the rest of the way over his head, pulling her attention back from what they could do on a countertop to what she could do with her hands. She was now free to explore what she'd only gotten a good look at earlier in the week. The man was built.

She roamed palms and fingers over him, enjoying the hot gleam in his hooded eyes as he watched her do it. When she reached his shoulder, a tingle raced down her spine as she traced over the pattern permanently drawn there. She saw it clearly now. The outline of an eagle was embedded in the center, and it struck her as so perfectly him. Alone and proud yet full of strength and courage. He'd had a rough childhood, and he'd made his own share of mistakes, but the man was strong enough to overcome. Strong enough to become the man she'd always thought he could be.

Gazing up at him, she saw the vulnerability he tried so hard not to let others see. He was wondering if she got the symbolism. If she'd figured out that he'd needed that permanent reminder to keep himself moving forward. Of course she did. She knew him.

With shaking fingers, she gripped the hem of her shirt and tugged upward. She wanted to be there with him, as vulnerable as he was, to show him that she thought no less of him for it.

Once she had her shirt off, she stood before him, jittery with nerves. He'd seen her breasts when they'd been younger. They'd made out as far as you could go without going all the way, but she was older now, and she knew he'd seen and done a lot more since those early years. She couldn't help but wonder how she compared to past women in his life as she stood there in her white cotton bra.

She also couldn't help but wish she'd invested in a few pieces of sexy underwear over the years.

Strong hands moved to span her waist as he took her in. His dark eyes went black. "You take my breath away, babe."

She smiled. Good response.

When she reached out her arms to him again, a noise sounded from another part of the house, and she remembered with clarity that they were in her own home on a Saturday morning, and her children were separated from them by mere walls.

What was wrong with her?

Before she could do it herself, Cody was pulling her shirt back down over her head and smoothing it into place. His hands lingered only briefly before he grabbed his own shirt off the floor and covered himself as well.

"Boss is in the house," he said, his voice tight enough she couldn't help but smile. She liked that she got him as worked up as he did her. "They're going to know I'm here."

She nodded. "And that won't take long."

As the words finished coming out of her mouth, Kendra yelled from the other side of the door. "Mom? Is Dad in there? Boss is out here, and there's syrup on the kitchen counter."

She looked up at him. "Syrup?"

"I brought pancakes."

"Then let's go have them." She forced a smile when what she really wanted to do was finish what they'd started. Looking longingly at the counter she had already determined to be the best spot, she sighed and answered Kendra. "We're coming out."

As she passed him, he reached out and snagged her hand. His gaze burned hot. "There'll be plenty of time later," he whispered. He cupped her jaw and laid another scorching kiss on her. "We'll make sure of it."

She nodded, giddy inside. He was darn right they would. "I'll get Joanie to keep the kids tonight."

"Then I'll take you out." He pressed his lips to the palm of her hand. "We're going out of town, though. I want you to myself, not sharing our time and everything we do with everyone who lives within a five-mile radius."

She grinned. "As long as we end up someplace horizontal."

She opened the door and walked out, leaving him gaping after her. He may have suspected she was ready for something more physical, but telling him outright was apparently a shocker. She couldn't keep her laughter inside. There were so many emotions running through her that some of them had to come out or she would combust before they got through breakfast.

CHAPTER

15

"These pancakes are delicious." Candy gave Cody a smile. He stood at the microwave, waiting for the last of the syrup to heat, but his daughters were already digging in. Lee Ann sat at the table beside them, watching him with quiet blue eyes. She'd been doing that since they'd all trooped into the kitchen. He was pretty sure she was as sorry as he that they'd been interrupted, and if her parting comment was anything to go by, they would remedy the situation that night.

"You think so?" He glanced around the table, forcing himself not to stand there staring at the woman he couldn't get out of his mind, and took in all of them. He then winked at Lee Ann. "Better than Supermom, here?"

"Hey!" She narrowed her gaze at him but did it without fire. "I don't do anything different than other moms. I do cook my own pancakes instead of bringing them from the diner, though."

He chuckled and lowered himself to the seat beside her. "You wouldn't want me to cook pancakes."

They'd come out of the darkroom earlier, doing their best to look as if they'd been in there working on photos only, but neither of the girls seemed to completely buy it. They'd worn the same suspicious gaze he'd seen Lee Ann turn on him more than once in the last few weeks. Yet they hadn't seemed upset at the possible conclusions they'd drawn. He'd taken that as a good sign to proceed with the discussion they'd planned.

"Let's see," he began, forking three pancakes and plopping them in the middle of his plate. "What do you do different than other moms? You work two jobs, volunteer for everything you can, and if I understand the gossip right, you're who everyone calls when they *just need some advice*." He slid an arm along the back of her chair. "I think it's time you quit the diner and focused more attention on your photography."

"Yeah, Mom," Candy piped up around a mouthful of sausage, and he couldn't think of anything he'd rather be doing on a Saturday morning than this. She slipped a bite of pancake under the table to Boss. "You're always saying how you don't have enough time to make pictures. You should do it."

"We've had this discussion already." Lee Ann gave him the evil eye, this time with intent. "Making pictures doesn't pay the bills. And as you can see, we do like to eat."

Cody dug into his food as he watched Lee Ann attack hers. "Do I need to give you more money?"

She jerked her head up. "That's for the girls."

"And providing a home and food *is* for them."

"I'm putting it into a savings account."

"If you're worried about savings, I'll set up some extra."

"I'm saving it for their college."

He fought the urge to grit his teeth. She was so intent on controlling every situation. "I'll still be around when they reach college. That money is for today, for all of you."

"I can't—"

"Quit your job, Lee, I've got you covered. Focus on what you really should be doing."

She lifted her chin. "Raising my daughters is what I should be doing."

Out of the corner of his eye he'd watched the girls' heads ping-pong back and forth, watching them as they'd argued. Neither had uttered a word, but he knew they could sense the difference in his and Lee Ann's relationship. There was a sharper edge now. He decided it was as good a time as any to tell them. Plus he needed to change the subject or he and Lee Ann really would start arguing, because he had a point. She needed to quit. She could rely on him now.

He focused on Candy and Kendra. "I asked your mom out on a date tonight."

Lee Ann gasped and jerked up straight in her seat. He probably shouldn't have caught her so off guard by putting it out there so bluntly, but there was no pulling it back now.

Kendra faced him, her eyes wide. "Really? A date?"

"Yep." Cody smiled and nodded before popping a bite of spicy sausage in his mouth.

Kendra high-fived him. "Way to go, Dad. Mom needs a boyfriend. She hasn't been on a date in years."

"Kendra Gayle," Lee Ann snapped, but Kendra didn't look her way. Good for her. She was independent enough to barely flinch as her mother tried to force her will.

"You agreed, Lee Ann. We're going to see where this can go, remember?" He winked. "See if you've still got the hots for me as bad as I have for you."

Her mouth flapped open and shut like a fish taking in water while both girls giggled.

"You also agreed to let our daughters know that we care for each other." His voice softened, took on more feeling, but he focused to keep it light. Wouldn't do for his daughters to see he was too big of a sap.

Kendra snorted, Lee Ann turned red, and Candy took pity on her mother and patted her hand.

He took in both of his daughters then and turned serious. "What do you think about that? You okay with your mother and me dating? We don't know where it may or may not go yet, but we want to try. See what's there."

And he couldn't help but think that it would work, because there was a lot there.

Once he headed to Florida, he'd fly them down occasionally, and he'd come back as well. His contract would put him off the clock at one on Saturdays and he wouldn't have to be back until Tuesday morning. With an early-morning flight, he could come up for two full days on weekends. That would have to be enough. For a while.

If he played his cards right, he might one day prove himself the man his foster parents had tried to make him into. Lee Ann had been right, they'd actually cared for him—unlike the foster parents in the other homes he'd been placed as a kid—and they'd been doing their best to see that he grew up to be responsible. If he were to be honest with himself, he could attribute a lot of what drove him through college to the Monroes, and until he'd found out they weren't around anymore, he hadn't realized that he'd wanted to run into them.

He would have liked for them to see that he'd made something of himself. See that their faith in him had paid off even though he'd been immature in the way he'd left, hurting and embarrassing them on his way out. They'd deserved an in-person apology, and the fact that he would never get to give it to them was something he now had to live with. Turning his mind back to the here and now, he pretended nonchalance as he cut off another bite of pancake.

"What do you say?" He looked from one girl to the other. "No promises at this point, but are you okay with us seeing if we can make a relationship work?"

Kendra answered immediately. "Will you promise not to kiss in public anymore?"

He was pretty sure his eyes bugged out as bad as Lee Ann's. "You saw us...uh...kiss?"

"Yuck, no," Kendra said, grimacing. "But Sadie texted us last night and told us her mom heard from her sister who heard from Gina Gregory that you two were practically eating each other's faces off on the porch. Not cool, Dad."

Lee Ann covered her face with her hand, but he suspected she was laughing as much as hiding embarrassment.

"And where..." he started, but had to stop and clear his throat. "Where did Gina Gregory hear it?"

Kendra shrugged. "Probably Grandma."

Yeah. Probably Grandma.

"Okay, no more kissing in public." He wanted to kiss Lee Ann any chance he got, but he had daughters to think about now. And he was in the middle of Gossip Central. He looked at Candy, aware she'd remained quiet throughout the exchange. "How do you feel? You okay with your mother and me dating if we promise not to kiss in public?"

Candy glanced at her mother, then back at him. "Does this mean you're not leaving at the end of the year? Or are we going with you?"

"We're not going anywhere," Lee Ann said, reaching over to pat the back of Candy's hand where it lay on the table. "Your dad and I are just dating."

He nodded, deciding not to bring up the idea of their visiting him yet. That might be too much to handle at once. "The rest we'll figure out when the time comes."

"But how do you date like that?"

"Well, I'll be here at least another four weeks."

Kendra rolled her eyes. "Dating for four weeks isn't enough. Candy's right. How do you date when you'll be somewhere else?"

"We'll talk on the phone," Lee Ann added. "And when he comes to visit you two, he and I will see each other then."

He glanced at her, hoping she realized that he'd be coming to visit all three of them, not just the girls. And then the thought of all the time he wouldn't be seeing them hit him. Being separated from any of them for weeks at a time would be rough.

Candy pursed her lips as she put thought into the matter. Before he could guess at what was going through her mind, she lasered her gaze on her sister. "I guess it's sort of like liking a guy you have no classes with. You rarely get to see him, but that doesn't stop you from going all silly every time he's near. Especially after he kisses you."

"Candy!" Kendra screeched and jumped to her feet. "You promised!" She was halfway across the kitchen before she stopped and muttered, "Can I be excused, Mom?"

Cody smiled into his hand at her manners, even though she was clearly distraught.

"If you think you have to," Lee Ann began, "but I would prefer if you'd come back to the table and tell us about this boy. He sounds pretty special, if you've let him give you a kiss."

Cody didn't point it out, but the deepening color on Kendra's face suggested it hadn't been a matter of her letting him.

"I'd rather not talk about it, Mom." Kendra remained in the center of the room, her arms wrapped tightly around her stomach and her head bowed. "Can't I just go?"

"In a few minutes." Lee Ann patted the seat where Kendra had been. "Come sit and tell us about him. Please?"

Kendra returned to the table and in very few muttered words, explained that he was an eighth grader who played basketball and that even though he'd given her just a tiny kiss, she didn't really think he liked her that much.

"He's the hottest guy in the whole school," Candy added for their benefit. Kendra shot her sister a deadly glare, but Candy only shrugged. "Well, he is."

Lee Ann rubbed Kendra's arm. "I remember the first boy I had a crush on. James Christian. I was in ninth grade and he was a junior."

A little sigh escaped from Lee Ann, and a tiny flare of jealousy breathed to life inside Cody. If he wasn't mistaken, James Christian was one of the two doctors in town. The unmarried one.

"But even though the thing I wanted to do most of all was run up and tell him how I felt, I knew that would just scare him off."

What? He eyed her. A seventeen-year-old boy would not be scared off if someone as hot as Lee Ann told him she liked him.

"Why?" Kendra looked at her mother, her face stricken as if she'd already made the biggest of mistakes.

"Because guys like to be the ones to take the first step. It makes them feel like they're in charge, but us girls have to be the ones to make it happen. We just don't let on that that's what we're doing."

What kind of asinine logic was this? "How old is this guy? Fourteen?"

Kendra nodded. "Almost."

"And you think fourteen-year-old boys are more comfortable making the first move?" he said, directing the question at Lee Ann. "While girls play some silly game trying to get their attention?"

"Of course." Her tone was short and to the point.

"Honey, at fourteen, boys don't need anything extra to notice girls." He turned his attention back to his daughter. "Whether you realized it or not, I guarantee you he noticed you well before you did him."

"But he didn't ever talk to me even though I waited near the boys' locker room three times."

He eyed Lee Ann. "That's because the *last* thing boys want to do at that age is take the first step and risk getting turned down. We're pretty fragile, even if we don't act it."

"I think you're too far removed from their age group, Cody." Lee Ann faced Kendra. "Trust me, sweetie. Be nice, smile, talk to him, but don't throw yourself at him."

He shook his head and stared straight into Kendra's eyes. "If you went up and kissed him first, he's already head over heels for you. Trust *me*. You've got his attention and he's wishing right now he had the nerve to call you up and ask you out."

Lee Ann gasped. "She's too young to date."

"That's not the point." He pulled out his phone. "Call him."

"Don't you dare. It's too early. She would have no good reason to call a boy this early on a Saturday morning."

"She calls him this morning because she likes him." He smiled at his daughter. "Trust me. That's reason enough, and he'll love it."

Kendra glanced at the phone in his hand, clearly uncertain about what to do. She chewed the inside of her lip and peeked at her sister. Candy shot him a look, studied him, then nodded. "I think you should do it."

"But what will I say?" Kendra whispered.

He opened his mouth to interject but caught Lee Ann's look. Instead of showing anger, the look was more tender. She shook her head and motioned at the girls as if to tell him not to interrupt the sisterhood while in the middle of a serious conversation.

Candy shrugged. "Our party is next Saturday. Ask if he'd like to go."

Kendra sucked in a breath. "You think he would?" She chewed the inside of her lip before asking, "You think I should?"

"He's hot, Kendra. And I think Dad's right. I saw the look on his face after you kissed him. He likes you. No doubt." Her eyes lit up. "I'll bet he'd dance with you."

Though he knew the last thing Lee Ann wanted was to see her daughters growing up, and certainly not by chasing after a boy, Cody was struck by the fact she didn't step into the middle of their conversation, even when Kendra tentatively reached out and took the phone.

She mumbled about having to look up the phone number, and then Cody glanced over at Lee Ann and winked. Their babies were growing up. Kendra liked a boy. A single tear in the corner of Lee Ann's eye was nearly his undoing. Had he messed up by pushing this? It didn't feel wrong. He stood and reached out his hand to her. "Let's give her some privacy."

Lee Ann followed without complaint, even putting her hand in his. He wrapped his fingers around hers and pulled her to his side. As they entered the family room, he bent to her ear. "Did I mess up bad?"

Shocking him, she turned into his chest. "Not at all. You're right. If she likes him that much, she shouldn't sit back and wait." She sniffed. "Though that boy's mother is going to kill me for letting her call so early."

"She'll get over it." He lifted her face and wiped away a tear. "Why are you crying? Did I overstep my bounds?"

She shook her head. "You were perfect. I was just moved by the thought my daughter is old enough to get her heart broken." More tears rolled from her eyes. "Oh, Cody. What if he breaks her heart? There's nothing I can do to make sure he doesn't."

"Sweetheart," he whispered and kissed the tears away. "You have to let them do it on their own."

"I know." Her voice wobbled.

"Trust me, it's not easy knowing what this boy thinks every time he looks at her, either." He gave her a slight grin before lowering his head and touching his mouth to hers. Warm lips quivered beneath his, and salty tears mixed with their kiss, but she didn't press for more, and neither did he. They merely clung to each other with the faintest of touches.

When they pulled apart, she tucked her head into his chest and he pulled in a ragged breath. She meant so much to him. Running a hand down her back, he struggled to find the right words to let her know how much he cared.

"Yuck," Candy said from the doorway, her smile negating the word.

Lee Ann made no move to pull away, so he gave her a little squeeze. "You and your sister never answered my question. Are you okay with me dating your mom?"

Kendra stepped into the doorway with her sister, a grin splitting her face. "We think it's the bee's knees."

He had no idea what "the bee's knees" meant, but it sounded like a good thing. And Kendra's mood seemed to have ratcheted up a couple notches. The call must have gone well.

Lee Ann grinned up at him. "We're the bee's knees. That's pretty darn good."

His throat grew tight as she glowed in his arms. "Fantastic," he mumbled. He needed to get her alone.

She put some space between them as if sensing his thoughts, but remained inside the circle of his arms. "So this boy, Kendra Gayle. What's his name and is he going to the dance with you?"

"Derrick Johnston. He said he'd love to." Her eyes seemed to melt as she confirmed what he'd suspected. "Is it okay that I said we could pick him up?"

"Absolutely."

Lee Ann's words and expression were exactly as they should have been, but her body was tense. Letting go was not easy for this woman. He tightened his hold in a quick, supportive way, and was rewarded with her body softening into his. She may not have liked letting her children make their own mistakes, but in the end she was willing to do the right thing.

"Now, I don't want to hear of you throwing yourself at him anymore, young lady," he said, his voice turning into what he suspected might sound like a father confronting his daughter's first date. All three ladies gaped at him, but he just shrugged. "He's a teenage boy. I don't want to have to hurt the kid before you get finished with him yourself. Any more kissing and he might think you're offering more than a *tiny* kiss."

Kendra's eyes widened, and she bobbed her head. "I promise." She gulped. "Can I...maybe...hold his hand if he doesn't do it first?"

Oh, Lord, he wasn't any more ready for this than Lee Ann was. He said "I suppose," but he wanted to shout "Keep your hands to yourself." "I'll go with you to pick him up. I'd like to meet him before he thinks he can dance with you."

She nodded, her head and long hair bouncing up and down once again, and he marveled at the fact he'd gone from having no connections to anyone anywhere to having two kids and was now going to be picking up a boy for one of them to take to a dance.

CHAPTER

16

It was nearing eleven when Cody turned his car onto Lee Ann's street and headed toward her house. They were as silent inside the car as it was on the darkened road before them. They'd driven the twenty miles over to the nearest town and had found a small but nice bar and restaurant with a local band. The music had been an eclectic mix, and Lee Ann had thoroughly enjoyed herself. If Cody's constant need to find excuses to touch her was a gauge, she'd say he'd enjoyed himself as well.

Though the night had gone perfectly, and conversation had never come to a lull, they seemed to have hit a rut. Neither had spoken during the last five miles as they'd neared her house.

Or maybe it was simply nerves. Lord knew she was nervous.

Should she invite him into her house? Suggest they go to his place? Were they actually going to make love?

She glanced across the cab at him and knew the answer to the last question. Yes, they were going to make love. She couldn't imagine either of them had the thought to do anything else. This was fourteen years in the making and she was more than ready for it.

He turned around at the end of her street and drove back up until they were directly in front of her house, then put the car in park and shut off the lights. He didn't turn off the engine.

Why did she feel like the seventeen-year-old she'd once been? "You're coming in, right?"

His fingers, wrapped tight around the steering wheel, loosened one at a time, and he seemed to be concentrating on breathing to match the moves. When the last finger released from the leather, he turned to her, and she almost melted on his seat at the look in his eyes. It was an enticing combination of desire, need, and desperate hope. But hope for her to *see* him—who he was, not simply that he wanted to be with her. "Yes, I'm coming in."

She nodded and reached for the door handle, but before she got it opened, his words stopped her. "You know everyone will know if I go in there with you, right? Are you okay with that?"

All was quiet on the street, and the few houses around them even had their lights out. That didn't mean one of her neighbors wouldn't wake in the middle of the night and notice Cody's car parked there or see it sitting right out front as they made their way to church in the morning.

Only thing worse than skipping church in a small town was skipping it to frolic with a man. Though she really thought she had a pass because, from what she heard, most bets were on her to win him over. They wanted to see her settled down with a "nice man," and the consensus was that Cody had grown up to be a nice man.

But everyone knowing also meant that the girls would find out. Not that they wouldn't guess anyway—they didn't live in the dark about such things—but she'd always been so careful to uphold good moral standards around them. She hated to relent on that now, yet there was no way she wasn't spending the whole darned night with Cody.

Her shoulders slumped as she plopped back against the seat and looked over at him. "What are we supposed to do, then?"

The streetlight caught his smile as he leaned across the cab and pressed a hard, quick kiss to her lips. "I need to run up to the apartment and let Boss out anyway. Why don't I let you out here, then I'll go get Boss, and he and I will walk back down. Either that or we can just go to my place. I just hate to leave my car in front of your house all night. It might embarrass the girls when they hear about it."

She liked that it was the girls he was concerned about and not merely the fact people would be talking about him. "Sounds perfect. I'll go in and..." She shrugged. "Freshen up."

He brushed his lips across her cheek, starting a trail of heat that quickly wound down her body, and she couldn't help but push closer and turn her face into his for a full kiss. He didn't disappoint. Too soon they were both overheating.

Getting caught making out in the car would be about as bad as having his vehicle parked in front of her house all night. "Go," she whispered, pushing him back from her. "Hurry. And bring back a toothbrush. I'm not letting you out of here until tomorrow."

His grin was lecherous. "Just don't plan on getting much sleep."

She fell one step deeper in love when he reached over and opened the door for her, then turned a serious face to hers. "Thank you," he said. "For giving us a chance."

🌸 🌸 🌸

Twenty minutes later, Cody neared Lee Ann's house, his feet dragging to the point that it almost made him laugh. He was a thirty-two-year-old man about to head inside and make love to the woman he'd never been able to get out of his mind, and he was more nervous now than the first time he'd been with a girl.

But these nerves weren't about performance anxiety or not knowing what to expect. They were about discussing the past, which he planned to do before they did anything else. He could see the love shining in her eyes. Love, he'd realized tonight as he'd sat across from her, enthralled by every move she'd made, that he felt equally as strongly. And because of that, he needed to share. He needed to let her see the real him if he ever hoped for this to turn into more.

He slipped silently inside the unlocked front door, Boss following at his side.

A light spilled out into the hallway from Lee Ann's bedroom, and after he got Boss settled in the front room, he glanced into the den where the Christmas tree glowed, white lights twinkling, and found Lee Ann standing there, waiting for him. He lost his breath at the sight.

She may have worn plain cotton under her clothes, but the thin robe that now draped her body did a fantastic job of molding to exactly the right curves. And if he wasn't mistaken, those curves were now unencumbered.

She stood nervously, her spiky hair looking as if she'd run her fingers repeatedly through it, then she pointed to the couch. "Let's sit. Talk."

Surprise registered as he realized she'd picked up on exactly what he had planned. He nodded and entered the room. They settled, both of them on the couch, and he grabbed her feet and tucked them in his lap as he'd done only the night before on her front porch. He knew she wouldn't think less of him when he was finished telling his story. She was too good a person to think that what happened to him was in any way his fault. But he couldn't help but worry she'd look at him and see someone different afterward. And he didn't want her to see the person who sometimes stared back at him in the mirror. The one no one wanted.

The lights on the tree cast the room in a romantic mood of soft light and shadows, but until he got everything off his chest, he had to ignore the ambience.

"You know I'm crazy about you, right?" he said. What a lame way to start. He almost apologized when her legs tensed under his hands, but he stroked a hand over her calves, soothingly, and plowed ahead. "I meant to say that..."

He paused. He actually wanted to tell her that he loved her, but found he couldn't quite put it out there like that. Something held him back. He switched gears, deciding to start another way.

"My first memory is with a couple whose last name was Franklin. I was four, and they had six other kids at the house, four of them like me. Foster kids. One of the real kids didn't like me and spent so much time harassing me that they finally had to send me back."

She scooted in closer and tucked herself against him. He felt himself relax. He dropped his head back to the couch.

"The second family wasn't much better. They had as many dogs as they had kids, and this time, it was one of the dogs that didn't like me. The rest of them were great, though. Even at that age I loved animals. I could escape the loneliness by hiding away with them, but every time I was in the same room with this one dog, he would almost take my leg off. Looking back, I suspect he had serious mental issues, because he did some other odd things, but nevertheless he and I didn't get along."

"What did they do?"

She asked as if she couldn't guess. He tucked his chin in and looked down at her. "They gave me back."

"Oh."

He put an arm around her and returned to staring at the ceiling. It was easier to think about the past if he couldn't see the sympathy in her eyes. "By family three, I was six. I started first grade with them. I was actually with them for a couple of years, me and another boy. And then they had a kid of their own."

Blue eyes looked up at him in question. He nodded.

"Yep, they sent me back. Both of us this time."

"Cody, I'm so sorry."

"Nah, nothing to be sorry about. It taught me a good lesson, made me tough. I learned early on not to depend. Not to want too much. It got me through."

"But it turned you into someone who eventually left the homes yourself, didn't it? Instead of waiting for them to tell you it was time to go."

Yeah, he thought. That's exactly what it had done.

"It had to have been tough," she nudged when he didn't answer her question. "Their sending you back. As a kid, I know how much you want someone to love you. How much not having that can mess with your life. Just like..." She stopped abruptly.

He glanced down at her, unsure what had caused her to stop speaking, and then he got it. "Like you wanted your dad to love you enough to come back?"

She nodded. "Yeah," she said but didn't elaborate.

"Tell me what happened," he urged. He had more to tell her, but he knew she needed to talk as well. That was the thing about the two of them, they'd always been so in sync with what the other did or did not need that it was scary. "I know he left when you were four."

She didn't speak for so long that he began to think he'd been wrong, but then she started, and his heart broke at the sadness in her voice. "He left because of me. I heard him tell Mom that. I'd been crying and throwing a fit about something earlier in the day, and that night I overheard him telling her that he couldn't take it anymore—screaming kids, everything a mess. He just didn't want to do it anymore, so he left. There one minute, gone the next. He didn't even say good-bye. And it was all because of me."

"Oh, Lee." Cody scooped her up then and pulled her fully into his lap. He pressed a kiss to her cheek and eyelids, wanting to comfort her, wanting to show her what he couldn't yet say in words. "It was he who had issues, babe. Not you. Never you."

One shoulder moved against him as she dipped her head and tucked her face into his neck. "Steph heard him, too. We were listening through the vent and heard everything. That's why she never quit hating me. I made him leave."

"No," he whispered. He closed his other arm around her and held her tight. "It wasn't you. Never could have been you."

🌼 🌼 🌼

The way his voice drifted off, Lee Ann knew he'd gone back to thinking about something else in his past. She hadn't meant to change the subject to herself, but she liked him holding her as she thought about her dad. It somehow made the memories hurt less.

And he was right. Her dad had been the one with the issues. But that didn't stop a little girl from wondering for years exactly what was wrong with her that someone who was supposed to love her could so easily walk away.

"Finish telling me about you," she whispered. She liked sitting there with him, and pressed a light kiss to his throat. "I remember you telling me about some of your later foster families one time, and I was struck by the fact that you always left within the first year. I thought you might have overreacted to a few of the situations, as if looking for a reason to blow up and walk out. I see why now—because of the pain of your early years. But I was right, wasn't I? At some point you started looking for excuses to leave."

He got the oddest look on his face before shifting his gaze to hers. "I never thought of it like that. I always believed I had perfectly good reasons to leave, but yeah, with years behind me now I can admit that maybe I blew some things out of proportion. I probably could have handled the situations better. You may be right."

She was pretty sure she was. His telling her about his early years had sealed it. The fact he still traveled from place to place now told her that not a lot had changed. Only this time he had his reasons lined up for leaving before he ever showed up in the first place. That way he didn't have to come up with one after he got there.

"Tell me about that day, Cody. I need to know what made you do it. What made you hurt me? What made you..." She sighed. *Walk away just like my dad.*

"Leave you?" he asked. "Aside from the fact that I messed up so bad you wouldn't want me around anyway?"

She nodded. "You didn't even stick around long enough to try to give me an excuse. You just left, almost as if relieved. I watched you from my bedroom window. You didn't look back. You walked out the door, got in your truck and drove away. I thought you'd come back later that day. Call me at least. But then I heard about what you were doing in town, and I knew. I knew before you even got out of town. You were making sure it was bad enough you couldn't stay. But why? Did you not want to be with me so bad that you'd have to do something like that?"

"No," he said, his voice heavy. "God, no. I loved you."

"You didn't. You couldn't have. Love doesn't hurt someone the way you did me."

"I did. I swear I did."

She shook her head, the sadness of years of loss filling her up inside. "You broke my heart, Cody. You destroyed me." And she wasn't sure she'd survive it if he did it again.

He pressed his lips to her temple and held them there. When he finally pulled back, his expression was grim. "I didn't like me very much back then. And even less that day. I loved you as much as I could, but maybe it's not possible to love someone enough if you don't like yourself at all."

Her vision blurred as she sat there watching him. He'd never made a habit of lying to her, but she felt as if he'd just been more honest than he'd ever been in his life, maybe even to himself.

"Then tell me what happened." It was no longer a question.

He paused, closed his eyes briefly, then opened them and locked his gaze on the tree.

"I'd just found papers Roy and Pearl had gotten somehow, about where I came from. I've no idea how they had them. Anyway, I found these papers and started reading. For some reason, I'd always had this image that my mother, when I found her, would explain to me that she'd wanted to keep me, but for some reason—money, a teenage pregnancy, whatever—she was forced to give me up. But I would find her, find out she'd regretted her actions and that she was thrilled to finally meet me."

"And I take it that isn't what the papers said?"

Cold eyes turned on her, and she could see that he was mentally somewhere else. She wanted to comfort him, yet he needed to get this out, whatever it was. They couldn't go beyond the physical if he didn't.

"What I read was that my mother kept me until I was two. And then she gave me away. Not when I'd been born, but after she had me for long enough to find out I wasn't worth keeping."

"Oh, Cody." She wrapped both hands around his face and pulled him close. She didn't kiss him, just caressed him and held him to her. "Maybe she had a good reason," she pleaded, not really believing it but wanting it to be true for his sake.

His entire body went rigid, and he once again focused across the room. "The other thing the papers said was that I had a brother, born on the same day. She kept him."

❀ ❀ ❀

Lee Ann didn't respond to his last statement, and he didn't know what to take from that. Was she horrified? His own mother hadn't wanted him but had kept another son who was apparently his twin. What in the hell had been so wrong with him?

And why had Lee Ann gone silent?

Finally giving in, he pulled his attention from the tree and shifted to look at her. Tears streaked down her face, leaving faint outlines of mascara tracking from the corners of her eyes.

"Shhhh," he whispered. He hated seeing her cry. She hadn't even cried when she'd walked in and caught him with

Stephanie. He hugged her tight, rocking with her against the couch and tucking her back into the crook of his neck. She made no sounds, but he felt the heat of her tears as they continued to run. "It's okay, baby. It was a long time ago."

She sniffled. "But how could she do that to you?"

"I don't know. I never did figure it out."

"You didn't seek her out then? Not even later after you'd calmed down?"

"What?" He reared back, pulling her out from him a bit at the same time. "Why would I seek her out? I hadn't been good enough for her once. I sure as hell wasn't going back for round two."

"But you have a brother. Didn't you want to know about him?"

The question made him stop. He tried not to think about that one. "There's a biological sibling out there, yes. But I don't know him, and he doesn't know me. There was no need to change that."

"Except he's your brother."

"And you had a sister. Did it make things any better for you?"

She flinched, and he felt mildly sorry about that, but it was the truth.

"She not only didn't care for you, but she blamed you for everything bad that happened in her life until the day that she died. And then she dumped her kids on you. Kids she'd had with *me*. On you." He shook his head. "Siblings aren't anything special, Lee. They're just additional people."

She nodded absentmindedly, then slowly eased back against him. "Maybe you're right, but I can't imagine the hole Candy and Kendra would both feel if they didn't have each other. There's a special bond there I can only ever dream about."

"They're lucky," he said, and he meant it. He brought a hand up to caress the soft skin of her cheeks, and she snuggled more deeply into him. "They not only have each other but they have you. They're lucky, Lee. More so than anyone else I've ever met."

"And now they have you." Her smile was small, but he appreciated the effort.

He nodded. "Now they have me."

Exhausted from the purging, and with Lee Ann seemingly just as drained, he lifted her in his arms. "Let me put you to bed."

"No." Her arm reached out as he rose, grabbing on to nothing but air. "Don't you dare leave me tonight."

"You're worn out. I'm putting you to bed. We'll have plenty of time later." Putting her to bed was the last thing he wanted to do, but it didn't seem like the time for more. Too much had been said between them tonight, and each needed to time to think, to adjust.

He reached her bedroom in a matter of steps and had a moment's pause when he saw the perfectly folded-down comforter and the crisp white sheets waiting beneath, both glowing in the muted light from the small bedside lamp. Beside the lamp was a clear vase holding a small bundle of fresh flowers. He'd seen similar ones at the local grocery store. The pragmatism of it all was so very typical of the woman in his arms.

Unable to keep the words in any longer, he peered down into her eyes. "I love you, you know. The right way this time."

A wobbly smile and more tears met his words. "I know. And I love you, too."

"No matter that you'd rather it be anyone else in the world but me?"

She shook her head. "That's not true. You have your flaws, but who doesn't? You're just as good as I always believed you to be. I couldn't pick anyone I'd rather love more."

He was the one who had to fight back the tears then. Without another word, he put a knee on the bed and set her gently in the middle of it. He tucked her bare legs under the turned-back covers, and when he moved to stand up, she reached out and stopped him.

"Lie down with me," she demanded.

There was no place he'd rather be. He shed the gentlemanly notions he'd had for all of ten seconds, then kicked off his shoes and stretched out on the covers beside her. "You're exhausted, baby. I've already kept you up way past your bedtime, and then I've put you through...all this crap." He kissed her temple and whispered, "You need to sleep."

"Maybe." Her eyelids drooped. "But you need to stay right here by my side. I'm not letting you run off so easily this time."

He chuckled, lightness knocking on his heart for the first time he could ever remember. Everything about his life was beginning to feel like it was falling into place. "I'm not running anywhere, babe. It's you and me. We'll figure it out together."

She let out a half laugh–half breath, and then she was asleep. He lay there for several minutes, replaying the conversation they'd just had through his mind and said more than one silent "Thank you" for having fallen in love with such a forgiving sort. Whether he'd found out his mother hadn't wanted him or not, he still didn't deserve to be forgiven the way he knew Lee Ann now had. Likely, he could never live up to the goodness that was her, but he had every intention of giving it his best shot.

After several minutes, he rose to turn off the lights on the tree, double-checked the locks on the doors, then returned to the bedroom and clicked off the lamp. He then undid the buttons of his shirt and stripped out of it and removed his belt from his pants. He climbed in beside her. He didn't want to be too forward, but he sure hoped they woke up in time to do what they hadn't gotten to tonight.

He may have the occasional gentlemanly tendencies, but he suspected he would have a very hard time following any come morning.

CHAPTER

17

Sunlight slanted through the open blinds, spearing Lee Ann's eyelids and letting her know she'd slept later than normal. She rolled to her side to check the clock and met Cody's sleeping face. Oh, yeah. She returned to her back.

The night before came back to her then, and she lay there soaking in the moment. What she hadn't told him was that she'd already forgiven him before he'd ever shared with her the why behind his actions. Though hearing that the boy who'd spent his life running—the kid who'd simply been trying to find a place to fit in—had found out that even his own mother didn't want him had cracked her heart in two. There was no way she could have held on to any residual anger after that.

Cody had been messed up when he'd come to town as a seventeen-year-old, and he'd been broken when he'd left. She'd only imagined she could tame him long enough to capture his love. The kind of love that stuck. But if his actions of late were anything to go by, he had finally reached a point in his life where loving him fully might be more than a pipe dream.

He loved her. And she him.

So where did they go from there?

She returned to lying on her side and watched him, appreciating the male form that lay beside her. He was on his back on top of the sheet, one arm thrown over his head, no shirt on, but his dress slacks from the night before still covering him from the waist down. The fastener and zipper had been loosened, though, and she caught a glimpse of what appeared to be navy briefs underneath. The sight made her mouth water as she wondered just what he'd look like without the pants.

The red digits of her clock showed that it was only seven, and that meant that since the girls were spending the rest of the day with Joanie—they were going to try out some cupcake recipes of Joanie's—she and Cody still had hours to make up for their change in direction of the night before.

She slipped quietly from the bed and padded to the bathroom, where she was horrified to look in the mirror and see traces of mascara running down to her neck. The man could have at least told her she'd dripped all over the darned place. She brushed her teeth and scrubbed her cheeks, then made a face at her reflection showing the bedhead she was sporting. Could she look any worse? Good thing she'd snuck out before she woke him up.

She did her best to fluff the flat side of her hair back into some semblance of order, then stepped back and took inventory. Not perfect but far better than when she'd entered the bathroom. It was the best she could do, anyway, without bringing out the heavy-duty stuff. And lazy Sunday mornings were not made for makeup and hair product. Cody would have to deal.

Flipping off the lights, she quietly opened the door but found herself staring at a hard chest and an eye-catching tattoo instead of a rumpled bed. His brown eyes were only half open, but he seemed to be awake enough to have the same thing in mind that she did.

"Good morning," he said.

Her blood heated. Yes it was. And she was tired of waiting.

She untied the robe and dropped it to her feet, standing there wearing nothing but the only pair of sexy underwear she'd been able to locate. It was a black-and-white thong Joanie had given her for her birthday a couple years ago as a hint that she needed to date. It may not have gotten any use before, but Cody seemed to be appreciating it very much now. He slowly scanned all the way down her body, and with each second that passed she got more turned on.

"Turn around," he said. The deepness of his voice caused her to involuntarily pull her shoulders back, pushing out her chest. It wasn't a large movement but enough to be noticed. Her nipples beaded.

"What?"

"Turn." He rotated his finger in the air in a slow, circular motion, indicating what he wanted her to do. "I need to see if the backs of those things are as hot as the front."

She was standing bare-chested in front of him, but he wanted her to turn around? She rolled her eyes. Whatever. Apparently he was an ass man. When she was facing the opposite direction, she bit her lip at his soft "Oh, yeah," then tossed him a look over her shoulder.

"That doing it for you?"

"Oh, baby." His eyes gleamed as they watched her. "Everything about you does it for me."

She completed the circle until she faced him once again. "Then please, tell me why you have yet to put your hands on me."

With a groan, he did exactly that. He reached out for her, clasping his hand on her bare rear, and pulled her into his own hardening body. His mouth fused to hers then, and she lost herself in the taste and feel of him.

Wanting still more, she slipped her hands inside the waistband of his slacks and pushed until they landed on the floor with a soft swish.

"They can keep my robe company," she whispered. She stepped past him before turning back to take in the full image. Then she took her own time perusing his body as he had done hers. She could spend hours doing this simple pleasure.

And it was navy boxer briefs, not plain briefs, but she liked them even better than what she'd imagined.

With an impish smile, she pushed down her thong and climbed onto the bed.

He was there almost before she was, sans underwear, and she laughed out loud, drunk on the thought of him— of them—and fell into his arms. The next second they were kissing and finished playing. His hands raked over her with a mission, touching her everywhere and setting her on fire.

"I want this, Lee." Intensity filled his words. "I want us."

She nodded and he reiterated, "I want us to work."

"I want that, too."

And she so very much did. Not only because he was the perfect man for her, but because he was the *only* man for her. No one else had even come close. She was as drawn to his loneliness and vulnerability today as she had been as a teen, and even more to the fact that he tried so hard not to let anyone see it. But she saw it, she always had. Because she had so much of the same running through her as well.

Not that she had ever been as alone as he. She'd had her mother after all, and everyone in Sugar Springs. But the fact she'd spent the better part of her youth pining for a father who wasn't worth the title had made her and Cody naturally migrate toward each other when they'd first met.

And it hadn't diminished a bit over the years.

Ready for more, she pushed against his shoulders and nudged him to the mattress. She rose up over him, one leg sliding over his stomach so that she sat straddling him. She wiggled against the hot flesh jutting against her backside and smiled when his eyes fluttered with pleasure.

"I have some exploring to do," she murmured, and she set about doing just that. She made sure there was nothing casual about it as she stroked and kissed and generally touched any which way she wanted. She was very meticulous.

"I love your tattoo," she said right before she leaned in and touched her lips and tongue to the pattern. The tips of her breasts brushed against his chest as she moved. She was feeling so much that it scared her, but she refused to back down. She didn't want this halfway. "It feels like you."

He grunted at her comment, but she didn't need him to say anything else. She'd already figured out the significance of the design the other night, and yes, the proud but solitary eagle suited him perfectly.

By the time she'd inched herself down to his thighs and eyed the part of him straining toward her, she was as turned on as he. She was wet and hot, and her thighs were like lava.

She dipped her head, making a low moaning noise as she moved lower, until she finally closed her mouth down over him. He groaned. Loudly. His hips lifted off the mattress as she stroked with her mouth, and she began to wonder if she'd pushed too far. He was ready to go.

"Though I appreciate your thoroughness," he said, his words tight and short, his breathing ragged. He gripped her shoulders. "I'm going to have to let you in on a little secret."

She looked up from where she was currently enjoying herself, feeling the power of what she was doing to him, then squealed when he flipped her over in one smooth move. She found herself flat on her back, her arms pinned above her head, and his free hand crawling down her body.

"You are not in charge here," he taunted. He missed nothing as his hand roamed, and she came darn close to losing her mind.

"Sure I am." She breathed the words. Her thighs parted as his fingers traced the lower perimeter of her abdomen. "I have you exactly where I want you."

Her body tensed from the core out. They'd played enough. She was going to come at the mere thought if he didn't quit teasing.

A lone finger stroked along the seam of her girl parts and she cried out.

"Hurry," she begged, suddenly desperate for him. But he didn't hurry. Instead his fingers continued to flitter over her, touching her everywhere but landing nowhere, while his mouth swooped in and latched onto a turgid nipple.

"Oh, God," she cried out again as she strained toward him. She thrashed her head against her restrained arms. "Cody, please." She couldn't catch her breath. His mouth was so insistent on her body, so perfectly right, and she was *so* ready. "Please. Now."

Blazing eyes captured hers, and he smiled wickedly. "I'm the one in control, babe. I could get you to do anything I wanted at this point."

She forced herself to focus on him and had to agree. And not just because of his skilled hands and mouth, but also because she loved him so much she wouldn't be able to say no if he asked. "Yes." She nodded. "Yes, you could."

A predatory gleam flashed on his face a second before he slipped a finger inside her.

The next instant, she exploded around his hand, her thighs clenching tight. He rocked the butt of his hand against her and thrust harder while she rode the wave until there was nothing left that could be wrung from her.

Her breaths were short and fast as she came back to earth, and she couldn't help teasing as she looked up at him. She smiled, but the action felt more like a satisfied oozing movement across her face. "Maybe I was in control the whole time. I am the one who just got off like a rocket."

A chuckle reached her ears, and then he leaned in and kissed her, both hands cupping her face and holding it captured beneath him. His touch was warm and familiar and so full of love that she knew she'd finally found someone she could put her trust in. Cody was there for her. And he loved her. She couldn't picture anything but happiness.

"If that was your doing, babe, I'm all for it." He reached for the wallet she'd noticed on her bedside table and pulled out a condom. "At this point, I can't imagine how anything will be better than watching you fall apart at my hands, so I'll take it. But you'll have to remember that I'm the one who gave that to you." He paused and held her gaze steady, his tone serious. "Me. I'm the one who makes you feel that."

She nodded. And she wanted it to be him forever.

Not ready to go there, she blinked and put a wide grin on her face as she reached for the packet. "Let's see what I can do for you now, shall we?"

His smile matched hers. "I'm all for that."

Instead of keeping it lighthearted, though, he slipped on the protection and stretched out over her. In one smooth motion, he joined them, and love pressed so hard against her chest it caused her physical pain. They moved together as they kissed, so perfectly in sync that it became difficult to breathe. She wanted so badly to believe she could have everything she'd ever wanted.

His hands reached for hers as he moved, his fingers sliding between hers, and he held them on either side of her head. "I love you," he whispered.

She nodded, unable to speak. He kissed her again, and this time they didn't let go until both of them were spent.

🌼 🌼 🌼

Lee Ann licked the buttercream icing from the tips of her fingers, then propped her chin in her hand and concentrated on Candy and Kendra in the adjoining room. They both sat in the middle of the floor with their legs curled to their sides as they smiled and cooed down at Keri's newborn baby. They'd all come over with Joanie. Instead of the normal Monday afternoon massage and girl talk at the salon, she and Joanie were bringing the party to Keri. With cupcakes instead of massages.

She turned her attention back to her friends and answered the question Keri had just asked. Was it good with Cody? A grin covered her face. "It was spectacular."

The other women sighed at the same time.

"But was it everything you'd built up in your head?" Joanie asked. She went for another dessert, picking out a chocolate cake with blue icing. "Was it the big wow we all are searching for?"

When she looked up at Lee Ann, there was no delay in the answer. Lee Ann's face heated in an instant. She nodded yes, it had been the big wow. And then some. She ducked her head in embarrassment as both Joanie and Keri squealed like junior high girls. All three of them busted out laughing when Candy shot them a hard look and shushed them. She was born to be a babysitter.

Kendra, on the other hand, turned from her spot in the middle of the oak-stained floor and watched the women, studying them with an air of interest. It was the same look Lee Ann's own mother often got when she was trying to decipher what was going on right under her nose for the sole purpose of sharing the info.

Oh, great. Now Kendra was joining the family business of gossip?

"Can I change his diaper?" Candy asked. Serious eyes burned steady on Keri. "I checked, and the strip on the diaper changed to green. He's wet."

Keri started to get up, but at the crestfallen look that came over Candy's face, she immediately lowered back down. "Sure," she said. "But do you know where everything is?"

"I figured that out when we got here. I checked out the nursery carefully as you showed us around." She nodded as if to assure Keri that she knew exactly what she was doing. "Is it okay if I take him in there and do it myself?"

Lee Ann sensed Keri's new-mother nerves over the thought of letting her baby out of her sight, but then also saw the relief that landed on her shoulders a couple seconds later. Candy was responsible, and Keri knew she could trust her to be careful. "It sure would be nice to have a break from diaper duty, even if it is just this one time."

Candy's eyes sparkled as she carefully scooped the baby up and turned to face them. "If Mom will bring me, I'll come over and help out all you want."

"You've got a lot going on the next couple of weeks," Lee Ann said. "But we'll try to get over another time or two."

Lee Ann watched her daughter as she stood with the child in her arms, and thought about the fact she'd been barely five years older than her when she'd had two of them to take care of herself. Sometimes she had no idea how she'd done it, and other times—times like yesterday morning as Cody had made love to her so tenderly—she wondered what it would be like to do it again. With him there this time around.

She shut down the thought for fear she would start depending on the idea of it, and he would decide his current life was more appealing than sticking around there would be. It was a conversation they would eventually need to have, but for now she wasn't worrying about it. She was in love, and things seemed to be going great. She was sticking with that plan until she couldn't.

Kendra hopped up and followed her sister to the other room, but not before glancing back at the women one more time. It wouldn't surprise Lee Ann to learn that her mother had put Kendra in charge of reporting back anything "juicy" that came out during the girls' afternoon.

"She sure is great with him," Keri said, her exhaustion evident. She couldn't hide the yawn that snuck up on her.

Pride gleamed from Lee Ann. "I'm not sure where she gets it, but yes, she is."

"Excuse me?" Joanie asked. "You're not sure where she gets it? Honey, that child is an exact replica of you. If I hadn't been there to know you truly hadn't given birth to her, I would swear she came from your blood."

Lee Ann looked at her, dumbfounded. "You think so?"

She'd often seen her mother in one or the other of them, as well as bits of Stephanie and Cody both, but she wasn't sure she'd ever thought about the fact each of them had traits that belonged solely to her. The idea made her happy.

Keri snorted and went for another of the cupcakes that Joanie had brought over. "You're blind, girl, if you can't see that. I wouldn't be surprised to see her carrying around a camera next."

She tilted her head at the SLR sitting at Lee Ann's elbow and gave it a pointed look. Lee Ann had made a lot of pictures when they'd first arrived, with the intention of getting the best ones back to Keri. She rarely went anywhere without at least one of her cameras with her.

"To tell you the truth," she replied, "she's already interested. I've been teaching her in our spare time."

"Of course you have." Keri reached over and squeezed Lee Ann's arm. "You're a great mother, Lee Ann. They're both terrific kids. I only hope I can do half as well as you."

It was as if the woman could read the niggling fear that had crept up lately. Being a parent wasn't easy, and with Cody in the girls' lives now, and seeing that they were learning new things and getting a more well-rounded life experience, she'd been worrying that she hadn't been doing a good enough job.

"Thank you," she said simply. "I appreciate that."

Joanie let out an exaggerated sigh but softened it with a quick one-armed hug. "Can we please get to the main subject of the day? Details, girl. We need details about the weekend. Make us jealous."

Lee Ann laughed, almost giddy to talk about the last forty-eight hours, the majority of which she'd spent with Cody, mostly just the two of them.

As she proceeded to share way more details than would probably make him comfortable, another part of her brain started working on the idea of what she might be able to do to convince him to stay. Of course he'd have to fulfill the contract in Florida first, but she was thinking about after that. She wanted to make sure he came back. And at this point, she couldn't convince herself his returning full-time would be a fact. He was too used to going. Running. And she caught that look in his eye occasionally that make her think it wasn't purely a thing of the past.

He didn't like to be in one place for too long, and with his past, she could see why, but she had to make sure he knew things were different now. She and the girls would never want him to leave. She only prayed he felt the same.

CHAPTER

18

Cody jabbed his fork into the coleslaw, his mind focused on one main topic. Lee Ann. How was he going to stand being separated from her for three months? And at the end of those months, what then? He knew what he wanted. He wanted her. Whenever and however he could have her. He wanted forever. Scary as it was, he couldn't imagine not knowing he always had her to come home to. But what he didn't know was how he was going to make that happen.

She would probably be reluctant to leave.

He looked around the diner, taking in the Wednesday late-lunch crowd, and admitted that staying wouldn't be the evil he'd once imagined. But it wasn't ideal either. There was not only the matter of being unable to step outside his door without hearing about it two hours later, but also the fact that he had no long-term job. He couldn't be the man he needed to be without a job that made him proud. He owed that much to his mentor.

The job situation, though, could eventually be remedied. There was more than one animal clinic or hospital within an hour's drive of Sugar Springs, so it would simply be a matter of being patient and waiting for an opportunity to open up.

Again, not ideal but doable.

The bigger issue was Sugar Springs itself. Did he *want* to commit to it? Forever? Because that's what it would be. The town was as much a person as anyone living in it. You couldn't up and move there if you weren't willing to deal with all its faults at the same time.

And, he had to admit, its bonuses. The place wasn't bad. Just nosy.

But what happened if the truce the townspeople seemed to have called on him was revoked for some reason? And yes, there had been a truce. It had started about the same time he'd realized he wanted more from Lee Ann than a past. He'd been pretending he hadn't noticed, but with the number of patients rapidly picking back up, he couldn't ignore it.

The thing was, there was zero chance he could go through the remainder of his life without making another idiotic, fool mistake. Would they turn on him when he did? He wasn't born and bred there, so he had to believe that would always be a possibility. He shoved a bite of shredded pork barbeque in his mouth simply to keep from growling out loud. Life could be so frustrating.

Then there was the other option. Could he convince Lee Ann to go with him? And if so, where?

He could see her not wanting the constant travel because of the kids, but he could also see benefits of that as well. As long as they weren't too disrupted during school, they would get a greater appreciation of the country than they could ever get there. And Lee Ann would be exposed to many opportunities for her photography. Though she claimed to be happy with her studio, he knew that deep down that wasn't making her the kind of happy she deserved to be.

So yeah, the idea had merit.

A plate of fries hit the table in front of him, and Holly plopped onto the opposite bench.

"You don't head over for lunch often," she said, stating the obvious.

He grabbed a couple of her fries. "Blocked the afternoon out to have a few hours off."

"That so? Wouldn't have thought you'd be able to, what with Sam Jenkins now singing your praises." She dumped a load of ketchup over the cut potatoes. "Heard business had picked right back up after you got his dog straightened out."

He grunted, not in the mood for company or to talk about Sam Jenkins. The day he'd come to the clinic, the man had worn him out. Cody must have proven himself, though, because from what he'd heard, Holly was right. Sam had been singing his praises.

That would stop, too, the moment he did something someone didn't like.

He peeked under the table to see what kind of shoes Holly was wearing, since he'd had to skip coming in for breakfast to get an earlier start. Well-worn *purple* cowboy boots went with today's ensemble. And nothing else about her attire was purple. He said nothing but noted her satisfied grin that he'd checked them out.

"I had some things I needed to do today," he said. He reached over and took another fry. "We rearranged the schedule, but you can rest assured no one was left untreated."

"I don't doubt your work ethic—that's been clear since you got here." Half her Diet Coke disappeared before she continued. "What I'm wondering is what's got the long look on your face.

After all, you're sleeping with Lee Ann now. Shouldn't you be smiling about that?"

Irritation burned in his chest. "Is there honestly nothing that can be kept secret in this town?"

She shrugged, looking a little put out at the fact herself. "Afraid not, Doc."

It didn't matter that people knew. He and Lee Ann were doing nothing he was ashamed of. But it did bother him that people were talking. It was nobody's business, but also it would get back to the girls. He didn't want them thinking less of their mother for a behavior he was pretty sure she'd do her best to discourage when they got just a bit older. Lord knew he'd be discouraging it.

He had to find a solution to the problem just to keep the kids from thinking his and Lee Ann's actions had to do with anything other than love.

"So what's eating you?" Holly's tone changed. It took on a deeper sincerity and he realized that when he left, he would miss her, too. She'd become a good friend.

"Just thinking about...things."

Grass-green eyes remained steady on him. "They've sucked you in, haven't they? You're going to stay. I can't say that makes me unhappy because I'd love to see Lee Ann and the girls with you. They deserve a guy like you. But man, am I the only one who honestly wants out of this place?"

"I didn't say that." The skin around his mouth tightened, keying him in on the fact he was frowning.

"But that is what you're thinking about, isn't it?"

He sent her a dirty look, but she only laughed.

"How the hell do you always know what I'm thinking?" he grumbled. Her mouth burst into a smile, and he realized she wasn't wearing her signature bright red lipstick. She looked good without it.

"I told you, I'm rarely wrong. I read people." One shoulder lifted in a small shrug. "It's a gift."

"Then what are you doing hiding it here? Thought you wanted to get out. Move to a bigger city, and you could find all number of people to read."

Why was he fussing at her to move? Was he afraid he wasn't going to get out, so he wanted to make sure someone did? That was a disturbing thought.

"I could," she told him. "And I will someday. Just need to find the right time. But I didn't sit down here to talk about me."

He ignored her. Not in the mood to put his feelings out on the table for her to pick at.

"What are you gonna do, Doc? You plan to make an honest woman out of our Lee Ann? Be a daddy to those kids?"

He looked at her then, and caught that she was once again serious. She was worried he was going to hurt all of them. Friend or not, he suspected hurting any one of them would be a nail in his coffin when it came to being tolerated in Sugar Springs. She would lead his march out of town.

"I'm already a daddy to those kids," he muttered. "And what I'm going to do is dance with them at their birthday party next weekend. Then I'll continue being the best father I possibly can, though I still don't know what I'm doing. I'm winging it, Holly. But I love it. I am a daddy to them, and I always will be."

She nodded, seeming to accept that he would be in their lives one way or another. A few seconds later, when he continued to ignore the other part of her question, she leaned down so that her face was directly in front of his. "And Lee Ann? What are you going to do about her?"

He shook his head. He had no idea what he was going to do. The thought of staying turned his stomach upside down. And, he had to admit, it was mostly fear that he didn't belong there and would never really fit in. But the thought of leaving was just as bad.

"I can promise you one thing," he finally said. "She has the power to hurt me as bad as I do her. So just keep that in mind as you're sitting there considering what catastrophes you want to befall me if this doesn't play out right."

She sat back in her seat and watched him through narrowed slits of eyes, then gave a small nod. "Oh, yeah, you've got it bad. That's what I thought."

With those words, she blew an air kiss in his direction and marched promptly back to the grill.

He grabbed another fry from the plate she'd left and shoved it in his mouth. Yeah, he had it bad. And if he didn't come up with a workable solution, he was either going to have to cave in and stay here—in a place that had already gotten rid of him once—or he was going to have to do some serious groveling and beg Lee Ann to come with him.

❀ ❀ ❀

Cody cursed as spaghetti sauce bubbled and splashed onto the back of his hand. It was Friday night, they'd gone to an afternoon basketball game of Candy's, and he now was attempting to cook a romantic dinner for Lee Ann. And it was turning into a huge disaster.

"Turn the heat down and it won't splash out like that," she suggested. She'd arrived a few minutes earlier, letting herself in, as he'd been trying to figure out how to get the spaghetti to go all the way into the water. He couldn't remember ever feeling like such a moron in front of someone.

He shot her a frown. "Maybe you should be the one cooking for me, since I clearly have no idea what I'm doing."

"Nah." She settled her rear against the back of the couch, looking sexy as hell in a straight knee-length denim skirt and pale yellow shirt. "I like watching you do it. It turns me on."

He checked the noodles and found them done, so he turned off the burner beneath the pot and returned to stir the sauce and meatballs one more time. The sauce splashed him again. "Damn."

A small hand glided around his waist and he jumped, the spoon following his movements and slinging sauce onto the floor. He hadn't heard her move across the room.

"I like it when a man cooks for me," she murmured. Her hands snuck under his shirt.

"Keep messing with me and this dinner won't be worth eating." If that turned out to be the case, he couldn't say he'd mind. Dating wasn't easy when there were kids involved. They'd managed to get together a couple times the week before, but it had now been nearly a week since he'd had her alone.

But he wanted to impress her tonight, thus his lame attempt at cooking. He had come up with a plan, and he was excited to talk to her about it, see what she thought. He sidestepped her wandering hands and went for the wine he had sitting out. After he poured two glasses, he watched her turn hers up. She drank it like a woman starved, then promptly returned to her prior journey. His chest.

And he was an idiot for trying to delay it. She had walked into his place turned on, and he'd done all he could to stick to the script. Screw the plan. He was a fool. He'd missed her, he wanted her, and best of all, she wanted him. There was only one solution to that problem.

He twisted the knob to lower the heat under the sauce as her hand dipped to the waist of his jeans.

"You'd really rather eat?" She pouted, which was so unlike her that he turned loose a very large grin.

"Hell, no." He palmed her ass and brought her to him. "You win, babe. But I get points for trying to be romantic."

The smile on her face struck him as a satisfied lion and he found himself wanting to roar. She wore that look for him. Nothing was a bigger turn-on.

"You can claim whatever prize you want for your romantic gesture," she said. "Just quit making me wait. It's been a really long week."

"That it has." He delayed no longer. He brought her body more fully against his, her toes dangling in the air, and searched out the secrets hidden behind her lips.

They broke apart a few minutes later, both needing air, but he didn't put her down. Instead, he searched her eyes and silently prayed she would like his idea, but that conversation was going on hold. Right now he had a woman he needed to love.

She locked her gaze on to his, and her eyes turned the color of the sky at midnight. "I didn't wear panties under this skirt."

"Oh, hell." Cody set her down temporarily, but only to reach to the bottom of her skirt and shove it up. He then scooped her back up, and she wrapped her legs around his waist. He shot a look at the kitchen table as he grew harder. "Not sure that table will hold us," he muttered.

"Take me against the wall if you want," she whispered. "Just take me soon."

He turned to the wall.

❀ ❀ ❀

Lee Ann twirled the waterlogged spaghetti around the tines of the fork and looked across the round pedestal table to Cody. He seemed about as impressed with the pasta as she was. She picked up the garlic bread.

"This is really good bread." She smiled sweetly when Cody narrowed his gaze on her.

"I didn't know noodles continued soaking up water if you didn't drain them soon enough," he complained. "I wanted to cook you a nice meal."

Lee Ann reached over and put her hand on the back of his. "You gave me something else even better, if that helps."

And he had. The round of lovemaking had been fast but powerful. Once they'd managed to free Cody from his jeans, he had in fact taken her against the wall. Then they'd showered, and he'd taken her against another wall.

After too many days without him, it was exactly what she'd been ready for, even if she had practically had to talk him into it.

Cody sighed and tossed down his fork. "That's it. Put your clothes back on. We're going out to eat."

"Out?" She hated to sound too excited, but the spaghetti was deplorable. "Well, okay. If you insist."

A hot smile covered his face and zapped the strength in her spine. Cody rose, snatched her skirt off the floor and tossed it to her. "Don't be cute or I'll make you pay for dinner."

"Yes, sir! Whatever you say."

His smile grew even wider with her words. "I like it when you talk like that. I could get used to it."

Lee Ann slid the skirt over her hips, then found her shirt and put it on as well. "Keep me a happy woman, Dalton, and you might have the opportunity to get used to it."

She'd meant it as a tease, but as the words left her mouth, she couldn't help but wonder what went through his mind when he thought about them and anything long-term. Did he really plan to come back after Florida?

Too many dreams were getting swept up in her mind, confusing her reality with what she wanted it to be. She had to know where they stood before she went much further. Otherwise she'd find herself heading down a path she'd ignored since high school, and she wasn't sure there would be a recovery from that one.

"What are we doing, Cody?" she asked. Her tone clued him in that the fun and games had come to an end.

He paused in the act of pulling on his shoes and looked over at her, then straightened to his full height. "I wanted to talk about that tonight, too."

A huge weight lifted from her shoulders. Good. They were on the same wavelength. That always made things better.

"I had an idea a few days ago," he started before she could say anything else. "One I think you're going to like. I already made a call to see if it would be possible and it is. They're just waiting for the go-ahead now."

Her breath caught when he'd said his idea was one he thought she'd like. And he'd already taken action to make it happen? Her breathing started up again, coming out in short bursts. "Is it not too late to get out of the contract? I wouldn't want you to leave someone in the lurch, like the previous guy Keri had lined up did to her."

Her words had grown slower as she'd caught sight of the look on his face. That was not what he'd been about to say. Dread curled in her gut.

"If not that," she started, narrowing her gaze on him, "then what?"

Cody crossed the room to where she stood in front of the door and took her hands in his. "I can extend my contract in Florida another two months, babe. I don't want to make trips back and forth all that time—I don't want any of us to. I want all of you to come with me instead."

Shock had her mouth hanging open before she got herself under control. "Why in the world would you extend it?"

"So the girls don't have to change schools in three months. Five months would keep them there through the semester. I confirmed this with the county down there."

"But you're okay with them changing schools now?"

"Wouldn't it be better to do it now than to wait for January or February? Plus, I want them to understand that what we're doing here"—he moved his hand back and forth between them—"it's not just casual. I want to set a good example for them."

She held up a hand, hoping to stall the words coming out of his mouth while her brain worked to catch up. He wanted her to uproot the girls—her—and just move to Florida with him?

"I want to marry you, Lee." He spoke quickly, as if realizing that she wasn't over the moon with his idea. "I want to be with you forever."

"Just not here?"

"No..." He cut off his words and tried again. "That's not what I meant. I think you'd like it in Florida. I've been there before, and there are so many beautiful places to explore along the coast. You could concentrate on your photography while the girls would get a chance to see another part of the country. We would be happy. I'm sure of it."

She shook her head at him, baffled. "Why do you think we'd like Florida better than we do here? And what are you thinking we'll do at the end of the five months?"

"Okay, wait." He held up his hand, and she had the urge to smack it out of her sight. He was ruining everything. "Let's slow down, and I'll start from the top."

"I don't think I want you to," she said. "I already know the answer. I can't take my girls out of their school, their home. Why would I do that to them?"

A look passed over his face that would have made her feel bad if she weren't already so ticked off. "You would do that for me. And you need to keep in mind they aren't just your girls. I have a say, too."

"Not in this you don't."

Dark eyebrows lifted, and she snapped her mouth shut. Was he threatening legal action if she didn't comply with his wishes? He'd better not be!

"Do not stand there and imply you could swoop in and take them from me."

"That is not what I'm saying." His voice had risen to match hers. "I've never hinted at that, and I have no intention of it. They wouldn't be the same if they didn't have you. There's no way I'd do that to them."

"Right. But you'd uproot them in a heartbeat. And then what? You'd want us all to follow you around every few months?"

"I'd want you to marry me and for the two of us to figure out how it can work. We have five months to get there."

"I don't need five months," she stated flatly.

At her words, his face grew taut. "Just like that? You're going to demand control and just shut down if you don't get your way?" He gave a harsh laugh. "You haven't changed at all."

"What are you talking about?" she said, spitting out the words.

"I'm talking about the fact you never give credence to anyone else's ideas but your own. You come up with something and barge forward without so much as a moment's consideration for what others involved might think."

"Is that so? And when exactly are you suggesting I've done this before?" She was yelling now, and so was he.

"When you made plans for us in high school! I didn't even know what I wanted to do, and you already had me mapped out to vet school and a marriage. I'm sure there were kids in there somewhere, too, but I never listened that far."

She gave a short, ugly laugh. "Yet aside from the marriage, which you made sure didn't happen by screwing my sister, you did exactly what I'd 'mapped out.'"

She air quoted the last two words, because she didn't think it had been as bad as he implied. It wasn't as if she'd railroaded over him. He'd been there. He could have told her he wanted something else if that was the case. All he'd had to do was say no.

But he'd never said anything. He'd only slept with her sister.

The thought brought her up straight. Was it her fault he'd slept with Steph? The irony that Stephanie had blamed her was not lost on her.

"I'm sorry, Lee." Cody had himself back under control now. "Let's back up. I shouldn't have said that."

"But you think it's true."

The movement was slight, but she saw his nod. "I was too messed up to be thinking about the future the way you wanted. And I had no idea how to tell you that."

"Is that why you slept with her then? Because of me?"

He reached out for her, but she stepped out of his touch. He sighed and dropped his arms to his sides. "I think I slept with her because doing that proved to me I was the worthless person I'd always suspected myself to be. The person I'd just learned I'd apparently been since a very young age."

She would have felt sorry for him if she didn't hate him at the moment.

Her breathing calmed, and she stood there in the middle of his kitchen, knowing that she was about to issue an ultimatum that had an almost perfect chance of backfiring. She was going to lose him again.

"Dammit, Cody," she muttered. "Why did you have to make me fall in love with you again when you weren't finished running?"

Hard eyes drilled back at her. "I haven't run since I left here the first time."

"You haven't ever stopped." She picked up the purse and coat she'd set down when she'd arrived and headed for the door. "I can't do this. The girls and I live in Sugar Springs. We'd love to have you here with us, but if you're too afraid you might have to face your own crap if you stay, I'll be agreeable to working out a deal where they can visit you on occasion. But they won't be changing schools and traipsing all over the country just because you're too scared to face your past. Where you came from doesn't matter. Things that happened out of your control don't matter. Who you are today is the only thing that will ever play into a future with us or anyone else you might let in. If you ever let anyone in."

Out of words, she turned to leave.

"Don't you dare walk out like that without giving me a chance to say my piece."

Hand on the doorknob, she turned slowly back to face him. In a flat tone she said, "Go on then. Tell me how it is."

"Dammit, Lee Ann." He paced across the width of the room, before spreading his arms wide and walking in a circle. "The entire town feels as small as this apartment to me. This closed-in. It's not me. Can't you understand that? This place isn't me."

"Why?"

He barked out a laugh. "I just explained. It's too small. I want more."

"You want to get lost in a place where no one knows you or has the thought to judge you. Because you're afraid you'll come up lacking."

"I'm afraid they'll be right!"

They both jolted back at the shouted words. Shock crossed Cody's face, and though the comment felt like it might be some sort of breakthrough for him, it was the end for her. She would accept nothing less than what she deserved. And that was everything. She'd spoken her mind, and now she needed to get home before she lost it.

She shrugged into her coat. "I love you, Cody. I couldn't hide that if I wanted to. I've loved you since the first day I saw you. But no, I will not uproot myself or my girls because you're too scared to do it right."

She yanked the door open. "Thanks for the offer of dinner, but I'll pass."

A thud echoed through the night as she slammed the door closed behind her. She'd just thrown down a gauntlet to the only man she'd ever loved. Take me or leave me. And she feared she knew the outcome. Her hands began to shake. She would soon have to figure out how to live without him.

Since she'd walked to his house, she had to make it all the way home before collapsing in misery. Ignoring any noises from houses she passed, she kept looking straight ahead and focused on putting one foot in front of the other.

How dare he be willing to give her a part of him but not all. He was so much better than he ever gave himself credit for, but she was tired of trying to convince him. She silently screamed at the injustice of it all, and as soon as she entered her house, she let the scream loose.

CHAPTER

The sound of canned air being pumped into latex was the only noise in the building as Lee Ann and Joanie inflated balloons. The birthday party was tonight. Cody would be there, would make Candy and Kendra ecstatic by helping make it *their best birthday ever*, and she would have to pretend her heart had not broken when she'd walked out of his place the night before. It shouldn't have surprised her that he'd not even given consideration to staying. He was a runner. Of course he would want to leave. But she'd honestly thought staying would at least be on his radar as a potential option.

Nope. He had only been concerned with figuring out how to get the three of them to follow him around until he decided he wanted something else. He may have loved them—in his own way—but if the man couldn't commit to settling down in one place, she couldn't see how he could ever fully commit to a person. And she didn't want only half of him. She'd rather continue on her own than go down that path. She'd already had a father who didn't stick around and a sister who'd hated her. She didn't need a husband who only gave superficially.

Lee Ann was content to remain silent, avoiding talking about the issue as she and Joanie worked, but she could tell Joanie had a different plan.

Joanie tied a ribbon to a silver balloon and attached it to the growing clump of pink and silver orbs the way Lee Ann had instructed before forcing the discussion Lee Ann had been doing her best to delay. "Okay, let's have it. What happened?"

Lee Ann kept her focus on the task at hand and her back to her friend. There was no point pretending she didn't know what Joanie was talking about, but she wasn't sure how to talk about it yet either. She also wanted to hold that pain all to herself a little while longer. It didn't seem fair to thrust it on someone else, no matter how well-meaning.

"Come on, Lee Ann," Joanie urged. She put a hand on her shoulder and squeezed, and that did it. The barriers were released. "Tell me what happened," Joanie begged.

Lee Ann's eyes filled with tears as she turned to her friend. "It's over."

She let the balloon go that she'd been working on, and as it squirted up through the air, she plopped down on the floor. "He wanted us to go to Florida with him."

Joanie lowered down beside her and nodded in a support-ing way. "But that isn't all that bad. He clearly doesn't want to be separated. Right? You could make something work. Go down there a few times, take some time off and let the girls spend spring break with him. It could work."

Lee Ann eyed her. "You aren't understanding. He wanted us to *move* there."

"Oh. Like, permanently?"

"Right, only not permanently either. We'd still leave after the contract was up, and then I guess we'd go wherever the whim struck next."

Her eyes rounded. "But you can't run all over the country chasing him."

"Exactly." Lee Ann nodded. "So I told him to choose. Me and Sugar Springs or not me at all."

"And he didn't choose well?"

Pain pressed inside her. "He didn't choose at all—not really. Just explained how he wasn't made for a town like Sugar Springs. So I put it out there, then walked out. I texted him this morning that I didn't need him to pick up the girls and the boy Kendra is bringing. I'll go get them myself. He simply has to show up and smile and be charming to his daughters' guests, then a dance or two, and as far as I'm concerned, he can go ahead and head on out to Florida."

"Except Keri still needs him."

Selfishly, she was hurt by that, too. She knew it made no sense. He'd signed a contract with Keri. But the thought that he'd stick around longer for someone else irritated her. If he wasn't going to be there forever, she was ready for him to be gone now.

Lee Ann rose and moved back to the helium tank. She had a party to prepare for, and sitting on the floor crying would not get it done. "He has to change, Jo. He's got to figure out that some things are worth sticking around for."

As she finished up with the balloons, her hands trembled with the thought of the hurt Kendra and Candy would soon feel. And there wasn't a darn thing Lee Ann could do to prevent it. She inhaled a shaky breath. It would be equally hard to help them while she went through the same exact thing herself.

❀ ❀ ❀

Cody took the stairs to his apartment two at a time. The party would start in less than thirty minutes and he was running late. He'd been finishing up some work he'd started the week before out at Buddy Sawyer's place and hadn't wanted to break before it was done. He was repairing a section of the man's fence around his property.

When he'd gotten the text from Lee Ann that morning telling him not to pick up the girls for the dance, he'd at first been furious. She couldn't just shove him out of their lives. But then he'd calmed down when it occurred to him she hadn't said don't come to the party, just don't pick up the girls. He could work with that.

So after he'd finished up at the clinic, he'd spent the afternoon doing manual labor and hopefully going a long way to making a man feel better. Cody didn't care what Buddy thought about him so much, but it did bother him that every time the two passed in town the older man still visibly shook with anger. That wasn't healthy, and it was his fault. He'd needed to fix it.

He'd also needed to keep busy purely to keep the argument between him and Lee Ann out of his mind. Because if he didn't do that, *he* was the one who got visibly angry. He was still ticked that she'd refused to even consider his suggestion. It had to be her way or no way. And that infuriated him.

It also scared him to death to think about the fact he was pretty sure she'd ended things between them last night. At least, if he didn't stay in Sugar Springs. He'd figured out after a busy morning at the clinic that staying focused on something else kept him from thinking too much about his own problems, and that's all he'd wanted today. Because walking away was going to be hard.

He couldn't quite convince himself he belonged in Sugar Springs, though, no matter what she'd said.

It would be nice if he did. That way he could stay and have a family. Have Lee Ann. Make her proud of him. He'd never wanted to let Lee Ann down again, yet it looked like that was exactly what he was going to do. Because he was afraid, just like she'd said.

He was terrified to invest 100 percent of himself in the place and have them turn on him once he couldn't go back. Losing everything at that point would kill him. And yeah, that probably meant he hadn't invested everything in himself and Lee Ann, either. Just like she'd accused.

It didn't make him stand up tall to realize that, but it was what it was.

He pulled his dirty shirt over his shoulders as he headed for his bathroom, then hung his head when he got there. Life without Lee Ann in it wasn't a life he particularly wanted to live. There had to be a solution. But right now he had to hurry. The *girls* were counting on him this time. Surely the least he could do was not let them down, too.

He reached in and started the shower but heard a knock at the front door before he could do more than turn the knob. His heart took off at a gallop. Lee Ann? Had she had second thoughts?

Since no one other than her ever came to his place, the chance of it being anyone else was slim, so he snatched a shirt out of the narrow closet and hurried to the door. But when he pulled it open, what he saw brought all the hurt and pain of the past back in a flash. The sight that greeted him was the same one he saw in his reflection every day. He was looking at his twin.

CHAPTER

Teenagers packed the building Lee Ann had rented for the girls' party. Music blared while boys and girls laughed with one another. A few ventured to the dance floor, but most hung back keeping the perimeter of the room company. Even Kendra had become too shy to ask Derrick to come out on the floor with her. They'd talked a lot of the night, but the boy looked terrified. Just like Cody had said. Funny how Lee Ann had never noticed that about them when she'd been that age.

She checked her watch and worked to keep a frown from her face. They should have cut the cake twenty minutes ago, but she hadn't wanted Cody to miss it. Where was he? She focused the camera and snapped more candids of the twins smiling over their gifts. Lee Ann had at least let them go ahead and open the presents.

Someone stepped quietly to her side, and the panic subsided. He was there. But when Lee Ann lowered the camera, it was Joanie she saw instead of Cody. And the look on her face was grim.

"He's still not here?"

Joanie shook her head but didn't make eye contact. Instead she nodded toward the heavy stove at the back of the room. "Don't worry about the fire. Your mom is keeping an eye on it."

The stove was the last thing on Lee Ann's mind. Yes, it was December and she didn't want the kids to come to a party and freeze, but the energy released from everyone in the room would keep them warm. All she wanted to know about was Cody.

"Where is he? We've got to cut this cake. Parents will start showing up within thirty minutes, and I can't have the guests going home without having eaten any cake." She glanced at her watch again, but only a minute had passed.

"Let's go ahead and cut it." A smile appeared on Joanie's face, her eyes a little too bright. "Let's do the cake and pictures, and then you can sit down and relax. You've been going all day. If Cody shows up..." Her voice stumbled. "He'll have to live with the fact he missed everything. And it was his own fault."

Lee Ann narrowed her gaze at the woman she'd known for most of her life. Joanie knew something else, so why wasn't she telling?

Before she could badger her for more, she watched Joanie's gaze latch onto someone across the room. Several couples were dancing now, and one of them was pushing the limits on appropriate. Reba surprised her by moving in to pull the two apart while giving them both an earful. Lee Ann wouldn't have even guessed her mother was paying that much attention.

She pressed her hand to Joanie's forearm, panic squeezing her and pushing a headache to the forefront, and whispered, "He's not coming, is he? What do you know?"

Joanie covered Lee Ann's hand and gripped it tight before finally replying. "I don't believe he is."

She couldn't speak. He wasn't coming. Joanie hadn't said why yet, but she didn't have to for Lee Ann to know it for a fact. With Lee Ann, she never said anything that might hurt her unless she was certain it was the truth. The air drained from Lee Ann's lungs. He had done to the girls exactly what she'd been afraid of. He hadn't been there for them. And they'd been counting on him.

How dare he? She would chop him off at the knees the next time she saw him.

"What do you know?" Lee Ann asked, her tone dead.

Again, Joanie didn't make eye contact. "I'm sorry, Lee Ann. I wish I didn't have to tell you this."

She'd never seen Joanie so afraid to say something. That alone made Lee Ann's words clipped when she spoke. "Just spit it out. What's he done?"

Joanie slipped her arm through Lee Ann's and led her to a corner where the music wasn't quite so loud. "I just got off the phone with Gina Gregory." Joanie gave a crooked smile. "What's the use of having the biggest gossip as a client of your shop if you don't take advantage of it on occasion, right?"

Lee Ann nodded as if she knew what Joanie was talking about. What did Gina have to do with anything? When she pictured the woman at the salon clinging to Cody as he came through the door, Lee Ann reared back, horrified. "He's out with Gina?"

"No, no." Joanie pulled Lee Ann close again and patted her arm. "No, nothing like...Well, I'm not sure...but it's not Gina. That's got to count for something, right?"

A brittle smile stretched across Joanie's face for a second before it crumbled. Lee Ann straightened her spine, outraged.

The man was out with another woman! Instead of at his daughters' birthday party! Instead of with her!

Her fingers shook as she pulled away and took a step back.

"Wait." Joanie's hand reached toward Lee Ann but fluttered back to her side when Lee Ann stepped even farther away. Joanie scrunched up her shoulders. "Don't you want to know the rest of it?"

A quick nod. "Oh, yes. Don't hide anything from me." The harsh voice coming from her throat surprised Lee Ann. "I'm not wasting one more minute of my life because of that man, so go ahead and spill it. Get it all out there."

Silence was the only answer for several long seconds, and then Joanie finally spoke in a low voice. "Gina said she'd just seen him at the Bungalow with Holly."

The Bungalow was the local watering hole.

"They were apparently...close."

Lee Ann paused and looked up. "Close?"

"Alcohol was involved, slow music, and no space between the two. In fact Gina said each of his hands had a butt cheek gripped tight."

Yep, that sounded like Cody.

Anger, jealousy, and humiliation all filled her at the same time, rolling her stomach upside down. The lying piece of scum. How dare he come back to town and do this to her again? She scanned the floor, where more kids had finally started dancing, and spied Kendra and Candy talking to some friends. The entire time they talked, they both kept an eye on the front door of the dance hall.

Doing this to Lee Ann was bad enough, but the girls would be crushed when they found out why he'd missed the party. She'd warned him not to hurt them. The man should have listened.

She snapped herself up straight. She was finished with Cody Dalton and would do everything in her power to ensure he never had another chance to come near her girls. They chose that moment to glance her way. She made eye contact while giving them the most encouraging smile she had in her.

Life would be okay for them—she would make sure of it. Just like she always did. She should have never even considered relying on anyone else.

She nodded to Joanie and moved toward the table. "Time to cut the cake."

❀ ❀ ❀

Bright light seared Cody's eyelids, forcing him to move from the bed, where he'd collapsed sometime late last night. The top of his head throbbed as he rolled over and checked the bedside clock. Ten thirty. Damn. He was too old for late-night drinking.

Remembering what he'd done the night before shamed him like no previous time in his life. He'd let his kids down. He'd let Lee Ann down. Rising, he dragged himself to the bathroom, splashed water on his face and squinted at his reflection. Red, hollow eyes echoed back at him. He was one dumb son of a bitch.

Dirty cotton had taken up residence in his mouth, so he brushed his teeth. After splashing more water on his face, he thought he could stand long enough to move through the apartment and see if his brother had returned or gone home with Holly. He made his way down the hallway, the space seeming more narrow than usual, then silently stared at the man sprawled out on the faded couch. Cody fought the urge to pack his bags and get out of town. Leave before facing anyone. But strangely, even though he had panicked last night at the sight of him, there was a small glimmer of hope deep in his gut.

He had a twin brother.

Nick Dalton.

And the man had wondered about Cody enough to hunt him up.

Cody scrubbed his hands over his face and opened the door to let Boss out to relieve himself. He needed to call Lee Ann. Apologize. Huh, like that would do any good. But he couldn't ignore her or the girls, and putting it off longer would only make it worse. When he located his cell phone on the kitchen floor, he found himself choosing a different number instead. Holly.

No answer.

He studied his brother and tried to remember exactly how the night had gone.

After Nick had arrived and the initial shock had ended, they had headed to the Bungalow so they could talk without having to sit and stare at each other the whole time. Long-lost brothers find each other? A night in the watering hole was apparently recommended. At least in his screwed-up mind. And yes, he had known exactly what he was doing at the time. No doubt he'd been subconsciously looking for an excuse to back Lee Ann off. He'd jumped at the first opportunity. Like he always did. Like he'd done with Stephanie.

He was bad. He'd known it his whole life, and Nick's arrival had only confirmed it. Seeing the brother his parents kept had sent Cody on a tailspin. Worthlessness, hurt, and anger had combined until all he could see had been bleak desolation.

Since hurting Lee Ann and the girls was inevitable, he'd figured he might as well do it last night instead of putting it off any longer. Quit waiting for it to eventually happen. *Eventually* had knocked on his door.

Holly had been at the Bungalow, scowling because Tucker Brown was dancing with the teacher and had yet to discover the true prize that was Holly. She'd seen Nick, checked him out top to bottom, then proceeded to welcome him to town.

Flipping through the tattered phone book he found in one of the kitchen drawers, Cody located the number for the diner. He told himself he needed to call Holly to make sure she'd made it home okay. He couldn't remember getting home himself and had no idea if Nick had been sober enough to drive. Given the way the man had been pouring them back, Cody doubted his brother had been the designated driver.

He told himself this was his reason to call Holly, but he suspected it had more to do with delaying the other phone call.

"Sugar Springs Diner. Can I help you?" Holly sounded fully awake, unlike the way he felt and the way his brother looked. Cody opened the door when Boss returned, patted him on the head, and moved to feed him his breakfast.

"Holly? It's Cody."

Silence followed his declaration. Finally "Hey, Cody. Everything all right?"

"Uh, yeah." He fidgeted with a dirty glass sitting in the sink. "I just...Guess you brought me and Nick home last night?"

She laughed lightly. "Yeah, I brought you both home last night. That man can't hold his liquor any better than you."

Silence again. He didn't know how he knew, but he was positive there was something she didn't want to tell him. And he was positive he didn't want to hear it. "Well, I just called to say thanks."

Nothing.

"Okay, I'll—"

A long sigh sounded across the line. "Cody, wait."

Sweat broke out on his upper lip.

"You know how we hear all kinds of gossip here at the restaurant, right?"

"Uh-huh."

"Well…" Holly paused and then blurted out, "Some of the people are saying that you not showing up for the party last night really upset the girls."

He closed his eyes. "I'm sure it didn't sit well with Lee Ann, either."

"Yeah, they're saying that, too."

"She's next on my list to call." He couldn't smooth things over with her. He'd known it last night as he'd pulled the door closed behind him on their way out. But he at least owed them all an apology. Hopefully the girls would still allow him in their lives. Maybe occasionally.

"That's the thing."

Pinpricks stabbed his neck from the inside out. "What's the thing?"

"They apparently left town during the middle of the night."

"Left town?" Fear scalded down his throat. "What do you mean left town? They don't leave town. That's what…"

He stopped. That's what he did. Holly's silence confirmed she knew it, too.

"They're coming back, right? They can't just disappear?"

He could almost see her shrug. "I assume, but I really don't know. She left me a text that she's quitting the diner, too. Word is that immediately following the party, they loaded up the car and took off."

"Her mom lives here. She has to come back." He sounded desperate, and for a man who'd just ruined his one chance for a happy life, he had no right to sound that way.

"Well, yeah, you would expect that, but I don't really know what's going on. Other than..." Another pause. "There was one more thing with the gossip I thought you might need to know."

Nick chose that minute to push himself up from the couch and peer around the room, his eyes thin slits. Boss watched from his food bowl, still weary with this new version of his owner, but he had quickly accepted it as fact the night before. He returned to eating, leaving the other man for Cody to deal with.

When Nick spotted Cody, he jolted as if shocked at finding himself in the same house as his twin brother. Cody poured a glass of water and passed it, and a bottle of aspirin, to him.

"Cody? You still there?" Holly asked.

"Still here. What's this one other thing?"

"They think it was me with *you* last night."

Eyes closed, he took in her words. Someone had confused him for his brother. Big surprise. And then the meaning registered, and his eyes opened wide. "Someone told her I was with you?"

"Yes." Her voice was small. "I'm sorry. I know Nick and I got a little carried away. It never occurred to me anyone would think it was you."

Lee Ann believed he'd stood up her and their daughters to go out and get soused with Holly. And he assumed Lee Ann

also imagined the evening had ended far differently than how
it had.

"I'm sorry, Cody."

"Not your fault." *What an idiot!* "I shouldn't have been
there in the first place. I had somewhere else to be."

"Yeah." The word said it all. He and everyone else in the
county knew he'd had somewhere else far more important to
be. And he'd blown it.

Nick came around the table and set his glass in the sink before
propping a hip against the counter. He watched Cody squirm.

Cody's gaze bounced from one wall to the next. The room
was closing in. He had to get away. Then his eyes landed on
the identical pair staring back at him. The man had his own
set of pain. They hadn't gotten into it yet, but Cody had seen
it last night, just as he could see it now.

Nick's life hadn't been the perfect picture Cody had always
envisioned. But the look said he was now here for Cody. And
that was an amazing thing to see.

Cody nodded and then realized Holly couldn't see him.
"Thanks for telling me, Holly." At the mention of Holly's
name, Nick's eyebrow twitched. "Don't worry about it,
okay?"

"Okay." Another sigh skipped across the line. "You two
are good for each other. And your girls need you, Cody. Don't
do anything stupid."

He already had.

"I don't want my accuracy percentage to go down because
of you," she finished up, trying to lighten the mood.

"Guess that means you betted on me staying, huh?" At her
soft agreement, he gentled his tone. That rating was about to
take a hit. "Take care, Hol. I appreciate the warning."

Cody slowly closed the cell phone and put space between him and Nick. The apartment was way too small for two six-four men.

"That was Holly?"

He gave a half laugh. "That was Holly. I can show you where she works if you want to catch her later."

"Nah." Nick scratched his fingernails over his jaw and eyed Cody. "I was just blowing off some steam last night. I take it my behavior with her got you into some trouble?"

Understatement of the year. "My own behavior before that got me into trouble. But it doesn't matter, it was over anyway."

"Why's that?" Nick grabbed one of the two chairs at the table and straddled it. After pulling two Cokes from the fridge, Cody did the same.

He guzzled half the can as he considered his next move. Nick was essentially a stranger, yet as soon as they'd set eyes on each other, nothing about the situation had felt strange. Cody wanted to talk to Nick. He wanted a brother. And for the first time, his desire for taking a chance began to outweigh his fear. He let his mouth tilt in a sarcastic smile. "Because my contract here is up in a couple weeks. I'm heading on to my next stop then."

"Ah." The word seemed to say so much more than it should have been able to. "So she was just a fling?"

Cody's vision blurred. She was so much more than a fling. He ignored the direct question. "It's not just her. She's also raising my twin teenage daughters."

That got his attention. Nick's eyebrows arched, but he didn't speak for several minutes. Finally, he said the last thing Cody had been expecting. "After Mom died last week and I discovered the papers where I learned you existed...when I found out she'd given you to someone else...I was jealous." He took a deep drink and when he set the can down, his words came out deadly and cold. "I wanted to be the one who had gotten to leave."

No words came to mind as both men simply appraised each other, circling with their gazes as if in the school yard waiting for someone to throw the first punch. Because someone always had to throw the first punch.

Cody couldn't figure it out. Nick had gotten to keep their parents and he'd wanted out? He was supposed to have been the one with the good life—the life Cody wasn't good enough to stay in. "You're full of shit," he said.

A simple shake of his head. "No. I was furious you had been able to escape." He broke eye contact then. "Mom was mean. A drunk, and a lousy person. Our father died from a bar fight not too long after we'd been born. From everything I could figure out, she changed almost immediately." He shrugged. "Or more likely, reverted back. My life was crap, and from what you told me last night, yours was no picnic, either."

"The papers I saw showed they'd both signed to give me away."

Nick eyed him. "The man died before we were one. I saw the death certificate and pictures of his funeral."

"Huh." The papers had been wrong? He wondered how that had happened. And then another thought popped into his mind. The documents had also indicated he'd been given away because he was a troubled child.

Cody considered everything Nick had said and tried to relate the description of his brother's life to the one he'd always imagined. It didn't fit. Through all the confusion, one question kept pounding through his mind. "Do you know why she got rid of me?"

Nick's hollow eyes looked as lost as Cody always felt. "You weren't the first one she did it to. It was all legal, but from what I can find out she sold you to the highest bidder. I suspect to support her cocaine habit."

"She sold me?" That made zero sense. "To the foster care system?"

"No. Apparently to some woman who planned to adopt you."

"Then how in the hell did I end up a ward of the state?" Anger colored his vision as he fought through the new information. His mother had given him away to another woman who, in the end, hadn't wanted him, either? Jesus, his life was fucked up.

Nick's shoulders moved in a shrug. "I've no idea, man, I didn't chase that rabbit. I was only interested in finding you."

Cody's breath slowed as he fought through his anger, then something else dawned on him that Nick had said. "Wait." He held up a hand in a stopping motion. "I wasn't the only one she sold?"

Nick raised his gaze and once again locked it on Cody's. "We have another brother."

The can slipped from Cody's fingers, but he caught it before it spilled across the table. He had two brothers? That hadn't been in the paperwork he'd seen, either. But if Nick had seen it…"Three of us?"

Nick gave a single nod.

"Have you found him yet?"

"No." His brother stood and paced. "After she died, I started with you. Figured being a twin, maybe there would be some great connection that would pull us together. I didn't even have to hire a PI. I found you on the Internet the first time I searched. As for our brother, though, he's proving more difficult. I've discovered he was adopted, and therefore likely had his name changed. Locating him hasn't been going well."

Two brothers. He had a family. "He the same as us, too? Identical?"

Nick shook his head. "He's a year older, almost to the day. From the people I've talked to, she sold him before our father knew anything about it. They weren't together at the time. Then they hooked back up for whatever reason, and next thing she knew it was her lucky day again. A chance to make another buck."

A family. Cody had a family. And then he realized he wanted to keep Nick in his life as well as help find the other brother. He was tired of being alone. He wanted this.

Reality hit with a thud. He'd already had a family. They'd been here waiting for him all this time. He'd finally found them, too, and then he'd shoved them away.

He had to fix it. He needed them. He needed their forgiveness.

Without them, nothing else mattered.

CHAPTER

21

Snow from the limbs overhead landed softly on Lee Ann's camera as she stretched out on the bough of the tree, the massive branch dipping low to run parallel with the ground. She framed the scene before her. She'd heard scurrying above and was thankful snow was the only thing tumbling down.

"It's beautiful," Candy whispered in awe as she squatted on the ground beside her.

Thanks to a light snowfall the night before, the stream she and the girls had visited the previous three afternoons now glistened, as purples and blues painted the sky beyond. Lee Ann clicked off more shots and agreed with her daughter.

"Do you think it'll be good enough for the show you just signed to do?"

Pride swelled as Lee Ann recalled the e-mail she'd gotten two days earlier. Cody had apparently contacted the gallery in Nashville he'd told her about. The e-mail had ticked her off at first, but then she'd taken her emotions out of it and looked at it from a business perspective. If she really wanted to make a go of it, she had to do that now. And since she'd quit the diner, she needed to make a go of it.

The manager at the gallery had wanted to see some of her work. After she'd sent the woman a sample, she'd been very interested in doing a show. They'd agreed to a small one to start. Come the end of January, her world would officially take a new turn. She nodded and reached out to stroke Candy's silky hair. "I think it'll be perfect."

Kendra had not crouched with them, as she wasn't as drawn to the artistic sight. She preferred searching for wildlife. And thanks to the hours they'd had in the Smoky Mountains the last few days, she'd been able to point out multiple animals, which Lee Ann had caught with her camera.

"Mom," Kendra whispered, her voice coming from directly behind Lee Ann.

"Yeah?" Click. Click. Lee Ann shifted and positioned the camera in front of Candy, allowing her to work the controls.

Kendra sat on the tree trunk and leaned close as she pointed to the other side of the stream. "I think I see something."

Lee Ann scanned the bank until she saw what her daughter had spotted. She couldn't make out what was hidden in the snow and leaves, but there was definite movement. She slipped an arm around Kendra. "Good catch. Let's wait a few minutes and see if anything comes out."

Candy rose from her position and followed their line of sight with the camera. Being the less patient of the twins, she whispered to her mother and sister. "It'll get dark soon. What if it doesn't come out in time? Let's cross and see if we can find it."

Kendra scowled at her sister. "You are so immature. Mom already taught us about disturbing nature years ago." She focused on the moving leaves and lost her condescending tone. "Anything we do could potentially harm the wildlife in any number of ways."

Lee Ann retrieved her camera in hopes of catching a nice shot, but she concentrated more on what having time alone with her daughters had done for them all. After the pain of having Cody not show up for the party, they'd all been too heartbroken to hang around for a lame apology. Together they'd made the decision that he'd messed up big-time, and none of them had wanted to stick around to see what happened next. All the girls knew at this point was that he'd skipped out on the party. She'd wanted to keep the Holly situation away from them as long as possible so as not to impact their decision about how they wanted to move forward with him.

With school out for the holidays, they'd packed enough clothes and essentials to keep them away from Sugar Springs until the first of the new year. This year they would do something different and celebrate the holidays in the Smokies. Just them and their grandmother, who was coming out today.

They'd spent the first night in a hotel on the main strip, but the following day Lee Ann had been able to secure a cabin that would be theirs for ten days. It cost more than she would normally be willing to pay, but these were trying circumstances. After checking in with her mother to remind her to mind the business messages and return any calls that couldn't wait, then texting Holly that she wouldn't be back to work at the diner, Lee Ann had turned off her cell phone and spent the days totally alone with her girls. She hadn't wanted to be made aware of any gossip or risk getting any calls she didn't want to take.

Along with spending each day scouring the woods together, they'd also shopped and enjoyed the holiday festivities along the strip. Come New Year's Eve there would be a huge fireworks show visible from the enormous deck of their cabin. Fireworks showering over the trees would make good portraits as well.

"Mom," Candy whispered, louder this time as she checked her watch. "We need to get back. Grandma should already be here."

Lee Ann's mom had resisted the idea of their leaving town and even suggested she come, too, but Lee Ann had known they needed time to lick their wounds. Lee Ann and the girls had talked about Cody and his actions during their daily hikes, and although no major decisions had been made, the wounds were already healing. At least they were for the girls. They were more resilient.

Although she'd refused to let Reba come, Lee Ann had promised to leave the key on the deck for her on Christmas Eve. Her mother planned to arrive while the three of them were out for their daily walk, bringing a fully cooked turkey along with her. They would make the side dishes together, and then they'd have their normal Christmas Eve dinner.

Her mother would spend the night so they could all be together the next day before she headed back home. She had to be at work the day after Christmas. City offices didn't close down just because some people needed to escape and hide in the woods.

Lee Ann glanced at her watch. They did need to head back. Not only did her mom need help with dinner, but also the sun was rapidly disappearing. She patted the log beside her. "Come sit with us a minute."

After Candy scooted in close, Lee Ann wrapped her arms around both her girls. The pain in her heart was still there, as strong as it had been Saturday night when she'd learned Cody had chosen Holly over them. She squeezed the girls to her, sorry she'd let him hurt them the same way. Each rested her head on Lee Ann's shoulder, and they released a sigh in unison. Lee Ann smiled. They were so similar. She wished she'd been closer to her sister and had some times like this, but some things just weren't meant to be. Like her and Cody, apparently. "We need to talk before we go back and see Grandma."

"Yeah, we know—" Kendra mumbled, and Candy finished for her, "we need to talk about how we're going to handle this issue with Dad."

Lee Ann's heart lurched. They were both so grown-up. "You know Grandma will ask how you're doing?"

Kendra tugged against the weight of Lee Ann's arm, so she loosened her grip but didn't let go. Both girls straightened and focused on a spot on the other side of the stream. Candy spoke first. "We've been talking about it, and we think we should give him another chance."

Lee Ann sucked in a quick burst of air. She was tired of giving the man chances. "But he might—"

Kendra nodded. "He might hurt us again. We know. But he's still really just learning this fatherhood stuff. He hasn't really messed up with us until now, so it's pretty much his real second chance with us."

"We owe him the chance," Candy added.

Lee Ann closed her eyes. Her girls were good, considerate young ladies. And they wanted to believe the best in everyone. But Lee Ann worried their hearts would be crushed over and over with this one. "Are you sure?"

They both nodded, then grew silent, but Lee Ann knew they had more to say. While she waited, she tried to discern how to handle Cody visiting sporadically for the next five years, maybe more. She was finished with second chances. As soon as she figured out how to get him out of her heart once and for all, she would move on herself.

Candy gripped Lee Ann's hand and held on. "We think you should give him another chance, too."

"No." She couldn't.

"Please, Mom, we know he loves you." Candy turned her pleading gaze to Lee Ann, and the irony struck her that this was the daughter who'd been so hesitant to open herself to him in the first place. "And we know he broke your heart a long time ago, so we totally get it if you can't. But we were thinking...maybe if you forgive him just this one more time, he'll stay in Sugar Springs with us."

Lee Ann's heart deflated at the sight of the hope on her daughters' faces. She cupped both of them on the cheek. "Sweethearts, he isn't staying. That's not an option."

"But..." Moisture deepened the brown of Candy's eyes. "But if you tell him you love him, and he already knows we love him, maybe he'll quit running."

Lee Ann's throat thickened. They recognized he was running? "Cody has..." How did she explain it? She licked her lips and tried again. "Cody has some issues that have nothing to do with any of us. I don't think he knows how to quit running."

"Then we just teach him." Candy stood before them, determination covering her face. "That's all we have to do. Give him some more time, but teach him he doesn't have to run anymore. He has a family here."

Sounded so easy. But Lee Ann knew differently. Kendra rose to mimic her sister's stance. "We can do it, Mom, but it would be easier if you would give him that chance, too. You do love him, don't you?"

Lee Ann thought about him choosing Stephanie over her, choosing Holly over her. Then she thought about him never choosing her again, and her heart bled. She nodded. "Of course I love him, but that's not enough."

Hesitant hope pulled at the edges of the girls' mouths. "Love has to be enough."

Adolescence was such a wonderful thing. Lee Ann gave a sad smile to her girls and wished she could keep them from ever losing their belief in love. "I'm afraid it isn't always that easy."

Kendra flipped her long hair over her shoulder. "Maybe if you just tell him you love him."

"I did," Lee Ann said, her voice cracking. She hated what she was about to do, but they had to know. He hadn't just skipped out on them, he'd skipped out on her as well. "Then we talked about the future Friday night, and I told him again. I begged him to quit running then." She took in a deep gulp of air. "But he went out with another woman instead."

Kendra's eyes bulged, while anger heated Candy's.

"He wouldn't do that to you." Kendra shook her head, not believing, but Candy glowered, fire brewing in the depths. "Who was it? There has to be some mistake."

"It's hard to mistake something like that when it happens in public."

"Did you see it with your own eyes?"

Lee Ann couldn't help the little smile, which lifted her spirits. Her girls would always be there to take care of her, but they wouldn't let her take the easy way out. "No, I was at the party all night with you. Joanie talked to Gina Gregory, who saw him."

Candy's shoulders slumped, and a little of the anger left her posture. "Gina Gregory? Even we know she's after Dad. Maybe she just made it up."

Lee Ann hadn't considered the idea. But now that she thought about it, she supposed it was a possibility. Gina would stoop to any level to get what she wanted.

"What did she say?" Kendra asked.

Shaking her head, Lee Ann rose and motioned for them to lead the way. They'd better finish talking on the walk or they would end up in the dark. "It doesn't matter. She may want him herself, but telling a lie that could so easily be checked out makes no sense. All I'd have to do is ask."

"But you didn't." This drifted back from Candy, and Lee Ann's head spun at the maturity of the simple declaration.

No, she hadn't asked. But it couldn't be fixed as easy as that. He'd skipped out on the party. Stood them all up. It had to be because of Holly. "Then why didn't he show up?"

"He's scared. He ran. He just didn't run all the way out of town this time." Kendra shrugged. "Maybe he managed to control his fear enough to keep him in town."

Lee Ann stopped in the middle of the path until both girls faced her, questioning looks on their faces. "How do you know so much about him?"

Candy gave her an incredulous look. "Anybody who knows anything about his past knows he's running from something that scares him."

Lee Ann shook her head as if to remove the cobwebs. "And how do you know so much about his past?" Other than an overview, she and Cody had chosen not to tell the girls too much.

Even in the dimming light, Lee Ann made out the blushes covering both their faces and she knew.

"The vents in the house?"

They nodded, sheepish, before both spoke quietly, "Sorry."

For the first time since this conversation began, Lee Ann laughed. If she'd been in their shoes, she would have kept an ear to the vent, too. "You're forgiven."

They began walking again, and Kendra asked, "So what's he running from?"

Lee Ann dropped back and snapped pictures of the girls as they walked ahead of her, scuffing their toes in the leaves too shielded from the overhead branches to have received any snow. "A misguided notion that everyone he gets close to will eventually want him to leave."

"Are you kidding me?" Both girls gawked at her.

Lee Ann snapped their incredulous expressions. With a grin, she silently thanked her sister for leaving her such terrific girls. They were part Stephanie, part Reba, part Cody, and a whole lot her. She couldn't ask for a better combination. "Nope. That's his theory. He did have a bad childhood, so he's got some reasons, I suppose."

Kendra began walking again as Candy shook her head at her mother. "Well, when's he going to grow up? You can't blame everything in your life on your childhood. Even we know that."

Lee Ann reached Candy's side and looped an arm through hers. "Tell me about it," she grumbled.

"So we just prove him wrong." They came out of the woods at a paved road, and Kendra stopped to wait for the others. "That's the answer, we stick to his side long enough to prove him wrong."

"But how?" Candy scrunched up her face in confusion. "He's leaving."

Lee Ann slowed her steps as she considered making the suggestion. If it wasn't for the unresolved Holly issue, it might be the thing to do. She pulled the stocking cap off her head and fingered her flattened hair.

"What is it, Mom?"

She had to put it out there. "He did suggest we follow him to Florida and then figure out from there where to go next. You could see him more often if we did that."

Of course, it would only add years of misery to her life, but for her girls, she would do that. She would spend the time working hard to make a name for herself and just let Cody pay the girls' way for a while. She had pride when it came to taking care of them, but over the last few days she'd realized that if nothing else, he owed her the chance to get on with her life. She'd put parts of it on hold years ago, but she wasn't doing that anymore. For anyone.

"More often?" Confusion flitted across Candy's face. "But not all the time? Is that because he doesn't want to be around all the time?"

Lee Ann lifted one shoulder and let it drop. "He and I would have to be together for that to happen. I'm sorry, hon, but I don't see how that can happen."

Kendra frowned. "That makes sense. Not if he cheated on you again."

"Yeah," Lee Ann agreed. "Not if he cheated on me again. I'll go if you want, but we'll both have to give a little. You'll have him near, but I won't have him in my house."

They were both quiet for several minutes as they thought through the options. Glances were exchanged, and once again she saw the connection between the two that she had never had with her sister. It made her glad that they'd been born together, no matter how hard it had been on her in the beginning.

Candy turned to her and stated. "But I love Sugar Springs."

"Me, too." Kendra sighed.

"How about another compromise, then?" Both girls regarded her when she spoke. "Maybe we could try something temporarily?

At the end of the school year we could move to wherever he is for the summer. If it works out, we reconsider where you'll go to school next year, but if it doesn't we come back."

Hope flashed across their faces, and though the thought of seeing Cody but having no relationship hurt, it would be worth it if the girls got the father they so desperately wanted.

Just as quickly as the hope had shown on Kendra's face, it disappeared. "But we can't do that to you unless you work out whatever happened the night of the party."

"Oh, sweetie." Lee Ann slipped both her arms through the girls' as they headed up the last hill. "I'll be all right. Let's just worry about you two right now."

"No, she's right," Candy said. "We don't want to do it if he really did that to you. You deserve better." She paused before continuing. "And we deserve better. We don't want him in our life if he's really that bad of a person."

Lee Ann had never been so proud of her girls. They refused to either desert their mother or lower their standards. They were turning out pretty good.

"Who was it he was supposedly seen with anyway?" Kendra asked, kicking at a clump of snow as they walked.

"Holly."

Kendra gasped and stopped in the middle of the now-dark road, the streetlight throwing shadows over her face. "Holly?" She shook her head. "Mom, Holly is not the type to do that to you."

"Yeah, she's not the type to do that to anyone, no matter how she much she flirts," her other daughter agreed.

Lee Ann hadn't thought so, either. But still, it was hard to say nothing was going on if he had her butt gripped in both hands.

"Nothing about it makes sense. We need to go back so you can ask Holly what happened." Kendra marched up the road, a young lady on a mission. "Maybe we should go home when Grandma goes tomorrow."

"That way we can see Dad on Christmas…" Candy stopped, probably thinking she sounded selfish for wanting to see her father on Christmas Day.

"You're right," Lee Ann said, nodding. "I need answers, and you two need to see your dad."

They reached the top of the hill, and the first thing Lee Ann noticed was her mother's car wasn't the only new vehicle in the driveway. Cody's SUV was also parked there. Her heartbeat sped up—she couldn't help it—and then she tamped down her excitement. He was probably there for the girls. She was happy about that, but she wouldn't let him see how bad she wanted him to be here for her, too. To tell her Gina had somehow been mistaken.

And then they saw him standing on the deck in the glow of light from the house. He stood unmoving, looking out over the woods. Kendra was the first to shout. "Dad!"

He didn't turn. Instead, it took Candy shouting at him again before he finally turned his head toward them, a look on his face as if there was no recognition whatsoever. He then glanced at the back door and said something she couldn't make out.

They reached the stairs to the deck, Lee Ann hanging back as both girls hurried up the steps. When Cody didn't come toward them, they stopped twenty feet away and stared. They rounded on Lee Ann and whispered, "What's wrong with him?"

Something was definitely not right. Lee Ann squeezed their hands and stepped in the middle of them. They would face

Cody together. They moved forward as the back door opened
and more light spilled onto the wooden slats.

And then Cody stepped out.

CHAPTER

22

Lee Ann's gaze bounced from one man to the other. She quickly picked up on the fact the real Cody was the man who'd just walked through the door. The girls seemed to catch on only seconds later, and they released her and hurried to his side.

His twin brother? Goose bumps covered her body. When had this happened? How?

Lee Ann glanced from one man to the other until the newcomer stepped forward and introduced himself. "Nick Dalton."

She nodded but couldn't keep her eyes from welling up. As she wrapped her fingers around Nick's strong hand, the puzzle piece fell into place and the bars she'd built around her heart years ago sprang free. This was the man who'd held Holly in his arms. Not Cody.

She looked to Cody for confirmation. As he held both girls in a hug, he peered over their shoulders at Lee Ann. When they made eye contact, he gave her a tight smile.

"Yes," he seemed to say. "I know I did wrong but I didn't do nearly as bad as you believed."

Reba emerged from the house. "Come on girls, your father and uncle have been helping in the kitchen for the last couple of hours. Let's give them a break now. You two can help me finish dinner."

If her mother was cooking dinner, it might be as good as Cody's spaghetti.

"Uncle?" Two sets of brown eyes sparkled in Nick's direction when the realization set in. Apparently it hadn't occurred to them that they now had an uncle.

Nick pushed away from the deck railing, clapping his brother on the shoulder as he passed. "That's right." He smiled at the girls. "Your favorite uncle."

Both girls giggled as they made their way into the house. "You're our only one."

When the door closed behind them, the light dimmed and the silence became deafening. Cody stepped to Lee Ann, and she let him snag her hands in his. She couldn't have stopped him.

"Lee Ann, I'm sorry."

"It was Nick, wasn't it?"

He hung his head for a second before looking back at her. "Of course it was Nick."

His back was to the light, so she couldn't see what was really in his eyes, and she felt vulnerable knowing he could so easily read hers. She shifted deeper into the shadows. "I knew it as soon as I saw him."

Her admission was as much as telling him she believed in him. Which meant she also still wanted it to work out between them.

"How did that...he...happen? Did you go find him?"

"No." He shook his head. "I probably never would have gone searching for him. But he found out about me last week and came looking for me. He's a good man. I was floored when I opened my door and saw him standing there."

"I'm sure," she said. "Must have been quite the shock."

"Oh, yeah," he agreed.

"And you're okay with this?" She motioned to the house where Nick now was. "I guess you are or you wouldn't have brought him out here, but really? You're okay with this?"

He nodded slowly, and she got the sense he'd been moved by his brother showing up. "I never thought I'd want it, but just in the few days he's been around I've already seen what Candy and Kendra have together. I won't lose contact with him now, Lee. He's my brother. And there's even another one out there we haven't found yet."

She gasped, both at the level of depth coming from him and also the fact he'd gone from having no one in his life a few weeks ago to having two brothers, two kids, and her—if he still wanted her.

"When did this happen exactly?" It had to have been Saturday. Or maybe Friday night after she'd left.

"About thirty minutes before I was supposed to be with you and the girls at the party." He released a heavy breath and pulled her against him. She allowed it but didn't soften. "I'm so sorry I let you all down. I'll make it up to the girls, I swear. I'll never do anything like that again." He peered down at her. "And I'll never do anything like that to you again, either."

The thought was bittersweet. "I get how having Nick show up at your door could knock you on your butt—I do, really. Maybe not exactly enough to go out drinking and forget to make an appearance at your daughters' party, but I get it."

"I didn't forget," he stated quietly.

She nodded. "You just chose not to go. Because you were looking for an excuse again, weren't you? And you found a good one. I'm honestly surprised you didn't leave town that night."

With little light to see each other, Cody pulled her tight against his chest and rested his chin on the top of her head. They stood that way for several seconds, until he tilted her face up and pressed a soft kiss to her lips. Then he separated their bodies.

"I love how you don't hide from the truth," he said.

She heard the smile in his voice.

"It's probably the thing I love most about you," he continued.

"That's nice to know, but that doesn't answer my question."

He chuckled. "It's hard to sidetrack you, too, isn't it?" He moved to the railing and propped against it. "I think last Saturday shamed me more than what I did with Stephanie."

Lee Ann remained frozen where she stood, unwilling to move until she heard what he had to say. He'd said it was Nick with Holly, but if it had been worse than Stephanie... Her heart constricted until she was sure it would never beat again. Finally, she forced words past her lips. "I thought you said it was Nick?"

His gaze shot to hers. "Of course *that* was Nick, but that's not what I'm talking about. I'm a grown man now, not a stupid teenager." He shook his head in disgust and began to pace. "I let down my entire family. My girls. On their thirteenth birthday. And yes, I did almost run. I'm not even sure what stopped me."

Lee Ann didn't move. It felt like he was heading to something really big, but she didn't want to get her hopes up as to where this was leading.

"I saw Nick, panicked, and immediately reverted to childish behavior, with the excuse that it's just the way I was." His laugh was hollow. "I'm surprised you ever had anything to do with me."

When Cody hit the strip of light splashing across the deck, Lee Ann quietly commanded, "Don't move."

He focused on her, and she could finally read his eyes. She took three steps—until she was within touching distance—and studied him. For the first time she didn't see the urge to run hiding anywhere in there. She just saw the desire to build. A family, a life. He finally seemed to get it.

She smiled then. Whatever other issues they might have they could work out. He was hers. And she was his, as she always had been. "I've been waiting for this man to show up."

Before she could move, Cody swept her into his arms. "I love you, baby," he moaned into the side of her neck, "so much there's no way I can ever live without you. Or my girls."

Lee Ann wrapped her arms around his neck and clasped them together. She savored the man and the love between them. "The girls and I were talking."

"Yeah?" With his lips on her neck, Cody began nibbling and moving her backward.

"About what you suggested the last time we were...uh..." She squirmed in his arms as his hot tongue dipped into the crease of her shoulder, heat spiraling through her body. "You know, the last time we were...together."

Cody leered at her before lifting her off the ground and trapping her against the side of the house. He locked a knee between her legs so she wouldn't fall, then began working on the buttons of her coat. "Whatever it was, I'm more than willing to give you anything you want."

A giggle bubbled out of her as his fingers worked frantically to get under her sweatshirt to the skin below. "I'm not talking about anything *sexual*," she whispered, certain her anxious girls were on the other side of the wall listening.

His fingers stilled on her stomach an inch from her breasts, and she couldn't help but thrust toward him, encouraging him to continue. But he didn't take the bait. Instead he readjusted her clothing and let her slide to the ground. "You mean about moving?"

She nodded but feared he didn't see the movement. "Yes. The girls and I talked and decided we could move with you at the end of the school year."

Cody didn't budge. They had talked about it and were willing to move with him? He closed his eyes, overwhelmed by the feeling of love. He had more than he'd ever dreamed. "You would be okay leaving Sugar Springs?"

He saw her nod again, but this time she didn't speak, just searched his face with her heart in her eyes. "I would do anything for those girls."

"But you love Sugar Springs. Your life is there."

"And we love you." Lee Ann reached out and trailed a finger down the front of his shirt. He'd walked onto the deck without a coat and hadn't been aware he'd grown cold until Lee Ann's heated fingertip scorched him through the cotton. "We want to give you the chance to get used to us. But it does come with a time limit."

A smile covered his face. His Lee Ann never gave in easily. And from what he'd seen, his girls were just like her. "Let me guess, they're in agreement with this stipulation?"

One quick nod, then she dropped her hand and took in a deep breath. She squared her shoulders. "We all stand together."

He laughed out loud. It was good to have his girls. All three of them. "I wouldn't have it any other way. Now, tell me about this stipulation."

"Well," she said, licking her lips, and Cody fought the urge to take her mouth with his. He'd had just about enough talking. "We all love you and want to give you time, but we'll only give you the summer at first. We'll reevaluate at the end of summer, but if things aren't going well, we're moving back."

He studied the woman he loved and thought about how close he had come to losing her again. Thanks to Nick, Cody's life was becoming the stuff dreams were made of. "What if I don't agree with the terms?"

Lee Ann gaped at him. He couldn't make out the look in her eyes, but he could guess what was there. She was on the verge of telling him to take a hike. He stopped the verbal attack before it could begin by closing his mouth over hers. Swallowing her soft moan, he pummeled her mouth.

He held her in his arms, and she finally wrapped those glorious legs around him as he'd wanted her to do earlier. When he had her trapped against the side of the house again, he didn't stop this time before his hands reached the soft mounds he'd come so close to caressing before. The feel of cool skin and hot body drove him mad. Even hot body covered in conservative cotton.

Cody pressed into her and deepened the kiss, and her moans became loud enough he was positive anyone in the room behind them would be able to hear.

She must have had the same thought because she reared back and tried to distance herself from him. He wouldn't let her. "Cody, stop it," she whispered. "We still have things unsettled, and I'm sure the girls are right behind us."

He scraped his teeth across her throat, and she melted a bit more. But not enough. He reached behind her and unhooked her bra before she could protest. "Nothing between us is unsettled."

Lee Ann's head dropped to the wall, the white skin of her neck glistening in the night. He slipped his hands over her naked flesh.

"You said you don't agree with the terms."

"So?" He pinched her nipples and groaned as he pulsed inside his jeans.

"So…we need commitment."

His tongue played across her neck and up to her ear. "Ever made love in the woods at night?" he whispered.

Lee Ann's heart pounded against his hands, and warmth spread through him. He had the love of his life in his arms, and he didn't intend to let her get away. She whimpered as he laved his tongue on her ear.

A thump directly behind Lee Ann had them jerking, killing the moment. Cody stared at the wall before whispering in horror. "They really are in there listening, aren't they?"

She nodded, a smile flirting with her lips.

He hadn't believed her, but was now mortified that his girls had heard him feeling up their mother. Geez. He lowered her to the ground and helped her adjust her clothes. "I'm sorry."

She shrugged. "It won't scar them for life. They're more grown-up than you can imagine."

Cody put space between them as he concentrated on losing his erection. The last thing he needed was for them to *see* what feeling up their mother did to him. "Give me a minute and we'll go in."

But Lee Ann shook her head. "We can't go in yet."

"Why not?"

She sighed. "We're still unsettled, Cody. What did you mean, what if you don't agree with the terms?"

Oh. That. The woman and her body certainly had a way of making him forget his plans. He leaned down and swept a soft kiss over her lips before brushing his thumb across them. "I don't agree because then I would have to tell Dr.

Wright I need to back out of my contract to buy into the practice."

Lee Ann's eyes grew round. "You're buying into the practice?"

He nodded. "I am."

"But why? And what about Florida?"

Cody grinned at the woman he loved. The look on her face made him hopeful. "First of all, because she doesn't want to come back full-time now that she has a baby. And before you ask, I already made arrangements for someone else to take over in my next contract. I'm finished doing that."

She simply stared, her mouth hanging slightly open.

"Secondly," he said, digging into his jeans pocket and fishing out the engagement ring he'd purchased the previous morning. He dropped to one knee and gazed up at the woman he hoped he would be lucky enough to spend the rest of his life with. "I needed a permanent job before I asked you to marry me."

A little squeak came from above him. "Really?"

He smiled and slipped the ring over her finger.

"Really." He kissed the back of her hand. "Would you, Lee Ann London, please make me the most insanely happy man for the rest of my life by marrying me at your earliest convenience?"

As Lee Ann smiled down at him and then at the ring on her finger, he knew what true happiness was. But before she could answer, the back door burst open, and Kendra and Candy flew onto the deck. "Don't forget us."

Lee Ann collapsed to sit on his knee as the girls slammed into him, wrapping their arms around both of them.

Cody hugged his girls to him. "Of course I wouldn't forget you. You're all my girls." Then he realized Lee Ann hadn't actually answered his question. His heart thundered. "Lee Ann? Are you going to marry me?"

She hadn't answered because tears were flowing down her cheeks. With the girls hugging them both, and Reba and Nick standing in the light from the door, Lee Ann finally smiled at him and spoke the two words that meant the most. "I will."

EPILOGUE

Lee Ann rested against Cody's chest, his arms wrapped around her, and smiled at her family. Christmas morning had arrived with another snowfall, and they'd started the morning with cocoa on the deck, Christmas carols playing in the background. Soon the cold had seeped in, moving them to the living room, where they opened presents by the fire. The cabin had been decorated with a tree when they'd arrived, so it was almost like home.

"Mom," Candy said without taking her eyes off the new digital camera her dad had gotten her. "When is Joanie getting here?"

Kendra sat down and snuggled up beside Lee Ann, the iPad her dad had given her in her hand. Cody reached over and rubbed Kendra's bedhead.

"Should be any time. Why?"

Candy shrugged. "I miss Boss."

Lee Ann closed her eyes and snuggled deeper into Cody's chest. She enjoyed hearing his heartbeat under her ear.

"Your grandma just happened to tell me Joanie was coming out today," Cody informed her. "So I thought it would be less hectic with him not showing up until then."

Lee Ann cracked her eyes open and smiled at her mother, who was sitting on the other side of the room, feet propped on the coffee table. "My mom just happened to mention several things to you she wasn't supposed to."

Reba shook her finger at Lee Ann. "I always told you this would work out. When he came to the house telling me how he had to find you and promised to never leave again, what was I supposed to do?"

"Just what you did, Mom. Just what you did."

She turned back to Cody. "I can't believe no one told you where I was before yesterday. And yes, there's no doubt they all knew. My mother has rarely kept a secret, and I couldn't see her keeping this one."

"I made sure no one told him, though," her mom added. "That was coming only from me, and only when I knew he was finished being an idiot."

"And yes, I tried everyone," he admitted. "It came out pretty soon that it had been Nick at the Bungalow that night, so I thought I'd get someone to break. Especially Ms. G. I thought she and I had something special with our daily gossip sessions. But that woman doesn't come off information if she doesn't want to. Neither would anyone else. They all knew I'd screwed up by skipping the party, and no one was going to give me the chance to do it again. They love you, Lee. All three of you. The whole town would die to protect you. There's no way I'd want to take you away from that. And no way I don't want to be a part of it myself," he said, his words spoken softly. "It's pretty darn special."

She had to agree. It was pretty darn special. But so was he. She snuggled deeper into him as the doorbell sounded. Nick headed their way from the connected kitchen wearing an apron and wielding a spatula. Thankfully, he'd been the one to do the majority of the cooking the afternoon before, and their dinner had turned out perfect. "The first batch of cookies is ready if anyone wants some."

Lee Ann began to push up off the couch to answer the door, but Nick waved his spatula in her direction. "Stay put. I'll get it."

"They haven't met, right?" She looked at Cody for confirmation as Nick headed out of the room. "She's going to be confused when he answers the door and doesn't recognize her."

Candy spoke from the floor, where she was currently wowing her grandmother with a magic trick. "She'll know. It's so obvious he's not Dad."

"But they're identical."

Cody pressed a kiss against Lee Ann's ear. "You knew."

His hot breath reminded her of last night. She had eventually gotten the opportunity to experience his wicked suggestion, and after everyone had gone to sleep they'd crept outside to make love in the woods.

She shivered and felt his lips smile against her neck. And though she didn't like the thought of leaving his strong chest and nuzzling lips, a good hostess would see her guest in. As she entered the foyer, the first thing she noticed was Joanie's stare at Nick. She glanced at Lee Ann, lifted an eyebrow, then refocused on Nick. Yep, Joanie somehow knew this wasn't Cody. It was probably the smell of warm chocolate drifting off him.

When Nick mentioned that he had to get back to his cookies, Lee Ann watched Joanie check out his backside as he went.

Lee Ann leaned in to her friend and whispered, "I feel like I should be upset."

Joanie shot her a quick confused look before straining her neck around the corner to get another peek. "Why?"

"It's like you're ogling Cody."

Joanie snorted. "Not even close."

Lee Ann shook her head. As they walked back through the rooms she took the time to check out the man, now sliding hot cookies on the cooling trays, and had to admit she couldn't find one glaring physical difference between the two men, yet there just seemed to be many things. And clearly whatever he had had attracted Joanie. Holly flashed through Lee Ann's mind. "You know, it was..."

"Him with Holly?" Even though Joanie's gaze was still fixed on Nick, her mind was right there with Lee Ann's.

"Yeah."

"I know." Joanie lowered her voice even more. "But that's okay. I'm just doing a little window-shopping."

Nick chose that moment to glance across the room, and narrowed his eyes at the women watching him. "Are you two talking about me?"

Heat filled Joanie's face.

He focused on Lee Ann's pink-faced friend and laughed out loud. "I guess so." He tossed the spatula to the counter and dug out his best smile as he sauntered across the room. "Tell me, ladies, what exactly are you two talking about?"

Lee Ann scrutinized her friend's blazing cheeks, intending on rescuing her, but when Joanie turned a teasing glance in Nick's direction, Lee Ann laughed out loud and decided to leave it to fate. Maybe she wouldn't be the only one to discover the excitement of twenty-degree, pitch-black, deep-woods sex. "Joanie can fill you in."

Lee Ann returned to the other room and stopped to take in the sight before her. The girls sat on the couch, each with an arm around Boss, while using their free hands to play with their favorite gifts. Reba flipped through her presents, pulling out the different earrings Lee Ann had picked up at a craft store earlier in the week, and Cody stood by the tree wearing the most content expression she had ever seen.

Finally, after almost fourteen years, her world had been righted and she got to have the life she desired. It wasn't what she'd dreamed of all those years ago, but it was exactly what she wanted now.

She moved across the room and stood by her fiancé. He shot her a wicked grin before lifting a chunk of mistletoe above them. She smiled. This was the man she'd loved her entire life, and nothing could be more perfect. She stretched to meet him halfway, and planted a kiss firmly on his lips.

The End

ACKNOWLEDGMENTS

Sugar Springs (the town) is a fictional place that I hold special in my heart due to the small town I grew up in, the wonderful people from there that I hold dear—and there are many—and all the lovely "main street" towns I've passed through and admired over the years. From these experiences, I've incorporated many elements into this book and into this town, and I can't help but smile every time I think about living right smack in the middle of Sugar Springs.

My love for the small-town life that I hope I've shown in this book comes from all the people in my past and present, and I thank every one of you. Especially my best friend since the third grade, Tonda. There are some special bonds in this book, and I couldn't help but think of you and me over the years as I wrote them. I hope you realize how much you mean to me and that though we don't always see nearly as much of each other as we'd like, I always hold you dear to my heart.

Also to my mother. There's a lot of you in everything I write, even if it doesn't always shine through. You're as much a part of Sugar Springs as I am, and I thank you for showing me so much love over the years that I know how to put it down on paper.

And now for *Sugar Springs* (the book).

Some of the best things in my life have come from finishing this book. I found the perfect friend and brainstorming partner when a relative newbie to my local writing chapter offered to beta read it for me. Thank you, Lara. I'm so glad you raised your hand when I sent out the plea (and have been there to read and reread every time since that I've asked!).

But mostly, I found a group of friends that I'm fortunate to not have to know what life would be like without them. This book was a finalist in the 2009 Romance Writers of America Golden Heart contest, and though it went on to win the award in its category, the best part about the final was the group of amazing ladies that formed from that year's list of finalists. The Ruby-Slippered Sisterhood is the best place I can imagine to belong, with some of the strongest and most giving women I know, and I thank each and every one of you for all the years of support, encouragement, and steady hand-holding any time I've needed it. I cannot wait to see how terrific we are in the years to come!

ABOUT THE AUTHOR

Kim Law wrote her first story, "The Gigantic Talking Raisin," in elementary school. Although it was never published, it was enough to whet her appetite for a career in writing. First, however, she would try her hand at a few other passions: baton twirling, softball, and music, to name a few. Voted Bookworm and Most Likely to Succeed in high school, she went on to earn a college degree in mathematics. Law spent years working as a computer programmer and raising her son, and she now devotes her time and energy to writing romance novels (none of which feature talking raisins). She is a past winner of the Romance Writers of America's Golden Heart Award and currently serves as president for her local RWA chapter. A native of Kentucky, she lives with her husband in Middle Tennessee.

Made in the USA
Charleston, SC
05 December 2012